'Full of comedy, pathos and great tunes' Hardeep Singh Kohli

'Warm, funny and evocative. If you grew up in the eighties, you're going to love this' Chris Brookmyre

'If you lived through the early eighties this book is essential. If you didn't it's simply a brilliant debut novel' John Niven

'Dark, hilarious, funny and heart-breaking all at the same time, a book that sums up the spirit of an era and a country in a way that will make you wince and laugh' Muriel Gray

'Like the vinyl that crackles off every page, *The Last Days of Disco* is as warm and authentic as Roddy Doyle at his very best' Nick Quantrill

'Took me back to an almost forgotten time when vengeance was still in vogue and young DJs remained wilfully "uncool". Just brilliant' Bobby Bluebell

'More than just a nostalgic recreation of the author's youth, it's a compassionate, affecting story of a family in crisis at a time of upheaval and transformation, when disco wasn't the only thing whose days were numbered' *Herald Scotland*

'*The Last Days of Disco* is a scream, an early 80s teenage dream of vinyl and violence, where *Phoenix Nights* meets Begbie – catfights and kickings at the disco, polis, payoffs, Masons, pals and a soundtrack "Kid" Jensen would be proud of … David Ross's debut novel punches the air and your face, hilarious and raging; a falling glitterball. Thatcher's Kilmarnock is the coalition's Kilmarnock, where the politics is bitter but the kids are alright; the last days of disco are the days we still dance in. This is a book that might just make you cry like nobody's watching' Iain MacLeod, *Sunday Mail*

'Ross perfectly plays the nostalgia card through the music and TV shows of the day, transporting readers back to the decade that, arguably, set the UK on the destructive political path it follows even now … By turn hilarious and heart-breaking, more than anything Ross creates beautifully rounded characters full of humanity and perhaps most of all, hope. It will make you laugh. It will make you cry. It's rude, keenly observed and candidly down to earth. You should read this, especially if you were 18 as the Falklands Conflict developed and recall the fear those call-up papers might be dispatched at any moment' *Scotsman*

'There's a bittersweet poignancy to David F. Ross's debut novel, *The Last Days of Disco*' *Edinburgh Evening News*

'The author himself grew up in Kilmarnock and his book gives a poignant portrayal of the humour and the horror of growing up in a small town in Scotland in the early 1980s. Crucially Ross's novel succeeds in balancing light and dark, in that it can leap smoothly from brutal social realism to laugh-out-loud humour within a few sentences. It is a triumphant debut novel, which announces a real new talent on the Scottish literary scene' *Press and Journal*

'Ross has written a great coming-of-age novel that is full of wonderful prose and characters who are instantly likeable. At times the book is reminiscent of Irvine Welsh; Kilmarnock takes the place of Leith and vinyl, rather than Heroin, is the drug of choice' Literature for Lads

'Set against a backdrop of rising unemployment levels and the brewing Falklands War, *The Last Days of Disco* – with its anger, wit and rebellion – is the novel version of an impassioned punk song. The humour is well-pitched and executed, in places even sublime – but David F. Ross has a talent for social angst, and it's this I'd love to see more of in the future' Louise Hutcheson, A Novel Book

'It's a strong premise and Ross handles the two threads skilfully, stepping backwards and forwards to follow the disco conflict through the local corridors of power ... Rather as Jonathan Coe does with the 70s in *The Rotters' Club*, Ross celebrates the music of the early 80s through the commitment and passion of Bobby and Joey to their favoured bands' Blue Book Balloon

'*The Last Days of Disco* strikes the perfect balance between weighty socio-political commentary and witty observation. I laughed out loud a great many times and shrunk in sadness during the harder moments. A tragic comedy of deep family difficulties and the comedic coping mechanisms, it makes for a strikingly authentic and enjoyable read' Publish Things

'David Ross captures the mood and spirit of the time impeccably, with a wonderful cast of characters and a fabulous soundtrack ... there are definite echoes of the late, great, much missed Iain Banks here – there are plenty of comparisons to be drawn, with a sprawling Scottish small-town cast, delicately intertwined plotlines, social commentary and a deft turn of often quite black humour' Espresso Coco

'*The Last Days of Disco* captures the decade in all its harsh monochromatic glory ... Filled with characters that will make you want to laugh and cry, often in the space of a single page, Ross has written a tragi-comedic novel that might topple *Trainspotting*'s crown and become Scotland's favourite book of the last fifty years' Andy Lawrence, Eurodrama

'From about halfway through the novel, the *Eastenders*-esque drum bash moments, revelations where your mouth will drop, come thick and fast. That said, Ross is the master of bad taste comedy. Fancy a children's entertainer who makes phallic balloon animals? Or sex in a shed involving a dry ice machine? Honestly, they say you couldn't make it up, but Ross really can ... Outstanding' Amy Pirt, This Little Bag of Dreams

'*The Last Days of Disco* is a thoroughly enjoyable, uplifting
and bloody hilarious book that's shot through with a clear and
knowledgeable devotion to music … In his first novel, David F.
Ross has given us a heady blend of social realism, tragedy, humour
and Paul Weller. There's not a dull moment in these pages and
I wholeheartedly recommend getting your hands on a copy'
Mumbling About Music

'I defy anyone not to be humming "Shaking Stevens" when reading
this. You will … This is a funny, charming, slightly crazy and
intelligent tale … retro comic magic' Northern Lass

'… completely exceeded expectations. I laughed out loud, I was
moved to tears and I couldn't put the book down. *The Last Days of
Disco* is a brilliantly written reminder of times past, good and bad,
and I would highly recommend it' Segnalibro Blog

'It is a tale of consequences, with heart and soul, a coming-of-age
tale set in difficult times. David Ross has written a terrific story
that will have you laughing out loud one moment and sobbing into
your pillow the next. The heart of it is emotionally resonant and
absolutely unforgettable. Highly Recommended. Get your dancing
shoes on!' Liz Loves Books

'*The Last Days of Disco* is a nostalgic, heart-warming tale of music
and gritty real-life set in Scotland in the 1980s … David F. Ross
excels in his weaving of humour and sadness into a novel which
will have you feeling a range of emotions but ultimately marvelling
at the signs of a great new author to follow' Reviewed the Book

'Ross uses the reader's benefit of 30 years of hindsight to set
up some fabulous gags. However, there are some very emotive
moments to share too. I was reminded of *Trainspotting* … but with
disco rather than drugs! I loved everything about this book and
have to award it 5/5' Grab this Book

'The turf war with Fat Franny who fancies himself as the Disco King of Kilmarnock provides the Scottish banter and laugh out loud moments. And it's the language – the Scottish vernacular – that really cements the book in the Scottish landscape. If you don't speak Scottish dialect then you'll have learned a few choice words by the end! When the tears flow, it's because of the Falklands war and what that means for the young men who are forced to go out there and fight. And the tears do flow for there are some sad moments, poignant moments and a realisation via the political reminders at the start of chapters of what the situation was like for so many' The Book Trail

'*Last Days of Disco* is the new *Trainspotting*, brilliant writing! Irvine Welsh you have a new jock on the block! Thank you David F. Ross for a fantastic read and music set to go with it' Atticus Finch

'This is David Ross's first novel but he demonstrates a gift for expressing life that surely has more to give. There is a real empathy for people of all kinds in the pages, there are "good" people doing bad things and "bad" people doing good things, because people are not good or bad they are just people dealing with what is in front of them, imperfectly. This book is worth reading for that truth alone, but it also takes you on an emotional journey that reminds you what it is to be human, a fabulous debut' Live Many Lives

'This is a high quality, extremely well drawn, and assured debut from this new author. Highly recommended' Books and Pals Blog

'Ross levers the various plot-twists and turns effectively. He also knows his music and the numerous references give the book authenticity. You will be thumbing through old records (or the modern day equivalent) as a result of reading this novel' Danny Rhodes

'Their adventures are hilarious, but life is not straightforward for most of the characters as it wasn't for most people at that time. With Thatcher constantly buzzing in the background, like an unwanted wasp, for one reason or another: unemployment, the Falklands; it takes you right back to that era with an authenticity that is rare to find' Sandra Foy, For Reading Addicts

The Rise and Fall of the Miraculous Vespas

The Rise and Fall

of the

Miraculous Vespas

DAVID F. ROSS

ORENDA
BOOKS

Orenda Books
16 Carson Road
West Dulwich
London SE21 8HU
www.orendabooks.co.uk

First published by Orenda Books 2016

ISBN 978-1-910633-37-3

Typeset in Garamond by MacGuru Ltd
Printed and bound by CPI Group (UK) Ltd, Croydon CRO 4YY

SALES & DISTRIBUTION

In the UK and elsewhere in Europe:
Turnaround Publisher Services
Unit 3, Olympia Trading Estate
Coburg Road
Wood Green
London
N22 6TZ
www.turnaround-uk.com

In USA/Canada:
Trafalgar Square Publishing
Independent Publishers Group
814 North Franklin Street
Chicago, IL 60610
USA
www.ipgbook.com

For rights information and details of other territories, please contact
info@orendabooks.co.uk

For Bobby, who inadvertently planted the seed.

Author's Note

The Rise and Fall of the Miraculous Vespas is a parallel story to *The Last Days of Disco*. Although not directly related, both books share certain characters and locations. The story that you are about to read may seem unbelievable. I doubt I would have believed it myself, had I not witnessed most of it with my own eyes. All I would ask is that you suspend your natural cynicism and justifiable disbelief, and acknowledge that even in the cultural backwater of Thatcher-ravaged, 1980s Ayrshire, teenage dreams (so hard to beat) can, and *did*, come true.

Beyond our prologue, the first person you will encounter is Max Mojo who, at the beginning of this remarkable odyssey, is named Dale Wishart. As our story begins, he lies in hospital, the apparent victim of a re-emerging war between three Ayrshire gangland firms.

A myriad of colourful characters will weave their way across your pages and into the deep recesses of your imagination as this tale unfolds. It falls to me, your storyteller and guide, to introduce them to you. In order, dear reader, that you can follow this snakes-and-ladders epistle with the clarity of thought necessary, I will briefly explain their various relationships and their place on Police Superintendent Don McAllister's 'Ayrshire's Most Wanted Bampot' list. In Ayrshire, in 1982 – when our tale is set – there are three dominant 'families', all working very hard to make a dishonest living.

In Crosshouse, to the west of Kilmarnock, the Wisharts hold sway. The Wisharts are money-launderers; a level of 'white-collar' organised criminality that places them lower down the local Police HQ totem pole than their immediate rivals. They are led by James Wishart, universally known as 'Washer'. Washer is Dale Wishart's father although Dale – who fronts an amateur band called The Vespas

– takes no active part in the family business. Washer's right-hand man, Gerry Ghee, is also his nephew. Benny Donald is notionally third in command, but his recent forays into Glasgow's dangerous drug scene are causing Washer concern. Frankie Fusi – known as Flatpack Frankie – is Washer's closest friend. They have a brother-like bond that goes back to their time serving in the Army together in Malaya. Frankie Fusi acts exclusively as a fixer for Washer, but is not a full-time member of the 'family'.

In Galston, over on the eastern side of Kilmarnock, the roost is run by the Quinns, a Romany family whose *modus operandi* is security and protection rackets. The Quinns are incomers … gypsies from Birmingham who took over the Galston rackets from the previous incumbents – the McLartys from Glasgow's East End – by force. Nobby Quinn is kingpin, but his fearsome wife, Magdalena is the brains behind the operation. The *muscle* is provided by their sons, of which there are almost too many to count. Fear not though, the only one *you* need look out for is Rocco, for reasons that will become apparent.

Which brings us to Fat Franny Duncan, of whom some of you may have heard. Fat Franny's patch is Onthank, in the North West of Kilmarnock. His crew are involved in everything from loan-sharking to entertainment contracts, although his once unassailable position as Don McAllister's *Public Enemy Number One* may be under challenge. Fat Franny's principal henchman, Robert 'Hobnail' Dale, is beginning to question his commitment to the Fat Franny cause. Des Brick, Fat Franny's advisor, and Hobnail's brother-in-law, has his mind elsewhere and Wullie Blair – also known as Wullie the Painter – is moonlighting as a decorator for Mickey 'Doc' Martin, one of Fat Franny's lone wolf rivals. To halt the slide, Fat Franny has brought in Terry Connolly to run the ice-cream vans. Terry is another with McLarty connections, as will become only too apparent to you.

So these are the three legs of a criminal cartel that, through an uneasy form of Mutually Assured Destruction, have maintained a peaceful equilibrium ever since the McLartys headed back north.

Dear reader ... for your entertainment, *that* peace is about to be shattered as the McLarty influence resurfaces ... and the glam-racket of an amateur band rehearsing in a nearby Church Hall stirs a sleep-walking community with their deluded hopes and dreams. But we'll get to their rise and fall in due course.

In the meantime, as Wullie (the Shakespeare, *not* the painter) might say ... all that's past is prologue.

DFR

The principal players

The **Wisharts** of Crosshouse

Dale Wishart (Max Mojo): *teenage frontman of the amateur band, The Vespas*

James ' Washer' Wishart: *Dale's gangster father*

Molly Wishart: *Washer's wife*

'Flatpack' Frankie Fusi: *Washer's closest friend and 'fixer'*

Gerry Ghee: *Washer's right hand man, and also his nephew*

Benny Donald: *a young, opportunistic Wishart family lieutenant*

The **Quinns** of Galston

Nobby Quinn: *Birmingham-born Romany gypsy patriarch*

Magdalena Quinn: *his domineering wife*

Rocco Quinn: *eldest and most vocal of their five volatile sons*

Maggie Abernethy: *his mixed-race girlfriend*

Ged McClure: *friend of Rocco and also connected to the McLarty crime family*

Fat Franny Duncan's North West Kilmarnock Crew

Fat Franny Duncan: *Onthank crime kingpin*

Robert 'Hobnail' Dale: *his friend since school, and principal 'muscle'*

Senga Dale: *his wife*

Grant Dale (Grant Delgado): *their son*

Des Brick: *Fat Franny's associate*

Wullie Blair (The Painter): *Fat Franny's associate*

Terry Connolly: *Fat Franny's newest associate, and still connected to the McLarty crime family.*

The **McLarty** Family of Glasgow

Malachy McLarty: *the most feared gangland leader in Scotland.*
Gregor Gidney: *the McLarty's number-one enforcer, and a known associate of Terry Connolly and Ged McClure*

The **Police** 'family'

Don McAllister: *Kilmarnock's Detective Chief Superintendent*
Charlie Lawson: *his colleague*
Mickey 'Doc' Martin: *an Ayrshire impresario who often acts on instruction for Don McAllister*

The **Miraculous Vespas**

Max Mojo (formerly known as Dale Wishart): *their manager*
Grant Delgado (formerly known as Grant Dale): *the singer, and songwriter*
Maggie Abernethy: *the drummer*
Eddie Sylvester (The Motorcycle Boy): *the guitarist*
Simon Sylvester: *the bass guitarist, and Eddie's twin brother*
Clifford 'X-Ray' Raymonde: *their producer*
Jimmy Stevenson: *their driver*
Hairy Doug: *their roadie and sound man*

*'Rock 'n' Roll doesn't necessarily mean a band. It doesn't
mean a singer, and it doesn't mean a lyric, really.
It's that question of trying to be immortal.'*

Malcolm McLaren

24th September 2014

On Christmas Day, 1995, The Miraculous Vespas appeared on the live festive edition of *Top of the Pops*. After more than ten years in the musical wilderness, the band's re-released, remixed debut single 'It's a Miracle (Thank You)', was back in the UK Top Five, and their long lost LP, 'The Rise of the Miraculous Vespas' was being hailed as one of the best British debut albums of all time. But their performance that day has gone down in musical history. As shocking as the Sex Pistols 'Bill Grundy' television interview and as iconic as Nirvana's famous appearance on Channel 4 programme *The Word*. Instead of playing their hit song live to a TV audience of 26 million people, lead singer Grant Delgado unplugged his guitar, took off his shirt and gaffa-taped firstly his mouth, and then that of his fellow bandmates. The act has been simultaneously hailed as the ultimate act of career suicide, and the greatest piece of confrontational performance art ever staged. Now, on the 30th anniversary of the band's legendary single reaching Number One, a new film written by the band's controversial manager, Max Mojo, charts the incredible story of the Rise *and* Fall of The Miraculous Vespas. It's a pleasure to meet you, Mr Mojo …

Max, Norma … ye can call me Max, hen.

Ah, okay. Thank you, Max … for agreeing to this interview. I feel very priveliged to be the only person you've decided to speak to.

Ah like yer stuff. Ah've mind ae ye fae The Tube. *That programme wis fuckin' pish, by the way, but you were great oan it.*

That's very kind of you to say.

Ah bet ye didnae know that The Miraculous Vespas were booked tae dae that bastart show. First episode, third series.

Really? No, I didn't know that.

Fifth ae October, nineteen eighty fuckin' four. That date's engrained oan ma memory like it wis fuckin' tattoo'ed there by Inkstain Ingram.

Who? That was a couple of years before I joined the show.

Disnae matter. He's deid noo, just like most ae them fae back in the day, ken? The Tube cancellin' us wis probably the point ah knew ah'd fucked it aw up. But lookin' back at that noo, ye've got tae laugh. They replaced us oan the bill wi' fuckin' Culture Club! The bloody irony, eh? They're oan dain' that 'War Song' pile ae absolute shite, an' efter that, the Boy George yin gets asked aboot gettin' fuckin' kidnapped. An' the cunt disnae deny it either. That caused us a load ae extra soapy bubble, the bastart.

Because of the trial, you mean?

Naw, no' really. The arrests an' the trials aw came later but lookin' back noo, it wis probably the point that ah knew there wis nae way back wi' Grant. Aw that crap in the papers meant The Miraculous Vespas had turned intae a joke. A one-hit wonder novelty record fae a band funded by gangsters an' fuckin' wallopers. Sad thing wis, the band would've been magic … ye'se aw ken that noo. Too fuckin' late though, eh?

Let's take our time, Max, if you don't mind. Can we go back to the very beginning of the story? The film starts with a strange psychedelic sequence. Was it a vision that you had … or a hallucination? Can you talk about Dale Wishart? Could you begin by explaining that transformation?

(pauses) So, ah'm strugglin' up this fuckin' hill … the Mount in Onthank, ken? Nae fuckin' idea how ah ended up in this shitehole, by the way. But ah'm carryin' a couple ae bastart four by twos nailed th'gither. Fuckin' skelfs aw over ma body. Agony, it wis. An' there's aw kinds ae bampots chuckin' stuff at us aw the way doon Onthank Drive. An' ma heid's gowpin' tae … worst fuckin' headache ah've ever hud, to be honest.

Anyways, the crowd parts like an Orange Walk's comin', an' through the gap, there's an auld cunt comes gallopin' towards us … but he's ridin' oan the back ae the biggest fuckin' Alsatian dug ye've ever seen. He's even got a fuckin' saddle oan the cunt, as if it wis the 3/1 favourite at fuckin' Aintree, or somethin'.

Ah starts shitin' it, but ah canny put the bits ae wid doon. Ken why? 'Cos some cunt's nailed them tae ma hands. Whit the fuck's aw that aboot? The auld boy leaps aff the dug, then says, 'Down Sheba.' Ah originally thought he says 'drown' Sheba, which is exactly whit ah'm wishin' some cunt wid dae tae it, by the by. Anyway, he speaks … Methuselah, ken … no' the dug:

'Yer wastin' yer talent,' *says this auld tosser. Tells me his name's Manny … Manny Wise.*

'Fuck dae *you* ken?' *ah says back … aw gallus an' that.*

'Ah ken mair than ye think, boy. Ah ken yer faither … an' ah can see the future, tae. *Your* future.'

Ah laughs at this, 'cos every cunt in Ayrshire kens Washer Wishart. A lot ae them probably wishin' they didnae. Ah tells him this, just as his massive fuckin' beast pisses up rna bare leg.

'Aw for fuck's sake,' *ah shouts, then the dug growls at us an' ah wish ah hudnae. But, anyway,* 'Look, auld yin, ah've been telt tae get this timber up tae the Mount. There's another big crowd up there waitin' for it … an' it's just aboot tae start pishin' it doon. So unless ye want tae grab an' end, fuck off an' let me dae ma job, eh?'

And then he says somethin' that bolts me … puts a shiver right through me, ken?

'Ye were born fur greatness, son. Remember yer Primary 7 essay? The yin where ye were a superhero … Max Mojo? The wan ye got that prize for?

'How the fuck dae you ken aboot that?' *ah says, suddenly ah've went aw* Elvis *… aw shook up. Ah'm regardin' him close noo, right in his face, tryin' tae work oot where ah've seen him before. An' then it dawns … it's the* Dale *cunt's fuckin' grampa – Washer's faither. Ah've only ever seen him in photies, cos,' get this … his auld fella died the same year the* Dale *yin wis' born … in the fuckin' 60s!*

So, ah'm properly fuckin' puggled, here … hands absolutely bastart uchin' tae they nails, an' then he hits me wi' it …

'Yer a leader ae men, son. So *lead.* Dae it right. Get fuckin' rid ae the *auld* you. *Dale Wishart?* Whit kinda arsehole name is that, son? Ye sound like a fuckin' carpet factory. Take control. Nane ae this fuckin' aboot at the front, tryin' tae look like a bloody lassie. Nae wonder the rest ae the band banjo'ed ye. Lead, ya wee prick … an' there will be untold riches.'

An' suddenly it aw makes sense. Ah'm Max. Ah need tae wake this fuckin' Dale *wanker up. Take control, jist like the aul' geezer says tae me. Ah've been dormant too long. Need tae shake it up! Lead … like this auld boy says. If ah dae … well …*

'It'll be …'

01: **I HOPE TO GOD YOU'RE NOT AS DUMB AS YOU MAKE OUT**

1

'*Miraculous.*'

'Eh? ... *whit* is?' The unexpected whispered sound being made by the bandaged figure in the bed was so faint that Bobby Cassidy wasn't entirely sure he'd heard it at all. He leaned in, carefully though, to avoid dislodging one of a number of tubes that might've stopped Dale Wishart from ever speaking *again* if he had. 'Dale. Whit did ye say there, pal?' But there was no response. He had been sitting at the side of the unconscious young man's hospital bed for almost fifteen minutes. Bobby assumed his bored imagination had simply made more of the unusual rhythm of the various bleeps and breathing interludes.

Bobby had dropped in to the Intensive Care Unit at Crosshouse Hospital, on the western fringes of Kilmarnock, to see Dale Wishart. He'd first checked that none of Dale's extended lunatic fringe family members were there but that became immaterial as he was no longer in critical care. He'd been moved earlier that morning when tests had determined he had suffered no lasting brain damage. His list of injuries was impressively extensive, mind you: broken ribs, damaged eye socket, fractured clavicle and an eye-wateringly painful-sounding twisted testicle. Two nights prior, the local amateur band Dale fronted had been bottled off stage at the start of a mass brawl that virtually destroyed the Henderson Church Hall. Bobby wasn't a close friend of Dale's, but the two eighteen-year-olds had shared some recent experiences, and they had had a love for the same musical influences.

Dale expressed these inspirations directly through The Vespas, his mod-influenced group; Bobby did so via the medium of mobile disco. His own fledgling DJ-ing vehicle, Heatwave Disco, had *supported* The Vespas on a few occasions. Last night was one of those occasions, although Bobby had – luckily for him, as it turned out – left the DJ-ing duties to his best friend and disco partner, Joey Miller. But he was here now because he felt a sense of obligation to check in on the battered singer. Dale Wishart had contacted Bobby to ask him to aid the band on what was ostensibly a money-making venture for Dale's gangster father, Washer Wishart. The gig had been dressed up as a charity enterprise and as a result Bobby wasn't going to be getting paid.

Bobby was shocked when he saw Dale, after being redirected and shown into the six-bed general ward on the third floor. The still-unconscious Vespas singer was hooked up to drips and wires as if he was the Six Million Dollar Man getting recharged. Bobby had just visited his *own* pal, Hamish May, who was suffering from hypothermia on a ward one floor above. Hamish had *also* been the victim of some mobile disco-related violence, although his fevered story that he had been abducted by smugglers, bundled into a rowing boat and despatched into the sea for Russian sailors to pick up, seemed delusional. That had been bad enough but at least Hamish was on the road to physical – if not mental – recovery.

Dale, on the other hand, looked like he had been run over by one of those daft new American monster trucks with the wheels the size of an Altonhill prefab. He was bare-chested, and the map of cuts, welts and developing yellow bruises that had been forcibly applied to their skin canvas made Bobby wince. Apart from the two perfectly formed black eyes – which were already turning deep purple – Dale's face was pale, but relatively unmarked. With the cream-coloured bandage obscuring his hair, Bobby sniggered at the thought of him looking a bit like Telly Savalas in *Kojak*; all FBI sunglasses and '*Who loves ya, Boaby?*'

Dale Wishart was a decent guy. He was one of life's eternal optimists. *Too* nice at times, Bobby thought. He had none of that '*dae you know who ah am?*' bullshit that usually went hand-in-hand with being a local bruiser's son. He actually seemed acutely embarrassed about his family business and despite the many understandable reasons for *not* doing so, nearly everybody liked him. Apart, it transpired, from his fellow bandmates in The Vespas. It was Dale's group, no doubt, but lately Steven Dent – his pal from early childhood – had been making a play for leadership. It was causing rifts between the two friends, and forcing the two other members into taking sides. Jamie and Andy Ferguson were brothers so they inevitably block-voted in times of dispute. Dale had previously avoided having siblings in the band. It didn't work for The Kinks or The Everly Brothers, he reasoned, and it wasn't really working for The Vespas. The Henderson Church gig had actually been a farewell of sorts and – as a result of the numerous arguments – a split had been acrimoniously agreed prior to the event. The Ferguson brothers were both naturally shy and normally shunned confrontation, so recent band arguments always became a question of which of the two more dominant personalities to side with. On the night of the Henderson Church gig, it was clear to Joey Miller just whose side they were on. Although he hadn't seen it personally, Malky Mackay – Heatwave's minder for the evening – had informed Joey, with some authority, that Dale hadn't been hospitalised as a result of the volatile crowd taking action, but as a direct consequence of his fellow *band* members taking it. Once Steven Dent's swinging bass had felled Dale, the three of them had battered the fuck out of him, and set his synthesiser on fire. They had then bolted off stage and out of the rear fire door of the church hall before the police had arrived and started 'lifting' everyone left in the hall.

'Musical differences,' said the taciturn Malky of the split, with no detectable sense of irony.

'Their fuckin' arms an' legs will be havin' differences of direction fae their heids once Washer gets a haud ae them,' being Joey's prosaic summary.

⚡

'Whit ye got ther', son?' Bobby turned his head round to see an old toothless man, gurning broadly back at him from the adjacent bed and pointing a shaky finger at Bobby's plastic Safeway bag.

'Lucozade,' said Bobby. 'It aids recovery, apparently … although it's gonnae have its work cut oot wi' *this* yin.'

'Gie it tae *me* then.' Bobby looked at the old man. The jaundiced skin visible on his body was virtually transparent, but his face had the telltale spidery blood vessels radiating out from a bulbous red nose. He had a thin tube coming across both sides of his fragile face, with an outlet going up each nostril. He had another, thicker one leading from under the thin pale-blue bedspread. Bobby watched the cloudy golden fluid it was now carrying work its way down the tube and into the bag that was taped to the metal sides of the hospital bed. The bag looked like it contained about a pint of Newcastle Brown Ale. The old fellow looked like *he* regularly contained about ten times that amount. Bobby figured he would be about fifty years old, but looked twenty more.

'It's no' booze, ye know?' Bobby told him.

'Ah ken *that*, son, ah'm no' a bloody eejit,' the old man whispered. Bobby stood up and went to the bottom of Manny's bed. He scanned the clipboard as if looking for a prognosis. He peered at the top of the chart.

'Manny, is it?' he asked.

'Aye, son. Manfred … but naebody ever calls me that. Stupid bloody name.' Bobby laughed. 'They don't gie me *anythin'* tae drink in here … 'cept bloody watter. Ye'd think ah wis a flamin' pot plant.' Manny sighed as much as his shallow breathing would permit. 'Nil by mouth … whit use is *that* tae an alkie, eh?'

'Sorry,' said Bobby.

'Dinnae be … just gie's yer juice!'

'Aye. Aw'right. Here. Ye'll need tae hide it, mind. Or they nurses'll find it.'

'No' worried aboot that, son,' said Manny. 'Ah'll huv that tanked the night.' Bobby laughed again. 'Yer pal'll be fine. Ah heard they doctors aw talkin'. Somebody gie'd him a batterin', and he's no gonnae look like Montgomery Clift ever again…' Old Manny paused, wheezing at the effort a few sentences had required, '…but ye dinnae need tae worry.' Bobby didn't have the heart to say that Dale was neither a pal, nor that he was particularly worried about his longer-term health. 'Ah've been talkin' tae him since this mornin' … y'know, tae help him oot the big sleep.'

'Cheers. Ah'm sure he'll huv appreciated that when he comes 'roond,' said Bobby. He looked at his watch.

'They three aul' wummin dinnae say nothin'. It's like they're affrontit tae speak tae a drunk. They shut the centre curtain ower and ah'm left masel. Aul' cows.'

'Ah need tae go, mate,' said Bobby. Hospitals freaked him out and he'd already been in this one about three times as long as he'd intended. 'Hope yir back oan yer feet soon, sir.'

'No' happenin', son. Ah'm no' gettin' oot ae here,' said Manny, with a wry, gumsy smile. 'End ae the line fur me, boy. But you make sure yer pal stays ootae trouble … just like ah've been tellin' him.'

'See ye, Manny,' said Bobby as he walked away from Dale's bed.

'Naw ye'll no',' replied Manny, lifting a quivering left hand to wave as he did so.

⚡

Bobby needed air. He couldn't understand why the wards always had to be so hot. *Did bacteria not fucking shag each other daft and multiply in warm conditions, like Scottish gadgies on holiday in Benidorm?* Everybody seemed to be sweating, *especially* him. Bobby walked down the corridor, under blinking fluorescent lights, alongside flaking paintwork and looking up at numerous gaps in the suspended ceiling tiles where cables and wires hung down. *Christ, why the fuck do hospitals have to be so depressing?* he wondered.

Noo, at this point in the story, Norma, ah'm only a Voice in the cunt's battered heid. Ah know he can hear me, but he's too fucked up tae really ken whit's goin' on, y'know? He's lyin' there, comatose, an' ah'm bawlin' away inside the wee bastart:

'Wake up, ya fuckin' moron!

Ah'm no' lyin' here any longer. Ah've got a fuckin' destiny tae fulfil … an' unfortunately for me, ah need your useless cunt ae a body. Immortality's waitin' just doon the next *Bruce Springsteen* motorway…

So, move yer fat arse, ya lazy bastart … or ah'll gie ye another fuckin' kickin' fae the inside.'

Musta worked, though. The daft wee ginger walloper wakes up, ken?

2

Grant Dale turned up the radio. He still made a regular appointment with the Chart rundown and tried to listen to the whole Top 40 on a Sunday, culminating with the Number One at five minutes to seven. It had been a while since any of his favourite records had actually reached the top of the charts, mind you. The year had started promisingly with the Human League dominating British music with *Don't You Want Me*. Grant had regularly considered the prospect of a New Romantic threesome with Joanne and Suzanne, while that *prick with the lopsided haircut* watched. That was the only downside of New Romantic music … all the guys involved in it looked like posh London *fannies*. It was a sure-fire route to a direct kicking up around Onthank, if anybody caught you buying the *Rimmel* out of Boots, that's for sure.

Grant had loved the Kraftwerk record, *The Model*. He had the 7-inch *and* 12-inch versions of the song, although at £3.99, the LP was a bit steep. Kraftwerk looked cool, if a bit *too* cool. Their look – Burton shop dummies meets Special Branch – might also result in a battering, although for totally different reasons.

Another favourite was Japan, although Grant was knowledgeable enough to know that they – like so many of the current crop – were just wannabe David Bowie impersonators. At least Japan's main man was a good-looking bastard, and occasionally played guitar as opposed to being *totally* synthetic. Grant had been growing his hair and had bleached and shaped it into a David Sylvian-type feather cut. Grant's dad, Bob Dale – known universally as Hobnail – had predictably hated it, but since he'd vanished off the reservation of late, *that* aggravation had gone at least.

In fact, Hobnail's incessant hounding of his son had initially per-suaded the boy to move out and start doing some strong-arm work of his own for Fat Franny Duncan, *the local loan shark heidcase*, and also his father's boss. If there was one way to completely fuck over his old man, it would be joining the Fat Franny fraternity. But in truth, Grant had neither the motivation for it, nor the neces-sary menace. Threatening to scald pensioners for late payments of a tenner seemed a bit over the top, even for an arsehole like Fat Franny Duncan. Grant was never going to win *Mastermind*, but he was sharp enough to know where the path followed by his father at the same age would lead, and astute enough to want to take a dif-ferent one. So, to his worried mother's delight, he had come home. He'd been gone for two weeks – only a day less, in fact, than his father – nevertheless, his prodigal return had seen Senga Dale bring out the best china and nip to the shops for a bit of Silverside while Grant returned to routine, taking a Sunday soak on bath night and listening to the radio.

'…and now, a *new* Number One, it's the UK's top-selling song … it's Captain Sensible, with "Happy Talk".'

Fuck it, couldae been worse, thought Grant. Irene Cara was hover-ing around the top three like the Childcatcher, waiting to brainwash more *Kids* into joining her sinister cult. That irritating song from *Fame* was a new entry at Number Four. Grant Dale was convinced *he* could have done better, given half a chance.

23rd June 1982

'Aye, ah hear whit yer sayin' … ye're right fuckin' there. How could ah avoid it!'

'Ah'm no' sayin' that. That's no' whit ah meant, man.'

'Stop puttin' fuckin' words in ma mooth. Ye don't ken whit yer askin' here. It's no' gonnae be as easy as you're makin' oot.'

'Naw … it fuckin' isnae!'

'Well, put it this way, there's nae *band* as of right noo. There's nae instruments, 'cos they've aw went walkin'. There's nae songs, nae money, an' frankly, nae inspiration. Ye need aw ae things tae start a band. Ah should ken, ah've been fuckin' tryin' long enough.'

'Aye? Like whit?'

'*Max Mojo*? Fuck sake, that sounds like that green an' white gadgie that helps weans cross the bastart road!'

'But every cunt'll be pissin' themselves. Jesus Christ, man.'

'Aye. *Aye*, ah said.'

'Where? That wee office oan John Dickie Street? Where Molly pays the rates?'

'Right. Fuckin' fine. Ah'll dae it after, man. Jist gie us a break, eh? Ma heid's loupin'.'

¶

Molly Wishart heard her son from the kitchen. She initially assumed that he was speaking to someone on the telephone, but when she leaned in closer to eavesdrop, it was apparent that he wasn't in the hall where the house phone was. Dale Wishart was in the front room of the manse. Molly peered through the gap between door and frame and saw him pacing back and forth. She hadn't heard the front door opening and, although she couldn't see the whole room, she assumed there was no one else in there.

'For God sake, son, it's like Blackpool Illuminations in here! Turn the big light off … everybody can see in.'

'Whit … 'cos ah've got *wan* fuckin' light oan?'

'Hey, watch who yer speakin' tae!' The doctors had told Molly Wishart to anticipate certain mood changes that were often the consequence of a severe concussion, but in the two weeks since he had returned home from hospital, she'd noticed these episodes increasing in both regularity and intensity. Molly had asked the specialist about this and she had booked him in for further neurological tests, but since he appeared to have made a remarkable physical recovery, the NHS urgency seemed to have shifted down a gear.

With biological tests ruling out other forms of psychosis associated with substance abuse or other mental-health conditions, a Pakistani consultant had eventually diagnosed Schizo-affective disorder. But he was non-commital about the Henderson Church beating being the cause. The consultant's colleagues casually suggested indulging in the young man's altered-state fantasy, and recommended acceding to his bizarre demands about his new persona. Molly and Washer were warned about delusions and hallucinations being the classic symptoms of this type of psychosis. Nobody said anything to them about the disorganised and profanity-strewn speech patterns.

In the subsequent days, Dale Wishart officially became *Max Mojo* via deed poll. When challenged, the individual now known as Max claimed his mum was imagining him talking to himself. He even shamefully hinted that *her* mental capacity might be called into question in this regard. But his left eye had also started fluttering and twitching uncontrollably when these periods occurred. Molly had convinced herself that with her son's previously carefree attitude on the decline, he was being slowly but surely overtaken by a darker and more malign force.

'Don't talk shite, Mam. That's the fuckin' plot ae *The Empire Strikes Back*,' he'd said to her. But the swearing in itself was indicative of a significant change. The teenager formerly known as *Dale* would never have spoken to his mother – or *any* woman for that matter – in that way. It was a positive trait he'd inherited from his father, who despite faults in other areas had never disrespected women in the manner so stereotypical of the working-class males of his generation.

Max's eye stopped twitching. He sat down. His demeanour seemed to relax as his mum stood before him.

'So, when's yer interview, again?' she asked him.

'Friday.'

'The 'morra, ye mean?'

'Aye. Christ … lost track ae the days, Mam.'

'Well, make sure ye get tae yer bed early tonight then, an' that ye've looked oot aw yer certificates, aye? It's a good wee job, doon at the Garden Centre. Plenty ae fresh air … nice flowers tae look after. It'll calm ye, son.'

'Aye, Mam. Ah will. Don't worry.' Max wasn't worried either, but mainly because he had absolutely no intention of going to this particular interview.

3

24th June 1982

'For *fuck's* sake!' Washer Wishart had stepped out of the back seat of the Volvo and straight into a muddy puddle. This wasn't a good start to what would surely be a difficult and confrontational situation. 'Who fuckin' lives like this, eh?' he said, scanning the agricultural wasteland of the Quinns' compound, where this summit meeting was being held. He wiped the brown watery *shite* from his brogues. He shook his head as he took in a destitute panorama containing scabby ducks, pigs and rabbits roaming free, four static caravans – three of which were on bricks as opposed to wheels – and a graveyard of rusting white goods, all underscored by a thick layer of slurried dung. Chickens moved tentatively, as if they were in the middle of a minefield. It was like an interpretation of *Animal Farm* painted by Hieronymous Bosch. Washer tiptoed gingerly through the muck, sighing and cursing under his breath.

'Fuckin' pikeys!' said Benny Donald in a sycophantic attempt to surf the mood. Washer didn't acknowledge him. Benny was still *persona non grata* for his peripheral role in the reason why Washer Wishart had to be in this god-forsaken Galston gypsy hovel in the first place. Washer aimed for the shed with the open door, where others had congregated. Benny trailed along behind, head down.

Nobby Quinn, the Birmingham-born gypsy patriarch, teased his wispy greying beard through nicotine-stained fingers. Magdalena, his domineering wife, stood right behind him, as if working him from the back. Three of their muscle-bound, tattooed sons sat on hay bales. They all looked like bored versions of David Essex in *Stardust*. They were the Quinns, ruling Romany crime family of Galston, a few miles to the east of Kilmarnock, and this was their gaff.

Actually, it was their gaffe in other ways that had necessitated this meeting. Ten days earlier, an angry mob acting under instruction from the Quinns had wrecked the Henderson Church Hall in Kilmarnock, during a faux charity fundraising gig by local band The Vespas. The reason for this had been uncertain until Fat Franny Duncan had admitted under some duresse that he had paid the Quinns to carry out this apparently incendiary act. The Fat Franny contingent – Bob 'Hobnail' Dale, Des Brick, Wullie the Painter, and the Fatman himself – were situated nearest to the large barn door. It was unintentional but it looked to Washer Wishart like they were bracing themselves for a quick getaway. Washer smirked at the thought of *milk* turning faster than Fat Franny Duncan.

The third leg of this Ayrshire crime triumvirate – Washer Wishart's crew from Crosshouse – were the current victims. There were three of them. Old man Washer, suited and business-respectable as usual. Flat-pack Frankie Fusi, the legendary dark-haired and smouldering fixer. Benny Donald, who was there ostensibly deputising for Washer's *consigliore*, his thirty-year-old nephew, Gerry Ghee. Gerry had called in sick that morning. Given the business of the day, it had raised a slight suspicion with Washer, but he hadn't pressed it. If he had, Gerry would've been forced to concede that he was having a vasectomy. It wasn't something he wanted widely known.

The summit had been called by the Quinns, at Don McAllister's insistence. A new gang war was the last thing Don McAllister wanted, so he had acted quickly. Regional enforcer, Mickey 'Doc' Martin had been cajoled into attending by McAllister, but purely as an independent witness.

So the meeting of the most powerful unelected men in East Ayrshire was taking place in a dung-filled cowshed. Washer wasn't impressed, but when in Romany territory…

'Thanks are due tae the Quinns for hostin' this emergency summit meetin'.' A muted, half-hearted round of applause broke out as Doc Martin opened proceedings. He wasn't expected to chair, but it looked like he'd have to. The inscrutability of the Wisharts, the

inarticulacy of the Quinns and the apparent determination of the
Fat Franny crew not to incriminate themselves had left no option.
The meeting should've started half an hour ago, but all present
danced around the subject with a prolonged discussion about the
morning's breakthrough news. Only Washer Wishart had an understandable interest in the Falklands War being declared over, given his
previous army service overseas. None of the others present could've
given a flying fuck about it, and their determination to drag the
stilted introductory smalltalk out for as long as possible was a clear
indication that this wasn't going to be as fruitful and conclusive a
discussion as Don McAllister had hoped. So – acknowledging the
digressionary tactics – Doc Martin cut to the chase.

'It's an emergency 'cos naebody wants a return tae the McLarty
era, right?' Doc waited for a response. He only got head shakes. It
was enough. 'So, Washer's been wronged, right?' No response. Doc
put that down to the confusing wording. These weren't the sharpest
tools in the box, he reckoned. 'Whit ah mean is that the Wisharts
were the victims ae an unfortunate fuck-up. Is that agreed? Nae mali-
ciousness wis intended towards them.' The seated leaders eyed each
other anxiously. 'For fuck's sake, it's no' the fuckin' *Deer Hunter*. Nae
cunts gettin' shot through the heid. Jist admit the fuck-up, apologise
an' we can get tae the compo.' There was some shuffling of feet and
a theatrical cough from Magdalena Quinn. Doc Martin was getting
annoyed. 'Franny, fuck sake, man. You're up.'

'Em … ah'm willin' tae … em, concede that ah only wanted they
two Heatwave DJ fannies neutered.' Fat Franny cleared his throat.
'Ah asked Nobby here for an … *accommodation*. But, as Doc says,
due tae an unfortunate breakdoon in communications…' Fat Franny
turned to look at Hobnail, '…the wrang instructions got passed.'
Fat Franny then turned to look directly at Washer Wishart. 'An' fur
that, ah'm sorry, Washer. As long as the penalty's fair, ah'll be fine in
handin' ower the lion's share.' Fat Franny had conserved a tidy stash
in his house safe, and while he resented giving it to Washer Wishart,
the price of protecting the ongoing calm was worth paying. Within

reason, of course. Hobnail would find his monthly cut docked for some time to come.

'Good,' said Doc Martin. 'Nobby? Anythin' tae add?' Nobby Quinn shook his head. But his fearsome wife spoke up.

'Washer, we're sorry about ye boy, but that wasna us. We didna touch 'im.' Magdalena's thick Brummie accent floated through the testosterone in the barn like a fart in a spacesuit. 'But inna spirit of keepin' peace here, we'll pey up too.'

'Thanks fur that, Mrs Quinn,' said Doc. 'Right, if you're aw'right wi' this, Washer, ah'll work oot a package an' let ye know once they've aw accepted it.' Washer Wishart nodded his acceptance. He'd got through this brief summit meeting without speaking. It would be clear that he'd accept the outturn penalty payments, but that he'd do so grudgingly. That should keep the others on edge until the *real* story of the Henderson night emerged. And he'd make sure it would. Meanwhile, the payments to him would hopefully sort out the Glasgow drug mess in which Benny Donald had landed the family.

'Could ye'se aw leave us a minute? Ah'd like a private word wi' yer bosses.' Doc Martin's request left all a bit blindsided. Hadn't they just worked out a resolution?

$$\frac{7}{2}$$

The kingpins all motioned to their subordinates to wait outside.

'There's rabbit stew in th' yard fur them's that want it.' And with that culinary threat issued by the fearsome Magdalena Quinn, the main part of the summit meeting of the Three East Ayrshire Crime Families concluded, blood unspilled. Des Brick knew Fat Franny had been hoping for a word with Doc Martin about his upcoming Metropolis nightclub residency. The suggestion that Doc was about to award that gig to Bobby Cassidy and his pal, Joey Miller, of Heatwave instead of Fat Franny had been the catalyst for the Henderson Church sanction. But after twenty additional minutes of private chat, Doc Martin had bolted first. He'd far better things to be doing than debating his *own* plans with subordinates, and nothing short of a red-hot poker up the arsehole from Satan himself would get him anywhere near that steaming oil-can with the boiled skinless rabbits.

'Whit wis that aw aboot, boss?' Des asked hopefully.

'Eh … nothin' important. Jist aboot the … em, method ae payment. The compo, like.' Fat Franny seemed distracted, but Des elected not to press the point further. The journey back to Onthank in the brown Rover was conducted in silence.

4

DI Charlie Lawson had elected to visit Senga Dale alone. His boss, Detective Chief Superintendent Don McAllister had suggested taking a young female copper, but Charlie figured that she'd just get in the way. The wee lassies at the Kilmarnock Cop Shop were useful at these types of difficult home visits, there was no doubt about that, but since Don McAllister specifically wanted this situation kept tight – and since it was after midnight anyway – Charlie didn't want this dragged out by a *Juliet Bravo* offering to make soothing cups of tea.

He rapped at the green door. Try though he always did to conceal or vary it, Charlie Lawson's door-knocking technique could only be *polis*. As he waited for the occupants of the house to stir, he mused on how often a police knock during the night prompted responses from adjacent houses more quickly than the one being knocked up. You could set your watch by it. Both of Senga Dale's terraced neighbours had illuminated their houses before hers. Net curtains on both sides twitched. The watchers would have instinctively known a police call was under way even though Charlie Lawson was unmarked both in clothing and in transport.

He didn't want to chap the door again, but just when he thought he would have to, an upper-bedroom light came on. He heard footsteps on the internal stairs, and then the door opened. *No locks or chains,* Charlie noted.

'Aw'right, son,' said Charlie, to the dishevelled teenager staring bleary-eyed into the gloom outside. 'Yer mam in? Ah need a word.'

'Eh … it's fuckin' three in the mornin', for fuck's sake! Can it no' wait?' croaked Grant Dale.

'Naw, it cannae … and naw, it *isnae*.' Grant looked puzzled, or *more* puzzled. 'Three in the mornin'.' Charlie Lawson moved up a step. 'Can ah come in? It's important. Go an' get yer mam.'

'Ah'm right here.' An unseen voice rattled down the stairs. 'Let him in, son.' Grant Dale stood to one side. He looked out into the street after Charlie Lawson had brushed past him.

'Fuck off, ya nosy aul' cunt!' he hissed at Mrs Trodden, the old woman who lived immediately to their right, and who was now out on her own doorstep for a better view.

All three moved from the small hall into the living room. No one sat. *In and out, basic details … condolences.* Charlie Lawson recalled his boss's instructions.

'Mrs Dale, ah'm very sorry to have to inform you that we've been investigatin' a fire in the town centre. A body was found in the building, an' we believe it to be that of yer husband, Robert Dale.' Senga's lip quivered a bit but she controlled it. *Show nothin' of yer feelings tae naebody.* Her son's eyes widened and he swallowed hard, but then his expression also returned to stoney-faced. They both remained standing. Charlie was relieved. Night shift was a bastard, particularly when you had to do house calls like this one, but it was beginning to look certain that he'd be back at his desk in less than half an hour. 'There are currently nae suspicious circumstances. It looks like a tragic accident,' Charlie concluded.

'Aye … fuckin' tragic,' said Senga, sarcastically.

'Do ye have any information relating to this incident that ye want tae tell me?' enquired Charlie.

'Naw,' said Senga. 'Boab an' me were … *separated*.'

'Separated?' said a surprised Grant. He thought his father had just nipped out 'for a message'. That was universal code in Onthank for a tactical fortnight-long withdrawal from public gaze. He sat down in his father's armchair.

'Aye. We'd split up,' said Senga, looking daggers at Grant. He got the message.

Charlie looked at both of them, back and forth and *again*. He suspected something was going on, but since there was a higher plan and he had already been informed of his role in carrying it out, he let a potential line of intuitive questioning drop.

'We'll need ye tae come tae the hospital for a formal identification. But, since this has clearly come as a massive shock tae ye…' It was now Charlie's turn to be sarcastic, '…we'll leave that until mornin'. That okay? Ah can send a car up tae get ye.'

'Ah suppose so. Whit time?' said Senga.

'Aboot nine?'

'Fine.'

'Ah'm sorry for yer loss, Mrs Dale,' said Charlie, heading for the front door. '*And* you, son. Ah take it he wis yer Dad?'

'Aye. He wis.' Charlie hadn't been expecting a grief-stricken display of emotional histrionics but, nevertheless, the reaction of Bob Dale's wife and son had been pretty callous. Charlie thought about his own wife, and their two teenage children. He'd often considered how they would react upon receiving the terrible news that some young prick with a blade and out of his head on smack, had killed him. *Certainly a lot more affected than this*, he acknowledged. *Fuckin' Onthank jakeys… nae heart at all.*

✦

'Whit the fuck wis that aw aboot, Mam?' Grant was angry. He had never connected with his father, but he never ever wished him dead. His mother's apparently calm, *laissez-faire* attitude shocked him though.

'Look, there's stuff ah need tae tell ye,' said Senga. 'But better waitin' until the mornin'. Ah threw yer dad oot, a few nights ago. He wis pretty abusive. An' really doon aboot everythin'. Ah couldnae be livin' wi' aw his shite anymore.' Senga sat down. 'Ah'm no that surprised he's topped himself.' Grant hadn't made that connection yet.

'Suicide?' Grant said. 'For fuck sake! Fuckin' coward.'

'Let's talk in the mornin', eh? There's somethin' else, but it can wait,' said Senga.

Grant sighed. His mother had got up and it was clear that he wasn't going to get any more clarity until Senga was ready to offer it. He knew only too well how impenetrably stubborn she could be. Grant sat in the living room with the lights out for an hour or so. As he passed his mother's bedroom on the way to his own, he could hear her sobbing.

⚡

6th July 1982

'Will there be time tae get the Revels? The pictures are shite without the Revels.' Rocco Quinn had moaned incessantly since meeting Maggie Abernethy at the bus-stop on the Ayr Road. It usually didn't bother her, but tonight it was particularly grating. It was her birthday, and she wanted to see *An Officer and a Gentleman*. Her boyfriend had made his objections clear, loudly and often. *Daft fuckin' lassie's film* or *Richard Gere's a bent shot* being his most often repeated observations. Maggie was now wishing she'd gone on her own. She was almost wishing she *was* on her own again. In the thirty minutes spent waiting for him to turn up on his motorbike, Maggie Abernethy had decided that the effort and commitment required to maintain a relationship with someone like Rocco Quinn wasn't worth it. This was her birthday, and he hadn't even acknowledged it. She wasn't the type of girl to expect diamonds and flowers, but a card would've been nice.

They had first encountered each other six months previously. Rocco had been driving his family's horse and cart, Steptoe-like, along Shortlees Avenue. The gypsies did the rag-and-bone routes around Shortlees once a week, but Maggie had never noticed the good-looking son of Nobby Quinn before. It was usually toothless, *baccy*-chewing old men who did the collections. Maggie had taken some of her mum's old clothes and shoes out to the cart and Rocco had given her a cheap, golden 'princess' ring in return. The tiny stone had fallen out of it that same evening but Maggie treasured the gift from the dark-haired, sallow-skinned, handsome young man and wore it still.

Rocco saw Maggie again the following week. He explained that his father had forced him onto the carts for a week as a punishment for losing a car in a poker game, but that *this* time, he was hoping he'd see her again. He was charming and polite in those early days. Maggie wasn't used to the close attention of young men. She had spent the majority of her twenty-three years in foster care. There were many boys sniffing around her through her school years. Her mixed-race background and her undoubted beauty guaranteed their attention, but she didn't court it, preferring her own company. She spent most of her non-curriculum time in the Music Department, battering seven shades of shit out of the school's only drum kit. Her favourite teacher, Mr Gamble, a hippyish muso, had gifted them to her when she left. He staged a break-in and testified that the drum kit had been stolen. It was the nicest thing anyone had ever done for Maggie.

The boys didn't really feature; they didn't have the attention span or the long-term commitment needed to break through her suspicious defences. She slept with a few of them, and once with Mr Gamble, but purely on her terms, of course.

As they walked from John Finnie Street, where Rocco had parked his motorbike, Maggie's mood was darkening. *His humourless jokes, his constant moaning and those stupid fucking Revels.* Being with Rocco was tiresome now. He took her for granted. They rarely laughed or joked or carried on anymore. They had sex like a middle-aged, unhappily married couple; sporadically, with repetitive, conventional positions and unsatisfied, bitter arguments afterwards. In only six months, their relationship had started to feel like an extended Youth Opportunities Scheme, only without the £23.50 a week to salve the pointless tedium and the lack of direction. She was going through the motions. It had to stop.

They reached the front doors of the ABC Cinema in Titchfield Street. A long queue had formed to the right of the narrow Art

Deco frontage. The building had a face like a beautiful old Wurlitzer Jukebox and Maggie loved going there. She first experienced the thrill of celluloid by going to the Minors as a child on Saturday mornings. She especially loved *The Time Machine*. It ran for weeks on end and Maggie was there every time. The dark-skinned women in it had long blonde hair, just like her. There was a curious magic about the ABC Cinema in Titchfield Street. It was like a portal to another world, and on this balmy evening, Maggie would escape to a world of crew-cuts, white-suited Marines and desperately optimistic factory girls looking to escape the humdrum existence that seemed to be their pre-determined destiny.

Rocco had insisted on getting the tickets. It was her birthday after all, he'd said. She had been despatched to get the Revels. The smaller hall, number two, to the left of the confectionary counter at the front was only a quarter full, with a higher percentage of men than a Richard Gere film might have been expected to attract. The lights dimmed. Rocco Quinn slumped down in his seat, his legs now drapped over the seats in front. There were no flashy Pearl & Dean advertisements, no encouraging message from Kia-Ora. Maggie Abernethy suddenly knew why. The British Board of Film Censors had certified *Flesh Gordon* as an 'X'.

'You fuckin' selfish *prick*!' shouted Maggie.

'Whit?' he pleaded, half-heartedly. Maggie stood up abruptly. She could hear male voices grumbling in the darkness behind her. She pushed past Rocco, knocking his legs to one side and his man-size bag of chocolate-covered surprises all over the cinema floor.

'Fuck off,' hissed Maggie.

5

'Could anybody know where ye are?'

'Naw.'

'Sure?'

'Fuckin' certain. Look, let's get this done, right? Whit's the deal?'
Wullie Blair – the Painter by nickname – had painted himself into a wee
corner. He was on an island of his own making, miles from any *other*
island. The sharks were circling. When Don McAllister had reached out
to him through a shared secret connection, it was initially like having
his own personal message in a bottle picked up by the coastguard.
Now though, the realisation that his 'saving' would come with onerous
conditions was dawning. They were sat in Don's car on the shale
hard-standing at the remote Laigh Milton Mill pub. Don had often
wondered how this old renovated Mill building survived as a boozer.
It was a beautiful old structure, no doubt, and its location on the very
edge of the origin of the River Irvine gave its context a sylvan character
that Don had rarely seen elsewhere in East Ayrshire. But you definitely
couldn't walk to it easily and the closest tiny village of Gatehead didn't
have enough regular bums to keep the tills ringing. Needless to say, the
Milton Mill had closed early and, although late, it wasn't yet dark.

'We're in a similar spot, you an' me,' said Don. He glanced over at
the access road where Charlie Lawson was standing guard. 'The fire
at Mickey Martin's nightclub was … *unfortunate*.' Don turned to
the side in the driver's seat to look directly at Wullie the Painter. 'Ah
need this tae disappear without suspicion, an' so dae you.'

'Ah had fuck all tae dae wi' the fire, or Hobnail,' sighed Wullie.
'Ye ken that.'

'Ah do, however, the Fatman might no' see it like that. Ah assume he still knows nothin' about ye workin' for Doc Martin.'

'Naw,' said Wullie anxiously.

'An' clearly ye'd like tae keep it that way,' said Don.

'Does the Pope wear a funny hat?'

'Right. So here's the script. Ah'm gonnae lock this doon. A fire started accidentally, by Bob Dale. Smokin', draps a lit fag near a tin of varnish … place goes up like a fuckin' Roman candle.' Don sounded assured. 'We'll dae the rest, right. You wurnae even there.' Wullie liked the sound of that part. Don's altered reality continued:

'The Doc's in. He's got his ain skeletons here, an' he needs ma help keepin' them hidden away. Ah don't want another turf war developin' here, so it suits tae get it aw done an' fuckin' dusted quick. Ah've spoken tae the parlour. The funeral'll be on Friday.'

'Fuck sake, that's jist the day after the morra! How the fuck did ye swing that wi' Senga?' said Wullie.

'Look son, naebody seems tae be greetin' many tears here for the fella. Better for this tae be ower wi' as quick as possible, naw?'

'Aye, ah suppose,' said Wullie. 'Is that us done here then?'

Don laughed. 'Eh, naw … no' quite.' Wullie's head drooped.

'Ah want regular updates on whit Fat Franny's up tae. You're gonnae be ma man on the inside.'

'For fuck sake, Mr McAllister. How am ah meant tae carry that aff?' said Wullie.

'Ye'll figure it oot. Fat Franny Duncan's no' interested in anythin' but himself. Let's be honest here, he never suspected ye were dain' that decorating work on the side for Doc Martin, did he? That disnae indicate a high level ae close scrutiny does it?' said Don.

'He's had a lot oan lately. Ah burst ae cash has jist went walkabout, an' we're aw in the spotlight,' said Wullie.

'Just be sharp then. We'll no' put ye in undue danger. That widnae be productive, would it,' said Don, patting Wullie's shoulder.

'An' whit if ah cannae?' Wullie enquired.

'Or *willnae*?' Don added. 'Well then, the tape ae ye leaving the

Foregate multi-storey wi' the date and time in its wee top right-hand corner might find its way tae the Fatman ... an' maybe even the Procurator Fiscal.' Don had played his shot well. Wullie the Painter now needed snookers.

6

Fat Franny Duncan stood tall. He was fully clothed in respectful black, save for a white tie. It was a horrendously hot day and some daft bastard had compounded the effect of this by leaving the St John Church central heating on overnight. Fat Franny also wore a black overcoat but he had draped it over the shoulders, like he imagined Don Corleone would have in similar circumstances. Mopping a sodden brow with a black monogrammed handkerchief, he breathed in deeply then looked up and began his tribute.

'Boab was like a brother tae me. A mair trustworthy man ah've yet tae meet. He cared deeply aboot Senga, his missus ... his life partner ... an' each of his weans, but 'specially his eldest yin, Grant there.' Fat Franny nodded in the direction of the front row left and touched his temple with a chubby forefinger. He pointedly avoided catching Senga Dale's eye. That she had been able to pay for this funeral service without approaching him for financial help had immediately raised his eyebrow. Fat Franny had recently suffered a break-in at the Ponderosie – the converted council house where he stayed with his mum, Rose. Almost forty grand had been taken from his safe while he had been called away suddenly. Anyone with more spending capacity than Fat Franny deemed them capable of having, he saw as a suspect.

He quickly looked right, to where his own team were yawning and looking bored. He pressed on.

'He wis a good man at heart, wis Boab Dale. Dae anythin' for ye ... if ye asked him tae.' Fat Franny heard a sarcastic snigger, probably from Senga, but let it pass without comment, apart from: 'He might've fu ... might've messed up his marriage, but mibbe that wisnae aw his fault, eh?' Senga Dale stood up calmly and walked over to the large wooden box that contained her husband's body. She leaned over and touched it tenderly, and then turned and walked steadily back up the same aisle that eighteen years earlier she'd walked down towards a new life as Mrs Robert Dale. And also as a new mother to the child who was already growing inside her.

§

Andrew and Sophie, her two other younger children, followed her out of their father's funeral service as if they were all connected by an invisible climbing rope.

'Ah … thank you, em, Mr Duncan. Thank you for that, em, touching tribute.' Reverend McKenzie had known this would be a tough appointment. As well as accusing virtually everyone – *including* the Church of Scotland – of taking his money, Fat Franny had turned up the heat on a large number of the minister's dwindling congregation. Henry McKenzie had hoped for … that new American term … a bit of *closure* with the burial of Bob Dale. But that now seemed highly unlikely. Fat Franny Duncan returned to his seat. With today's job almost done, a thin-lipped smile concealed an anger that had grown steadily since he had been robbed ten days ago.

Rev. Henry McKenzie wrapped things up sharpish. With Senga having left the building, it seemed pointless recounting the tale of how they met. Little point in telling of the few happy memories the minister had been made aware of in the days following Bob Dale's identification as the victim in the fire that burned down the Metropolis nightclub before it had even opened.

§

Senga had waited for Grant, her eldest, out in the Church car park. Her heels were making indentations in the soft steaming tarmac. It was a ludicrous offer, but Fat Franny made it anyway. 'Senga, we're huvin' a wee *do* for Boab doon the Portman. A coupla bottles ae Pomagne … some sausage rolls an' that, nothin' else but. Ah'm no' fuckin' made ae money, ken?' Senga's expression remained impassive. She was determined she would give nothing away about the package she'd received from her late husband. She knew the money was Fat Franny's, and she also knew that it was Hobnail's way of ensuring she understood that he *too* wanted Grant to find a life far from the Fatman's clutches. Senga turned away without reply. 'Well, dinnae say ah didnae ask,' and then when she was beyond earshot, 'ya fuckin' midden.' He called out to Grant Dale. 'Whit aboot you, son? A wee dram tae yer faither's memory efter the graveyard?'

'Naw Franny. Thanks, but. Ah'm just gonnae head up the road wi' ma mam. She's in a bit ae shock wi' aw this,' said Grant.

'Aye,' said the Fatman, softly. 'Ah'll bet she is.' Grant turned and started to walk after his mother. 'Ho, Grant,' shouted Fat Franny. 'A couple mair days ae compassionate leave, then it's back tae work, right?' Grant stopped. He paused. He turned to face Fat Franny Duncan from twenty paces away.

'Ah'm no' comin' back, Franny.'

'Oh … izzat right, son?'

'Aye. It's no' for me, man. The life an' that.'

'Mibbe ah'll decide … like yer faither wanted me tae.'

'Ah'm thinkin' ae goin' tae College. Mibbe tae dae music.'

'Aye, aw'right Elvis,' said Fat Franny before heading towards his own orange Ford Capri. 'We'll see.'

That morning, as he was putting on his father's black tie, to go to his father's funeral, Grant's mother told him about the money that his father had sent her. She also told him where it had come from. She explained what she intended to do with it, and – with regard to Grant – the strict conditions that came attached with those plans. Distance placed between the Dales, and Fat Franny Duncan was the constant in all of them.

⚡

7.48 pm

'The nick ae that cunt, Fagan, eh?' Wullie the Painter was obviously impressed.

'Aye,' said Des Brick. He'd been pretty quiet for the majority of the day and Wullie had been acutely aware of it. It was understandable, after all, Hobnail had been his brother-in-law, and even though he no longer spoke to Senga, his sister, the funeral had been awkward for all involved. The burial had been a bit less tense, but nonetheless, Wullie had history with Senga, too, and he couldn't help but feel a little sorry for her, even if she wasn't exactly demonstrating any obvious sense of loss. His current job was to try and shake Des Brick out of his morosity, and in turn, add necessary deflection to his own unintentional role in the big man's demise.

'Fuck *talkin'* tae her, or drinkin' tea wi' her … ah'd huv slipped her the boaby,' said Wullie. Des smiled. The ice was cracking. 'Ah mean, fuck sake, how many ordinary folk wid get tae say they'd knobbed the Queen, eh? He had opportunity, a bed, an' by all accounts a willin' gash.' Des laughed. Job *nearly* done. 'Her nightie was up 'roond her neck an' she's gaun *"Stick one's boaby right up one's Blackwall Tunnel"…*' Des Brick was guffawing at this. '…an' whit does yer man Fagan dae? He bleats oan like a wee fuckin' lassie aboot his missus leavin' him. Nae bloody wonder she did, if the daft cunt carries oan like *that* durin' a hoose-breakin'.' Wullie the Painter had his arms outstretched, like one of the Queen's own Counsel appealing for sanity to prevail in a black-and-white case.

A voice boomed: 'An' while ah remember it, where the fuck huv you been these last few days? Everythin' fuckin' kickin' off an' you *disappear* fur a whole week, eh?' Fat Franny had come in through the side door, taking both men by surprise, especially the Painter. 'Been tryin' yer hoose constantly, so we huv. Whit the fuck, Wullie!'

'Aye, sorry aboot that, boss. Had tae vanish, *sparko*. Got word that the polis were efter a chat aboot aw they wee bottles ae Belgian beer an' aw the fags that ah did the deal oan, 'member?' Wullie had rehearsed this bit with Charlie Lawson, in case it needed verification.

For the moment though, Fat Franny seemed to have other things on his mind. He let the explanation stand.

Des Brick had realised the awkwardness of his own situation the minute that Hobnail's death had been confirmed. Hobnail was a miserable cunt, of that there could be no dispute, but Des felt his brother-in-law had been badly treated by the Fatman over the years. Hobnail and Franny had been close friends through school, but when Franny's influence and control had begun to rise, and as his band of foot-soldiers started to coalesce through the 70s, Des Brick watched Hobnail's position diminish from equal into that of purely Thug Numero Uno.

'Hey, Mr Benn!' Wullie's high-pitched taunt shook Des out of his daydreaming. 'Away intae that cupboard an' come oot dressed as Desmond fuckin' Brick, eh?'

Des laughed and stood up.

'Right, fuckface. Let's get oan wi' it,' said Des.

'Whit's Franny goat lined up fur us then?' asked the Painter.

'We've tae pick up Terry Connolly at his hoose,' Des confirmed, now back in the zone. 'It's his initiation, th'night.'

Wullie the Painter gagged a bit. He recalled *his* only too well. But given his current situation, a strategic AWOL was out of the question.

⚡

7.58 pm

Wullie the Painter looked at the Polaroids. His heart sank. He already had a set of similar ones, from his own initiation into the fraternity of Fat Franny. It was a ludicrous and embarrassing thing to have to go through. Terry Connolly came back from the Portman's narrow bar with a tray of drinks, even though he and Wullie were the only two in the pool room.

'Expectin' company, pal?' Wullie was still cagey around Terry, and vice versa. Terry Connolly's introduction had been limited to

'This is Terry. He's a guid yin. Dinnae gie him any fuckin' grief.' The Fatman hadn't explained Terry's role or responsibilities within the inner circle so, since the previous evening's events, a degree of paranoia had developed on all sides. At least Terry was trying to make a connection.

'Jist thought ah'd get a few in, save us huvin' tae go back up while the fitba's oan.'

'Aye. Ah suppose,' said Wullie, resigned to a strained evening of teeth-pulling conversation while the World Cup Final deserved his full attention. Wullie lifted two of his four pints of Lager and placed them directly in front of him as if deciding which one to tackle first.

'Hope ye don't mind me askin', wee man,' Wullie suspected what was coming, but let Terry finish in the slim hope that it wasn't what he thought. 'Whit the fuck wis aw that shite wi' us gettin' our knobs oot?' *Fuckin' bingo,* thought Wullie. There really wasn't ever any doubt, was there?

'Look, it's fuckin' Franny. He's ay suspicious that wan ae the inner circle is a plank, know? The fuckin' *knobs oot* business is wan ae his ways ae tryin' tae make sure nae cunt goes rogue.' Wullie was embarrassed at having to say this. He was even more affronted at having had to rub the exposed end of his cock against Terry Connolly's – a man to whom he'd only properly been introduced two hours earlier.

'Is he a fuckin' bent shot, then, the Fatman like?' Terry instinctively lowered his voice. He was a hardman, but not one without tact.

'Naw. He's ridin' that Theresa Morgan yin … that blondie yin wi' the magic tits, ken?'

'Can she make stuff disappear wi' them, like?' laughed Terry.

'In a manner ae speakin',' said Wullie. Terry looked puzzled.

'If she catches ye gawpin' … one word, and a flash ae them tae Fatboy Franny an' they could make *you* fuckin' disappear.' Terry laughed at Wullie's joke, without appreciating he wasn't joking. Wullie drained his pint and then belched loudly.

'Fat Franny makes us aw drap oor troosers, pull back the foreskin and touch knob-ends wi' any new inner circle member.' Wullie sipped from pint number two then continued. 'He takes photies ae it aw an' makes copies for every cunt. If anybody drifts aff the plan, copies ae them are sent to every fucker he kens. Nae boaby … nae wedge, the following month. It's a bit like being blood brothers … only … no'.' Wullie looked up at the screen willing Paolo Rossi to kick off and get him off this subject.

'Mair like … *boaby* brothers,' said Terry. Wullie smiled.

'Aye … boaby brothers. Ah like that.' Wullie lifted his glass, and Terry Connolly reciprocated with a clink. *Maybe this cunt isnae aw bad,* he figured.

'So,' Wullie the Painter ventured, 'whit's your gig gonnae be in the FF Universe?'

'The vans mainly. Ice-cream yins aroon' Onthank. Got five lined up … aw sellin' jellies an' blues an' that oot the back,' said Terry, matter-of-factly. 'Yer ma's wee helpers. Oot they come in their slippers fur a pack ae fags, a '99 an' a bag ae Temazapam. Ye could write the fuckin' script. In fact, if their *doctors* wrote the script, we'd be ootae business.' Terry sipped his pint. 'They vans are like travelling junkie shops. Customer comes tae you. Fuckin' piss easy.'

'Where are ye' gettin' the stock?' asked Wullie.

'Cannae tell ye, brother,' said Terry, smiling. 'Ah'd have tae kill ye!' Wullie the Painter frowned. Terry relented, but only a bit. 'It's a big source. Ah cannae reveal the name, honestly, ah *cannae*. They're expandin' their gig intae Ayrshire. It'll be good for us in Onthank, though … for *aw* ae us.' Terry supped his pint and then continued, unsolicited. 'Ah could cut ye a slice, wee man … if ye were intae it, ken? The Fatman disnae need tae ken anythin' aboot it.' Wullie the Painter sensed that Terry Connolly's understanding of discretion might not be the strongest. 'Ah mean, ah coulda done this maself. Fat Franny's oan the way oot … but he still casts a big shadow ower Onthank. Best tae pay the dues at the start, ken?' Terry laughed. 'An' if that means rubbin' ma baws against *other* guys' baws, then fuck it. Ah had tae dae *much* worse in Polmont Young Offenders!'

Wullie was relieved. Terry wouldn't be a threat, he'd concluded. He was too open with information which, given Wullie's new covert initiative, would certainly come in handy. Wullie had never liked the ice-cream vans anyway. Despite Terry's over-confidence, Wullie felt there were far too many personal risks in dealing with desperate addicts needing a score. You were trapped in a metal box for one. It only took one out-of-their-head moron with a perceived griev-ance and a can of petrol and you were toast. *Literally.* Plus, Don McAllister's squad might've turned a blind eye to some of the activi-ties but they still dropped the odd unpredictable raid on all of the organisations. The vans were the easiest and most public targets. And Terry Connolly was *already* in the crosshairs of the likes of Charlie Lawson over this new Metropolis nightclub business. Wullie the Painter figured Terry Connolly might not actually be around long enough even to *become* a threat. Unless, of course, he was on the same restrictive deal with McAllister that Wullie was. In the world of the small-time hood, suspicion was the default setting.

'Who've ye got here?' Wullie asked, turning to look at Terry for the first time in the conversation.

'Italy ... 3–1,' said Terry. 'Got a tonne oan wi' Wullie Hills.'

'Ye've nae chance,' said Wullie.

'Ye reckon?'

'Aye. Italy huv had their peak wi' the Brazil game. Nae way they can raise it again.'

'Ach, shite. The fuckin' Gerries shouldnae even be *in* the Final efter whit Schumacher did tae that French boy.' Terry folded his arms as if the defence had rested. But it was the German defence that ultimately rested, and two hours later Terry Connolly whooped and hollered as Dino Zoff lifted the golden trophy. Goals from – predictably – player of the tournament, Rossi, followed by Tardelli and Altobelli had Italy home and dry. Terry Connolly shifted his allegiance and prayed for a German consolation, and with seven minutes to go, Paul Breitner provided it. *Fuckin' lucky bastart*, thought Wullie the Painter. He put the Polaroids back in the brown envelope and stuffed them deep into his inside jacket pocket. Maybe some of Terry Connolly's good fortune would shine on him too.

$$\maltese$$

Tae gie ye a wee insight intae the … dynamic, at this point, the cunt wis tryin' his best tae ignore me, ken. Like a wee wean that yer shoutin' at … gie'in intae trouble for some fuckin' shite. Ye know … stickin' its fingers in its ears an' singin' 'La La La … ah'm no listenin'.

There wis' resistance … nae fuckin' doubt. But ah had the scent ae ma destiny in ma nostrils, an' nae wee poofy bawbag host wis getting' in the way, ken?

Molly an' Washer – the Ma and Da – they didnae get whit wis goin' oan. This transformation ae their wean fae a wee cunt that widnae say 'BOO' tae a goose intae a musical Master *ae the Universe … they couldnae cope wi' it aw tae start wi'.*

No' really their fault, tae be honest. Aw that initial resistance … it musta looked like the cunt wis goin' aff his heid, y'know? Aw that 'inner turmoil' that his specialists went oan aboot. It did me a favour while ah moulded the wee bastart intae a leader tae be reckoned wi' … jist like Washer, actually, but wi' a better line ae patter, ken?

Anyway, it started spillin' intae the music around aboot this time tae. The cunt's still clingin' oan tae the notion that the New Romantic's the thing. So ah booted his baws aboot that yin, so tae speak. We went the full twelve rounds oan it, ah have tae admit, but gradually it wis back listenin' tae the Ramones, Bowie, Curtis Mayfield … even The Jam. Stuff that it had grown up oan but had disowned for aw that Visage an' Spandau Ballet bollocks. A couple ae hunner listens tae 'Blitzkreig Bop' though, an' we were back oan track. Meanwhile, Molly made another doctor's appointment for the two ae us tae go tae. Ah wis as happy as fuckin' Larry tae go tae that … as ye can imagine.

7

15th July 1982

'Are ye ready, son?' Molly Wishart called up the stairs. She knew that this doctor's appointment for her increasingly erratic son was essential, but also that he would endeavour to avoid it at all costs. Surprisingly, he responded in the affirmative, and said that he would be there in a minute. As he came into view at the top of the stairs, her heart sank.

'Yer no' goin' oot wi' me, lookin' like that!' she sighed.

'Whit's up wi' it?' he said. Max Mojo was dressed in a pair of striped pyjamas. One of the legs was rolled up to just under the knee. Underneath the top, he wore a cream-coloured chunky knit sweater. He wore black DM boots with white laces. His hair had been dyed emerald green, which obviously accounted for the strange smell that had been wafting around the upper hall all morning, Molly reasoned. He had glasses with different-coloured lenses on, and he had drawn a CND logo on his forehead in blue ink. A 'Fuck EVERYTHING' button badge was pinned to the pyjama jacket's lapel. He looked like Rupert the Bear as an acid casualty. It was a test, Molly acknowledged. Despite all her instincts telling her not to, she called his bluff.

'Right, then. Let's go. We've only got half an hour to get there,' she said. He looked deflated.

Most people on the bus from Crosshouse to the surgery in Dundonald Road just stared. A couple laughed. One old woman fixed her gaze on Molly and seemed to shake her head indignantly for the whole journey. Once in the doctors' waiting room, the response of others was virtually identical.

They waited an uncomfortable twenty minutes. The buzzer went off. Dr McManus's room. Max had been summoned. He got up slowly, slouched towards the door and headed dramatically down the hall as if being asked to walk the green mile. The number of 'headshakers' trebled. Molly wanted the ground to open up and swallow her, but at least she had got her son here: a task that looked like being beyond her without the assistance of a straightjacket only two days earlier.

Max looked for the door with Dr McManus's name on it. He went straight in without knocking, surprising the young male doctor who was sitting at his desk writing notes. 'Ah, hello ... Dale, is it?' asked Dr McManus, doing a distinct comedy double-take. Max was also blindsided. The young doctor was either Indian, or Pakistani, or something other than an obvious 'McManus'.

'Naw ... it's no'. It's Max. Max Mojo. Fuck's sake, man ... keep up!' The young doctor looked down at his notes, and then at the front cover of the file.

'Em, could you wait here a moment? I'll just be a second,' he said, before leaving. Max looked around the small, windowless office. A doctor's examination table took up most of the room. A tiny desk sat at the end of it. Projecting cabinets on the wall meant the doctor had to watch his head as he stood up. It was almost certain that this was once a store cupboard. *Fucking NHS cuts,* thought Max. The door opened. Dr McManus came back in. The puzzled look had gone.

'Hi Max,' he said, all bedside-mannerly. 'How are things, son?' The 'son' grated with Max. This doctor didn't look much older than *him*.

'Fine,' said Max. 'Jist fine.'

'You've come through quite a trauma. Can you jump up on the bed and we'll just take a quick look at how you're healing?' The doctor's English was really good, Max had to concede.

'Aye. Aw'right,' said Max. Sooner be out and getting on with more important plotting. Max lay back.

'Okay, let's just have a look at this testicle,' said Dr McManus as he eased back Max's pyjama trousers and put his hand down the front, cupping his balls briefly. Max sprung up and head-butted him.

'Hey … ya fuckin' poofter!' he yelled. 'Get yer fuckin' hands aff ma baws, ya cunt!' The stunned young clinician slumped to his knees holding his head. Max briefly thought about swinging a boot, but held back.

'Ah'm gettin' the polis onto you! Ye'll be fuckin' shipped back tae Bombay oan the next boat, ya bastart … touchin' *me* up!' He stormed out of the consultant's cupboard-sized room. 'C'mon Mam,' he shouted into the waiting room. 'We're fuckin' ootae here! Some bent cunt masqueradin' as a doctor's jist felt us up. We're gaun tae the polis. Ah'm gettin' this place shut doon.'

⚡

Later that evening, deep within the bowels of Kilmarnock Police Station in the centre of the town, Max Mojo accepted that Dr Ranesh was not a 'Paki molester', who had broken into the doctor's surgery, stolen a white coat and posed as a *Dr McManus* in order simply to feel up innocent, law-abiding people like him. In turn, Dr Ranesh – who was merely filling in for his older Scottish colleague while he was on sabbatical – accepted that Max Mojo's complex medical condition had contributed to his unreasonable behaviour. Although Max still maintained he was the victim, a potential assault charge against him was dropped. With Washer and Molly nodding furiously in agreement, Max was instructed to take the medication he had been prescribed. If he didn't, and a repeat of any similar behaviour ensued, it was made clear he wouldn't be let off with a warning next time.

⚡

17th July 1982

'Get me Flat-pack Frankie.'

'Aye, righto Uncle Washer. Whit'll ah tell um it's for?'

'Just tell him he's wanted. That'll dae it.' Benny Donald nodded and exited stage left. Jimmy 'Washer' Wishart was 'donating' some money to have the Crosshouse Church Hall roof fixed. Washer lived in the old Manse immediately adjacent to the church itself and – since he rented the hall back to the church for their occasional use – had finally acknowledged the landlord's obligation to provide a wind-and-watertight envelope. Benny Donald had entered through the back door as instructed, and had burst onto the low platform like a triumphant vaudevillian, returning for one more encore.

'When's the boy gettin' oot?' asked Gerry Ghee.

'He's been hame for a wee while. Thought he wis gonnae be eatin' through a fuckin' straw for a bit at the beginning. Ah'd never ae heard the end ae it fae his maw, if that had transpired, ken?' Gerry Ghee looked surprised. 'Sorry, Gerry. Ah huvnae telt folk 'cos he's been acting a bit mental, ken? Some fuckin' schizophrenic thing. The daft cunt's been holed up in his room listenin' tae music tae slash yer wrists tae. Plays it fuckin' non-stop, tae. Bangin' oan constantly aboot bein' immortal. It's gettin' embarrassin', tae be honest wi' ye. He's painted the whole fuckin' room black. Ye'd think Dracula slept in there durin' the day, manky wee bastart.' Gerry nodded, and then shook his head immediately afterwards. It was intended to demonstrate empathy, to reinforce that he too didn't know what to make of it.

'Ah dunno … mibbe he's still sufferin' some form ae trauma efter the Church riot, y'know?' said Washer. 'His ma's up tae a hundred wi' it aw.'

'Aye. Fuckin' mental night, that yin, wi' aw they bastart gypos turnin' up. Ye got tae the bottom ae it aw yet?'

'Aye,' said Washer. 'Just aboot joined up aw the dots. That stupid fat cunt Duncan ordered a hit oan the two DJs but his arsehole ae a sidekick … the yin that cannae even fuckin' speak right … he gets the message wrang, an' Dale … ach fuck it, ah mean *Max*, and his group got targeted.' Gerry nodded sagely, as if this was an everyday fuck-up that regularly befell stuttering sidekicks.

'So who we efter, then?' said Gerry.

'Naebody. Ah want this yin left for a while.' Gerry Ghee was surprised at Washer Wishart's calm. Of all the local East Ayrshire hoods, Washer Wishart was known for his mature and sound judgement in the face of challenge, but still, his only son – on whom he had always previously doted – had nearly been rubbed out. Gerry Ghee couldn't understand his boss's quiet composure … unless a bigger plan was emerging. Gerry acknowledged the complexity of the situation that now involved three rival gangster gangs. There had been peace in the valleys of East Ayrshire since the McLartys had been forcibly evacuated years ago, back to the Glasgow swamp from whence they'd emerged.

The Quinns had enjoyed the other families' gratitude for that, but the resultant détente was now being threatened because one had apparently paid another to ambush a third. The initial summit meeting, held to identify cause and ensure calm, had been inconclusive. Someone was holding back, and although reparations had been agreed, Washer separately suspected that the real reason for his boy's battering was being covered up. Something about it didn't feel right to Washer Wishart. He'd had no reason to suspect anyone moving into his territory in Crosshouse. Everyone – even Ayrshire kingpin Mickey 'Doc' Martin – looked down on Crosshouse. It was regularly joked that even the Twix chocolate bars in Crosshouse had webbed fingers due to inbreeding.

So Washer instinctively knew something didn't fit. Head *polis* honcho, Don McAllister had been on the telephone the day after the gig. He had urged Washer to let the dust settle, and not to declare war on the Quinns. His sharp sense for human behaviour suggested that this was a misunderstanding … and that, furthermore, the damage inflicted on Dale would have been opportunistic, and not premeditated. Washer saw some sense in this viewpoint and acceded. But somebody was answerable for his son, and with the other family heads vigorously maintaining innocence, Washer would need to dig around a bit. Don McAllister accepted this and provided the consequences remained confined to the community's unseen underbelly, he'd turn a blind one. Washer needed to find out more though. And that's where Flat-pack Frankie came in.

$

Frank's nickname was the subject of some dispute. He had performed strong-arm duties for his close friend since the early 70s, when the power and reach of Washer Wishart really accelerated. It was believed that Frank Fusi had made two young corner boys disappear by killing them and packaging their dissected body parts in wooden boxes that were part of an entrepreneurial business dream based on ready-to-assemble furniture. He hadn't, of course, although they *had* been persuaded to move on. The citizens of Ayrshire couldn't get their heads around how money could be made from a joinery business that required them to build their own cabinets, but Frank Fusi was convinced he was onto something with the flat-packing idea. The name stuck, and pub legend did the rest.

Keep ootae Frankie Fusi's way, or ye'll get fuckin' flat-packed.

Steven Dent and the Ferguson brothers needed to take note.

8

The green had gone. His ginger hair was now dyed a more vibrant orange. He seemed to be working his way through the colours of the Rowntree's Fruit Pastille spectrum. He wore badly applied black eyeliner. He wore black leather trousers. He wore a white shirt with a large expressive picture of Sly Stone's face covering its front. He wore the black 12-high DM boots. He wore the confidence born of knowing Washer Wishart's reputation protected him from any adverse reactions. Max Mojo strode down John Finnie Street with a sense of purpose that no one who had seen him during the previous six weeks would've considered he still possessed. Though they might have been concerned that he *was* possessed, such was the increasing regularity with which he seemed to be in conversation with himself. Initially, on coming out of hospital, he had been highly irritable; the dark voice in his head never letting up, always driving and *droning* on, but as Max – and the Lithium compounds he was taking – had become more accustomed to it, he began to respond differently to the voice and its insistent promptings.

'*Ye got the cards?*'

'Aye. Ah've got them here. Vocalist. Guitarist. Moe Tucker-type stand-up drummer. Bass, but no' a bass-tard.'

'*Influences? Ah fuckin' telt ye tae note the influences, ya prick. Fuck sake … dae ah huv tae dae everythin' fae in here?*'

'Naw. Gie's peace, eh. Ah hudnae finished.' An old woman standing at the lights waiting to cross regarded Max and his outer monologue in conversation.

'Ye aw'right, son?' she asked, with a smile.

'Fuck off, grandma. If we wanted your opinion, we'd tell ye it!'

'Sorry about that,' said Max, immediately. The difference in tone persuaded the old woman that he was indeed, on something. One to be studiously avoided. She crossed. Max Mojo kept on, another Kilmarnock striding man. He was headed for his destiny … via English Dave and the RGM Music shop, a local Mecca for fledgling bands.

⚡

3.14 pm

At precisely the same time, Flat-pack Frankie Fusi was opening the boot of his rusting Vauxhall estate car. He had driven south down the A76 to New Cumnock with the window wound down, and Radio 1 blaring from the single dashboard speaker.

It was a stiflingly hot day, another in a long line of them, yet Frankie still wore a pin-striped mohair suit. He was conducting business for his friend Washer Wishart. That business was presently lying petrified in the extended folded-down boot space of his car, under tarpaulin. It had been pretty easy to secure an independent account of the events that transpired on the night Washer's son had been felled. Bobby Cassidy, Heatwave Disco's absent chief, referred him quickly to his sidekick, Joey Miller. He'd hastily passed on the contact details of Heatwave's minder for that evening, Malky MacKay. Malky had neither allegiances nor agenda so his testimony that – an initial lobbed bottle from the crowd apart – the subsequent damage to the Vespa's frontman had been solely down to those sharing the stage was enough for Frankie Fusi.

Earlier that morning, his 'men' had rounded up the three ex-Vespas. Now, five hours later, they were stripped, topped and tailed, hooded and their arms were bound behind their backs with Gaffa tape. Oh, and as might be expected by such a scenario, all three of them were absolutely *shiting* themselves.

⚡

3.20 pm

Grant Dale was genuinely excited. He'd never spent as much money on anything as substantial as this before. Not by a *long* distance. Since his mother had made it clear that the money she had secured for him was his to do as he wished, buying an electric guitar had gone straight to the top of his list. Grant hadn't been academically clever. He had always been interested in English, especially poetry, but he had never tested that interest in exam conditions. He'd left school at sixteen with two O Levels; two more than any other male in his extended family had ever achieved. They were low grades, and in Art and Music. *No' real subjects like widwork*, according to his unimpressed father. It was yet another example of the growing rift between Hobnail and Senga. One disappointed, the other exalted, by the same outcome.

But Grant had something of an aptitude for music, and guitar in particular. He had initially been ambivalent. All of his early guitar lessons seemed to involve learning the chords to dull Eric Clapton songs, rather than the more limited – but far more exciting – range offered by bands like The Clash or The Ramones. However, he surprised himself by sticking with it, and now, with the allocation of the Fatman's money from his mum, he was off to buy a guitar – a shiny black Rickenbacker, just like the one Paul Weller sometimes played.

⚡

3.53 pm

'Aw'right, Inkstain?' Frankie Fusi walked towards the parked Harley Davidson, where the dismounted Ernie Ingram extended an illustrated arm. Frankie shook the hand that was at the end of it. Ernie simultaneously hitched up his leather trousers with his free hand.

'Howdy, Franko. What's the story?' Ernie 'Inkstain' Ingram was a regular collaborator of Washer Wishart. When the Crosshouse Kingpin wanted a message sent, he usually did it in indelible ink inserted artistically into the recipient's dermis. Ernie was the

Galston-based tattooist with no conscience. He'd mark anybody –
and with *anything* – for the right money. He had a relatively normal
clientele of young servicemen looking to express their new 'brother-
hood', or Masonic Lodge members affirming their allegiances, or
football fans, or band groupies, or daft wee lassies in the first flush of
love. But Ernie also had a lucrative sideline. He did call-outs, mainly
for stag nights or drunken 18th birthday parties. And – as was the
case on this beautiful summer's afternoon – he responded to short-
notice calls from Washer Wishart.

'Where are they, boss?' asked Ernie.

'In the shed, on the hooks … jist waitin' for the pen,' said Frankie.

'The message?' said Ernie.

'We'll have three of yer 'specials' from the *future bender* menu,'
said Frankie.

'Right, ye are, Franko. Tell Washer ah'm askin' efter his boy.'

'Will do, compadre.' Frankie Fusi shook Ernie 'Inkstain' Ingram's
muscular hand again. As he did so, he noticed a small Tweety Pie
tattoo on the rocker's thumb. *Cute,* thought Frankie Fusi.

'I'll be a coupla hours,' said Ernie.

'Aye, nae worries. Ah've strapped them up so there shouldnae be
any strugglin'. Once yer done, jist cut them doon an' take the straps
aff their feet. The cunts can walk back tae Killie, lettin' everybody
know they *take it up the arse*. Big capital letters, mind. Bigger than
yer usual.'

'Aye. It'll be noticeable.' Ernie grinned. Frankie laughed and
walked slowly back to his car.

He hadn't even reached the vehicle before the muffled screams of
the barn's inhabitants increased in volume. It sounded like a tortuous
harmony of slowed-down Kate Bush vocals recorded backwards. The
petrified source of those sounds had caught sight of Ernie Ingram
strolling in with his wee generator and a suitcase full of pigment.

⚡

4.09 pm

English Dave *was* actually English, and his name was David English. He was a local Kilmarnock celebrity. His shop – RGM Music – had been a fixture in Nelson Street for longer than anyone could remember. Locals joked that English Dave had sold the first set of bagpipes in history. That he'd been there at the crossroads as Robert Johnson bartered for his soul with the devil using an acoustic guitar bought from Dave. That Keith Moon had battered the fuck out of a set of RGM Music drums at Woodstock. That Paul's Hofner Bass was originally loaned to the Beatle by English Dave himself.

Dave did tell great stories and nobody particularly cared if they were true or not. His shop was a great place to be for kids of all ages – kids who were interested in the sounds instruments made. There was always someone hammering away on a Fender as if they were Hendrix, or blowing one of the saxophones at the rear like they were the soloist on 'Baker Street'.

When the newly named Max Mojo entered the shop, 'Should I Stay or Should I Go' by The Clash was blaring. English Dave was startled by the young man's transformation, but then appeared genuinely happy to see him. Dave had obviously heard about the Henderson Church fiasco. The synthesiser that the band was using that night was borrowed from RGM. *Sale or return*. Sale was clearly the only option now, since fire had reduced it to a pile of ash. English Dave was hoping the young man was here now to settle. Sadly, he was mistaken.

'Dave,' said Max Mojo, nodding.

'So, ah've heard that's it's not Dale anymore. Max something … that right?'

'Aye. Mojo … Max Mojo.' The old man smiled, indulgently, as if listening to a toddler playing at being a *Batman* villain. 'You okay, son?' asked English Dave.

'Aye … *look, fuck that aul' yin, ah'm pinnin' these cards up in the windae, right?*'

'What did you say?' English Dave was taken aback. 'What's happening with your eye there?'

'Ach, sorry. It's nothin' Dave. Ah'm just a bit irritable. The headaches an' lack ae sleep an' that, y'know?' Max had covered his twitching eye with his hand.

'So, cards you were saying? You starting up the band again?' said English Dave.

'Fucks it got tae dae wi' you, ya aul' duffer?'

'Look, son. Take that tone with me again an' you can get out my shop. You owe *me* money for that synth in case you've forgotten.' English Dave was flustered. Max Mojo, the body, was embarrassed. The *Voice* inside its head wasn't. His face had gone bright red. Four other people in the shop, previously minding their own business, were all now staring at him.

'Dave … ah'm really, really sorry,' said Max. He turned away. Dave heard him whispering. It wasn't easy to hear clearly but the teenager appeared to be arguing with himself. '…jist *you* fuckin' button it just now, ya cunt!' said Max, more audibly. He turned round to face a confused English Dave. 'Right, sorry Dave, where wur we?'

'No idea, son,' Dave admitted.

'Ah'll square ye up fur the synth, man. Ye ken ma da's good for it. Ah'm just lookin' tae put a new band th'gither. Could ah put up the cards and a poster?' Max asked, as politely as his tormented brain would allow him. 'An' if ye could point any talent in the ma direction, that'd be magic … *ya prick*! … AAARRGH.' Thankfully, Dave seemed to have misheard the last insult.

'Sure pal. You got a name yet?'

'Naw. Got a few ideas … *wanker…*' he coughed loudly. Again, he seemed to have gotten away with it. 'Ah'm managin', no' playin'.'

⚡

English Dave looked at the poster and smiled:

NEW BAND EMERGES FROM THE ASHES OF LEGENDARY BAND...

**IF YOU'RE FULL OF THE SPIRIT OF IGGY, THE PASSION
OF THE CLASH, THE GROOVE OF THE DELFONICS &
THE CLOUD'NT-GIVE-A-FUCK ATTITUDE OF LYDON ...
PHONE ME. I CAN'T SAY I'LL DEFINITELY PHONE YOU
BACK ... BUT ... YOU NEVER FUCKING KNOW!**

SIMGER – GUITARIST – BASS (BUT NOT A BASS-TARD!) – DRUMS

CALL MAX MOJO. TEL: 36890

Given the earlier outbursts, English Dave thought the better of pointing out the spelling mistakes and instead, simply taped it to the shop window behind him. The cards went into polythene sleeve pockets that held adverts for various secondhand guitar parts, amplifiers, speakers, cymbals, and one – Max Mojo noticed – for the sale of a full mobile disco unit – the *Heatwave* Disco unit.

'So,' said English Dave, holding in the mirth. '*Max Mojo*, is it?'

'Ah needed a new start. New *name*. Somethin' the London Labels wid pick up oan, like.'

'Well, it *is* different,' said Dave.

From the back of the shop, an almighty drum racket shook the walls of the small, narrow space.

'Maggie! Knock that off, eh?' shouted Dave. Everyone in the shop turned to face the blur of bleached blonde hair that contrasted with ebony skin. The girl looked up contemptuously. Max observed that she was stunningly beautiful. And, moreover, she could obviously play those drums. She wasn't standing up, and she made Moe Tucker look like the Elephant Man, but that apart, he figured he might just have found his drummer. He went over to speak to her, hoping the *Voice* would shut the fuck up for at least the next ten minutes.

'How much is the Rickenbacker, man?' English Dave's attention was drawn back by the tall, handsome, pale-skinned youth standing in front of him.

'Six hundred, son,' he said casually. He anticipated that would end the conversation. It was by far the most expensive one that RGM Music had in stock.

'Aw'right, mate,' said Grant Dale. 'Cash dae ye?' English Dave's eyebrows arched. *What a fucking bizarre half an hour,* he thought. Grant Dale brought the cash out in fifties. And there was clearly far more in his wallet than what he had just laid down on the counter. Max Mojo also caught the moment and instinctively glided back over towards the transaction.

'Fuckin' brilliant song this, eh?' he said. Although Max appeared to be speaking to no one in particular, his comments were very specifically addressed to Grant, who was now beside him.

'Eh … aye. Orange Juice, intit?' said Grant. He was only vaguely aware of the identity of the person tapping his feet and drumming nervous fingers on the counter. He knew he was connected to an Ayrshire big man, but he couldn't think which one.

'*Ah-ah … I can't help myself.* Fuck me, that's the story ae ma life, right noo,' said Max, fishing.

'That right?' said Grant, trying to avoid the bait.

'Used tae be in a band, me.'

'Aye?'

'Aye. Headed for a wee bit ae stardom tae.' There was a pause. Max took a different tact. 'Can ye play that?' Grant turned round and held up the new guitar.

'Aye. A bit. No' bought it yet though. Jist waitin' for the aul' fella tae come back wi' a case for it,' said Grant.

'Go oan, then … gie's a wee tune. Can ye pick up the vibe?' said Max. He appeared to be struggling with an internal twitch. *Either that or he was holding in a massive fart,* thought Grant. English Dave was still through in the back shop. So Grant pulled it up and strummed along in tune with the *Sound of Young Scotland* that was coming from the shop's sound system.

'*Fuck, cunt looks good holdin' that.*'

'Whit?' said Grant.

'*Cocksucker.*'

'Whit d'ye call *me*?' Grant put the guitar down and squared up.

'Nothin' man, ah'm sorry. Involuntary spasms. Cannae control them sometimes.' Max had suppressed the *Voice* again. His left eyelid was fluttering madly, like a bedsheet drying on a Girvan washing line. 'Can ye sing? Ah'm gettin' a band th'gither, like. Fancy it?' asked Max.

'Dunno. Mibbe,' said Grant. It had already occurred to him that sitting in his bedroom plucking away at this new toy was probably a bit sad. What was the point of the investment if he didn't play it in public? And since busking was totally out of the question, a band was a distinct interest. The bizarre individual facing him was unusual to say the least, but when you considered the likes of Adam Ant, Grant reckoned that *unusual* could be a definite advantage in the music business. This opportunity had emerged much quicker than he'd been ready for but *fuck it*, what was to be lost?

'Who else is in it?' Grant enquired.

'Well, *her* ... probably,' said Max, indicating the barely clothed, blonde-haired female sitting at the drum kit. The driving blues-glam sound of Bryan Ferry's 'Let's Stick Together' oozed out of English Dave's sound system. Grant picked up the rhythm, and so did Maggie Abernethy, sitting at the shop's drum kit. A light bulb was instantly lit above Max's orange head by the *Voice*. It took until the end of the song for its significance to be fully acknowledged by Max, the *Voice's* host. English Dave's mix tape ploughed straight into 'Where Were You?' by the Mekons. The two players got it instantly; slow, monotone rhythmic strumming gradually giving way to an accelerating drum beat. Max watched mesmerised at the intuitive synchronisation between the pair, and when Grant sang '*Could you ever be my wife ... do you love me?*' at the end of the song, Max Mojo's dark heart leapt. He'd been watching the eye contact between the two, especially the salacious wink thrown back by the funky female drummer in response. If he could keep the *Voice* in check and avoid calling Maggie *a darkie*, he might just have half a group identified on the first day. Max went back over to speak to her. Grant returned to the business of wrapping up his new axe.

Max shouted over to Grant. 'Hey mate … she's up fur it. Whit aboot you … *ya fuckwit.*' Max anticipated the inevitable insult and stamped his feet to obscure it. Maggie winked at Grant again. On that basis alone, Grant was in. He walked across, shook Max's hand, wrote the phone number on his own, and headed out of RGM Music with his guitar case over his shoulder. Max Mojo looked like he was about to have an epileptic fit.

'See ye … *YA FUCKIN' MANKY ONTHANK CUNT, YE!*' Thankfully, a passing Fire Brigade siren meant that Max Mojo's part of the farewell went unheard by Grant Dale; newly installed guitarist and potential singer with a new Kilmarnock-based band destined – according to the *Voice* of their Lithium-addled, delusional teenage manager – *for the very very, motherfuckin' top.*

02: **THE NAME OF THIS BAND IS…**

Ah ken ye'll be thinkin' it wis aw fuckin' plain sailin' efter they two hooked up, but wis it fuck. Months went by an' nuthin' happened. Ah'm puttin' that doon tae they doctor cunts upping the dose ae the medication. Ah wis like a fuckin' zombie for weeks. Ken like Nicholson at the end ae 'Cuckoo's Nest'? Well, that, but withoot some big fuckin' Indian squaw tae pit us ootae ma misery. An' ah wis absolutely fuckin' miserable, man. Like Morrissey oot for a walk an' findin' that some cunt's locked the Cemetery Gates. Aye, that bad!

Anyway, eventually it passed. Ah got the vibe back. It wis aboot this time that ah started wearin' the patch. Couldnae concentrate on talkin' tae folk wi' the eye actin' like a drunk uncle at a weddin'. So ah fuckin' covered it up, Captain Hook-like. Ah got back in touch wi' Grant an' the darkie lassie. They were still intae it … the band, an' that, ken? We aw met regular like, at Washer's church but tae tell ye the truth, they two just pissed aboot like a coupla weans, ken?

Don't get me wrang, Norma, ah'd've fucked her tae, back then … In the back door, like. Obviously. She had yer typical darkie's erse. John Brown's coulda launched a ship doon the middle ae it.

I ken whit yer probably thinkin', but hey, ah'm no' ootae order here, it wis different times back then. Nane ae this fuckin PC shite ye get noo …an' ah'm no' a hypocrite either, ya cunt. Ah telt her tae her face, but we'll fuckin' get back tae that later.

Problem wis, Grant thought he wis in love, but she'd been knobbin' one ae they Quinn pikeys. Don't think it wid ae stopped her, mind, dirty fuckin' hoor that she wis … But Washer didnae need the additional aggro fae they blacko cunts, ken? Plus, ah needed Washer's money, so Grant hud tae be telt tae stop sniffin' roon her crack.

Anyway, we're sittin' in the Manse, practisin', meant tae be, but actually gettin' naewhere fast.

They last few months ae 82 … fuck me, wis ah glad tae see them go.

Weller chucks it wi' The Jam, every cunt's oan the dole an' ye cannae walk doon the street for fear ae a fuckin' car explodin' aff ae aw they Irish bastarts. So … wi' the drummer an' the singer actin' more like the fuckin' Carpenters than they two fae the noo … whit are they called again? They White Stripes? Aye, them! … well, we needed a bit ae focus. Ah jist didnae fuckin' expect it tae come fae where it did, ken?

9

'So where are ye fae?'

'Ah'm fae Shortlees, for Christ's sake, ye've been to the hoose.' Maggie laughed. She knew what Grant meant, but even though they had been officially going out with each other for three weeks, he was still a bit awkward when they were alone. She found it endearing though.

'Ye ken whit ah mean … *originally*.'

'Ma dad was from Jamaica originally. He was a fitba player. He played a few times for Celtic tae, in the early 50s. Met ma mam at a dance up in Glesga. She wis only twenty. They went oot a few times, up the dancin' an' that, then he signed for an English team. They stayed in touch though an' she went doon tae see him quite often. He went back tae America in the mid 50s.'

'Did she go wi' him then?' asked Grant. She could see him doing the arithmetic in his head.

'Naw, he came back at the start ae the season in 1958. Tae see some pals. He wrote her a letter. *Loads* ae letters, actually. She saw him … ended up the duff. Ah burst oot in July 1959,' she said, 'so, tae answer yer question, ah wis born at Irvine Central … jist like you.' Maggie smiled, as if she had concluded a children's story on *Jackanory*.

'Fuckin' hell. Dae ye still see him?' said Grant.

Maggie drew in the breath through her teeth. '*No* … no no no no no.'

Grant looked perplexed.

'No' interested,' said Maggie. 'An' he disnae ken aboot us, anyway.'

Grant was surprised at this story. It was definitely not what he had expected when he casually asked about it. He felt a bit sad for her, but she definitely didn't feel sorry for herself. It probably explained her mustang-spirited independence and confidence. Although he didn't dare say it, Grant also thought it explained her impeccable rhythm and timing – both on the drums *and* in the back seat of his mum's new car where they had shagged each other for the first time three days ago.

He really liked her, and he was sure she liked him. But there remained rough, unpredictable edges to her. The relationship with Rocco, son of Galston gypsy crime boss Nobby Quinn, had ended, according to Maggie. But Grant had recently been advised by his dad's former colleague, Wullie the Painter, to stay out of Rocco's way. But Maggie was a uniquely wild proposition. For Grant, who wasn't massively experienced with girls, it was both a challenge and a source of constant excitement.

Kid Creole & The Coconuts were singing 'I'm a Wonderful Thing, Baby' on the radio at the side of the church hall stage.

Maggie got to her feet.

'C'mon, lets dance!'

'Ah'm pish at dancin'… just like God, both ae us move in mysterious fuckin' ways,' he laughed.

'We'll need tae fix that then,' she said, pulling him closer. 'Cannae have the wee lassies wettin' their pants 'cos the lead singer moves like a three-legged dug!'

Maggie moved effortlessly; Grant like he was a puppet whose strings were being operated by Stevie Wonder. At least he was enthusiastic and keen to learn. In fact, she could feel the full extent of his growing enthusiasm as he pressed against her.

'Right then, my lad, let's have another quick go at "Thirteen".' Maggie walked over to the drum kit that had been a permanent fixture on the stage of Washer Wishart's church hall for four months. She knew this would please Grant because he had loved the song. And he had long-since perfected the chord structure. It was also the song that, back in early August, had persuaded Max Mojo that the tall, handsome Grant was going to be the band's singer.

Now though, he wasn't on the ball enough to realise that Maggie was talking about sex. Big Star's 'No. 1 Record' was playing in Senga's car's tape deck as Maggie sat astride him, grinding into his cock and slapping his face rhythmically with her coffee-coloured tits. Her nipples were like blackberries on large, brown saucers. Grant had only ever seen brown-skinned breasts on BBC reports from Africa about starvation. Maggie wasn't dark brown but the number of coloured people in Kilmarnock could have been counted on the fingers of one hand, and they all worked at the new hospital. It was a resoundingly white environment until the sun shone and turned most a patchy lobster pink.

Maggie walked beyond the drum kit and stood against the curtained back wall of the stage. She summoned him with a long-nailed forefinger – the same finger she'd so deftly shoved up his arsehole a few days ago. He got up and glided over to her as if he was metallic and she was magnetic, his heart thumping away furiously. She slid down the velvet as she opened her legs, her knickers now draped around her left ankle. As Grant reached her, she grabbed for his belt and undid it quickly. His jeans slid down. The contrast between his white skin and her rich, butterscotch tone was marked. In the dark shadows of the back stage, he appeared ill; spotty-arsed, and with fading sunburn lines where his shorts stopped. She looked ludicrously healthy in comparison. No wonder human milk bottles like him lay out in the sun until it made their pale skin flake like a giant's dandruff, thought Grant, catching a glimpse of his arse in a side-stage mirror as it pounded away. He had lifted her up and supported her weight. The biceps on his wiry arms flexed. She wrapped her legs around him. Grant's arse hammered like a pneumatic road drill until they both came together.

At the back of the hall, Max Mojo was watching all this through a crack in the door. His own stiff cock was in his hand and he was beating away at it furiously. He had come back early, and with some good news. He had suspected that Grant and Maggie were already an item. And although he feigned indifference in front of them,

Max had heard from 'Audrey wi' the Big Hoose' that Maggie was still seeing Rocco Quinn, and *that* was a potential complication they could all do without. Nevertheless, he finished masturbating into an empty crisp bag, dumped it in a bin, wiped his cock on his shirt, and – when *they* were also finished – burst into the hall to tell them he'd found a lead guitarist and a bass player.

10

'Des?' Fat Franny was surprised to see his colleague standing inside the front door of the *Ponderosie.* 'Fuck ae you doin' here? We're no' due a meet until Friday. It's only Monday, Des.'

'It's yer mam, Franny.' Des looked pale.

Fat Franny instantly dropped the bottle of milk in his left hand. It smashed on the top step. He pushed past Des Brick.

'Mam!' he shouted. He ran to the living room. Her slippers were on the floor, and *Neighbours* was on, but his mum wasn't in that room. She wasn't in the kitchen either, although there was a strange, smoky smell in there. With Des Brick pursuing him up the stairs, Fat Franny eventually found Rose lying asleep in her bedroom, where Des Brick had taken her after calming her down.

'Whit the fuck's been goin' oan?' Fat Franny demanded.

'Boss, ah jist came roon tae pass oan a wee message an' yer front door wis' open so ah jist came in.'

'Aye, *and*? Get tae the fuckin' point, will ye!'

'Well, Fran … yer mam wis in the kitchen. Ah came in looking for ye, an'…'

'An' *whit*? So fuckin' help me, Des…'

'Yer mam wis tryin' tae fry lettuce an' yoghurt in a pan … an'…' Des had thought twice about the next bit, but with Fat Franny Duncan glaring at him there was no holding back now. '… she turns roon an' says it's a dinner she's cookin' … for JFK an' Jackie O.' Des Brick sat on the stairs, halfway down, the pressure of that reveal taking its toll.

Fat Franny turned and went back into his mum's room. She had stirred.

'Mum? Are ye okay? Ah wis jist oot at the shop for two minutes. Ah told ye tae stay in yer armchair, remember?'

'Ach, ah'm sorry, son. But we were havin' guests round. Somebody had tae go an' see tae them.' Rose Duncan smiled at her son and reached a tiny hand from under the covers to touch his cheek. 'Yer such a good boy, Francis. Yer dad would be so proud ae ye, son.'

Tears welled in both of Fat Franny's eyes. He rubbed them away quickly.

'Go an' see tae the Kennedys, son. Ah don't want them thinking ah keep a tardy hoose.'

'Aye, ah'm jist goin', Mam. You get a wee rest, noo.' Fat Franny pulled up the covers and tucked his mum in under them. Just like *she* used to do for him.

Des Brick was sitting at the kitchen table when Fat Franny came back down. His eyes were red and moist, but Des knew better than to draw attention to them.

'She okay, Franny?' he said.

'Aye,' said Fat Franny.

'Ah'm sorry. Ah didnae mean tae startle ye when ye came back earlier.'

'Aye, ah ken. Thanks.'

'Ah got a bit ae a fright myself, like. Ah mean the place was aw smokin', ken?'

'Aye. Look Des, ah get it. Thanks for comin' roon. Ah appreciate it. Away and see tae Effie,' said Fat Franny. He was genuinely thankful, but he was also ashamed that he'd left his old mum in the house by herself, even if it was only for the fifteen minutes or so that it had taken to go and get the milk.

'Okay, mate. Look, ah'll see ye after. Later in the week, like,' said Des. He got up and walked to the front door. He looked back briefly to see the Onthank main man stare blankly out of his rear kitchen window to the open green fields beyond. Des Brick let himself out into the descending gloom of the brisk November evening.

✦

Fat Franny sat upstairs in the darkness of his mother's bedroom. He watched the covers around her small body gently rise and fall. When he was a wee boy, she seemed so strong, so protective. So *immortal*. Especially the night she put herself in the way of a beating from Fat Franny's drunken waster of a father. She'd taken the punches and kicks that were meant for her son. Later that evening, a quarter of a century ago, Abie Duncan had come at the boy again, this time with a broom handle. Again, his mother had shielded him, and only the intervention of a neighbour stopped Franny's dad from putting his mum in intensive care. There were other times in the four years that followed, but none left their mark on Franny like that night; his eleventh birthday. On the 5th September 1961 – Franny's *fifteenth* birthday – he and his best friend, the six-foot, four-inch teenager, Bob Dale, battered Abie Duncan to a pulp. After it, an out-of-breath Franny took a ten-bob note that he'd received earlier in the day from his granny, and put it in his father's top pocket. He told him that if he ever saw him again he'd kill him. It was his birthday present to himself. Rose Duncan never asked her son about where her husband was, and they had never mentioned his name from that day to this.

Fat Franny now felt totally alone. He had made bad calls in the last year and now felt stranded on an island of his own making. Des Brick had his own, all-consuming problems. Wullie the Painter was only as loyal as the next big job that would pay better. And he wouldn't trust Terry Connolly as far as he could throw him. Only Theresa, his young girlfriend, could really be trusted now. His business had virtually evaporated in the short time since Bob Dale's death. That's why this new tape business had to work. Fat Franny knew he'd taken his childhood friend for granted. He'd abused him, and selfishly assumed he'd always just *be* there; that he'd always just take the increasingly mean-spirited abuse.

Paradoxically, it had been Hobnail who had the power all along. People were afraid of *him,* not Fat Franny. With him gone, the regular payments stopped and the threats went largely unheeded. Everyone's takings were down. Only Terry Connolly seemed to be making progress. But Fat Franny had made *his* deal deliberately different to the others, allowing Terry to keep a far greater percentage of the ice-cream van business because he accepted there were higher risks. That was Fat Franny's necessary cover. Connolly wouldn't have trusted him otherwise.

Fat Franny couldn't believe how quickly it had all deteriorated, although time was a strangely fluid concept in such circumstances. It seemed to him only a few months ago that his mum had started getting confused about the identities of visitors to the house. In actual fact it had begun five years ago. At first the deterioration had been slow, and they'd both laughed, putting it down to normal absent-mindedness. She put clean dishes in the fridge. She went out and left the doors wide open. She began to forget the bus routes into the town centre. She also got lost on the way back to the *Ponderosie* and Fat Franny had to grovel with gratitude to a young police sergeant who had brought her home. That was two years ago now. Since then, there had been a few other sporadic incidents culminating with the break-in to the house and the theft from the safe of Fat Franny's money. Fat Franny had been saving that sizeable sum to pay for his mum to be looked after properly, but he couldn't stop all the bampots turning up at their house, silently judging him for not putting his mum in an old folks' home years earlier. Now, the money was gone, his income was dramatically reduced – and *reducing* – and his mum's decline was accelerating.

'Ah'm sorry, Mam. Ah've let ye doon. Everythin's turnin' tae shit. Ah dinnae want tae be doin' this anymore.' Fat Franny Duncan was in tears. He hadn't cried since that night in 1957. Now he felt he wouldn't be able to stop. His mum couldn't hear him. He sat in the darkness running his hands through thinning hair and down to the tied-up, greying pony tail. Empires crumbled, and just like Brando at the end of *Apocalypse Now* he now faced the heart of his particular darkness.

11

'Everybody here?' asked Washer Wishart.

His nephew, Gerry Ghee stood up gingerly to answer. 'Aye, boss. Aw assembled,' he said before sitting down again on the big cushion.

Washer Wishart sat at the top of the long table. He looked out at the faces of his colleagues. He remembered many of them sitting here with him on this same wooden floor forty-odd years ago, singing Jesus anthems, glum-faced, since none of them were religious. These older, wiser faces were still glum, but for different reasons.

The drum kit was immediately behind him. One of its high-hat cymbals lay on its side. Washer had kicked it over in frustration at his son's attitude on being informed that the church hall couldn't be used for rehearsals that evening. More important issues had to be debated. Since Max Mojo couldn't conceive of *anything* more important than the destiny of his band, an argument had ensued. Washer tried to keep his anger in check, but eventually it was either the cymbal or Max's head.

'Ah don't fuckin' need this pressure on!' Max had exclaimed.

'Wait … wait. Ah've got it,' said an excited Gerry Ghee. 'Spandau Ballet. "Chant No. 1"!'

'Who rattled *your* cage, ya cunt?' shouted Max.

'Hey. Enough. Dinnae fu … Don't speak tae yer cousin like that. Ah need the hall, right? Ah've got a bloody business tae run here. Ye'll need tae go somewhere else the night.' Washer had turned away from Max, indicating that the conversation was over.

When Washer wasn't looking, Gerry Ghee made a slow, waving motion with his hand which worked its way into a two-fingered salute. Max booted an empty paint tin. It flew up and caught Gerry in the groin. He dropped to his knees like James Brown at the Harlem Apollo.

'Ooyah wee bastart! Fuck sake, no' again!' he groaned.

'Fuck off, dickhead!' said Max, as his father launched a boot at the cymbal stand, sending it flying. Max Mojo left, slamming the heavy wooden double doors of the church behind him.

'That yin needs a good fuckin' slap, Washer,' whined Gerry.

Washer Wishart just grunted. More important things were on his mind.

With his full extended crew assembled, the meeting began. The table to the side contained only a few bottles of Emva Cream sherry, and about six open boxes of Finefare Yellow Pack Mince Pies. As a measure of the potential festive bonus to come, this was not a good sign to the twenty or so footsoldiers now seated adjacent.

Washer stood to deliver his state-of-the-nation address.

'Lads, there's nae hidin' that business has been tough this year. Thatcher might be claiming that the unemployed are aw oan benefits but she disnae live in Crosshoose. Naebody has any money an', as a result, naebody's doin' any business, legit or otherwise.' Washer looked at everyone. As a unit, their heads were visibly drooping. He had no upbeat conclusion to this preamble. It would be a lean, lean Christmas in the Wishart camp.

As the meeting went on Washer's frank appraisal of the direction for his business was quickly forgotten; the 'Nae Christmas bonuses' bit stuck fast with each of the men present, though. It was understood in advance that profits had been down for all of the individual businesses through which cash from various discreet sources, known only to Washer, was filtered. But most couldn't really comprehend the parallel between a nation with high unemployment and increased numbers on benefits, and the black economy. Logic suggested to them that lack of legitimate employment opportunity would lead to criminality or desperation simply as a means of getting by. But the Wisharts weren't money-*lenders*, they were launderers. The former racked up relatively small amounts, by threat, intimidation and ridiculous levels of compound interest from folk with no disposable income to fund whatever lifestyle or craving they needed. The latter attempted to legitimise *other* people's illegal proceeds. It was obviously criminal in its own right, but it allowed Washer, and his assembled cabal of incorporated small businesses to feel that their proceeds were no more ill-gotten than those of white-collar tax evaders who most probably contributed to the Tory Party election funds in the first place.

'No' a good night, boss,' said Gerry Ghee as he watched the last car leave the Manse car park. Frankie Fusi walked up the path, hands stuffed deep into his Crombie coat pockets, collar turned up against the developing wind.

'Aye. Ah know. Cannae dae anythin' about it jist noo', though,' said Washer. 'We need tae take stock, son. Diversify an' that. Christ, even the bloody laundry's takings are doon. Aw'right Frankie?'

'Fucking Thatcher … nae bastart can even afford tae get their *clothes* washed, never mind their funny money.' Frankie Fusi summarised the problem succinctly with his only contribution of the evening.

Gerry Ghee smiled, and eventually Washer Wishart did, too. 'Ah'm gettin' too auld for aw this, ken?' said Washer, ruefully.

'Aye, man. Things are tougher than they've been since ah joined ye,' Gerry agreed. Washer opened a bottle and poured each of them a sherry into a paper cup. 'Maybe yer daft boy an' his band'll hit the big-time an' ye'll be able tae retire?' Washer Wishart laughed at the thought. He had always been a decent kid, Gerry. The ongoing business with Max had taken Washer's eye off the ball; there was no doubt about that. Washer was aware that his cohorts at the meeting would all have been thinking it.

'Take they mince pies back tae yer Ma, son,' he said to Gerry. After the meeting had ended, Washer's offer of a Christmas sherry and a pie had been ignored. He wasn't especially surprised. All of these local Crosshouse businessmen were taking massive risks to be part of the Wishart consortium. They had just been told that right now there would be no reward for that risk. Their patience wouldn't last long into 1983. Washer wished he could trust them with the bigger picture. As the first snowflakes of the year began to fall on Crosshouse, Washer Wishart and his inner circle had some big decisions to make.

✦

9.27 pm

'Fuck sake, get that shite aff!' Max Mojo's mood hadn't improved by the time he'd reached the Wee Thack. Maggie and Grant were already there. It was a Wednesday evening and the pub was relatively quiet. The three had the back area, where the Jukebox was located, to themselves. But, as they waited for the band's new guitar and bass player to appear, Maggie's choice of records was irritating the fuck out of the young music-mogul-in-waiting.

'Don't push me, 'cos I'm close to the edge...' she sang, into his face. *'I'm tryin' not to lose my head ... a ha ha ha.'*

'Bugger off, ya n...'

'Don't even fuckin' think it, boy,' said Maggie, deadly serious. 'Ah'll end you, if ye ever say it.'

Max looked immediately at Grant. Grant was clearly angry but said nothing. The song faded out and The Jam's swansong, 'Beat Surrender', replaced it. The collective mood improved immediately. That song united them all, including the brothers Sylvester, who had entered the pub just as Paul Weller announced the opening title.

'Where the fuck have you two been?' asked Max Mojo.

'Ma Da didnae pass oan the message,' said the taller Simon Sylvester. 'We ended up oan the bus tae Crosshoose. Stuck ma heid in through the door ae the church an' a fuckin' Masonic meetin' or somethin' wis goin' oan.' Simon and his brother, Eddie sat down. 'Some local tit wi' webbed hands telt us ye were here.'

✦

'Fuck off!' said Max, as he walked to the bar to get them a drink.

It had been almost a month since Eddie Sylvester had pressed his dirty, chocolate-marked face up against the RGM Music window, before taking Max Mojo's card home. Eddie was nearly three years older than Max. He was quiet and sensitive, but he had taken the initiative in phoning Max's number to enquire if the guitar and bass positions in his band had been filled. Fortunately, Eddie hadn't made it clear during their phone call that Simon was a relation. If he had, Max would've said *no* to both of them on the spot. Max had gone to the Sylvester family home in Caprington. Eddie was there – in a garage that resembled an Aladdin's cave of white goods and motor-cycle parts – playing a Hendrix riff expertly. Max couldn't place it at first, but he knew it was Jimi's. And he also immediately knew that this kid could really *play*. When he'd asked Eddie when his pal was going to join them, Eddie casually told Max that Simon was his twin brother, and that he was still upstairs in his bed. Max Mojo was presented with an immediate dilemma. He'd been looking to complete the classic band line-up for months with no realistic can-didates, and now, a guitarist of genuine talent had materialised, but potentially only available as another fucking sibling double-act. Max waited patiently for the other Sylvester brother to show face. He'd earlier decided that, regardless of Eddie's skill, the deal would be off if Simon was a prick.

It was four in the afternoon but it took over an hour for Simon Sylvester to get up. That didn't auger well but in the intervening period, Eddie Sylvester demonstrated agility with a guitar that left his potential band manager stunned. The twenty-one-year-old had challenged Max to name a song that he couldn't play. Max came up with The Byrds 'Eight Miles High', Mott the Hoople's 'Roll Away the Stone', 'Another Girl, Another Planet' by the Only Ones, and Wire's 'Outdoor Minor'. Eddie knew them all. By the time Simon Sylvester appeared, unshaven and uninterested, Max Mojo had decided that the cunt could be the bass-playing Yorkshire Ripper, but he'd *still* be in. At least they weren't identical. *That* was something.

Max nipped out into Grange Street for some fresh air. Although he also smoked, the thick density of the fug in the Wee Thack was bringing on another brutal headache. He felt inside his denim jacket pocket for his fags. He found them and brought one out but his zippo lighter was gone. He reflected on the three days of rehearsals the full band had undertaken since the Caprington accord. They hardly rivalled Chuck Berry in terms of hard work, but various personal interruptions had curtailed their progress. Grant developed laryngitis and then, having recovered from that, promptly twisted an ankle playing *kerby* in the street with Maggie. Maggie had subsequently gone into a brief spell of hiding, having informed Rocco Quinn that any relationship they once had was now definitely over. And – in a portent of the future – Simon Sylvester had given his brother a black eye after losing a hotly contested game of *Buckaroo*.

When he came back to the table with a tray of drinks, a piece of paper with a list of names was written on it:

The Bisciut Tins
Bisciut Tin Mentality
Scattered Showers
Scattered Showers + The Bisciut Tins
Buffalo Bisciuts
Buffalo Springside
Jam + The Mallows
Peek + The Assorted Freans
Gari + The Baldis
THE VENUSIANS

'Well?' said Eddie Sylvester. 'Whit yin dae ye like?'

'Like for *whit*? said Max.

'The name ae the band, man,' said Eddie, arms outstretched. Maggie sniggered.

'The name ae *this* band … is The Miraculous Vespas. End ae story,' asserted Max.

'Whit kinda fuckin' name's that, Max? Folk'll think we're a parka-wearin' trapeze act fae Billy Smart's!' said Simon Sylvester.

Max picked up the paper and looked disdainfully at it. The first nine were written in a childlike scribble; the final one written in more considered – and mature – capitals. 'Some cunt got a fuckin' biscuit habit or somethin'?' They all looked at Eddie Sylvester. 'Mighta kent. Ye cannae fuckin' spell either. Who came up wi' the last yin?' said Max. Grant raised a hand, mid-drink. 'At least that yin *sounds* like a fuckin' band!'

'Well, The *Mekons* were from Venus, ken? So...' said Grant, tailing off.

'Aye. It's good ... but naw. *Ah'm* namin' this band.' Max had spoken.

'But should we no' go for somethin' simple?' said Eddie. 'Look at aw these stupid bands comin' oot noo? Orchestral Manoeuvres in the fuckin' Dark? Blue Rondo à la Turk? One the Juggler?'

'Who the fuck's *One the Juggler* when they're at hame?' said Maggie, laughing.

'They were in the *NME*,' said Eddie confidently.

'An' also ... Scattered Showers & The Biscuit Tins? The only simple thing aboot that name is the cunt that came up wi' it!' said Simon Sylvester. This time they all laughed.

'Talkin' ae names, ah'm changin' mine.' They all looked at Grant. 'Grant *Delgado*,' said Grant. Simon laughed so hard a snot bubble formed on his top lip. Eddie was in mid-slurp and gave himself hiccups. Maggie just smiled.

'Fuckin' beezer!' said Max. 'Max Mojo an' Grant Delgado.' Max Mojo raised his pint glass.

'Here's tae the rise ae The Miraculous Vespas,' he said. They all clinked his glass, and repeated the toast. As they sat down, Madness began singing about the House of Fun, and the males all joined in, nutty-dancing around the back of the Wee Thack like four versions of Chas Smash. Maggie Abernethy remained seated, regarding them proudly like Olivia Walton watching John-Boy, Jason, Ben and Jim-Bob horsing around at a barn-raising hoe-down.

12

'Surprise! Merry Christmas, babe'

'Eh, Jeezo! ... aye, Merry Christmas, Mags.' Grant Dale kissed his gorgeous girlfriend. She was standing at the front door in a short, sleeveless dress, even though the snow lay thick on the ground outside. 'Wasnae expectin' tae get ye today, hen,' he added, showing her inside.

'Jist thought ah'd come up and see ye.'

'Fuck, Mags ... ah huvnae got yer present yet,' he admitted.

'It's fine, honestly.' Maggie kissed him again, this time on the cheek.

'Who is it, Grant?' Senga Dale called down from the top of the stairs.

'It's, em ... jist a pal ae mine, Mam,' said Grant, his pale cheeks turning the shade of Rudolph's nose.

'A pal! A *pal*?' said Maggie, teasing him.

Senga came downstairs.

'Whit's this? Ye didnae say yer pal wis a lassie!' Senga smiled at Maggie and introduced herself.

Maggie told Senga she was the drummer in Grant's band and Senga showed Maggie into the living room, raising an approving eyebrow in Grant's direction as she passed him.

'Sorry aboot the mess, hen. The weans are up the stairs wi' their presents but they jist leave aw the wrapping at their arses, ken?'

'Aye,' said Maggie. 'Ah've got a few sisters ae ma own.'

'Ye staying for Christmas dinner, Maggie?' said Senga. 'There's more than enough for five ae us.' She already suspected Grant and this girl were more than just bandmates. Although she was a different shade than that usually witnessed in Ayrshire, they looked like a well-matched couple – both tall and with chiselled cheekbones.

Senga made tea and brought it through from the kitchen on a tray with a small Munro made out of chocolate Hob-Nobs. Grant was kneeling in front of the televison set, flicking between an animated cartoon film about racoons that had Leo Sayer voicing one of the characters, and *The Island of Adventure* on the other side.

'Telly's pish as usual,' he concluded. 'Bugger all on 'til *Top ae the Pops* at two.'

'3–2–1's on later,' said Senga. 'Ah love that Ed Roger.'

Grant laughed.

'Whit?' she said.

'It's Ted *Rogers*, Mrs Dale,' offered Maggie.

'Well, hen ... ah dinnae care if there's two ae them. Ah still love 'em,' she laughed.

'Whit did he get ye then?' said Senga, sipping at her mug.

'Eh, well…'

'Ah huvnae got it yet, Mam. Ah ordered it fae the Embassy catalogue ... but thanks for bringin' that up again, eh?' said Grant.

'It's fine, Mrs Dale. He didnae know ah wis comin' over today. Ah jist wanted tae surprise him.'

'Ach, that's lovely, hen. In't that lovely, Grant?'

'Lovely, Mam,' said Grant, now back with the racoons.

'Wid ye leave that dial? Christ, are ye tryin' tae watch both programmes at the same time?' said Senga. 'Jist put it off tae the Queen's on. You young folk ... always got tae have the telly boomin' away in the corner. Nae time for chattin', eh?'

'Yer right, Mrs Dale,' said Maggie, as Grant shot her a glance.

'God knows whit it's gonnae be like wi' *another* bloody channel. Four ae them, an' oan aw bloomin' day jist aboot! Your generation isnae gonnae be able tae converse with itself soon,' said Senga shaking her head ruefully.

Grant switched to the test card on BBC2. 'That better for ye, Mam?' he said sarcastically.

'She's pretty, that wee lassie,' said Senga in a whisper.

'Aye, but she's probably older than *you* noo,' he said.

'Cheeky wee get, ye!' Senga got up and gently cuffed her son's ear on the way past.

'Actually, ah've got somethin' for you, Grant,' said Maggie moving closer to him.

'Ach, bollocks. Yer determined tae make me feel shite, aren't ye?'

She laughed. 'C'mon outside a minute,' she said. They stood up.

'Jist nippin' out a minute, Mam,' shouted Grant.

'But she's just got here, Grant.'

'A minute, Mam … we're stayin' for dinner.' The door shut behind them. It had just started snowing again. Grant put his black Harrington jacket over Maggie's bare shoulders. Contrasted against the pristine snow, Maggie's skin seemed darker than it was. Grant caught her gaze as she reached the end of the path. She looked like a blonde Donna Summer. He couldn't believe the way his fortune had turned around in these last six months or so. From constant rucks with his aggressive father, and taking the pocket-book money away from the weak-willed and infirm on behalf of that fat fuck Franny Duncan, to having a new name and being in a band – albeit one that hadn't played a gig yet and had a delusional manager – and having regular sex with its beautiful drummer. Quite a turnaround, indeed!

Maggie walked him to the end of the cul-de-sac and put her hands over his eyes before they reached the corner.

'Right, are ye ready?' she asked him.

'Eh, aye. Ah think so,' he replied nervously.

Maggie drew her hands back and Grant opened his eyes. Parked at the back of the turning-head was a pale-blue Volkswagen Campervan. It was in decent condition, with gleaming chrome and no obvious rusting. It had been decorated with CND logos and slogans, such as 'Anti-Complacency League, Baby'. It looked very cool.

'Holy fuck, Mags!'

'Dae ye like it?' she said, with child-like exuberance.

'Aye … but fuckin' hell, ah wis thinkin' of gettin' you a bottle ae Rive Gauche!'

'Ha ha, it's cool. This is for you *and* me,' she said. 'It can be a joint present.'

Grant was stunned. Although he still had most of his secret Fat Franny stash, officially they were both on the dole, and it would have taken her about a decade to have saved enough from what was left out of her weekly government allowance.

'Look, ah dinnae want this tae come oot wrang, but where did ye get the money for it?'

She looked instantly hurt.

'Fuck, Mags … ah'm sorry. It's great, really. Please jist forget ah asked that, eh?'

'It didnae cost me anythin'. Ah won it in a poker game,' she said.

That prompted even more questions in Grant's mind, given Maggie's prior history with the gypsy Quinns of Galston. But he decided to hold onto them for now. He could inquire more after Ne'erday. They had only been going out for about two months. This initially seemed like a big step, but Maggie hadn't exactly asked him to move into it. And she wasn't giving him a set of keys. It was just a convenient – and mobile – place for them to go, for them to get hammered and high, and listen to John Peel, and for them to shag each other. He decided it was nice for her to make such a commitment.

In a few days, he would be off to Austria with his mother. Part of the money her late husband had sent her was paying for her to fulfil *her* dream of seeing the Vienna Philharmonic Orchestra play the traditional New Year's Day concert. She had asked Grant to go with her, while her mother looked after her other two children. What the future held for Grant and Maggie could wait until 1983; after the fat Austrian lady had sung.

13

18th January 1983
7.33 pm

'Happy birthday, darlin',' said Fat Franny Duncan.

He didn't routinely dine out in Kilmarnock. Not for fear of a rival hit against him while he was eating and at his most vulnerable. No, it was because he wouldn't dream of dining out with other men. So he only ate out with Theresa, his girlfriend, whose twentieth birthday they were celebrating.

Fat Franny was a big man. Theresa was slim, good-looking and had big breasts. Guys her own age looked twice at her. *Three* times when they realised who she was with. Their age gap would've suggested they might be father and daughter, and Fat Franny was acutely aware of this. But the Coffee Club in Bank Street had a downstairs basement section and it was relatively discreet. It was also mid-January, when the restaurants of Kilmarnock had their toughest – and *emptiest* – times of the year. The tables were arranged in three small zones and the lighting was always dimmed in the evenings. Despite everything, Fat Franny Duncan still cared what people thought about him, but principally because if they thought ill, then Theresa might leave him.

'Thanks Francis,' said Theresa.

Fat Franny held out his right hand. Theresa extended her left. Fat Franny took it and raised it to his lips. He kissed it gingerly, and with his left, brought up a small package from under the table.

'Aw, Fran … that's no whit ah think it is, is it?'

'Open it an' see,' said Fat Franny. Theresa carefully peeled back the shiny gold paper around the small, square parcel. Fat Franny watched the moisture develop in her eyes.

'Aye, Francis … aye, ah will.' Theresa knew that Fat Franny hadn't actually *asked* her to marry him, but they'd talked about it recently, and the ring that she was now holding was exactly the clustered diamond with the yellow gold band that she'd seen in Henderson's window in King Street. She'd told him about it, but hadn't really held out a strong hope that he had been paying enough attention to have acted on the information. Again, he had surprised her. He was doing that more and more often, lately. She liked the new, different Fat Franny. People who looked at them and regarded them as an odd couple didn't know these transformative things about him.

They had met at a function Fat Franny was DJ-ing at almost two years before. Theresa Morgan was there with two of her friends, Janice Fallon and Lizzie King. Janice and Lizzie had left early when Danny Keachie – Theresa's *then* boyfriend – had turned up uninvited. At the end of the night, Fat Franny had encountered the resultant argument between Theresa and Danny Keachie after she'd broken it off with him. Danny Keachie had punched Theresa in the face. Fat Franny – or rather Hobnail acting on instruction – had ensured that he spent the next two weeks with his jaw wired shut in Crosshouse Hospital. In the days that followed, Fat Franny sent Theresa flowers and chocolates, and a month after that first, brief encounter, Fat Franny Duncan and Theresa Morgan went for a drink together at the remote Craigie Inn.

Theresa, Janice and Lizzie had been inseparable back then, but only Janice said hello when their paths now infrequently crossed. The fallout with Lizzie was public and painful, and also irretrievable. Lizzie was now pregnant with Bobby Cassidy's baby, and since Bobby had been a major DJ rival of the Fat Franny empire, the die had been well and truly cast.

The waitress brought their food over to the table in the darkest corner of the Coffee Club's basement. They had both ordered gammon steaks and pineapple, with chips: their usual.

'Ach, that's beautiful, hen. Congratulations.' She'd seen enough strange-looking relationships in her time working there to avoid making assumptions. She waited to see Fat Franny's reaction and then added, '…to both ae ye'se.'

Fat Franny said thanks. A decent tip was assured, thought the waitress as she returned to the kitchen.

'Well, *there's* a coincidence,' said Theresa, as Earth, Wind & Fire came through the Coffee Club's speakers. 'Whit aboot September, then?' said Theresa. Fat Franny spluttered his drink.

'Aye, eh … plenty ae time, like? Ah'm that excited, Tre. *Really.* Ah'd want tae dae it right. Nae rush like, darlin'.'

'Ach, ah suppose,' said Theresa. Fat Franny felt like he had dodged a bullet on the timing.

'Is it jist aboot the money an' that? Ah ken losin' aw that cash wis a big blow.'

'Hey, don't you worry aboot aw that. Whatever you want … ah've got it covered.'

Fat Franny took Theresa's hand; the one with the new ring.

'Tre … there's somethin' else ah wanted tae talk aboot.'

'Whit is it?'

'It's Mam. She's gettin' worse. She forgot *ma* name the other day, thought ah'd fuckin' broke in tae the hoose. She wis aw agitated. Ah burst oot greetin'.'

'Aw, Francis. Ye've done aw ye can for her. Ye maybe need tae think aboot…' Theresa hesistated. '…gettin' her looked after. Properly, ken?'

'Whit dae ye mean … *properly?*' said Fat Franny, with more aggression than he'd intended.

'Hey, ah didnae mean anythin' by it. She's jist … a worry.'

'Well, ah wondered how ye'd maybe feel aboot maybe movin' in? Helpin' us wi' her, ken?' Fat Franny navigated the minefield he was in skilfully. A miscalculated step and Theresa would have cause to suspect his motivation. But he *did* love her, in so far as Fat Franny loved anything beyond himself, and his old mum. He genuinely wanted her to be around him, to be around *for* him. But he wasn't prepared for what she said next.

'Whit aboot a bigger move? Maybe tae the coast … Troon, Prestwick? Bigger hoose. Somewhere fur us aw tae … y'know?'

Fat Franny wasn't good in these circumstances. He was a reactive man, and one who normally reacted in a way that maintained the status quo. Proactivity was a much harder leap into the unknown for him. He'd rehearsed the now-unneccesary engagement speech in the mirror, just as he'd imagined Don Corleone might, in a similar situation. But her unexpected suggestion now made him feel vulnerable. He didn't like it.

'Ach … eat yer dinner, an' let's talk aboot it efter, eh?' Fat Franny now wished he hadn't raised the subject of his mum. He could have taken this a step at a time, like the Don would've. But his fragile old mum's shorter-term future was becoming interlinked with *their* longer-term one, and he couldn't separate them in his own mind.

'Christ, Fran … ah'd love us tae move away. Whit's *actually* here? Things'll jist go back tae normal when ma dad gets oot. Ah cannae watch that again. Ah've gied up wi' ma mam. If she wants tae be an emotional punchbag the rest ae her life then that's up tae her.' Theresa lit up a cigarette. She drew it in and a third of it turned to ash. She blew the smoke out the side of her mouth to avoid it going across their food. 'Ah'm no' movin' in wi' ye. God, ye live jist aroon' the corner fae me as it is.' Theresa hated the *Ponderosie*. It smelt of piss and stew and old people. And as a house clubbed together crudely with its neighbour, it was as appealing as Siamese twins created in Dr Frankenstein's laboratory. 'Troon sounds magic, d'ye no' think?' she said.

Despite the generation gap, Fat Franny Duncan and Theresa Morgan had much in common. Both were only children in a community where that was unusual. Both had grown up witnessing their mothers suffering domestic abuse, although that, sadly, wasn't so unusual. The legacy it had left them was different for each, though. Theresa was desperate to escape from the memories of a father addicted to gambling, returning nightly from a place of high spirits to the realisation of the paucity of his domestic life. He had never taken out his inability to control his frustrations directly on his family. Instead he represented mental torture for Theresa and her mother. His imprisonment for assault and handling stolen goods had given them eighteen months of unexpected respite, but her mother had apparently already forgiven his past transgressions. She was willing to forget the psychological torment of repeated visits from bailiffs, the stress of paying bills out of unpredictable pay packets – although with a criminal record, paid employment of *any* kind was going to be a new challenge – and was ready to take him back in a few months when his time was served. Theresa wasn't going to be around to see it; she was planning to be long gone. And therefore the conversations with Fat Franny about getting engaged had been instigated by her.

For his part, in the days and weeks that followed, when he considered it more fully, the idea of moving away and making a fresh start began actually to appeal to Fat Franny. He'd long wanted to become legitimised in business. The original idea of a roster of entertainment acts had fallen on its arse due to the lack of available talent. The follow-up initiative – a residency at the new Metropolis, with Fat Franny Duncan as DJ – also now looked out of touch, following the fall-out with Doc Martin the day before the place went up in smoke. So Fat Franny was now pinning everything on his new venture. He'd told no one about it, apart, obviously, from Terry Connolly, who had the initial connections, and even to him only the barest minimum. It was a risky business, but as one that tapped into the basest male instincts, it was a potential grower. A few years of *that* and *a big fuck-off hoose in Troon* became a distinct possiblity.

14

Max burst into the church hall, all profane excitement and anticipation of what he was about to reveal.

His enthusiasm evaporated quickly. The band was ploughing through a half-arsed jam of the Velvet Underground's 'Run, Run, Run'. The Sylvester brothers looked bored but, harangued and marshalled by Grant, they were methodically falling into line.

'Hey, fuckin' listen up,' shouted Max Mojo for the third time, annoyed that none of the foursome had taken particular notice when he'd come in, even though Maggie was looking straight at him. He was doubly aggravated because he explicitly told them to work on two of the three new songs Grant had written. Immortality wouldn't fall at the feet of a fucking covers band, especially one with such stereotypically limited tastes.

'Gie's fuckin' peace wi' that Lou Reed shite, eh?' The lifeless jam ground to a halt. 'Ah've got news … *great* news. Ah've got us a gig. Next week. At the Metropolis.'

'Aye?' said Grant, sounding more surprised than he'd intended.

'Aye, smart arse,' said Max. 'A gig. Yer a fuckin' band. Gigs are whit yer *supposed* tae dae.'

'Ah jist didnae expect … well, ken…' Grant tailed off.

'He jist didnae expect a useless pale-faced prick like *you* tae get us one,' said Maggie. The Sylvester brothers laughed in unison. Various phrases ran through Max Mojo's head at this point, almost all of which would've been considered by Alf Garnett's scriptwriters as going too far. He managed to hold them all inside, though. Maybe the anti-depressants *did* work, after all!

'So, ye'se up for it? It's decent money, an' it'll help pay for a bit ae studio time.'

'Aye Max. It's good, man,' said Grant. 'Really, it is.'

'*Man?* You some kinda fuckin' hippy throwback noo?' said Max.

'How long we gonnae be on for then?' asked Simon, leaning over to light a cigarette for Maggie.

'Hey, where the fuck did you get that?' Max shouted.

'It's a fuckin' lighter, mate. Calm doon,' said Simon calmly.

'It's *ma* fuckin' lighter, ya thievin' bastart!'

Simon examined the lighter as if he had never seen it before, and then lobbed it at Max. 'Well, if yer gonnae act like a wee wean ower it...' he said.

'Max, for fuck sake ... tell us aboot the gig,' said Grant.

'Two sets, aboot four or five songs each ... either side ae The Heid.'

'The Heid?' said Maggie. 'Who the fuck are they?'

'*He* ... no' they,' said Max. 'Who the fuck is *he?*'

'Dinnae be so pedantic,' she replied. 'Jist tell us.'

Max drew in breath and puffed his chest out with pride. 'The Heid is the foremost proponent of the mystical art ae ... hypnosis.'

Simon Sylvester laughed loudly. 'Ye've got us supportin' a bastart hypnotist? Fuck sake, man, that's hardly The Clash oan before The Who at Shea Stadium, is it?'

'Well, at least the second half'll be a piece ae piss. Every cunt'll be fuckin' zonked,' said Grant.

'Yer a bunch ae ungrateful wankers, so ye'se are!' Max was irritated. This was a breakthrough. It was the first Miraculous Vespas gig beyond Washer's coterie hanging about the church hall waiting for increasingly sparse work details and listening to their rehearsals. The band should've been more excited. The local press would be there as The Heid was still a reasonably big draw on the Ayrshire club circuit, by all the accounts Max had checked. He didn't normally work with a band. DJ Bobby Cassidy had been earmarked but had had to pull out unexpectedly. Bobby had called Max that morning at the house and they had met up in town that morning. He said he had some daft evening pregnancy breathing class thing to go to and he couldn't get out of it. Things had been going reasonably well for Bobby at the Metropolis and he didn't want Mickey Martin to have any reason to consider calling in Fat Franny Duncan as a late 'second-half substitute'. He'd pitched the idea to Mickey's bar manager, and he'd simply shrugged his shoulders and told him that any fuck-ups would be totally down to Bobby. That was enough for him and he'd thought of Max. In a previous existence, Max had given Bobby's fledgling Heatwave Disco some paid gigs supporting the original Vespas, and Bobby Cassidy still felt a tiny bit of responsibility for the Henderson Church fiasco, so – reciprocity being the substance that oiled the gears of the black economy – a big, long-standing favour could now be returned.

15

The following morning the band members assembled as usual at the Crosshouse parish hall. But, as Max watched them walk up the path – Grant and Maggie arrived as if joined at the hip in the peace-loving Campervan, but Simon and Eddie had travelled on separate buses even though they still lived in the same house – he detected a definite spring in their steps. Gradually, the dream that Max had painted for them all had been *adopted* by them all. They were a decent outfit, no doubt. He had them rehearsing for four hours a day, four days a week. Eddie was a potentially brilliant guitar player. *Ugly bastard*, Max acknowledged, but then Keith Richards was no oil painting. Grant Delgado had developed into an interesting singer. He was still shy and the vocals were a bit frail, but with the right songs he could sound like Jonathan Richman, which in Max Mojo's opinion would be no bad thing. His movement and confidence with the guitar and the mic stand was also improving. Maggie – it would clearly take a long time for *her* to accept Max's suggested name-change – was a competent drummer. She'd never be a female Ginger Baker, but Max figured she was already better than Moe Tucker. She was undeniably captivating into the bargain. With Maggie, they would have the *Smash Hits* teenage wanker market cornered, should they ever get that far. Only Simon Sylvester remained a constant concern. He was uncontrollably volatile, particularly when drunk, and a compulsive thief when sober. These could have otherwise been attributes, but Simon was a poor bass player, even by the standards set by the likes of Sid Vicious. In the absence of anyone better, Max resorted to hoping that an equally mental future groupie simply *stabbed the cunt*, bringing fame to The Miraculous Vespas through a more well-trodden rock 'n' roll route.

'Right, we need ten songs … jist in case, ken? Probably only fuckin' dae eight, but,' said Max, rubbing his hands together. 'The two best new yins, obviously…'

'*Obviously*,' said Simon sarcastically.

Max shot him a glance. 'An' the rest, jist the best ae the covers, aw'right?'

'Aye, Max,' said Grant. 'It'll be fine, man.'

Grant seemed calm. Max was surprised. He initially feared that, of the four, the most likely to be struck by stagefright was Grant Delgado. But as they rattled through 'Here Comes the Sun', Grant's vocals started to glide and soar through the rafters. It was like a switch had been flicked and the skinny, black drainpipe had morphed into Jim Morrison overnight. He'd obviously been practising outside of rehearsals, as Max had encouraged him to. He also seemed to Max to have bulked up. It was an illusion but it was truly amazing what burgeoning self-confidence could do to someone. The other three needed a kick up the arse though.

'For fuck sake, that song's aw aboot the joy ae bein' alive. It needs tae be light. It needs tae fuckin' glisten,' shouted Max. 'Feel the fuckin' vibe for Christ's sake. Take a lead fae Grant … follow his arc.'

'Aw, the wee teacher's pet,' mumbled Maggie.

'*Whit* did ye say?' asked Max accusingly.

'She said *"you'd like tae follow yer boaby right up Grant's arc"* … or somethin' like that,' said Simon.

Max pulled off his eye-patch and ran across the wooden floor. He launched himself straight into Simon's body like Andy Irvine making a Grand Slam-saving tackle. They landed in a flurry of arms and legs and thick bass strings. A few dull punches were thrown before the two were eventually separated, but beyond a few bleeding cuts and scrapes the principal damage appeared to have been suffered by the bass. It lay in two pieces, held together by two of its four heavy cables but it was in a critical condition. Its neck was broken.

'Ya stupid cunt, ye. Whit did ye dae that for?' yelled Simon.

'Jesus Christ, Max!' said Grant. 'They were only fuckin' kiddin'!'

'Ah've had it wi' aw the fuckin' aboot,' said Max, seemingly unaware that blood was steadily dripping from his nose onto a previously pristine white Levis t-shirt.

'You're a fanny,' said Maggie calmly.

'Ah'm ploughin' aw ma money and energy intae...'

'Haud oan ... aw *your* money?' said Grant.

Max began again; this time with a more considered, conciliatory tone. Inside, though, he was raging. 'Ah'm spendin' serious time tryin' tae get us a shot at somethin' special here. We might only get one shot, so ... if it's aw'right wi' you four ... let's no' fuck it up oan day one, eh?'

There was silence; a pause developing so far into its third trimester that its head was crowning.

'Are we doin' this gig or no'?' Max Mojo's arms were outstretched like a pleading Jesus on the Mount of Olives. The medication was working overtime, as deep down inside, the *Voice* wanted to rip the heads from each of them. Ozzy Osbourne and the bats would be nothing compared to *this* ritual slaughter.

'Will there be Tunnocks Tea Cakes an' Irn-Bru oan the rider?' asked Eddie innocently.

It was enough to defuse the tautness. They all laughed. Max reluctantly forced a thin-lipped grin, but it was enough. The tension of the moment had passed.

'Aye ... of course we're doin' it. We'll be ready. Jist gie us some time tae sort oot the set. Let me deal wi' the music side, you sort out the money. Aw'right?' said Grant.

'Aye. Fine.' Max pawed at his dripping nose. Grant looked at them individually until they had all said yes. He then motioned with his head, and Simon reached over and offered a hand.

Max took it, and shook it. 'Yer a fuckin' arsehole, Sylvester,' he remarked with sincerity, but with enough disguise as to be taken differently. He re-patched his fluttering left eye.

Max Mojo left them to it as the sunlight worked hard to penetrate the dark interior of the church hall. He turned back. A sudden shaft of it caught Grant Delgado and held him in its natural coruscating spotlight.

'Little darlin', it's been a long cold lonely winter...'

Grant Delgado was a superstar in waiting. Pride swelled in Max Mojo's heart while longing stirred in his pants.

16

'How we gettin' there again?'

'Ah fuckin' told ye a hundred times, Jimmy Stevenson's pickin' ye'se up. Jesus Johnny … gonnae listen when ah'm talkin' tae ye?'

Grant was enjoying playing with Max's increasingly frazzled mindset. Max had met The Heid earlier that afternoon for the first time and far from drawing comfort from the encounter, had left it with more concerns than he'd had over his own band of misfits. The Heid was already pissed for a kick-off. He looked like a Buchanan Street tramp with a *Lord of the Rings* obsession. Four neat whiskies were despatched in half an hour, during the audience with Max. After passing the obligatory questioning about his age, the teenager had grudgingly bought them all. The deal was that The Miraculous Vespas would be paid from The Heid's fee, which it now emerged was based on takings at the door. The *Ayrshire Post* had heavily plugged the gig, mainly building on the growing reputation of the Metropolis as Ayrshire's newest superclub. Bobby Cassidy was doing well, and his music, as well as Kilmarnock's unusual four am licence, was now slowly drawing weekend punters from outside the region. The club had an official capacity of three hundred but it regularly took six hundred people, jammed in like a London Central Line tube train at rush hour. Mickey 'Doc' Martin was a happy man, and when that was the state of affairs, those positive vibes generally washed down and bathed others in the same line of activity. But sales for The Heid had been slow. The old show pony had an undoubted reputation but it was on the wane. There were only so many times you could watch some poor, overly-suggestive sod eat an onion and it remain funny, regardless of how much El Dorado you had in your belly.

'It'll be fine, son,' said the sixty-year-old Heid. 'We'll divvy up efter the show, like, eh?'

Max couldn't quite place the accent. It seemed like a weird combination of Ayrshire and Edinburgh. The legacy of a life of playing wee smoky clubs and shiteholes up and down the Central Belt, no doubt.

'Aye. Fine,' said Max. He stood up to leave. He'd spent well over a fiver on this old tosser already. Any more would eat into profit, although The Heid seemed to be preparing him for bad news on that front.

'Whit's yer real name, incidentally?' asked the standing Max.

'Head … Harry Head,' slurred The Heid.

'*Fuck* off!'

'Fuckin' is, son,'

'Ha ha ha … ya aul' prick.' Max left the Metropolis laughing. He thought of the Quarrymen playing at a church fete, Elvis on the back of a flatbed truck … and then The Miraculous Vespas supporting a *miroculous* Heid. The stuff of legend.

The Heid gig wis a mistake. Cannae fuckin' expect tae get it right aw the time though, by the way. Jist seemed like the right bastart thing tae dae, ken? Ah kent a guy that kent a guy that knew he wis lookin' for a support act. Nae cunt in oor band had ever heard ae him though. So it gets relayed back that The Heid's been oan Opportunity Knocks. Kicked oot early doors though like. A comedian back then … but noo the cunt's reinvented hissel' as a fuckin' hypnotist, ken? Fuckin' arsehole that he wis…

Cunt comes in, dressed like fuckin' Zorro's Grampa … ah near pished maself. He's aw in black … an', back then in the fuckin' day-glo eighties, that marked the cunt as a major league fuckin' kiddie fiddler.

17

Jimmy Stevenson's van blocked the Foregate, but the few shops in it that still operated had long since closed, so nobody objected. In any case, it took the band only fifteen minutes to get their gear unloaded – including Simon Sylvester's brand new bass guitar, purchased from the Grant Delgado Emergency Fund. Having deposited them, Jimmy Stevenson disappeared into the crisp night air. Since the terms of his probation restricted his activities to that of driver only, he never now entered any venues where alcohol would be served.

Inside the Metropolis, taped soul music was playing, and the lighting had been set to a pre-programmed choreography. The Miraculous Vespas would be playing to the immediate left of the dancefloor, on a slightly raised podium. The Heid's show would use the dancefloor as its stage. The punters had ample space to move about, especially since it was clear even this early on that the first gig of the 'Greatest new band in Scotland' wasn't going to be a sell-out.

The Metropolis had only been open a few months but it had already acquired that stagnant pub odour of smoke, vomit, stale perfume and spilt beer. Its carpeted areas felt like they had been coated with adhesive. Its wooden floor was already dappled with embedded fragments of broken glass.

As The Miraculous Vespas tuned up, Max counted just six people in the club. Two seemed to be with The Heid's entourage, although he was nowhere to be seen. Max had recalled The Heid saying he'd be in his 'dressing room', so Max went to look for it. It was a cleaner's cupboard. Its door was slightly open but Max could hear the old trouper in there, still pissed but talking to someone.

'Aye, just like that … slow doon a bit tho', ah'm no' as young as ah used tae be, hen.'

Max peeked through the gap in the door. The Heid was sitting on a Belfast sink, black trousers and big, off-white y-fronts at his ankles, while a much younger, blonde-haired woman's head bobbed up and down between his pale, veined, corned-beef legs. Max stuck his head in further. The Heid had a black shirt and black jacket on. He wore a long but skinny white leather tie, which he had cast over his left shoulder, presumably for fear of it getting tangled up in the action happening down below. His eyes were closed. His wispy grey hair and beard were combed. He was holding a massive, lit cigar in his right hand while his left propelled the woman's head, helping it keep the rhythm. A bag of onions sat at his feet.

'Where's the Heid?' asked Grant, when Max returned to the main room.

'In the back gettin' a gobble affa some poor wummin' he's obviously pit a spell oan,' said Max. 'Ah left him tae it. Good luck tae the auld cunt.'

18

'Good evenin' Kilmarnock. We're The Miraculous Vespas…'

Maggie's drum thudded into action and Grant's casual strum built up speed afterwards. They had tried to vary their cover of 'Where Were You?' but it was such a strong song that the band inevitably retreated back into a more faithful rendition. Max Mojo was standing at the back of the Metropolis, trying to gauge both sound quality and audience reaction. Both fell into the 'mediocre' category. The band had no mixing desk to speak of; for future gigs that would have to be rectified. In a quarter-full club context, their sound was muddy. It was distorted and the volume was difficult to set as a result. More bass but less amplification would have been the starting point, Max now reckoned. The club was partially underground and had a mass of concrete surrounding it, but the crispness Max heard in his head was totally missing. One thing that did stand out though was Grant Delgado. He moved like an anaconda, draping himself around the microphone stand, rhythm guitar barely used after those opening chords. Max heard a few girls in the crowd talking favourably about Grant, and what they'd like him to do to them.

The band's covers of 'Song from Under the Floorboards', and 'Run, Run, Run' – which Max had advised against – sounded only marginally better. Then Grant introduced 'Your Love Is a Wonderous Colour'; the first of their two original songs. Grant had written it a month ago. Maggie liked it because she assumed it was about her. The Sylvester brothers also liked it, as they both had interesting parts. Eddie had a cyclical guitar part not dissimilar to the Beatles 'Dear Prudence', and Simon had a bass line that took a few twists and turns of its own. Admittedly, he had relied on his brother teaching him the nuances, but Simon Sylvester was definitely improving. For a first song, it was pretty accomplished, and while lyrically, it wouldn't be giving Leonard Cohen any sleepless nights, the band considered it to be a cut above the dross being peddled by the Club Tropicana set.

The three-and-a-half-minute song ended with the same apathetic response as the three that had gone before. It had been Grant's task to introduce The Heid, but he'd forgotten, and they'd walked off calmly but in a descending storm of ear-splitting feedback. The Heid was not amused.

'Big hand fur the band, lays an' gennulmen…' The Heid sarcastically slow-clapped until the squealing sound had gone. He strode to the DJ booth and angrily flicked a switch. *This* was to have been Max Mojo's job, but he was still at the back of the club eavesdropping. A burst of dry ice covered the stage, briefly obscuring the black-clad hypnotist with his shirt now open to the navel.

Max saw this and laughed at the thought of the skinny, white-leather tie being his everyday-wear. He emerged through the fog to the sound of the theme from *Star Wars*. It would have been reasonably impressive as an entrance had The Miraculous Vespas not fucked up the illusion.

A deep voice that reminded Max of the Wizard of Oz burst through the Marshall amps. 'I am the amazing and mysterious Heid,' it said. 'Prepare to be shocked and astonished at my powers of suggestion.'

'Ah'm fuckin' shocked an' astonished any cunt actually pays tae see this!' whispered Max to an adjacent stranger who had earlier paid to see it. She moved away from him.

'You're gonna see people do things you'd never believe possible…' said the Heid.

'…like eat a bastart onion, thinking it's an apple?' whispered Max, to no one in particular.

'You'll see them act out their fantasies … with no inhibitions at all,' said The Heid. 'You'll be telling people about this next forty-five minutes for the rest of yer life…' The Heid stepped back a few paces, to be briefly obscured again by the diminishing mist. With the majority of the fifty or so people in the audience currently smoking, this was less impressive than it might otherwise have been. The Heid re-emerged to a brief burst of Black Sabbath's 'Paranoid'. *Another fuckin' desperate cliche*, thought Max.

'I want you all to think of a happy place,' said The Heid. He twisted his long grey beard with his right hand and appeared to Max to be scratching his arse with his left. But The Heid was looking for a 50p coin; performance prop number one.

'Ah'm gonna toss it…' said The Heid, waiting patiently for the laughs and sniggers that always followed this line. 'And, because my mind is controlling *yours* now … those that can answer my question are gonna be the stars of tonight's show.'

'Aye, right', 'Tosser' and 'Ya prick' came back at him from various standing hecklers.

The Heid flipped the coin and it landed. Max cynically assumed he'd simply ask people whether it had landed heads- or tails-up, but the old entertainer surprised the teenager by saying, 'Those who know the identity of the person on the side facing upwards … step forward and come to the edge of the stage.'

Max sniggered. There was no stage, just a rough edge where sticky carpet met wooden dancefloor. The Heid had a rehearsed script though, and context didn't alter it.

Max watched four people from different parts of the crowd move forward. It was, perhaps predictably, an equal gender split. He was sure that one of the women was the same woman that he saw earlier, on her knees and administering head to The Heid. She was now wearing a different top, though, and since Max hadn't seen her face in the cleaner's cupboard, he assumed he was mistaken.

The four made their way to the dancefloor where four wooden seats were now waiting for them. Out of the corner of his eye, Max noticed Eddie being restrained by his brother. Max headed down through the crowd to join them.

One by one, the four wrote the words 'Britannia, seated with a lion' on pieces of paper The Heid had handed them. After he held each piece up for the audience to examine, he asked the four what they had just written. One by one, the four said that they didn't know. They had a look of total bemusement on their faces, as did most of the audience. The Heid declared them to be the most suggestible people present, and that he had planted the words. They were ignorant to the question but that he … The Mysterious Heid … was now controlling their minds.

Another simple mind seemingly being controlled was that of guitarist Eddie Sylvester. He was now being bundled by the rest of The Miraculous Vespas back into the same cleaner's cupboard that had earlier doubled as The Heid's un-dressing room.

'Whit the fuck's up wi' him?' shouted Max Mojo.

'He wants tae be oot oan the dancefloor,' said Grant. 'That auld prick's hypnotised him.'

'Has he fuck! That's aw a load ae shite, man,' said Max.

'His eyes are spinnin' like a bloody kaleidoscope,' said Maggie.

'Has he been oan the mushrooms?' Max demanded.

'How should ah know?' said Simon, before theatrically adding, arms outstretched, 'I am not my brother's fucking keeper.'

Grant and Maggie both laughed.

'Gie it up, you'se two … an' get him fuckin' sorted oot, eh?' said Max. 'Ye'se are back oan in twenty minutes!'

The Heid's act was indeed predictable. After warming up the crowd by having the four believe they were the new ABBA, with unsurprisingly awful voices, it progressed to the four 'volunteers' acting out a scene in a hotel restaurant. Each man was dining with the other's wife. At the click of The Heid's nicotine-stained fingers, *that* became suddenly apparent to all four. Hilarity was supposed to ensue. This running theme of swapped partners led to the subsequent 'adjoining bedrooms' scene, in which each 'couple' was challenged by The Heid to out-vocalise the other during role-playing sex. In one corner of the dancefloor an older woman was yodelling like Johnny

Weissmuller while her much younger 'partner' barked during an energetically simulated doggy-style. In the other corner, the blonde Max thought he'd seen earlier shouted 'Yee-Haw' as she sat astride a bearded, dark-skinned boy, riding him to what seemed to her to be Grand National triumph. Only when the women were down to their underwear did The Heid step in and touch their heads, saying '*Sleeeeep*' as he did so. All four instantaneously capitulated to The Heid's will.

As a reward for their efforts the two males were given juicy 'apples', and the smell of raw onion filled the Metropolis. For his finale, the two women were running free, through the flower-filled meadows of Austria, singing 'The hills are alive with the sound of music' at the tops of their voices. Until The Heid suddenly intervened and reminded them that they had a profound fear of open spaces.

Both women shuddered and dived into the corners and crevices of the dancefloor. Max saw them both look genuinely fearful. He thought about this gig, and now reckoned on why Bobby Cassidy was so keen to get out of it. *Fuckin' walloper*, he thought as he imagined Bobby's smiling face. He went back behind the bar to gee up the band for their final four numbers. The Heid had just brought the two women back into the room, so to speak, and was bringing the 'performance' to a close. Max annoyingly heard more applause proffered for The Heid's clapped-out, tired act than for the band. Still, it was a start. He'd get to work on the local pubs in the morning and get a proper, wee Ayrshire tour of their own going. He might try and approach Billy Sloan from the radio to come down in the hope of a bit of coverage. He even considered banging on Simple Minds' manager, Bruce Findlay's door. A future support slot with them would be fantastic, once the singer had written a few more original songs. Into the bargain, Findlay owned a few independent record stores around Scotland.

'We'll need tae just dae a few acoustic versions, Max.'

All four of them stared at Eddie Sylvester. He had wedged himself under the Belfast sink. He was shaking and sweating profusely.

'Whit?' said Max.

'He thinks he's … *aggra*-phobic,' said Simon.

'Fuck does that even mean? Is he jist angry?' shouted Max.

'Naw. Cannae go ootside intae open spaces,' said Grant.

'So how did he fuckin' get here th'night then? Beamed straight doon fae the bastart Enterprise?'

'Look, leave him in there. Let's go, eh?' said Maggie impatiently.

'Get up ya stupid cunt!' shouted Max, aiming a kick at Eddie's coiled body.

'Hey, fuckin' leave him alone!' Simon jumped in to defend his brother, qualifying the action with, 'he might be an arsehole, but he's *ma* arsehole tae batter, no' yours.'

'Fuck off. Get him oot oan that stage noo or yer both history,' screamed Max Mojo. Grant and Maggie had already headed down the narrow corridor.

'That auld wanker's fuckin' done the voodoo shite oan him. That's *your* fault, Mojo! He's never gonnae get ootae this cupboard.'

'Don't talk shite!' Max could hear Grant and Maggie tuning up. 'Ah'll be back,' said Max. As he turned away, Simon gave him the fingers.

Out in the club, Grant was introducing Maggie as the best drummer in Scotland. Some people had drifted away, but around thirty remained. It was now one am on a Wednesday morning. That in itself was worthy of celebration. Tuesday night was the worst for any type of event. It was just beyond consideration as part of a previous extended weekend hangover, and too early to be regarded as part of the run-up to the next one. The most miserable of all days, Tuesdays.

'We're gonna soothe you into Wednesday with a few wee classics,' whispered Grant Delgado. Shorn of the uncontrolled amplification, Grant's voice, light guitar strumming and Maggie's brushed strokes made 'Here Comes the Sun' sound fantastic to Max Mojo. It was the best they had ever performed it, in his opinion. They followed that with a glistening 'Life's a Gas', and then a slowed down 'Touch Me', with Grant channelling Bolan *and* Morrison in a way that gave Max Mojo his second hard-on of the evening. The duo's newly adopted theme song, 'Thirteen' rounded off the covers.

'We'd like to leave you wi' this. It might end up being our first single. It's somethin' called "The First Picture".'

Max Mojo was astonished. He didn't even know such a song existed, far less that they would be revealing it tonight. It was a fragile, delicate number full of soaring melodies and unexpected chord changes. Max could hear it in his head, with the full band in flow, and with some decent production. For Max, It stood comparison with the four stonewallers that had preceded it. It was an instant classic. Grant Delgado was a fucking superstar in waiting. Max's cock was now bulging out of his tight, pin-striped jeans. As soon as the song finished – and the best cheers of the night were its reward – Max Mojo dived into the gents and relieved the pressure.

19

When Max Mojo came out of the toilet, Grant and Simon were carrying the stricken guitarist out to Jimmy Stevenson's parked vehicle.

'Whit happened tae him?'

'Ah thought aboot whit ye said, Max,' replied Simon, '…an' ah want tae be in the band, ken? So ah jist leathered the cunt a dull yin. Knocked him oot, like.'

Max looked down at the unconscious Eddie.

'It wis' either that or break the big sink aff the wa'!' said Simon, logically.

'Aye … ah suppose.' Max scratched his head and went to look for The Heid, and payment. He was to be disappointed on the second count. There had been a bit of a scuffle earlier in the cupboard between The Heid and Simon Sylvester, and now The Heid entourage was already outside in the small service yard at the rear of the Metropolis.

'Whit d'ye fuckin' mean *"No payin"*?'

'Ah'm no' payin' ye,' said the angry Heid. 'Ye'se fucked up ma intro, an' then didnae turn up for the ending.'

'Aye we did. That wis the best bit, ya dick!' argued Max. 'Plus, ye fuckin' hypnotised ma guitarist. Daft cunt's feart fae his ain shadow noo. We want compensation for that!' Max pushed the old man backwards against his small van. Immediately, two men got out the back of it.

'Everythin' aw'right Da?' said one … the *same* one who had earlier slithered his way to Red Rum-like victory across the Metropolis dancefloor.

Max moved slowly to one side and peaked in the back of the van. The other two 'suggestible' audience members were in the back of The Heid's small van. It was a travelling show in every sense. The Heid's look and shoulder-shrug to Max said it all. The older woman stuck her head out.

'Hey, Long John Silver, beat it ... or ye'll end up like a fish supper fae Ferri's ... battered an' boggin'.' Max took a step backwards.

'So, as ah think we can aw agree ... ah didnae hypnotise yer man, did ah?' said The Heid, a look of aged resignation on his face. 'A wee bit ae advice, pal. In future, get the dosh up front. It's much harder for folk tae get it aff ye *efter* a bad gig, then for them tae *gie* ye it efter wan, ken? Jist sayin', like.'

The Family Heid got in the van and it spluttered off, leaving Max to ponder who the blow-job artist was. The older woman might have been Mrs Heid. The boys were probably both sons. Which left a 'daughter-in-law'... or maybe even a daughter!

'Dirty aul' bastart!' Max Mojo shuddered. It had been that kind of night.

'Look everybody, it's bad fuckin' biscuits. That auld cunt fucked off without payin' us,' said Max. 'Jimmy, ah'll need tae owe ye, man.'

'For Christ's sake, son. Ah don't dae 'tic. Ah trusted ye earlier.' Jimmy's van screeched to a halt, throwing the band in the back forward and into the partition dividing the driver's cabin and the rear of the van.

'Did ah hear that right?' shouted Grant through the small open window. 'Nae money? For fuck sake, Max. *That* wis your one job, man!'

'Aye, aye ... ah fuckin' ken. Gie it a rest, eh? Ah feel as bad as everybody else ... well, apart fae *him* obviously.' Max pointed through the window at Eddie Sylvester, who was out cold and draped bizarrely over the components of the drum kit on the back shelf. 'Has anybody got any cash tae sort oot Jimmy?' There was no response. 'Ah'll square ye'se up the morra.' Simon Sylvester shuffled in his seat. He brought out a thick black wallet.

'Jesus,' said Maggie.

'Ye fuckin' kept that quiet when ah wis' at the bar, ya cunt!' said Max.

'How much?' said Simon.

'Fifty,' said Jimmy, sticking a sweaty mitt through the hole. Simon opened up the wallet and pulled out a few twenties. Max spotted The Heid's tiny picture inside the wallet's inner sleeve.

'Ya fuckin' dancer,' said an excited Max Mojo. 'How the fuck did ye get that? An' more tae the point, when were ye gonnae let on?'

Simon tapped his nose. He gave Jimmy Stevenson sixty pounds and told him to keep the change. Simon handed Max Mojo another hundred, telling him to 'divvy up'. The remainder of the stolen wallet's contents remained with its new owner.

The van headed off under the railway arches and back up to Onthank to drop Grant and Maggie off.

Max Mojo was experiencing a mix of emotions. Exaltation at realising Grant Delgado's potential, disappointment at his own inexperience in failing to secure payment, and uncertainty over the various pros and cons of having an untrustworthy kleptomaniac as part of the band. But at least it *was* a band. The road to Max's destiny had been charted. The rise of The Miraculous Vespas had surely begun.

03: **PLEASE PLEASE PLEASE, LET ME GET WHAT I WANT...**

That shoulda been it ... right there. A bit ae fuckin' shared commitment, ken? Fuckin' determination? But naw. Every cunt jist sloped back intae being a lazy bastart. None ae them had the fuckin' imagination, back then ... apart fae mibbe Delgado. An' even then, jist mibbe.

BB fuckin' disappeared in that daft van ae hers. By the way, we called her Butter Biscuit by then. It drove her fuckin' mental ... which wis an added bonus in ma opinion, ken? The dopey cunt Eddie came up wi' it. 'Cos Grant had Delgado us his ither name, heid-the-ba reckons wi' aw needed tae change. Ah says 'Ah'm no' changin' ma name fae Max Mojo.' That prick Simon told him tae away an' fuck himself up an entry. The lassie's second name wis Abernethy, so wi' the stupid cunt's obsession wi' biscuits, and him thinkin' her first name wis short for Margarine ... Butter Biscuit. Ah telt ye he wis a fuckin' moron, didn't ah? Ah wanted tae rename it Chocolate Biscuit, but that wisnae oan the cards, like.

Anyway, where wis' ah? Oh aye ... she shot the craw 'cos some cunt tried tae set fire tae the van wi' her in it. Bound tae be they pikey wankers fae Galston, ah tells her.

An' then she's aff ... as if they daft cunts wi' the pillows oan their heids were chasin' her ... only, in a smokin' van, like.

The fuckin' bass player gets lifted for shopliftin' jackets ootae DM Hoey's ... an' his fuckin' marshmallow ae a brother cannae leave the hoose 'cos that Heid cunt had mangled whit little brain he had left.

Plus, ah had a wee bit ae trouble maself, truth be telt. Came aff the Lithium. Cauld Christmas Turkey, ah wis'. A week later, ah'm runnin' doon Dundonald Road, fuckin' starkers wi' three wee dugs ah'd nicked affa two pensioners, an' a gnome ah stole oot the Provost's garden, aw in a FineFare shopping trolley. Ah'm shoutin' 'They'll be bigger than the bastart Beatles!' Ah pushes the fuckin' thing through the Co-op's windae. So they telt me, anyway. Don't fuckin' remember a thing aboot it.

Net result: confined tae fuckin' barracks, Norma. Aw leave cancelled ... an' back oan an even stronger set ae Jack an' Jills. Whit a cunt, eh?

20

'Long time, Senga.'

'Aye, Des. Bob wis still livin' last time, eh?' It was a bitter comment, aimed to hurt her brother, who hadn't even spoken to her on the day of her husband's – and *his* colleague's – funeral.

'Look, Senga, ah'm no' efter a fight, right. Too much water under the bridge for aw that noo.'

'So whit ye here for then? Jist helpin' me oot tae the motor wi' ma messages? Got a new job as a supermarket trolley attendant, is it? Lean fuckin' times wi' the Fatman?'

'Gie it up, eh, Senga? Ah'm concerned aboot Grant,' said Des.

'*Grant?*' said Senga. 'Grant's doin' jist fine away fae aw the pish that happens aroond here.'

'Fat Franny kens ye took his money aw they months ago,' said Des.

'Eh?' Senga was suddenly flustered. She tried but couldn't hide it. 'Dinnae ken whit yer talkin' aboot, sunshine.'

'Ye cannae kid a kidder, Seng,' said Des. 'If he disnae ken for certain yet, he's got real suspicions it wis you.' Senga pulled her shoulders back. She now *knew* her brother knew.

'How?' she said.

'Yer wee trip tae Venice wi' the boy … for Hogmanay, an' that. That didnae go unnoticed.'

'How did ye ken aboot that? An' it wis *Vienna*, no' Venice, by the way.'

'Same fuckin' difference. Point is, it wisnae Ayr Butlins, wis it?'

'Big bloody deal, Des. Ah could've been savin' up for that for years. Bob coulda been insured for thousands!'

'Aye,' said Des. 'But ye wurnae ... an' he *wisnae*. An' Grant's oan the Broo for Christ's sake, but he's buyin' guitars like they're goin' ootae fashion ... an' a fuckin' Campervan!'

'Hey, it belongs tae his girlfriend. That's no' his. Jesus Christ, Des, ye widnae be much cop as a bloody detective.' Senga was fuming but trying hard to hide it. They had reached her car. She struggled to unlock it with all the bags she was holding. She dropped her purse. It opened as it fell. Des could see the thickness of notes in there and that there weren't many green ones. Their eyes locked together but he said nothing.

'How's the weans? An' Effie?' she asked him, breaking the silence.

'The *weans* are fine, but no' weans anymore,' he replied curtly. 'Senga, ah'm no' here for the small talk. It's way too late for that noo. But ah don't want Grant gettin' drawn intae aw the bullshit. He made the right decision last summer ... in *ma* opinion, any road. But things are goin' south wi' Franny. He's suspicious ae everybody, an' noo he's realisin' jist how much Bob protected him. His maw's oan her last legs but he cannae accept it. He says that money wis hers. An' he cannae let that go. He's weaker withoot Bob, but still dangerous.' Des sighed. 'Look, tell Grant tae watch hisself. And you tae.'

'So, why are you still wi' him, then? Why dae ye no' jist bugger off an' dae somethin' else ... somethin' *straight*?' she asked him.

'Disnae matter. Ah jist don't want...' He tailed off. '...the blood's thicker than the water when it aw comes doon tae it, right?'

Senga looked straight at her younger brother. He was trembling. He seemed to be holding something back and, as a consequence, he looked vulnerable. She suddenly felt sorry for him, although she didn't really know why.

'Effie's got cancer,' he finally said. 'They've gie'd her six months ... a year tops.'

'Aw Des, ah'm sorry.' She felt she should hug him, but it had been too long. It would have felt like false emotion, and neither of them needed that.

'Ah'm havin' to draw back oan the work, dae less, ken. But Franny's looked efter us. He's no' as bad as folk think. Honestly, we'd be fucked withoot him.'

'Aye. Well, Des … ah better get goin'. Grant'll be hame for his tea soon.' Senga touched her brother's forearm. 'Tell Effie ah'm thinkin' aboot her, eh?'

'Ah will, an' mind Senga … get Grant tae knock the daft spendin' oan the heid okay? Keep under the radar for a while. Folk might think he's an arsehole maist ae the time, but there's nae benefit in rubbin' Fat Franny's nose in it.' Des turned to walk away.

'Des.' He turned round. 'Who telt ye aboot us bein' away for the New Year?' Senga asked.

'Disnae matter,' he said.

'It does tae me.'

Des sighed deeply. Having given her the warning, he felt she deserved to know why. 'One ae they Quinn boys fae Galston telt the Painter. *He* telt me,' said Des. He had hoped to leave it at that, but dots still needed to be joined. 'Grant's lassie … the half-caste yin … she went oot wi' Rocco Quinn. Bad break-up last year, an' aw kind ae shite went oan. Apparently she wis braggin' aboot the money Grant had.'

Senga looked furious.

'Look, speak tae him. Jist tell him tae lie low, eh? Ah'll see ye, Senga. Take care ae yerself.' And with that, he was gone.

She stayed and watched him walk the length of the car park back down to Glasgow Road, and away back in to the heart of Onthank. She wasn't quite sure what else to do.

21

'Mam? Whit's the matter wi' ye?' Grant had just taken Senga outside to show off his new purchase. He could tell she really didn't approve. 'Look, it's safe … it's no like it's a Harley Davidson or somethin'.'

'Come in the hoose,' she said tersely.

'Christ's sake, Mam. Ah'm no' a wean,' Grant pleaded.

Senga slammed the door behind him. 'Then stop fuckin' actin' like yin, Grant!' she yelled. 'Sit doon.'

'Ah'm no' sure ah want tae, if you're gonnae be bawlin' like a banshee,' he said.

'*Grant!*' He sat down as instructed. 'Ah told *ye* aboot that money … where it came fae. An' ah told ye no' tae be makin' a show ae spendin' it,' she stressed.

'Aye, an' whit? Ah huvnae!' His arms were outstretched, pleading ignorance.

'So where did ye get that bloody motorbike then … The Multi-Coloured Swap Shop?'

'It's no' a motorbike … exactly,' said Grant. 'It's a scooter. A *Vespa*. That's for the band, Mam. For press photographs an' that.'

'So, ye didnae buy it then?'

'Well, aye … of course ah *bought* it! They wurnae givin' them away, Mam. Look, whit's the issue here?' Grant was getting annoyed. Nine months ago, his mum had told him that his father had left him an inheritance of £20,000. She'd told him it was dodgy money, but she'd been economical with the truth. She'd put it in a bank account for him. It was his to do as he liked with. She'd told him other money left to Sophie and Andrew had gone into a trust fund for them when they turned twenty-one. He was getting his early on strict condition that he cut ties with Fat Franny Duncan *and* that he told no one about the money. Last Christmas, when she'd told him about the plan to go to Austria for New Year, she'd told him the full story. That the money was actually Fat Franny's, stolen from the safe in the Fatman's house by Grant's father to give to them. He'd asked her if that was the reason he was dead. She'd told him she didn't think so, but she couldn't be completely sure. Fat Franny Duncan was a nasty piece of work, she'd said, but she couldn't believe that he'd be capable of having his oldest friend killed. But you just never knew, she'd warned him.

'How much ae it's left, Grant?' Senga now asked. 'An' whit've ye spent the rest oan?' She had looked out a notepad and a pen, figuring it might be a long list.

Grant told her about the guitars: three for him, and one new bass guitar to replace Simon Sylvester's own one, broken in the flurry with Max. He also told her the hire of Jimmy Stevenson's van, the amps and sound gear from the Hurlford shed of Hairy Doug in preparation for a couple of upcoming gigs that Max was working on. He omitted to tell her that the hire of the latter had now become a purchase, since Max had put his boot through a Marshall speaker during yet another violent disagreement with the bass player. He also avoided telling his mother about the whole Campervan story. That Grant had been forced into paying Rocco Quinn settlement money to prevent him destroying it. Needless to say, Maggie's poker-victory version of the story was violently contested by her ex-boyfriend. Max Mojo was with Grant when Rocco and his baseball-bat-wielding brothers came a-calling. Max had brokered the pay-off after seeing Grant's reaction when the Quinns explained their knowledge about the depth of his funds, but not before a mental calculation of how he might make use of such a surprisingly handsome sum. This clearly wasn't the time for Grant to enlighten his mum about *any* of that.

Another omission was that he'd subsequently been manipulated by Max Mojo into paying the band a modest weekly wage to supplement their dole money, and to ensure they kept turning up for rehearsals. Grant wasn't even sure himself how that had happened but he had reluctantly agreed to it in return for a future 35 percent of all band-related profits. Max Mojo might've been a teenager but his ability to exploit those around him was truly strange. Max believed himself to be the reincarnation of Brian Epstein, Kit Lambert, Don Arden, Col. Tom Parker etc, and often the conviction with which he held to that belief was perversely inspiring.

But Grant's mother wouldn't have appreciated that at this point. So he had to lie. He felt bad about it, but he couldn't have told Senga that more than half of the money she'd given him nine months ago was gone. And that he'd told not only Max Mojo about exactly where it had come from, but also his unpredictable and untamed girlfriend, Maggie Abernethy.

22

Max Mojo couldn't sleep. He paced his bedroom floor. It was strewn with seven-inch singles. He was trying to galvanise an image in his mind of the band as they would appear on the poster for their first proper gigs. The Heid debacle a month before had now all but been erased for his memory as a gig, although Max knew it would reappear in countless biographies after The Miraculous Vespas had broken America. After they had played the Budokan. After they had been on *Top of the Pops* for four weeks running.

Max Mojo had absolutely no doubt that all of these things would ultimately happen. First though, the band needed an image, and one that could compete in the eyes of teenage girls with those two pricks from Wham! He looked at the various pairs of stonewashed jeans and checked shirts he'd scored from the girls who worked at Jim Beam near the bottom of the Foregate, but nothing was jumping out at him. The shirts were a bit too Big Country or U2 for Max, although Eddie Sylvester fancied himself as The Edge, prior to his recent hypnosis. Maggie – or BB as Max now constantly referred to her – was never going to wear *anything* suggested by Max, but since she was in the back, and insisted on showing more flesh than not, Max felt he could compromise. Leather was a potential answer. Maggie, looking like she'd just crawled out of the jungle with Annabella Lwin, fronted by black-clad leather guitar heroes; *that* could work. But the music wasn't rough or especially rocking. And since Max was insistent on keeping 'Vespas' in their name, the leather didn't particularly fit.

Paul Weller's new look – European coffee-house modernist

chic – was interesting, and 'Speak Like a Child' was a phenomenal opening statement of new intent in Max's informed opinion, but he needed something more original. Weller copyists were everywhere, and charlatans like Secret Affair or The Lambrettas hadn't faired well in *that* slipstream.

Eddie Sylvester's condition remained a concern. He had always been considered strange, especially by other kids at Kilmarnock Academy. His teachers branded him disruptive and aggressive, and in his second year he had been moved to the nearby Park School. It was formally referred to as a school for *special* pupils, but kids who went there were relentlessly and unfairly stigmatised for being stupid. Eddie and Simon's mother had been killed in a gardening accident right outside their house, when the boys were only ten. The blades of the electric lawnmower with which she had been mowing the wet lawn had cut through the protective sheath of its electric cable. She hadn't realised the live wires were exposed and had been electrocuted after reaching down to examine the damage. Much of Eddie's short-attention span and belligerence had been put down to the trauma of seeing it happen from his bedroom window. As a result, his erratic behaviour was simply tolerated or often even ignored by his continuously stressed father.

Simon Sylvester explained all of this to his fellow band members, not to excuse this latest mental hiccup, but simply to stop the aggravation Simon was receiving from the others. Eddie wouldn't come to the church hall in advance of their first real gigs. He still wanted to be in the band, Simon confirmed, but he just wouldn't be able to leave the house.

This presented Max Mojo with a real difficulty. He'd just confirmed that a three-gig mini-tour of Kilmarnock pubs had been secured. Grant's money had paid an advance in order to book them, and it would also fund the promotional material for it, but more than seventy people paying £1.00 a ticket at each venue and the returns would wash the venture's face.

Max had no time to recruit another guitarist, and Eddie's skill was one of the most immediate things about their emerging sound. It was a real conundrum.

Ah'm a fuckin' genius, by the way. That mornin', wanderin' aboot ma room, listenin' tae Bunnymen an' Simple Minds an' that new Aztec Camera record, it came tae me. Eddie 'fuckin' Sylvester … The Motorcycle Boy!

Ah fuckin' hated the school for the maist part, but ah wis aw'right at English. A couple ae fuckin' books that ah had nicked ootae the library had always stuck wi' me. Ah read them loadsae times back then. Wan wis called The Outsiders *an' the ither yin wis* Rumble Fish. *Both written by the same geezer. Some fuckin' Yank dude called Hinton. Anyway, the Motorcycle Boy's this character in one ae them. Ah cannae remember which wan noo though. Every cunt thinks he fuckin' mental … so, right up dopey Eddie Sylvester's street, ken?*

Thing is, he isnae mental at aw. Jist nae cunt knows that he cannae hear right, 'cos ae a fight he wis in, once. The Motorcycle Boy's got a heidcase brother, an' his ma's buggered off tae. Ah'm thinkin' 'this is too fuckin' good tae be true!'

So, we call the daft cunt 'The Motorcycle Boy' an' we aw agree that we'll never tell any bastart whit his real name is … aw mysterious, like. But the best bit … the bit ye obviously ken aw aboot noo … we put a full-face motorbike helmet oan the cunt. Tinted visor, ken? Tae deal wi' his aggravated-phobia. Daft bastart's brain thinks he's still inside his hoose. Fuckin' genius!

See that prick oan Top Gear, *wi' Jeremy fuckin' Clarkson … the Spiv or somethin' … well, ah invented that idea. An' some daft indie band called themselves efter him tae. Ah shoulda fuckin' sued the baith ae they* them *anaw.*

Any road up, at least we had an 'image' ae sorts.

23

27th March 1983

'Everything alright, William?'

'Aye, hunky dory. Mr McAllister. You?'

'Well, ah'd been expectin' the pleasure of your company a bit more often these last few moths, but apart fae that … aye, couldnae be better, son.'

Don McAllister had shifted the regular rendezvous about in the last month. Wullie the Painter thought all of this was a bit over the top. He was hardly *Huggy Bear* after all.

'So, whit's the gen?' said Don. It was so dark on the golf course that Wullie could hardly see his face even though it was only a few feet from his.

'This no' a bit … ah dunno, too *Watergate*?' asked the Painter.

'Would ye rather we met in the driveway ae the Fatman's hoose?' said Don.

'Ah'm no' that sure it wid actually matter, mate,' said Wullie. 'Franny's doin' fuck all these days. His Ma's aff her heid, an' he cannae go oot an' leave her in case she burns the street doon. Dinnae get me wrang, ah'm no' complainin' but yer payin' me for nothin' at the minute. Fat Franny Duncan's a busted flush. He's old news, sir. Jesus, that's why ah had tae take the P an' D job affa Doc Martin in the first place.'

'Aye. Ah know aw that,' said Don calmly.

Wullie the Painter was surprised. 'Look, it isnae the bloody *Cosa Nostra* up in Onthank, ken? It's wee stuff, man. Pounds, shillings and pence. A wee bit ae skag on the vans, mibbe, but that's the limit. The rest ae it is jist sharkin', an' that shouldnae be botherin' you. Maybe five, ten years ago, when the McLartys were aboot, an'

there were chibbins every week, but no' noo. Every bastart's skint …
even the crooks,' said Wullie. 'Fuck, *especially* the crooks,' he added,
pulling his trousers pockets inside out.

'The McLartys are comin' back,' said Don, lettin' it sink in. 'Ah've
known for a while. Big deals goin' doon in Glasgow, son. An' noo
they're lookin' tae move the money oan ootae the city an' back doon
here.'

'Fuck sake,' said Wullie. 'Ye sure?'

'Fairly certain, aye. So you're role is gonnae change, wee man.'

'Ach, Christ,' said Wullie, head drooping.

'Never mind Christ, son. Ye've had an easy ride so far. Ah'm
boostin' ye two hundred a month. There wis always gonnae have to
be payback. In the words of the famous Glasgow prophet, 'Staun up
Wullie, your time has *came*!' Don McAllister laughed. 'Charlie'll fill
ye in … mibbe literally, eh boy?'

Don walked back towards the ninth tee and the small clearing
behind it where his Jaguar was parked. As he disappeared completely
into the darkness, Charlie Lawson emerged. Once again, he was
only about five feet from Wullie before the painter could even see
his outline.

'Right, Mr Lawson, whit's the script?' said Wullie.

'The boss wants ye tae get close tae Washer Wishart and tae they
Galston gypsies as well. The McLartys are lookin' for a route in, an'
word is they've got an angle wi' each crew already. Mr McAllister
wants tae know who it is. Any clues?'

'Fuck sake, Mr Lawson, he's jist told me aboot them comin' back
… ah'm no' that quick aff the mark,' said Wullie.

'Well, here's a few,' said Charlie Lawson. 'That dipstick Terry
Connolly in your mob, for one. He's gettin' bigger and bigger stashes
oan the vans. It's comin' fae somewhere.'

'Pick the cunt up then! Whit d'ye need me for?' pleaded Wullie
the Painter.

'Connolly's still small beer. An' he might be the road in tae the
bigger gig. Mr McAllister's plannin' a major clampdown in East

Ayrshire. He retires next year, an' a big score would virtually guarantee a CBE or mibbe bigger.'

'A *CBE*? Whit … aff the Queen, like?' Wullie the Painter was impressed.

'Aye. So things are gonnae get rough. If the McLartys move back, an' if it's off the back ae the drugs, well that isnae good for the Man. Got it?' said Charlie Lawson.

'Aye. Ah think so,' said Wullie. Charlie Lawson handed him an envelope, which the Painter put in his inside pocket.

'Jist keep yer eyes and ears open. Washer's man, Benny Donald … he's intae the McLartys tae. Spent too much up at the Clydeside Casino. Fucked, so he is. Washer disnae know. Get close tae him. Tell him yer lookin' for a new gig 'cos Fat Franny's oan the wane. An' also, there's Ged McClure fae the Quinn contingent. A bit ae *intel* on him tae. Anythin' unusual, bring it back tae us. Okey dokey?' Charlie Lawson smiled. His teeth were surprisingly white for a West of Scotland male, Wullie thought.

'Ah suppose so, eh?' said Wullie. Charlie Lawson patted his shoulder.

'You take care now, y'hear?' he said, patronisingly.

Wullie the Painter waited for five minutes, like he'd been told earlier, and then he too walked back to the same clearing. His car was parked a couple of miles further on, in the village, and it had just started raining. As he reached the clearing an owl hooted loudly over his left shoulder, causing him to dive down instinctively.

'Jesus fuckin' Christ! Aw the President's Men, right enough, eh?' he sighed, as his heartbeat slowly returned to normal.

24

2nd April 1983

Despite a bit of the post-Rocco Quinn tension remaining between Maggie and Grant, rehearsals had been going well and Max Mojo was happy. Well, in between the random periods when the paranoia took hold, at any rate. When these happened he simply went out and shot at the arses of cows in the field at the back of the manse with his .22 air rifle. It wasn't exactly a hobby but it was certainly therapeutic. It de-stressed him, allowing him to focus and get some equilibrium back. This morning was one of those times. As he waited for the band to turn up at the hall, he hung out of the rear casement window, firing intermittently into the crisp, spring air and scattering the Friesians. Iggy sang 'No Fun' on the Dansette, but on this occasion, Iggy was wrong.

The drummer and the singer appeared. Separately, and half an hour apart. Her in the Campervan; him on the Vespa. The Sylvester twins turned up in a taxi, *The Motorcycle Boy* now apparently warming to the full-leather, *Mad Max* vibe that his teenage manager had fashioned for him. The helmet stayed on and the visor stayed firmly shut until he was in the hall, on stage and surrounded by the others. Max Mojo was unsure whether the daft bastard actually had any form of open-space phobia, but he already saw the media angles of a mysterious guitarist who never spoke to the media and played, unidentified, with his back to the audience.

It was crucial that The Miraculous Vespas now started to realise the emerging potential that Max Mojo saw in them. The often insouciant band members were crying out for his relentless energy and drive, although the flipside of that was the aggression and tactlessness that propelled him. They also needed his seemingly vast musical knowledge. Whilst Max was unable to play traditional instruments himself, and his singing was, for the most part, flat and tuneless, Max understood melody. Like a discount-store Phil Spector, he shaped their opinion about style, attitude and lyrical content. Max Mojo had gradually educated his older colleagues. Washer had gotten him a VCR from *some fat guy who owed him a favour*. With it Max recorded as much music as he could from The Old Grey Whistle Test, pouring over the stances of such as Tom Verlaine from Television, or using the unique 'pause' facility to write down – and then analyse – Vic Godard and Ian McCulloch lyrics. Over the last few weeks, he'd fashioned the four into a group; not simply four disparate individuals, all of whom were now competent enough in their own right. Max Mojo had learned that, in the recent punk context, managers were as important as lead singers. Dale Wishart might have been deluded in terms of his perceived musical talent, but Max Mojo had no time for such fantasies. Management was his forte. It required control and it would need a sharp rise in profile. If Scotland was the arse-end of the music business world, Ayrshire was halfway up its colon; out of sight and – unless someone had cause to stick an investigative finger up there – completely out of mind.

Max acknowledged that a lot of the great music he valued had spluttered out of a band's cack-handed attempts to copy the best parts of their dads' record collections. Such alchemy often resulted from the most spontaneous and unplanned process; from the lowest of expectations. He knew his band needed to establish precedents; accepted touchstones that could be referenced in interviews. Grounding foundations that would give the band a shared musical anchor. Such things were important. He'd rehearsed being asked 'Who are your influences?' by a succession of star-struck *Sounds* journalists. In these temporal conversations, he struggled to be consistent or concise. His choices changed daily. This wasn't good, and God only knew what the others would say if asked unrehearsed. Focus was required.

45s and LPs charting the development of popular music lay

scattered around Max's portable record player, its lid open as if it had just exploded. Elvis Presley, gazing sideways from the cover of his first LP towards The Clash's *London Calling*, like a proud father regarding how similarly handsome his son had become. *Never Mind The Bollocks* and *Parallel Lines*, *All Mod Cons* and *Closer*. The Beatles 'Penny Lane/Strawberry Fields Forever' – the sonic equivalent of the Sistine Chapel ceiling – lay next to 'Ghost Town' by The Specials. Seminal singles by Marc Bolan, Mott the Hoople and Elvis Costello & the Attractions ... all were the subject of detailed analysis as if Max was studying them for an upcoming PhD examination. They were all small, vital pieces in the jigsaw puzzle he was trying to assemble; the musical lineage of The Miraculous Vespas.

Max had brought the small, black record player down to their rehearsal space. He'd also carried boxes of the records that he'd been acquiring of late with funds from the band's bank account. There were now two signatories to the account – Grant and Max – but each could draw money from it independently, provided they filled in the ledger book accurately. For all Max's obvious faults, he was initially diligent in recording the debit expenditure. Unfortunately for The Miraculous Vespas, there was little to nothing in the credit columns. Max Mojo reckoned that all that was about to change, though. Orange Juice had finally hit the UK Top Ten with 'Rip It Up', and Max was convinced that this alone would bring the majors flying up to Scotland, wallets bulging and blank cheques already endorsed. He had sorted out three showcase gigs in local Kilmarnock pubs in the last week of April. Letters written to various radio-station DJs, such as 'Tiger' Tim Stevens and Billy Sloan up in Glasgow, and Mac Barber from Ayr-based West Sound, had received responses. They were tentative acceptances, admittedly, but still, enough to be feeling upbeat about. Max had also written numerous letters to former Postcard major-domo, Alan Horne, asking for advice. His one reply, in bold, massive capitals ... on an *actual* postcard ... of 'AWAY AND FUCK YERSELF, SON!' had led to an agricultural shooting spree to rival The Glorious Twelfth. Similar correspondence to Paul Morley at the *New Musical Express* and Dave McCullough at *Sounds* had so far gone unnoticed. Max figured the route to the London-based music industry could only come through the music press, so patient perseverance would have to become a learned characteristic.

Max had asked the foursome to bring in their favourite records, like a lazy music teacher trying to pass a bored period with delinquent pupils. If they didn't have their own, they were encouraged to pick from Max's burgeoning collection. His objective was to try and understand them better, musically; to work out their passions and what fired their collective imaginations. Simon Sylvester had initially told him to fuck off after he realised that part of this would also involve explaining to the others why the choice of record was so personally special. 'Ah'm in this band tae play ... an' shag women,' he'd argued, 'No' tae dae *your* fuckin' homework, mate.' However, he'd relented, and all four now sat on the stage around Max Mojo's piles of records.

'Ladies first, eh?' said Max, in a rare expression of chivalry. 'BB, you're up.' Maggie sighed. She passed around the one record she had brought with her. It was a twelve-inch single. Max examined it like it was the Holy Grail.

'Hey, nae fuckin' LPs, Maggie. *That's* cheatin'. Make her dae lines, Max!' said Simon. Maggie smiled.

'Shut up, an' let her play it, you,' said Grant. 'On ye go, Mags.' He smiled at her. Maybe whatever ice had recently formed between them was now thawing. Just in time, thought Max.

'It's jist a new yin. Ma mam bought it for me. It's Gil-Scott Heron ... "B-Movie". Any ae ye'se heard it?'

'Aye. *Me*,' lied Max. He hadn't, but didn't want to admit it. Maggie put it on the turntable. Even for five individuals with such eclectic tastes, 'B-Movie' was a bizarre choice of record to kick off this bonding session.

'Is there nae fuckin' singin' in it?' said Simon.

'Naw. It's a socio-political poem, set tae music,' replied Maggie. 'A protest against Ronald *Ray-gun*.'

'So whit dae ye like aboot it, mainly?' asked Max.

'It *means* somethin'. It's no' just about love or any ae that short-term shit,' she said. 'Plus, the groove's kinda hypnotic.'

'Aye … ah get that,' said Max nodding. 'Ah prefer "The Bottle" though.'

'Twelve minutes ae that an' ye'd be *turnin'* tae the fuckin' bottle,' said Simon.

'Hey Si-mone?' Maggie extended her middle finger. 'Mandate *my* ass!'

'Anytime, hen … anytime,' he said.

'Whit you got, Eddie?' said Grant sharply.

'Ah'll go last,' said Eddie, through the visor. 'And it's *Motorcycle Boy*.'

'Sorry, man. Right, ah'll go next,' said Grant. Grant Delgado played 'Roadrunner' by Jonathan Richman & The Modern Lovers to universal approval. 'It's intelligent, timeless, cool and disnae give a fuck!' he said.

'Just like you, ye mean?' said Maggie.

'Aye. Just like me,' he replied, laughing. The record was Max's. Grant reflected on how much influence Max had had on his musical direction. They'd known each other for less than a year but in that time, Grant had moved from fledgling New Romantic to desperately hip beatnik. It was all really down to the younger man's sometimes aggravating promptings.

'Ah mind the first time ah heard this,' said Simon, as The Jam's 'Start' played. 'Radio Luxembourg, it wis. Ah wis in the bath, havin' a Sherman Tank, when this yin came on. Damn near pit me aff ma fuckin' stroke. Listen tae the bass.' It was the most familiar of the three so far played. Again, they all loved it.

'It's a bass line nicked fae The Beatles,' Max pointed out.

'Is it fuck!' said Simon.

'Aye. "Taxman" affa *Revolver*,' said Grant. Max dug out the LP and played its opening track.

'Fuck sake! Ach who cares, eh? Still great, though.'

Max Mojo played his track next. It was 'I'll Never Fall in Love Again', by Bobbie Gentry.

'Listen tae the weird lyrics, Grant. *That's* a fuckin' heartbreak song, pal.' said Max, 'an' that bizarre song construction. It's really fuckin' minimalistic.'

'Ah don't even ken whit that means, mate,' Simon admitted.

'There's fuck all wasted. Fuckin' Bacharach, man ... makes every bastart second count,' said Grant. Once again, it received the thumbs up from the Crosshouse Juke Box Jury.

'Motorcycle Boy?' said Grant Delgado. Simon sniggered as his brother finally took off the helmet and reached into a bag he had brought with him. The Motorcycle Boy pulled out a battered seven-inch single. Its cover was torn and had been sellotaped many times.

'This is the only thing ah can remember aboot ma mam. Her singin' away tae this in the kitchen ... thinkin' naebody wis listenin'. But ah wis. Sittin' at the top ae the stairs. She had a great voice, didn't she, Si? Ma Da loved *Country & Western*. Johnny Cash and Merle Haggard, mainly. An' they baith loved aw the crooners. Sinatra, Como, Dean Martin, ken? Remember that big, broon Marconi, Simon? Ah fuckin' remember aw they LP covers they had. Aul' Blue Eyes, wi' his hair fallin' oot, oan the sleeve ae 'My Way'. That big fuckin' red lipstick kiss oan the Connie Francis record. The Everly's shiny white teeth and matchin' Arthur Montford jaickets. They fuckin' hated each other more then me an' you, Si!' He put the seven-inch single on the record player. 'Anyway, efter she died, ma Da threw them aw oot. Apart fae this yin. Ah kept it separate.'

Glen Campbell's 'Galveston' came on.

'If only we could dae somethin' as fuckin' brilliant as this, eh?' said the Motorcycle Boy, as his brother stood up and walked to the rear of the hall. He touched his brother's shoulder gently as he went.

'Too right, boy,' said Max. 'That's the basic challenge right there. Making music that's as fuckin' vital an' brilliant as aw ae they five we've jist listened tae. If we can dae that, we'll *aw* fuckin' live forever.'

⚡

2nd April 1983

Maggie gave them a lift out to Crosshands Farm. She had fallen out with her mum again, and was happy to have somewhere else to be.

'Ah'll wait for ye here,' she said, looking at the warzone that was the rubble-strewn driveway leading up to Hairy Doug's shed.

'Aye, probably better,' said Max. 'Stick oan yer Black & White Minstrels tape an' we'll be back before it's by.'

'Fuckin' pack that shite in, you! Ah'm no' gonnae tell ye again,' warned Grant.

Max had been to the farm many times before. The original Vespas hired most of their speakers from Hairy Doug, but this trip was for a different purpose. The two teenagers tramped stealthily as if moving through the dangerous green fields of First World War-era France.

'Ah'll chap, an' you can speak, right?' said Max.

'No chance!' said Grant. 'This is aw you, pal.'

As they were about to deliberate this further, the corrugated metal door opened and the massively framed biker squeezed himself through it.

'Alright, son?' said Hairy Doug as they approached gingerly for fear of stepping on something unidentified.

'How's it goin', big man?' said Max. 'Tried tae phone earlier. Hoped we'd catch ye in.'

'Come on in, boys. I'm Doug, by the way,' he said to Grant, extending a sweaty, oil-stained paw the size of a baseball catcher's mitt. Grant shook it, then wished he hadn't.

'What can I do fur ya, son?' Hairy Doug said.

'Can ah offer ye'se a cuppy tea? A wee Jaffy Cake mibbee?' Max and Grant looked around. It wasn't immediately clear where the high-pitched voice was coming from. Hairy Doug's place only had two rooms, and it didn't immediately appear to be coming from either of them.

'...or mibbe a wee Top Deck Shandy?' The owner of the voice popped up like a jack-in-the-box from behind an old wooden barrel that doubled as a table. It was surrounded by clutter. Max got a fright and squealed.

'Sorry, sonny. Didnae mean to fricht ye. Was just doon feedin' the cats.'

'Boys, this is Fanny,' said Hairy Doug. Grant spluttered. Max elbowed him.

'Naw, eh ... Fanny, I'm fine,' said Max.

'So, boy,' said the hairy roadie. 'Mixing desk, was it? Sixty quid all right?'

'Fuck sake, Hairy ... April Fools' Day wis yesterday, big man!'

'Come on through, an' Hairy's not my first name, by the by,' Grant laughed at Max's embarrassment. 'You hiring then?'

'Eh, aye, but ah've got a wee proposition tae!' said Max.

'Oh yeah? I'm intrigued,' said Hairy Doug. 'Fanny'll see to *you*, son,' he said to Grant, who again struggled to hold the laughter in.

Fifteen minutes later and they were back in the Campervan heading for Crosshouse.

'Fanny?' laughed Grant. 'Hairy Doug and Hairy Fa...'

'Well, ah dinnae think she'll be changin' *her* name tae that if they get married! Fuck sake, Grant ... grow up!' said Max. But Grant was in hysterics.

'...an' she wis actually hairier than him, Billy Connolly and The Grateful Dead put th'gither! Did ye see that moustache?' Maggie was laughing so hard she had to pull the van over to the side of the road.

'Jesus Christ! Is naebody takin' this seriously? If anybody's interested, the big yin said he'd dae it. Forty quid, an' he'd bring the sound an' light desk tae. That's a fuckin' result, in ma opinion, naw?' Max was getting aggravated.

'Aye ... yer right, Max. A result, deffo,' said Grant.

'You're the Master,' said Maggie.

'You're Yoda,' said Grant.

'The Capo di Tutti Capi,' said Maggie. Max's face was growing redder.

'Fuckin' shut it, the pair ae ye'se! Yer actin' like a pair ae ... *fannies!*'

Grant and Maggie lost it again.

25

Wullie the Painter's first day on the vans was unremarkable. Since he'd asked Fat Franny for an introductory accommodation on one of Terry Connolly's more lucrative routes, he'd anticipated countless wired, half-cut jakeys 'waitin' for their 'ice-cream' man. All he got was a shifty-looking dude asking how much for number 32 for a week, and when Wullie the Painter asked him to elaborate, the guy clammed up and said it was the *chip* van he'd wanted. Wullie thought this a little bizarre since the unmistakably tuneless sound this one made – allied to the massive 'Ice Cream' writing all around it – seemed a sure-fire giveaway. Onthank was full of strange characters though. By the end of the shift, Wullie the Painter was starting to wonder if it was all just a ruse; some sleight of hand to deflect Don McAllister's Keystone Cops away from where the *real* action took place. It was a warm day, mind you. The Embassy Regal and '99 count was substantial. He'd also gone through four boxes of flakes and had completely sold out of Tudor tomato-flavour crisps. The thru'penny bags were the top seller though. A wee scoop of Kola Kubes and white chocolate mice and other bizarre gummy crap that stuck to your false teeth were the uncontested Onthank winner. Ironically, there was even jelly fruit-flavour 'false teeth' sweets sold to kids who'd soon need the real thing. Maybe sugary confectionary was the real addiction after all? A tiny wee boy had almost run in front of the van trying to get it to stop. Wullie leaned out and shouted at him.

'Ya stupid wee shite, ah nearly ran intae ye there!'

'Mister, ma mam says ye only sell cigarettes efter tea time,' the boy said. 'Izzat true, mister?'

Wullie laughed. 'Naw it isnae. Yer ma's talkin' pish,' he said. 'Here, ah'll gie ye a '99 for free!'

'Ma mam says it's too close tae tea time for a '99,' the boy said sadly.

'Just take it ... she'll no' ken.' The wee boy's eyes lit up as Wullie the Painter handed the ice-cream cone over the counter. 'Have ye got a phone in the hoose?' he asked the boy.

'Aye, mister.'

Wullie handed the boy a piece of paper with numbers on it. 'If she talks pish again, phone this number an' ask for Esther Rantzen!'

Wullie the Painter lamented Bob Dale's passing more and more with every day. Why could the stupid bastard not just have accepted his level in the Fat Franny empire? Wullie had enjoyed a cosy, stress-free existence these last three years since signing up. He'd paid his dues, got his *own* Wullie out, and was just starting to reap the rewards. There was no going back now, though. Fat Franny's grip had slipped immeasurably in just nine months. Added to this, Des Brick had also gone 'off the boil'. Fat Franny could still command a bit of respect simply because of past reputation. There remained a number of the young, up-and-comers straight out of school expulsion who wanted into the firm and were willing to do the Fatman's bidding. But there were new, potentially more organised factions emerging in Onthank, ones that quickly understood that Bob Dale was the foundation on which Fat Franny Duncan's tower was constructed. Although still standing, the removal of this big sturdy block left everything else above it in a precariously unstable position. All it would take would be a big gust of wind blowing down from the big city.

Wullie had reached out to Benny Donald in Crosshouse through an old football team mate. The approach was actually an honest one: *The Fatman's fucked an' ahm lookin' for a transfer*. Benny's initial response – filtered through the same contact – was that everybody was feeling the pinch, but if Wullie the Painter could bring an income stream with him, Washer Wishart would consider it. It wasn't a massive earner, but Wullie the Painter had cultivated a private sideline with a Kilmarnock removals driver. The driver brought back substantial amounts of beer and cigarettes from Europe, smuggled in through compartments in the vans. They were bought from 'sources' he'd established in Calais and Zeebrugge, and sold on in Ayrshire at a tidy profit. Wullie the Painter provided the purchasing funds and organised the sell-on. The driver took the risks at customs. The split was 50/50. It was decent business, but with Washer's connections, the initiative could perhaps be expanded. Regardless, it was enough to get Wullie an audience, and that was his primary motivation right now.

The Quinns would be much harder to infiltrate. They were relentlessly suspicious of outsiders and since Wullie wasn't planning to get married to one of Magdelena's mental daughters, another route in would have to be considered. Ged McClure was the only non-family connection Wullie the Painter knew, but Ged was a headcase. The scams he ran were ridiculously dangerous and increasingly involved substantial personal risks, being associated with bigger and more ruthless organisations outside of Ayrshire. It was entirely likely that Ged McClure was one of the conduits to the McLartys and their apparent desire for Ayrshire resettlement; perhaps even the *only* one. Wullie had tried to contact Ged but had been informed ominously that he was 'out of town on important business' and that the timing of his return was 'uncertain'. Wullie was certain his request would've gone on record. One way or another, Ged McClure would find out Wullie the Painter was looking for him.

26

21st May 1983

Max Mojo reflected on a very successful week. The Miraculous Vespas had played a great, incident-free gig at The Hunting Lodge on the 16th. It was their first real gig, Max having already exorcised The Heid fiasco from his memory. The band were spending more time together and a real gang feel had been the result. Although originally grating, Maggie and Grant's propensity to finish each other's sentences was a clear indication to Max of just how in sync they were. Max had taken them all up to Paddy's Market in Glasgow and they had come back with a range of individual stage clothes. Having initially asserted his control of their aesthetic, Max had relented a bit. Maggie had her own style and much of it appeared to involve showing bare skin. Grant stayed true to the monochrome of his new hero, Lou Reed. The Sylvester Brothers experimented. Max had given them photos of Orange Juice. Simon appeared at The Hunting Lodge looking like all four of the Glasgow band members at once. He had bought boxing boots, calvary trousers held up by braces, and a sailor's shirt. He'd also stolen a Davy Crockett hat but Max prevented him wearing that; it was too Edwyn Collins.

Max had Xerox'd blue fanzine-style posters with a photo of the band standing around Grant Delgado, who was seated on the Vespa. Even Maggie had applauded the personal effort Max had expended in taping hundreds of them to every lamppost and derelict-building hoarding in the town. However, he blew off this credit with a thoughtless observation that the copying process had apparently made the boys faces darker but Maggie's whiter. *A fuckin' anti-apartheid photocopier*, he'd called it, with no discernible trace of humour.

Unlike the brief slots when they had supported the hypnotist,

Grant Delgado was a bag of nerves for their first gig. He vomited so loudly in the toilet behind the small stage, that Max was certain those out front had heard him. Max overheard Grant telling Maggie he was scared, but mainly because he now felt that they had something. He'd assumed the previous performance at the Metropolis would've been the band's one and only gig. Now, with three real ones lined up, it automatically seemed much more serious and important. With some soothing words from the drummer – which Max couldn't decipher – the singer regained his composure.

With Hairy Doug newly installed as sound-and-light technician on a 5 percent future profit share, the band – and Grant especially – had looked and sounded fantastic at The Hunting Lodge. Their set now consisted of an equal number of Grant Delgado original compositions and cover versions re-interpreted to fit their emerging sound. Grant had started writing and playing with a Gretsch 'Country Gentleman' guitar, having seen a tape of the Monkees' Mike Nesmith playing one. The Miraculous Vespas' music now took on both a contemporary *and* a retro vibe. With the guitar's bluesy twang to the fore, 'The First Picture' was a stand-out song. The Miraculous Vespas opened with it, and encored with it, such was its immediacy and strength. None of Max's celebrity pen-pals turned up, but the pub was full.

The second Kilmarnock gig, two days later at The Charleston in New Farm Loch, was also a success, despite the band appearing more than an hour late due to Jimmy Stevenson's van getting stuck in the flash flooding that obscured the ford at the Dean Park. Max had insisted Jimmy try and cross the flowing water even though it was almost a foot deep. Max had to wade out through it to get to a nearby house and beg to use the telephone. An irate Washer Wishart arranged for a tractor to get there and pull them out before the police arrived, so the gig could proceed. Mac Barber did show for this one and – despite the memory of a previous threat by Washer's people when the band was in its previous incarnation – admitted to Grant that he was impressed. He asked if 'The First Picture' had been recorded yet, and to get in touch again when it had been.

And now, here they were, at the end of their mini-showcase tour of local pubs. The Miraculous Vespas were half an hour into their set at Pebbles in Troon. To Max's delight – and surprise – many of those who had come to the previous two nights had made the ten-mile trip west across to Troon. Although perhaps smaller than the other two venues, there was a much better atmosphere, and as a consequence everyone connected to the band seemed to be in a good mood.

Earlier that day in Glasgow, Max Mojo had finally been granted an audience with Billy Sloan. The Radio Clyde DJ couldn't get to the gig, but provided Max bought the lunch, he'd spare him half an hour or so in order to impart some advice. Billy had been intrigued by Max's promo description of The Miraculous Vespas:

'Fronted by bona-fide rock God, Grant Delgado, The Miraculous Vespas from Ayrshire are the past, present and future of intelligent rock n' roll. Mysterious guitar hero The Motorcycle Boy plays it left-hand ... Butter Biscuit, effortlessly cool and tribal, battering the drums ... and don't leave your scepticism lying around; bass-hound Simon Sylvester will just fucking nick it..!'

Max had started experimenting with a fanzine to help promote the band. He'd impressed his mother by the amount of reading and research he was doing. He had even turned his furniture into components of the band's office. His clothes were strewn around the room, while his wardrobe was now full of organised posters, letters, address books and music papers. His drawer unit now housed his overflowing record and cassette-tape collection. Molly and Washer had to admit a grudging respect for his determination to succeed and the untutored organisation with which he was now pursuing that goal. He was so different to the laid-back, carefree, optimistic kid who had gone into hospital after the Henderson Church beating. He was still only nineteen but now he acted – and looked – so much older.

Billy Sloan had been surprised when Max extended an upward arm and introduced himself at the door of the Stakis-owned restaurant, The Berni Inn, on Hope Street, where Billy had suggested they meet. Based on their limited correspondence, the Glaswegian DJ had expected someone much older and more connected to the burgeoning Glasgow scene. There were a fair few mavericks in that scene already, but even Billy Sloan was stunned when Max strolled in without shoes on his feet. Billy didn't anticipate this meeting would last long.

'Some cunt just mugged me for ma fuckin' brogues, man,' a stunned Max explained. 'Nipped up the lane for a quick pish tae get rid ae the nerves an' that ... an' a wee prick wi' a blade jumps oot fae behind a bin. *Whit size are ye,* he says. Ah thought he wis askin' aboot ma knob!' The DJ was warming to Max. '*Yer shoes*, he says. Ah says, *ah'm a 6*,' Max continued. 'The cunt pulls oot a list ae names wi' numbers next tae it! Ma fuckin' brogues have just been nicked tae order!'

Billy Sloan was roaring at this. 'Glesga, eh?' said the DJ.

'Aye,' sighed Max. 'Couldnae beat it wi' a big stick.' Max took his seat at the table, socks sodding wet. He hadn't intended it this way, but the ice had been broken.

As they waited to be served, Max Mojo surprised Billy Sloan. This couth, young man had an extensive knowledge of music lineage that was highly impressive. Max admitted he hadn't been to many gigs but the ones that stuck – U2 at Tiffany's, Blondie at the Apollo, The Clash at the Magnum – had all left him with a vision of how to compose a stage presence. As he explained to the influential DJ over a rare steak, 'We jist need the fuckin' break, man ... so go oan, fuckin' *gie* us it!'

When the rest of the band asked, Max Mojo was deliberately non-committal about how the afternoon meeting in one of Glasgow's most popular restaurants had gone. Max had thought *tartare* was a kind of sauce, just like HP. So he didn't dare tell Grant that the advice given by Billy Sloan as they chewed through 'a plate ae fuckin' cow meat so raw that it prob'ly got its arse wiped an' stuck oan a bastart plate' had just cost the band nearly fifty quid. Especially when that advice had already been freely given by numerous others: 'Get yersel a demo made. Decent sound studio. Bring it back tae me then!'

Nevertheless, Max reflected that this week-long campaign of profile-building had been highly successful. The next move would definitely be getting 'The First Picture' recorded. There was a small place down near Glencairn Square accurately called Shabby Road Studios. Another emerging Ayrshire band, The Trashcan Sinatras, occasionally used it. He'd contact them in the morning and try to forge a possible touring and recording alliance. Meanwhile he leaned back on the bar, supping his fourth pint of the evening and watched The Miraculous Vespas' glacial interpretation of 'Pleasant Valley Sunday'. Life was good.

And then Max Mojo felt suddenly unwell. He instinctively looked at his glass. *A bad pint,* he thought. But no ... thunderous rumbling and bubbling in his stomach hinted at something more substantial. And immediate. *That fuckin' scabby roadkill* that he'd earlier eaten off what looked like a piece of broken toilet cistern, most probably. It tasted awful at the time; it was surely going to taste even worse coming back up. Max shoved his way through the heaving throng to head for the toilet between the bar and where the band were playing. The room was packed and it appeared that its walls were actually sweating. Max felt like he was hallucinating, but not in a good way. He remembered the scene in *Midnight Cowboy* when Jon Voight took the drugs. Max put his hands up over his mouth, unsure of whether he'd make it to the bowl in time. He burst into the tiny gents. Thankfully, no one was at either of the two urinals, and the single cubicle door was slightly open. He instinctively opted for the cubicle. He pushed it open and vomited. But someone was already sitting on the seat, trousers at their ankles and drunken head down between knees as if braced for an emergency airplane landing. Reactions dulled, it was a few vital seconds before the seated man realised he had been spewed over. Before he'd raised his head sufficiently to see who his assailant was, Max Mojo had delivered a right hook to his jaw, knocking him backwards off the pan.

Max Mojo watched the resultant carnage from behind The Motorcycle Boy's guitar amp. The man in the toilet had eventually burst forth, covered in vomit and swinging indiscriminate punches in every direction. His arms were rotating like a swingball with two ropes. He connected with a barman, a woman and – most unfortunately for him – a bouncer. In such a confined space, a chain reaction was set off and Pebbles quickly turned into a Wild West-style brawl. Max Mojo pulled his band members behind the bar. Only The Motorcycle Boy remained on stage, still strumming furiously, his back to the melee and in full-face helmet. A thrown glass smashed against it, which was the sign for him to join the others in retreat. Max led the band out of a rear fire-exit door and the five of them ran across Templehill carrying guitars and drumsticks like the Beatles in *Help!* Max looked back from a safe distance and watched the fighting spill out on to the street. Sirens sounded in the distance.

'Fuck me,' said Grant breathlessly. 'Whit sparked that aff?'

'Dunno,' said Max, sheepishly. 'Some cunts jist cannae handle their drink, man.'

'What aboot Hairy Doug?' said Maggie.

'Ach, fuck it. He's a big geezer. He'll be aw'right,' said Max.

'Whit we gonnae dae, noo? Jimmy's no' due here for another hour and a half yet. Plus, the amps and the drums an' shit are aw still in there … well, whit's left ae them.' They turned and looked at Simon Sylvester. He was also carrying a large bottle of Johnnie Walker.

'Fuck sake, you,' said Max. 'No' gonnae let a riot get in the way ae the thievin', eh?'

'Opportunity knocks, Mr Mojo,' Simon replied, unscrewing the top of the bottle.

The Miraculous Vespas sat on the grassy mound watching the police herding people into the assembled vans, and the catalytic *shiter* being escorted into an ambulance. Despite the chaos of this last gig, they toasted its apparent success with whisky. *Controversy sells*, Max had reminded them and, by Ayrshire standards at least, they were now controversial. With a bit of prompting from Max, the local press would surely report their gigs as essential, unpredictable, and a wee bit dangerous. After all, it hadn't done the Sex Pistols any harm, had it?

The bigger issue facing Max was how Hairy Doug had fared. They had only rented his mixing desk but since he was now a *de facto* shareholder in the band, a difficult conversation might have to be had highlighting that shares can go down as well as up. Pebbles' owners would also be looking for Max Mojo in the days to come and since Doc Martin had an interest there, he was praying that the pub had suffered only limited damage. If not, the *Grunt Delgado* slush fund would be taking as much of a kicking as the recently-vomited-upon drunk guy who just went to the toilet to take an innocent shite.

Maybe, for Max Mojo, avoidance was better than cure over the next week or so.

27

Max Mojo was agitated; more so than normal, although normality in such a context was measured by a very wide gauge.

'Sit doon Max, for Christ's sake,' said Grant Delgado. His band's manager was moving around the church hall as if he was a remote-control car being played with by a hyperactive child on Christmas Day.

'Ah'm fuckin' beelin', so ah am!'

'How?' asked Grant.

'That bastart, Mac Barber,' said Max. 'Some daft wee lassie at the paper jist phoned an' said he couldnae make it this mornin'.' Max was raging. It had been Mac Barber who had contacted Max after word of the Troon riot had reached his desk at the *Ayrshire Post*, where he contributed a weekly music column. Max had initially played up the chaos as the inevitable outcome of massive over-demand to see The Miraculous Vespas. Unsurprisingly, he had made no reference to his own part in the proceedings.

'Ah gets aw ready an' everythin', an' then he fuckin' calls off … an' sends some other daft wee lassie called Farrah!'

'Might be Farrah Fawcett-Majors,' said Simon Sylvester.

'Aye. Might be,' said Max sarcastically. 'She'll be takin' a break between episodes ae *Charlie's Angels* tae fuckin' moonlight by writin' aboot make-up an' tampons for the *Post*!'

Maggie looked over sharply at Max. 'You're a prick, ye ken that?' she said.

Max ignored her.

'Whit ye moanin' aboot? It's still an interview, intit?' said Grant, but Max had left the room and the questions hung in the air, unanswered.

§

Simon Sylvester was experimenting with another new look. He had found a pair of glasses on that morning's bus out to Crosshouse. But their lenses were strong and he was having trouble focusing on his hand, which he had held up two feet from his face. He stared at it like an amputee regarding a new prosthetic.

'Whit dae ye think?' he asked. Grant walked towards him. Through the frames, the singer looked like Marty Feldman in the final stages of a NASA G-Force test.

'You look like Mr Magoo,' Grant said.

Over his shoulder, Simon could only vaguely discern the shape coming back through the vestibule door. He took off the glasses. His natural focus readjusted and as it did, he burst out laughing.

'Holy fuck, Max! Is it Halloween aw'ready?'

The rest of the band turned round. Grant and Maggie also laughed. The Motorcycle Boy raised an impressed eyebrow.

'Sup wi' it?' said Max, aggressively. He looked down at his clothing. It looked fine from his perspective. More than fine. He was wearing the baggy denim dungarees that he'd picked up at Oxfam last week. He initially thought they would make him look more like Geoffrey from Rainbow than Kevin from Dexy's, but, to Max, that fear was now without foundation. They looked fucking great, in his opinion. Below their turned-up legs, he wore his DM boots, but a black one on the left foot, and a tan one on the right. He wore an orange Led Zeppelin t-shirt under the dungarees, and one of Washer's tweed Hacking jackets with the corded elbow patches over it. Hair that Max had bleached only last week was now teased high in a yellow-hued quiff that resembled Grant's in shape if not colour. It was, however, the wearing of a monocle and the reintroduction of the cane that was the standout observation from Grant Delgado's point of view.

'Is it an interview yer gaun tae, or an audition for *The Archers*?'

⚡

'Haw, wee man … *chase* me!' The fat driver of the number 11 bus, which ran from Ardrossan to Kilmarnock through Crosshouse, thought he was a comedian. He shouted through the open door and edged the bus slowly away every time Max stepped towards the footplate. The bus was at least fifty yards beyond the stop by the time Max was actually permitted onto it. The lower-deck passengers were laughing.

'Gets him *every* day, the wee balloon. It cracks me up, so it does.' Max glared at the passenger in the seat reserved for the disabled. *Auld cunt's no' fuckin' disabled at aw.* The words formed but Max kept them in his head. It had just started raining. An enforced walk across the no man's land between here and the town in these clothes wasn't going to be on the cards today.

'C'mon then … *chase* me!' taunted the fat Larry Grayson driver, 'aw hing oan … ye aw'ready did!'

'Ha. Funny. Duncan Norvelle, right?' Max had to endure this repetitive cycle of cringing banter almost every day. It was as if Western SMT only employed one fucking driver. There were six of these buses an hour, yet Max had only ever been on 'Duncan's'.

'Ah telt aw the men tae sit at the rear … but tae keep their back's tae the wa', ken?' said the fat driver.

'Aye. Ah get it. Ye think ah'm a poof. Big fuckin' laugh.' This was as aggressive as Max was now permitted to get. Months earlier, he had been banned from the number 11 for calling the same driver *'a useless fat baldy cunt'*. But it was a forty-minute walk into the town centre from Crosshouse with no shelter from the Scottish microclimate, so in the same week, he swallowed his pride – and copious medicinal compounds – and publicly apologised. The homosexual jibes amid an excruciating daily Bernard Manning routine were his penance.

The bus pulled around the sharp corner at the Arches and Max got off to the sound of wolf-whistles and jeers. He resolved to buy Western SMT with the band management royalties and – as Maggie Thatcher had commanded – he'd privatise it and fire that fat prick as his first private-ownership act. He'd make the buses run once a week instead of every half an hour. Then we'd see who thought the bus journey to Kilmarnock to spend their giro money was the highlight of their day. *Fucking intolerant, narrow-minded wankers.*

Vengeful thoughts occupied a restless mind as he climbed the shallow incline up to The Black Hoose. When Mac Darbei had changed the interviewer, Max Mojo retaliated by changing the location. *Two can fuckin' play at that game! This 'Farrah' lassie had better be sharp.* The Black Hoose was no place for shrinking violets. It was the undisputed OK Corral of Kilmarnock boozers; a *spit an' shite-hole* throwback to the halcyon days of industrial drinking dens. A place where the working man of Kilmarnock would go straight from work, if he had any that is – via the bookies, naturally – to avoid the nightly hassle and interrogation from his 'ball and chain'. On that basis alone, The Black Hoose was a happy place for hard men to relax and in the company of other hard men. It was a place for men's men. So if a woman entered, the balance shifted. A female presence reminded the regulars what they had at home, or in the unlikely event that she was pretty, exactly what they *didn't* have at home. Max was taking a risk himself. He was the sartorial antithesis of a Black Hoose man, especially today. But his deepening sense of annoyance was overriding any fears for his own safety. A point had to be made. And it would be made here, amid the lingering, fuggy stench of stale smoke, spilt beer and sawdusted vomit.

Max bought a pint of McEwan's Lager. He wasn't asked for proof of age. Of all the things the Black Hoose bar staff cared about, underage drinking wasn't one of them. He wasn't a big drinker – even before the hospital stay – and he simply selected the keg that caught his eye first. It had a picture of a bearded cavalier on it, a bit like Adam Ant might look when he started drawing a pension, Max thought. After the cursory stares and 'Who the fuck are *you* lookin'' at?' salutations had died down a bit, he sat in the corner furthest from the door. The 'Farrah' lassie would have to walk right past the hardened mid-morning boozers. *Serve her right.*

'Aw, for fuck's sake, man!' Max had spotted 'Farrah' hovering by the main, swing doors. So had everyone else. Their interrogative gaze had shifted from him to her. She was young; even by Max's standards. She was dressed unusually; again even by his standards. And she was foreign. She looked around, the disgust registering as the odours assaulted her. She saw Max, waved hopefully and, when he lifted his head in acknowledgement, moved gingerly towards him.

'Hi, I'm Farah. Farah *Nawaz* … from the *Ayrshire Post*.'

Max looked around the bar. Everyone was staring at them. The developing scene was a massive shift from what passed for daily normality in The Black Hoose. Max hadn't considered this scenario. He was already eyeing up the available options. He could ignore her; pretend that he wasn't who she was looking for. But that might rule out a future conciliatory interview with Mac Barber. He could tough it out and fall back on the *Hav' you cunts heard ae Washer Wishart?* threat. But he was secretly proud of never having resorted to lighting that particular 'Bat signal' high up in the Ayrshire sky.

'You must be Max?' said Farah, more as a question than a statement.

Max hesitated. *Fuck it*, he thought. *Batman it is, then*.

'Aye,' he said quietly.

'Can I sit down?' asked Farah politely.

'S'a free country, hen,' he replied.

Farah dusted what looked like abnormally large flakes of dandruff off the seat. She took off her long, colourful knitted scarf and put it down before sitting on it. She had a silky, multi-coloured, kaftan-type shirt on and tight-legged, blue, pin-striped jeans underneath. Her black hair was long and as she rummaged in her bag, it fell forward, briefly covering her face.

When she lifted her head the action was accompanied by a hand throwing her hair backwards like she was in a shampoo commercial. She was very pretty, Max noticed. But he was still in *unbending obstreperous arsehole* mode, and she'd soon appreciate how deep that particular emotional well could be.

'Well this is a little … *unusual*,' said Farah nervously.

'So are you!' he replied. Her expression changed.

'What, because I'm not white? Or because I'm not a man?'

'Hey … dinnae be havin' a go at *me*! Ah've got a black lassie in ma band.'

'Good for you,' said Farah angrily, 'but I'm not black, I'm brown … like the sauce you no doubt pour over everything you eat.' She stared at him determinedly.

Max blinked first. 'Look, ah'm sorry. Ah've nothin' against…' He paused.

She waited for those unintentionally thoughtless words. The ones intended to salve but which only made things worse. Different, more threatening ones came from behind her though. It hadn't taken long.

'Haw Boaby, look at these!' A slurred voice, dipped in anger and hard-boiled in hate. 'Twa P's in a pod, here. A poofter an' a Paki!'

The bar's occupants sniggered.

Max looked at Farah Nawaz. She had a look of sudden resignation in her eyes; one of knowing dismay. Max was suddenly ashamed at himself for drawing her to this ironically named place. For putting her in such a situation simply to make what Max had considered to be a principled point to Mac Barber. He looked around the bar room, taking in more than he had when he had first entered. A sign behind the optics read *'Nae Blacks, Nae Irish, Nae Dugs'*; an attempt at territorial humour. A signed Jim Davidson concert poster. A framed portrait of the recently victorious Thatcher. A picture of Enoch Powell pointing an accusatory finger directly at Max. Sentiments and figureheads appropriated from England's rise of nationalistic intolerance during the previous decade. Menacing reddened faces were suddenly everywhere, it seemed. The Black Hoose was a pub for the right-wing, racist drunkard. He hadn't been aware such a place even existed in East Ayrshire. Sectarian boozers, *aye* … they were ten a penny if you looked hard enough, but this? A pub full of monosyllabic, pitchfork-wielding morons; the Washer clause would cut no ice here, he reckoned.

'Let's go,' he whispered to Farah, rising and placing himself between her and the rest of the bar. He motioned behind his back and Farah stood and moved closer to his right-hand side.

'Haw … John Inman, ah'm gonnae teach ye a fuckin' lesson, son!'

'Hah-YA!' Max adopted a stance the bemused barflies had only previously seen on an episode of *Hong Kong Phooey*. 'Dinnae fuck wi' me, man … ah'm a Karate Black Belt, seventh Dan,' he lied.

'Fuckin' *Desperate* Dan, mair like,' said one.

'You're fuckin' gettin' it, ya cunt … you an' yer Paki burd!' shouted another.

Max pushed Farah towards the door and lifted his cane. The advancing boozer tripped and fell over it, headbutting the solid wooden bar top. Max looked at the cane. It was about to save him from a Black Hoose battering. Propelling Farah through the doors, he turned and wedged the cane between the handles and listened briefly from the street as the pub regulars leapt to the aid of their fallen colleague.

Max and Farah ran down the hill. It was – or rather had *been* – a good and loyal cane, but it wouldn't hold the back the Black Hoose bampots forever.

Out of breath and out of Black Hoose reach, Farah Nawaz vented her anger at Max Mojo. He again attempted to assure her that it was nothing personal, that his choice of meeting venue had purely been to display his annoyance at Mac Barber's disrespect. Farah responded by informing him in terse, formal fashion that Mac loved the band, but that a close relative of his had died suddenly. Rather than post-pone the interview, Mac had suggested to his editor that Farah be given a chance. She had looked upon their meeting as an honour, and a big opportunity to show what she could do. Max Mojo felt dreadful. His emotional range was a daily pendulum swing between unbridled aggression and soft-hearted empathy. Right now, it was firmly in the latter sector.

'Lemme buy ye a cup ae tea, eh? A bacon roll an' that ... ye dae eat bacon, right?' he asked anxiously.

Apparently satisfied with his numerous apologies, Farah Nawaz accepted. 'A pot of tea will be fine,' she said.

They walked to the Garden Grill in the centre of the town, in sight of the Cross. If the Black Hoose search party had left their home turf to hunt for the pair, there were enough coppers patrolling the nearby Burns Mall to provide official protection. As he considered this, Max dismissed the threat. Those bastards were *homing* drunks; they'd leave the pub reluctantly, sometimes with a message written on their wrists, but they never ventured too far from home base for long. Nevertheless, Max insisted they sit at the one table in the Garden Grill that had a clear view of all possible approaches. A young waitress brought over their order. She looked disdainfully at Max and pitifully at Farah Nawaz.

'See the looks ye get, eh ... just for being a wee bit different?' said Max, shaking his head. Farah's own 'tell me about it' expression needed no more elaboration.

'So where are ye from, originally like? asked Max.

'Lahore,' she replied before clearing up his evident confusion by adding 'Pakistan.'

'Is that in India?'

'No. It's definitely *not* in India.'

'Whit brought ye here then?'

'I was at school in England, going home for summers, but my father has been gradually moving his business to Scotland.'

'Ah ... ah get ye. How long ye been livin' in Killie then?'

'I don't. Live here, I mean. I live in Glasgow. My family are there ... and my future husband's family too.'

'A wee bit oan the young side tae be gettin' married, are ye no'?' said Max. 'Could understand it if ye were fae 'roon here. They get hitched at thirteen, oan average.'

It was a joke. Farah knew it and she laughed. It was the first time Max had noticed her teeth. They were absolutely perfect, just like her skin. *Fae a well-aff background, nae question.*

'Ye like it here, then?' Max asked. 'Ye must find it absolutely fuckin' freezin, naw?'

'I'm getting used to it, I suppose. Although I had only been living here permanently for a month when I got caught out in the worst snowstorm I had ever seen.'

'Nae snaw in Le *Hoor* then, ah take it?'

'No. Never. I didn't know what to do. The car wouldn't move. I was stuck and it was nighttime and … I don't know what I would have done if an old couple hadn't stopped and helped. The old man got out a shovel and dug the car out.' She looked out of the window. '*Most* people are lovely,' she said.

Max slurped a large mouthful of tea. 'Can ah ask whit yer dain' workin' for the *Ayrshire Post*, then?'

'I'm doing a bit of work experience before university. To help with my English, you know?'

Max nodded, but her grasp of the language was already exemplary, unlike his.

'I have an older brother in a band … back home,' said Farah, taking out a small tape recorder. It seemed that the formal business was about to begin.

'Aye?' said Max.

'You sound surprised,' said Farah, 'that I might be related to such people.'

"Naw,' said Max. 'Whit type ae music?'

'Heavy rock, mainly,' said Farah.

'AC/DC and Black Sabbath an' that?'

'No, Foreigner or Rush. He sings with a high-pitched voice. My father can't stand that type of music.'

'Aye … ah ken *that* feelin',' sighed Max, not talking about his own father, but empathising with hers.

'So what made you form the band, Max?'

Over the course of almost two hours, Max talked enthusiastically about destiny; his and that of each individual Miraculous Vespa. He spoke honestly of the dreams that were relentlessly propelling him towards something significant, he was sure. Of how he had put the band together, and although the potential for unforeseen fuck-ups languished around almost every corner, it was worth it, because the four of them were already individually great. It was his job to make sure they were collectively greater.

But they talked about Farah's dreams too. Her natural anxieties about her upcoming arranged marriage, and her fears about losing her burgeoning identity along with her name. Her wish to do something significant to help young, disadvantaged women in Pakistan receive proper education, and give them the chance at the life of opportunity Farah had had herself. She went further, into her hidden dream of owning a powerful motorbike and driving it, unburdened by time, from America's East Coast to its free-spirited West. She confounded herself. Max Mojo was the first person she had told of such private, personal things. He promised to keep it to himself. And she agreed to keep his secret fears – that Grant would leave the band, and *him* – out of any future print. They had known each other less than three hours, but already they had made a pact. It was a surprising morning.

⚡

The following week, a full-page report on 'The West of Scotland's best new band' appeared in the music section of the *Ayrshire Post*. It was a beautifully written piece, in Grant's opinion. And much more positive than Maggie and the Sylvester twins had dared hope for. Farah had captured the band's restless desire, their raw talent and the inspirational drive of their complex and contradictory manager. It was the first public break The Miraculous Vespas had had. Max Mojo wouldn't forget it.

28

Ye were askin' there about the point where ah kent we had it. Well, Norma, there wis two things that really fuckin' kicked it aw oan, ken? Hearin' the Smiths for the first time ... an' Wembley. An' baith ae them happened in the same bastardin' week, tae. Fuckin' mental.

28th May 1983
10.25 pm

'Mon, lets jist fuckin' go, ya prick. Whit's stoppin' ye? Yer maw?'

'Why the fuck would ah want tae go tae London, jist tae see a daft fitba match?'

'It's no' jist *any* fitba match, G ... it's fuckin' Scotland an' England, at Wembley. It's a fuckin' rite ae passage, boy.' Max was getting annoyed. Grant's antipathy to the plight Max was currently in meant that the band's manager would have to elaborate. He might even have to hint at the truth.

'Look, don't fuckin' make me spell it oot here, eh ... ya fuckin' bastart, ye!' It often felt like virtually every sentence uttered by the teenage would-be music mogul to his band's singer now ended with a cursed insult. Grant was no longer offended. And Max had long since ceased to give a fuck anyway.

'Ye need tae disappear for a few days, aye? Ah'm no' fuckin' stupid, Max. Hairy Doug, Doc Martin *and* noo some cunt wi a tractor ... aw your doin'. Am ah right? Why dae ah need tae come tae though?' said Grant. The thought of three or four days – or maybe *more* – cooped up with someone as high maintenance as his band's manager didn't in any way appeal.

'Cos ah've got two fuckin' tickets, ya cunt! Whit ah'm ah meant tae dae wi' the ither yin? Shove it up ma *erse*?'

A week earlier, the day after Pebbles, Max Mojo was on the hunt for a copy of 'Stoned out Of My Mind' by the Chi-lites. He'd loved the song since first hearing The Jam cover it on their farewell single the previous year. It was on a rare EP, which also featured 'Have You Seen Her', 'Oh Girl' and 'Homely Girl'. A record fair in Glasgow city centre seemed to offer a decent opportunity to find it but Max was to be disappointed, although he did pick up some other obscure records. Some of those that left the Merchant City Hall with him that day were 'I'm on My Way' by Dean Parrish, Esther Phillips' 'Just Say Goodbye', and Curtis Mayfield's seminal 'Superfly'.

Max was offered a lift home by the owner of a local lounge bar who knew Washer and Frankie Fusi. The bar owner had been to the fair to get shot of stocks of old vinyl for which there was now little space and even less audience.

On the drive back through Thornliebank and Whitecraigs, he offered Max two tickets for the upcoming England v Scotland game at Wembley. The lounge bar owner had to attend a funeral on the Wednesday of the game and consequently couldn't go himself. Max acknowledged that the offer – of the lift *and* the tickets – wouldn't have been forthcoming had Washer Wishart not been related to him. Nevertheless, it did present a welcome window through which to vanish just as an irate Hairy Doug was closing in.

Grant was right; Max didn't care about the football. He wouldn't have known many of the players, although he did know about the match's recent history. Six years earlier, this footballing fixture had achieved worldwide notoriety when – in celebration of an unlikely victory – the Scots hordes descended from the terracing, broke the goalposts and took large sections of the pitch home with them. The legends that followed suggested that there were around 400 penalty spots on the pitch that day, the Scottish daily newspapers uncovering numerous revellers all claiming they now had one of the two legitimate ones planted in back gardens from Banff to the Borders. This was all done in the supposedly good-natured spirit of Bannockburn, 1314. Unsurprisingly, the local residents of North West

London didn't welcome the bi-annual intrusion. In the aftermath of this particular match, various suggestions from the English FA hinted that the oldest international fixture in football's history had finally run its course. There was a fine line between the happy drunk and the football hooligan, and Scots fans in particular walked that line many times in the years that followed 1977. Between this match and the infamous Old Firm Cup Final of 1980, the reputation of fans north of Hadrian's Wall suffered badly.

It was against this background of concern from the media, the government, the police, the burghers of Wembley Park and his hypertensive mum, that Max took the tickets for the game. He eventually persuaded Grant to go with him, by promising that they would go and hang about outside the BBC's Broadcasting House, waiting for John Peel.

Max prepared a hopeful mix tape of the new records. After a fair number of false starts – and some industrial-strength swearing that resulted in Molly Wishart's brush handle banging her annoyance from the kitchen downstairs – the tape was made. To record vinyl onto C90, a conventional tape recorder was positioned next to the main speaker of Max's old record player. The 'record' button was depressed – it now shared *that* characteristic with the rest of the occupants of the house – along with the 'pause' button holding the recording sequence until just before the point where needle made sound. Max pondered the Luddite nature of this recording technique. He'd read about compact disc technology revolutionising music, and now the first ones were being sold down south. He knew that essentially all recording was similar, but he now longed to be in a proper studio with real equipment and a qualified sound engineer. Mix tapes, enjoyable though they were, only made this longing more pressing.

This new tape – self-titled *Philly Soul Sounds of the 70s* – was to go with Max to Wembley in the hope that the two strangers who would be providing him and Grant with a lift as part of the ticket deal, would play it at some point on the road trip. Having sourced the tickets, Max delegated the task of sourcing the kilts; *de rigueur* for a Scotland away fixture. Reluctantly Grant took up the challenge. His find was less kilt, more tartan blanket with big belt holding it up. Max Mojo and Grant Delgado would eventually leave Kilmarnock the day before the game looking like walking advertisements for the Russ Abbot Madhouse for the stereotypically Scotch.

Big Jock and the wee Pie-Man were to be their front-seat chaperones for the journey. Max knew neither of them, but since the lounge bar owner had arranged it, Max wasn't complaining. The altered Wednesday-night date for the game affected Big Jock's hospital porter shift patterns, so they had decided it would be best to drive down overnight on the Tuesday. Max and Grant would be dropped in the city and picked up first thing on the Thursday morning, even though a return journey wasn't part of the original deal.

29

10.43 pm

'Jesus fuckin' Christ!' Max shouted from his room. He opened the windows and shouted it again and again. It brought both parents running upstairs.

'Whit is it, son … are ye' aw'right in there?'

'Eh? Aye. Ah'm fuckin' fine. Gie's peace, for fuck sake.'

'Hey! Knock that oan the heid, right? Ah don't care whit they doctors say, speak tae yer Ma like that again an' ah'll separate yer heid fae yer shoodirs.'

'Sorry, Dad!'

'It's nearly flamin' midnight … get a bloody grip, son.'

Max Mojo had felt like a ton weight had been lifted from his shoulders. He thought back to the dream about carrying the cross up to the Mount at Onthank; back to the first thing he could vividly remember before all the headaches had started. It was as if someone had just relieved him of that burden and then given him a blow job into the bargain. He felt euphoric. He felt dizzy. He wasn't on drugs, at least not recreational ones anyway. He'd just listened to the greatest record he'd ever heard.

It wis 'What Difference Does It Make?' Fuckin' bolted me tae the floor, man. Ah wis gettin' ma stuff th'gither for goin' tae Wembley an' Peel's oan the tranny. He's wafflin' oan aboot aw kinds ae shite, an' playin' fuckin' pish music like Steel Pulse or tunes that'd make ye slash some cunt wi' a blade jist tae make it stop. Wisnae a great Peel night, ken, but then he puts on this band that's in session, ken? Fuckin' guitar, man. Fuckin' Johnny. Jesus Christ, ah wis aboot greetin' at the end ae it. Couldnae fuckin' get ower it.

'You need tae watch yersel' noo, aw' right?' Max's mum had many reservations about her damaged son heading down to London, but, as Washer reminded her, his doctors encouraged them to treat him as normally as possible.

They had reluctantly accepted that he had changed his name by deed poll, and that he was – for the mid- to longer-term at least – now a different person. Washer wasn't entirely demoralised by it. Max Mojo was driven and determined, whereas Dale Wishart had been a plodder. One to whom life just happened. Max might've been an obnoxious, foul-mouthed wee bastard, but at least he seemed to know what he wanted. It was an odd brew of emotions that Washer Wishart now experienced when regarding his son. Although he despised the thought of it, Max was *actually* the type of character Washer had once anticipated handing the family business over to at some future point. By default, he had become the son Washer had never had, and previously didn't know he even wanted.

'Aye. Ah will,' said Max, curtly, while jamming a white t-shirt into the recesses of his blue Adidas bag. He was already dreaming of a new band sound, all jangly guitars but still with a soulful Mod groove. The Postcard records of Orange Juice offered a bit of a template, but Grant had developed into a decent singer, and for all Max loved them, he couldn't describe Edwyn Collins as the type of singer he'd wanted in *his* band. How he hoped against hope that Grant – but perhaps more importantly, The Motorcycle Boy – had also been listening in to the John Peel show.

Ah mind ae leavin' the hoose that night as if ah wis' oan speed, ken? Like some daft drunk cunt stumblin' through a railway tunnel an' spottin' a wee light awa' at the end ae it. Mibbe that's a bad analogy, but ye'll ken whit ah mean, eh, Norma? Thousands ae fuckin' weans aw stuck in their bedrooms wonderin' who the fuck they were an' whit they were aw aboot, were aw oan the verge ae fuckin' life-changing enlightenment.

'All men have secrets and here is mine.' *Fuck sake, the quiffed cunt wis singin' right at me, man.*

Ah didnae ken it at the time but they lyrics were exactly how ah felt … 'But still I'd leap in front of a flying bullet for you.' Fuckin' hell. Grant loved it tae. That song felt tae me what 'Heartbreak Hotel' probably felt like tae aw they millions ae wee American lassies aw desperate for their first shag. It wis the future fur us … the band, ken? Bumblin' aboot tryin' to find a kinda common ground, ye know. We were definitely gettin' there by that time, mind you. But there wis still different fuckin' styles … vibes, an' that, an' then aw ae a sudden, it's right there in front ae us. Guitar. Drums. Bass. Voice. Nae need to bother wi' fuckin' trumpets or banjos or synths or any ae that fuckin' JoBoxers shite.

Otherwise, it wis generally gettin' a bit fuckin' mental, ken? Too much pressure, *as the wee* Selecter *lassie used tae sing. Too fuckin' right, hen! Ah needed tae get ootae Dodge or else any number of wide cunts wid ae pannelled us. The debts were risin' faster than Neil Kinnock's blood pressure. This wis' aw before Grant's stash came intae full public knowledge. Only folk that knew wis me, him, the pikeys … an' as ah only found oot later, the Burundi drummer. An' ah couldnae tell Washer, like. An opportunity tae fuck off doon tae that London presents itself, like a big fuckin' safe, warm, wet fanny at the end ae a night oan the batter … or at least that's how ah felt aboot it at the time, like. So ah dives right in. Who fuckin' widnae, eh?*

30

Grant left his house in Onthank to rendezvous with Max Mojo at the Broomhill Hotel just before midnight on Tuesday with more than just Morrissey's mercurial lyrics ringing in his ears. Senga's three-point interrogation still reverberated as much as Johnny Marr's guitar.

1. Why was he going at all?
2. What did he know about the two strangers?
3. Where was he going to sleep?

Grant lied about the first two but number three left him stumped because, to be honest, neither he nor Max had even considered the question. Big Jock and the Pie-Man were sorted for digs with friends of the smaller man with the unusual – and unexplained – nickname. The wee man kindly phoned his contacts from Abington Services on the first stop en route to ask if there was room for the two kilted teenagers as well. The shaking of the tiny bald head inside the phone booth indicated no sanctuary.

'Nuthin' dain', boys,' said the Pie-Man. 'Sorry.'

'Ach, nae worries. Thanks fur tryin' at least, eh?' said Grant.

'Baldy wee basturt.' The engine started just as Max Mojo made his feelings on the subject known. General Johnson's vocal intro on 'Give Me Just a Little More Time' thankfully also concealed them or the trip would have been over before they had crossed the border.

'Ah'll try another couple ae folk fae Galston at the next stop. Viviani might put ye'se up,' said the Pie-Man optimistically. 'No sure if he's still *in* London, mind, but if ye'se can keep *schtum* aboot it, he might dae ye's a wee turn, ken?'

Tony Viviani was a Galston man of Italian descent. His family had originally come from the same region as Frankie Fusi's but the adopted Ayrshiremen had never met. Tony had operated an ice-cream van as part of his father's 'Emporio Viviani's'. During his 'rounds', he charmed a number of young Galston women into the back of his van with the promise of a free double nougat. For him, this utopian existence continued for years until he unwittingly plundered a fifteen-year-old niece of Nobby Quinn. Amid rumour and counter rumour that he had actually raped her, and fearing ending up in the foundations of the Auchinleck bypass, he'd bolted around eighteen months before, surfacing in London. There he would have probably stayed in anonymous bliss had he not sent a postcard from London to the Standalane pub in Galston asking the landlord to send on a reference for a labourer's job. The card was posted up behind the bar and before Judith Chalmers could say *Wish You Were Here*, everyone knew where he was, including his fearsome wife Deirdre, who, with four kids and another due, headed south for the Big Smoke. Tony hadn't so much as said goodbye to her. Deirdre, like many others in Galston, was also aware of the rumours that her fecund husband had stolen a large sum of money from a rigged fist-fighting tournament run by the Quinns.

This was the back-story that new Smiths fans, Max Mojo and Grant Delgado headed into on that sunny Wednesday morning in old London Town. By the time they made it over to Hammersmith it was close to opening time. Tony Viviani wasn't in the pub the Pie-Man had given the teenagers the directions to, but someone knew him and where he was staying. That same someone then spent what felt like about an hour telling them a story that was to reveal where he had been sitting when an IRA bomb had gone off in the corner of the very same pub two years earlier. As it happened he had been sitting at home watching television. Max called the old man a *soppy old cunt* for wasting their time on such an anti-climactic story.

Grant got his arse kicked by the owner, and the two kilted Scotsmen were unceremoniously booted out on to the street.

'Fuck sake, eh? Knock that fuckin' shite oan the heid doon here, or ah'm headin' back hame oan the train. We're gonnae end up gettin' an absolute doin' affa somebody if you cannae fuckin' button it.' Grant was raging.

Did the body rule the mind, or did the mind rule the body? Ah dunno!

Ye'll appreciate here, that ah couldnae fuckin' help aw that shite, right? Back then, a lot ae the time, whatever wis in ma heid jist came right oot. Still does tae a certain extent, an' by the way, ah dinnae think that's a bad thing, ken? There should be mair folk plain speakin'. We widnae be in aw this fuckin' mess wi' they towel-heids in the Middle East if we'd aw sat doon at the beginnin' an' telt each other the plain facts. Fuck aw the 'Bootros Bootros Galley' bollocks. Somebody calls me a cunt, an' can back up the reasons why ah'm a cunt, then ah'm happy wi' that. Ah'll be a cunt tae him, an' ah'll stay oot his fuckin' way as a result. Ah'm a wee bit like that auld gadgie … the Prince Philip.

Each tae his ain, ken? Que Sera…

'Get yersel tae fuck,' said Max. 'Widnae be in this fuckin' position if ye'd let us book a hotel like ah said.'

The rest of the journey was conducted in silence and on foot. Tony Viviani was living in a two-bedroom, second-floor flat right next to Battersea Power Station. This iconic structure was like an old English pub table overturned after a brawl; the urban decay at its base resembling all the things that had dropped from it as it had fallen over. As Max and Grant approached the front door, a sense of doom began to build. *What if Tony Viviani hadn't actually spoken to the Pie-Man's contact? What if he had said it was okay but had been so pissed at the time that he'd forgotten he'd said so? What if he was a mental case?*

Grant's steps were noticeably slowing, letting Max take the lead. After three sturdy knocks, the wooden door opened. A look-a-like of Ringo Starr in the film *That'll Be the Day* looked them up and down. As if to reinforce the metaphor of a man living beyond his sell-by date, he wore a faded yellow t-shirt with the words 'I SHOT JR' screen-printed on the front. The two kilted strangers in front of him could only have been those referred to him by pals of wee Paddy Bolton, the Pie-Man.

'Whit team dae ye'se support?' Tony asked, with an eyebrow raised. It seemed like a trick question.

'Don't really like fitba,' said Max.

'If ye *did* like fitba, whit team wid ye support?' Tony wasn't to be denied. Grant was beginning to think the correct answer was the password.

'Christ's sake … whit is this, the fuckin' *Krypton Factor*?' Max was becoming agitated, but Tony defused the tension with a smile. He was simply enquiring on the assumption that Scots travelling to Wembley would have club allegiances. Ayr United was his.

'You two the mates ae the Pie-Man, then?'

'Aye. You Tony the Pony fae Galston?' said Max, suppressing the urge to call him a prick.

Tony looked outside and beyond them. 'Naw. Tony's no here jist noo. He's em … away in Benidorm for the summer. Ah'm his cousin … *Terry*. C'mon in boys,' he said warmly. He was evidently the worst liar on the planet.

Grant figured he wouldn't stay on this informal home-made witness protection programme for long. Tony/*Terry* beckoned them in. Grant was relieved that he was so welcoming. This sense quickly evaporated when the penny dropped about the biggest 'What if' of them all. *What if Tony Viviani hadn't told his missus?*

Naturally, he hadn't. Deirdre more than lived up to her billing, going absolutely *mental*.

'You're fuckin' jokin', ya daft tally prick! Two fuckin' clowns in skirts ye've niver even met afore … steyin' … in *ma* hoose? That'll be fuckin' right! Get rid, or I'll make that call tae Ged McClure, an' let *him* tell Nobby Quinn yer here.'

Max and Grant stood motionless next to the living-room window.

Tony the Pony tried to reason with his irate wife. Stammered pleas about how he couldn't let the Pie-Man down, that they were homeless and defenceless lads from the old country, that they had come all this way and finally – the one that had Grant move instinctively to a concealed position behind the curtain – that he and she would only need to sleep on their folded-down sofa for one night.

'Have you loast yer fuckin' marbles, ya greasy walloper? Bad 'nuff them bein' here at aw' but you've telt them they can huv *oor* bed!' Deirdre drew breath. Another assault seemed inevitable. 'Yer a fuckin' lazy bastart! Couldnae even stick the buildin' site withoot aw the screwin' aboot.'

This last jibe seemed unrelated to context but spoke loudly of the darker malaise at the centre of their relationship. There was a brief few seconds of calm, then an almighty smash as the mirror above the electric two-bar fire shattered on contact with a flying plate.

'Ah'm takin' the weans tae Brenda's. Ye can dae whit the fuck ye like wi' they two clowns, but if the three o' ye are still here the morra mornin', Quinn's crew'll fuckin' kill ye 'cos ah'm phonin' McClure right noo! *Thomas, Joseph, Maria, Mary*! Get yer stuff, we're goin' tae yer Aunty Bren's.'

Fifteen minutes of uncoordinated banging and swearing later and they were gone.

Tony Viviani had wisely stayed in the living room with Max and Grant, clearly thinking the better of any further appeals. When the noise had dissipated to an extent where Deirdre was evidently more than a block away, Tony smiled and rubbed his hands together. 'Fancy a beer then lads?' he said.

Max and Grant had somewhere to stay for the night. Despite the mess he'd made of his life, Tony Viviani had clearly retained a degree of magnetic charm. He seemed like the kind of guy that everybody generally liked until *they* were having an off-day, whereupon his constant glass half-full attitude became a severe irritation. He didn't seem unduly concerned about the prospect of hospitalisation at the hands of the Quinns, although Grant in particular wanted to ensure that he didn't come into contact with them. The whole caravan business with Maggie had eventually died down, but only after he'd handed over two thousand pounds. He was in no mood to rekindle bad feeling with Rocco Quinn by associating with Tony Viviani.

'Dinnae worry aboot the missus, eh? Time ae the month, an' that, ken?' said Tony, convinced that Deirdre would cool off, realise she really loved him and come home in a different mood next morning, having left the phone safely housed on its cradle.

31

Max and Grant made it to Trafalgar Square as the sun seemed to be at its warmest. The fountains were boarded up but that didn't stop the Scots fans from again treading that very thin line. The large crowd with whom they travelled towards Wembley tipped burger vans over, a small group of English supporters were chased outside a tube station in a hail of bricks, and a policeman's helmet was stolen, causing quite a serious *stramash* and resulting in around ten arrests. All in all, it was quite an intimidating atmosphere even though all of the supporters outside the stadium appeared to be in blue and tartan. This dark mood continued inside the ground. From all around Max and Grant, empty quarter-bottles of vodka and whisky were thrown at the police patrolling the running track around the pitch. Thankfully, none hit their intended targets. The mood worsened as England went 1–0 up and then, in the second half, deservedly doubled their lead. Glenn Hoddle had torn Scotland apart and the Tartan Army's golden boy, Charlie Nicholas had been a nightmare.

Max and Grant's trip back into the city centre was surprisingly muted. Trains full of drunken Scots bemoaning another defeat at the hands of the auld enemy didn't auger well for the London Underground staff on duty that night. However, the teenagers didn't see any real trouble. Grant was convinced he saw two older guys pointing at them as they came out of the stadium and trudged down Wembley Way. It was of note because he was sure he'd seen them at Trafalgar Square earlier in the day as well. He became more suspicious when he saw them in the same subway carriage. Max and Grant got off at Piccadilly and immediately the two older guys got off too. Attack being the best form of defence, Max approached them with a 'whit's yer fuckin' problem, ya cunts? We're no' rent boys, ya fuckin' arsebandits, ye'se!'

The older of the two men laughed and informed them that he was Gregor, from Irvine, and that he knew Max, albeit when *he* was known as Dale Wishart. They were initially confused by his dismissal that he had ever been called by that name, but eventually they simply shrugged, uninterested. Nevertheless, they offered to buy the boys a drink, *provided yer baith ower age*, they joked. Grant wasn't enamoured with the idea but Max persuaded him and they all went to Soho for a pint in an exclusive-looking basement pub next to the Raymond Revue Bar. The two elder men had stuck a fifty in the doorman's top pocket in order to get their two younger, kilted compatriots in.

Inside, Max could barely see his hand in front of his face, everything was so dark. Grant was sure two guys were kissing each other in an adjacent booth. The noise from the sound system was booming. It helped conceal Max's uncontrolled smalltalk wherein he eventually suggested Gregor's mother was *'a hoormaister'*. Gregor agreed, and said 'Thora Hird's'. He'd thought Max had asked if she needed help with the stairs. A topless waitress came over and took a shouted order for four pints. When she returned, it was with a bill for forty pounds. Max choked. The two older men weren't fazed at all by the ludicrous cost.

'So, Dal ... sorry, *Max* ... whit's yer da up tae these days? Still dain' the washin'?'

'Dunno whit ye mean, man,' said Max. Instinct kicked in that he should tell strangers nothing about Washer.

'C'mon son, dinnae be so fuckin' coy.' The older, fatter man, who said his name was Gregor, wasn't going to be easily put off. 'Ah've got a big deal comin' up. Ah need some dirty shit hidden, ken? We spotted ye'se oan the train earlier, an' ah says tae Ged here "ah ken him ... that's Washer Wishart's boy". Ah did, didn't ah, Ged?'

'He did,' said Ged.

Grant considered that there was something odd about the two men. He couldn't put his finger on what though. Gregor was bald, with manicured nails and he was casually – but soberly – dressed, while Ged looked like a jakey, biker busker. Gregor was assured, Ged was obviously agitated. They were different ages, but not sufficiently different to be father and son.

'You two jist doon for the game then?' asked Max, trying to shift the focus.

'Aye an' naw,' said Gregor.

Max waited for elaboration but there was none. 'Whit did ye think ae it then?' he asked.

'Whit?'

'The match, like. It wisnae the best, eh? Stein should've taken Nicholas aff even earlier. He wis absolutely pish,' said Max.

'Who the fuck are you, aw ae a sudden? *Archie McPherson?*' Ged hadn't looked interested, but all of a sudden his intervention shifted the dynamic.

'Lighten up, pal,' said Grant. 'We're jist havin' a pint wi' ye'se.' Grant already knew that they didn't have the money on them to get the next round, but he sensed a bigger problem emerging. It might have seemed like the ultimate in opportunistic meetings but Gregor and his buddy Ged were obviously keen to take advantage of bumping into a close relative of Washer Wishart.

Gregor put a hand on Ged's forearm. 'It's aw calm, boys. We're aw pals here, right? Scotsmen abroad ... the famous Tartan Army, ken?' Gregor smiled broadly. 'Ne'er mind Ged, here. He's oan a separate mission. Been looking for an Ayrshire cunt that's absconded doon here.'

Max and Grant looked at each other across the booth's table.

'In fact, it's a job for a pal ae yer da's,' said Gregor. 'Nobby Quinn, fae Galston. Ken ae him?'

'Aye,' said Max, 'but he's nae pal ae Washer's.'

'Ah'm jist rowin' yer fuckin' tail, son. Don't get oot yer pram!' Gregor refocused. 'Since we've bumped intae ye, aw casual an' that like ... ah'm efter a big favour. We've got ye'se in here, got ye a pint ae the maist expensive fuckin' beer oan the planet, an' ye've had a lassie's nipples in yer ear while she served ye ... so whit ah want...' Ged snorted. 'Whit *we* want ... is an opener wi' yer faither. We've moved oan a large quantity ae gear up in Glesga an' we're sittin' oan aw the readies. Ah need it distributed. Yer da's the fuckin' top boy.'

'Ah'd like tae help ye, honest ah wid, but ah'm no' part ae his business. Ah'm in the *music* business. Band management, an' that, ken?' Max was breathing heavily, and then gulping his pint. It seemed to be the only thing preventing him from calling Gregor a cunt, although it had given him the hiccups.

'Even better,' said Gregor. 'A demand, supply *and* cash deal! Everybody's a fuckin' winner.' Gregor sat back and put an arm around Max's shoulder. 'You ken it makes sense, son. By the way, where are you boys stayin' th'night?'

Grant got up to go to the toilet. Ged watched him intently all the way there. Grant was sweating and he was sure that Ged could sense his growing anxiety. He went into one of the cubicles and sat on the toilet seat. He didn't actually need to go, although paradoxically, he was now *shiting* himself.

Grant heard the door open.

'Wanna go somewhere else, George?'

'Yeah, after this line, sweet. Only here to speak to Kenny but he's fucked off earlier. I'll page my driver, man.'

Grant peered out through a gap in the door. The toilets were lit by an ultravoilet light giving only marginally more clarity in the darkness than the lounge area itself. Grant could see what looked like two long-haired, heavily made-up women kissing. Then the door opened and the curly-haired Ged burst in. He briefly thought he had walked into the wrong toilets.

'Ootae ma fuckin' way, ya benders,' he shouted at the two. They separated, and Grant could see it was two men in drag, and he was almost certain one of them was the Culture Club singer, Boy George.

'Not want to join us, pal?' said the one who probably wasn't Boy George.

'Fuck off, ya poofy basturts. Ah'll fuckin' *do* ye'se!' shouted Ged, scanning the small, tiled, L-shaped room, presumably looking for Grant. The one who probably *was* Boy George laughed and touched Ged's shoulder. He spun round, fist clenched.

'Aw, do you really wanna hurt me?' said the one who probably was Boy George.

The one who probably wasn't laughed a high-pitched camp laugh. Ged drew his arm back as Grant burst out of the cubicle. Ged spun again, but too late to see Grant bring the ceramic cistern top down on his head. Ged slumped and blood ran, slowly at first but then the pressure from the source burst the cut and it flowed like the sluice gates had been opened at the Hoover Dam.

'Fuckin' hell,' said Grant. 'Sorry aboot that.'

'Happens more often than you'd think, mate.'

'Fuck sake,' said Grant.

'Yeah, if only we had you to protect us all the time, sweetie,' smiled Boy George.

'Are you fuckin' Boy George by the way?'

'Yes. I am. And he's bloody *great* in bed, lemme tell ya.'

The one who wasn't Boy George sniggered, and then he snorted the line of white powder that both had been protecting when Grant had exploded out of the cubicle. Grant had a beamer.

'Thanks, man. I owe you.' Boy George put a small packet of the white stuff inside Ged's denim jacket pocket. They bundled Ged into the furthest cubicle, and locked it from inside. He was still breathing at least. Grant clambered over to the next one and the three of them went quickly back out into the main room.

'He looking for you then?' said Boy George.

'Aye probably, but no' for whit ye think?' Ah'm the singer in a band. He's jist some fuckin' ned lookin' for *another* geezer fae Scotland.'

'I like your skirt,' said Boy George. 'Tartan's quite big again. Even the Bay City Rollers might make a comeback.'

Grant smiled nervously. He was now desperate to get Max's attention and get the fuck out of there before someone else discovered Ged.

'Manager's a friend. I'll let him know about this angry fuck,' said Boy George, nodding in Ged's direction. 'He'll sort it. Clear it up.'

'Cheers. Better get aff. Fuckin' karma, eh?' said Grant, patting his own top pocket.

'Karma … yeah,' Boy George laughed. 'I like that.'

'Darlin', we'd better hustle,' said the giggling *Not* Boy George.

'Yeah, coming.' Boy George touched Grant's cheek. 'Fucking great cheekbones, sweetie. You any good?'

'Eh?' said Grant.

'Your band … are they any good?'

'Aw, right. Eh, aye. Indie stuff but wi' a wee bit ae dance in there tae. Ye'd like us.'

Boy George smiled. The one who wasn't Boy George told him a driver would be outside.

Boy George reached into his bag and pulled out a card. 'Give this geezer a call, sweet. Tell him I recommended you, and tell him *you know the bones are buried in San Sebastian.* He'll know you really *did* meet me.' Boy George leaned over and kissed Grant on the cheek. 'Good luck, em….'

'Grant. Grant Delgado,' said Grant.

'Great name, man,' said Boy George, and then he was gone.

Noo, ah never believed aw that shite aboot it bein' the Boy George back then. The basturt wis oan the front page ae every fuckin' paper in Britain in they days. Why the fuck wid' the cunt have been in some scabby Soho shitehole oan a Wednesday night, eh? It made nae fuckin' sense whatsoever. But throw a fuckin' stick in the middle ae the London in 1983, an' ye'd ae hit some daft cunt wi' a knob wearin' a bloody lassie's dress an' make up, ken? Gender Benders, The Sun called them. Still, Grant wis totally high oan the whole thing, so it wis guid enough for me, like. Ah went alang wi' it…

Grant caught Max's eye through the dense clouds of cigarette smoke and eye-bursting laser light beams. Gregor was being distracted by a waitress into whose G-string he was trying to insert another large note of apparently corrupt currency. Max bolted. They both made it up the stairs and out into the warm June air. It was just before midnight. They ran through the crowds to catch the late tube back to Hammersmith.

2nd June 1983
0.51 am

Tony Viviani was still waiting up and had brought a few of his own mates back from the pub. Still the life and soul, he wanted the two teenagers to sing some songs about Scotland for his English compatriots. There was to be no putting him off. The marital bed – so much the centrepoint of the earlier argument – would lay unused and Max and Grant left the house at around four am, having not slept at all. They left without washing or doing anything that might've woken the party. Max's hair looked like Ken Dodd's after standing on a live electric cable. More worryingly, Grant's voice now sounded like the sonic signal used to detect life on other planets. Tony and his mates were sound asleep on either the chairs or the floor in the living room. Tony had figured that, if Ged McClure's gang was going to turn up he would at least have had some assistance, or more likely someone to take him to hospital. Although he couldn't be certain, Grant felt sure Ged wouldn't be troubling the Viviani household for some time.

Max and Grant made it back to Euston Station on time to catch up with their return journey drivers, who bought them both some breakfast before they were on their way. They *did* play Max's mix tape repeatedly on the way back but he slept through most of the nine and a half hours it took to get home.

'Some fuckin' place, the London, eh boy?' said Max, as the car drove away from Kilmarnock's bus station.

'Aye ... ye could fuckin' say.' Grant laughed, and so did Max.

For perhaps the first time, it felt to both like a real connection had

been made. Like they were in it together, and that the 'it' could actually be something really special. Boy George had given Grant the
card of Morrison Hardwicke, an A&R man from London Records.
Max had called him from Carlisle and, after a few false starts – Max
thought A&R stood for *Albums & Records* – and then the code words,
had got through and been given some direct, if unsurprising, advice.

'Get a fackin' demo made … four songs, yer *best* songs, good
quality studio recordings, mind … no' fackin' bullshit. Bring it
back down an' ah'll see ya. But just as a favour to Georgie, mind.
Alright?' Hardwicke had said. It was more than alright … it was a
real fucking breakthrough. They needed to knuckle down and get
the twins totally focused. But it was exciting, and before they parted,
they hugged. Immortality beckoned.

04: **YOU CAN'T PUT YOUR ARMS AROUND A MEMORY...**

Ma cousin Gerry met some decorater gadgie ... Wullie somethin', cannae remember ... aboot a month later at a Kilmarnock fitba match. He'd been telt by a mate that Tony Viviani had been remanded for trial for attempted murder. Deirdre, his missus, had came back efter aw, the next mornin' but even fuckin' angrier than when she'd left. The folk next door had heard screamin'... 'Ah'm gonnae fuckin kill ye...!', an' stuff ... an' they phoned the polis. When they turned up, Deirdre wis lyin' oan the kitchen floor wi' blood gushin' fae a heid wound. Tony wis sittin' in the living room watchin' Countdown an' drinkin' a cup ae tea.

The weans were still at Brenda's. Ye couldnae fuckin' make it up, man!

What did you take from that?

That Galston folk are pure mental, eh?

32

The train pulled in to the station. Fat Franny Duncan, his mum and Theresa got off on the platform and walked slowly out to the turning circle outside the ticket office. Des Brick was nowhere to be seen. Fat Franny put his suitcases down and walked over to the railings. He looked down the length of John Finnie Street from his elevated viewpoint. He sighed; *still* no sign. The traffic was all heading towards him. He remembered the time – he must only have been about four years old – when Abie brought him up here. They watched the cars and buses having brief passing conversations with each other as they moved up and down the street. He was on his dad's shoulders. He felt like he was higher than anyone else on earth. John Finnie Street was now a one-way system. Vehicles didn't seem to converse anymore. They just jostled impatiently for room. They prevented people crossing. They were a barrier. Everything changes. Nothing stays the same.

'Francis, ah'll just get a taxi. It'll be for the best.'

'Aye. Ah suppose.'

Fat Franny watched Theresa lift her own suitcase and struggle around the corner into the wind. He couldn't even go and help her with it. To do so would have meant leaving his mum and it was clear now that he couldn't do that, even for a few minutes. She would just wander off; into the toilets, or into the traffic, or even off the platform. Theresa Morgan, Fat Franny Duncan's fiancée of only six months, disappeared from his view. He wasn't sure when he would see her again. Or even *if.*

Three weeks earlier, she had been overjoyed when Fat Franny

suggested they go on holiday. It was ludicrously short notice, but Theresa was used to that with Fat Franny. He was impulsive at the best of times, but she wasn't innocent to the nature of his business. Sometimes being out of the firing line for a brief period was an occupational hazard in his line of work. Theresa anticipated Torremolinos, or maybe Majorca. She already had a one-year passport as a result of a hint Fat Franny had given when they got engaged. Fat Franny had been obstinately cagey about the destination and that increased her excitement. But he'd talked about Spain quite a bit lately, although mainly when laughing about Manuel, the waiter in *Fawlty Towers*. Based on this – and the powers of deduction of her old school pal Alison at AT Mays – she spent good money on new clothes. She bought a beach towel the size of the Rugby Park pitch. She bought Factor 50 sun lotion, even though she was already quite sallow-skinned. She'd even laughed when Fat Franny had said that it was only one factor lower than emulsion paint. That was his opportunity. But he didn't tell her until the day that they were leaving.

They were going to Margate. By train. And with old Rose in tow. Fat Franny had also talked previously about a place where English-speaking people would be, and where you could get an English breakfast. Theresa never thought for a minute that the place would actually be *in* England. She was livid. It wasn't even Blackpool. She could've coped with that. He was taking her to some old folks' home by the sea. And using her as a *de facto* nursemaid. She contemplated telling him on the morning of their departure that she wasn't going. But then she'd have to explain his actions and her disappointment to others. Her pride would get in the way of that. Plus, with everyone else away for the fair, Kilmarnock would be Tumbleweed City. So she sucked in her cheeks, boarded the train south from Kilmarnock railway station and waved bye-bye to the future she'd imagined over the course of the previous six months. Everything changes. Nothing stays the same.

'Jesus Christ, Des. Ah telt ye two o'clock! Been waiting here for half an' hour.'

'Sorry Franny. It wis Effie. Ah couldnae leave her the day. Old Aggie fae next door wis oot an' ah couldnae get haud ae anybody else tae come for you.' Des Brick was as agitated as Fat Franny Duncan but for opposing reasons.

Des felt Fat Franny should've just got a taxi back to the Ponderosie. It wasn't that far from the station. Fat Franny on the other hand felt it only fair that Des Brick pick them up, given the latitude Franny had extended him lately. Checkmate.

The fifteen-minute drive to the north-west corner of the town was conducted in silence apart from the occasional 'House!' shouted out by Rose. When they arrived, Des commented on how much chirpier Franny's mum seemed compared to the last time he'd seen her. Franny felt guilty about dragging Des away from his terminally ill wife at such a difficult time, but he couldn't admit to it. He handed Des a package.

'Got this for Effie,' said Fat Franny.

'Cheers. Ah'll tell her ye were askin' for her,' said Des. He didn't have the heart to tell Fat Franny that Effie could no longer chew food conventionally, far less eat brittle Margate rock. It was the thought that counted though.

'Aye. Dae that,' said Fat Franny, as he helped his old mum out the rear of Des Brick's car. 'When ye track the Painter doon, can ye tell him ah want tae see him?'

'Aye. Ah will, boss.'

Theresa Morgan opened her case. She tipped it up contemptuously. They had been away for a week but three-quarters of the contents had remained unworn. The ten new bikinis were a complete waste of money, as were the skimpy tops aimed at late-night Mediterranean beach clubs. She had spent the week in the jeans she had travelled in. It was originally a protest, but Fat Franny didn't even cotton on. He just assumed that she was feeling the blustery winds that blew daily along the promenade, picking up speed as they rounded the Old Clock Tower. Had the weather been kinder, Theresa may have been able to tolerate the endless bingo halls, the

Scenic Railway, the boredom of the Dreamland Amusement Park, and Fat Franny in a 'Kiss Me Quick' hat. But it rained. And it was cold. And ultimately, it was miserable. As her frustration reached its peak, Fat Franny admitted he only thought of Margate after hearing Chas & Dave extol its virtues the previous year. *That*, Theresa concluded, was the last straw.

And now she was back home, or to be more accurate back at her *mum's* home. In Onthank. A whiter shade of pale than she'd been before she left. She stared at the walls of what she'd recently thought would soon be her old bedroom. The same old posters of Adam Ant, Nick Heyward and Simon Le Bon smiled back at her. Once they had filled her with hope of a different life; now they seemed to be sneering in disdain.

She slumped on the bed, clean and dirty clothes all around her, and cried.

Nothing changes. *Everything* stays the same.

33

'Whit's up wi' you?' asked Washer Wishart. His nephew Gerry Ghee had a face longer, and more twisted than the M74.

'Allie's pregnant,' he said. *'Again.'*

'Haw, congratulations, son!' said Washer, extending his hand. 'Ye'll have a five-a-side team, then. Provided some cunt invents fitba for women, that is.'

'Aye. Cheers.' Gerry Ghee wore the look of a man who had won the pools and lost his memory of the coupon's location, all on the same day.

'Fuck sake, ye dinnae need tae be so overjoyed aboot it, though.'

'Ach … ah've had the snip aboot a year ago. It wis as sore as fuck, an' it's aw been for nothin'.'

'Jesus,' said Washer, '…ye kept *that* quiet.'

'Ah had tae … in case anybody telt the wife, ken.'

'Whit … ye didnae even agree it wi' Alison first?' said Washer, staggered at this. Gerry shook his head silently. He now looked like a man who'd just been informed that his appeal against an imminent death penalty had just been thrown out.

'Well, sorry son, but ah've nae sympathy for ye. Ye need tae trust yer missus, in ma opinion.'

'Washer, ah need a rise. Ah ken it's no' the best timin'…'

'No' the best timin'?' Washer interrupted. 'Son, It's up there wi' Michael Foot comin' tae ask for a campaign donation!'

Gerry didn't know what to say. Four kids and another one on the way required a bit more financial stability than his uncle was apparently able to provide. His options were limited.

'Aye, sorry. Had tae ask, Washer. Hope ye can understand,' he said. 'An' obviously if anythin' decent ... or *unusual* comes up, gie's a shout, eh?'

'Why don't ye sue the doctors for yer fucked-up procedure?' said Washer, trying to be helpful. 'Chase a couple ae ambulances?'

'Cannae. They told me "nae shaggin'" until ma semen tests were clear. But, fuck me man ... it wis' takin' months! An' it wis ma thirtieth birthday ... ah wis pished, blah blah fuckin' blah.' Gerry looked like he was going to cry.

Washer suppressed a laugh. 'How far oan is she?'

'Five months,' said Gerry.

'Holy fuck, son.' This time Washer *did* laugh.

'For the first three ae them, she says *she* didnae even ken!'

'Nae luck, pal.' Washer got up. He was going to be late for meeting Frankie Fusi. 'Here,' he said. 'They'll help ye. They're specialist lawyers.' Washer handed Gerry a piece of paper he'd written on.

'Aye. Cheers,' said Gerry Ghee sarcastically, as his uncle walked away chuckling. '*Messrs Sioux, Grubbit & Runne.* Aye ... big fuckin' laugh!'

Washer Wishart was on his way to the pub. It wouldn't take him long to get there. You could see its front door from the upper front-facing bedroom of the manse. Many times in the past he was grateful for that proximity; that perverse feeling of community belonging; of being central to the way things worked. Now, though, it seemed like a curse. When a business – even one that traverses legality like a tightrope walker over a bear-pit – gets into trouble in a one-horse town, there's no hiding it.

He reached the front door of the Portland Arms. Three small children were sat outside, leaning against the wall. All three had a bottle of Coke and a packet of ready-salted crisps. They looked like they had accepted that they would be there for a while. Washer peered in through the casement windows. As he'd anticipated, the pub was full of his business comrades. The same ones who were now struggling with the twin impacts of a developing miners' strike and the reduction of benefits washing their way down from the local laundry. It was a Tuesday night. He just wanted a quiet pint away from the questions and the suggestions. Washer spotted Frankie Fusi sitting in a corner. He walked along the street to the window closest to where Frankie was seated. Washer rapped lightly on it. Only Frankie noticed him. Washer motioned for him to come outside.

⚡

Flat-pack Frank Fusi and Jimmy 'Washer' Wishart were both born in 1931. Frank – or Francesco – began his colourful life in the cloistered courtyards of Lucca and fled Italy with his family in 1933. Washer – or James Walter – was born in the very minister's house where he still lived.

Their thirty-year friendship was founded during eighteen months in the ludicrous humidity of the jungle villages surrounding Kuching, Borneo, where they were both performing their National Service. Both young men saw action; both returned with commendations for valour. In Washer's case, his contained a special mention for saving the lives of two colleagues. One of them was Frankie Fusi.

For a few months when they returned to Ayrshire in early 1951, the two twenty-year-olds were lauded by their small parish.

'Fancy gaun for a walk, Franco?' asked Washer.

'A walk? Where tae?'

'Jist roon aboot here, mate. Cannae be arsed wi' the pub the night. C'mon, pal. A wee stroll doon the lane ae memories?' said Washer.

'Fuck it. Aye. Aw'right,' said Frankie. 'But you're buyin' the chips!'

'Deal.'

The two old friends wandered along to the Cross and turned right heading up the Kilmaurs Road towards the nearby village of Knockentiber. It was a beautiful evening.

'So many changes, eh?' Washer looked at the commemorative plaque. 'Mind ae the time ma da wis tryin' tae get you an' me oan this badge?'

'Aye,' said Frankie. 'You deserved it though. Ah didnae.'

'Ach, pish!' said Washer.

They leaned on the old stone bridge looking down at the Carmel Water, lazily meandering under it. They walked on.

'The place is only famous for the hospital, noo,' said Washer.

'Worse things tae be well known for though,' said Frankie. 'We could be livin' in bloody Greenham Common, eh?' Washer laughed.

'Ah suppose, although there's times when ye look aboot an' think a nuclear bomb wid make some improvements roon here.' He sighed. 'Fuckin' Thatcher! How the fuck did she get back in, eh? Are folk really that bastardin' shallow?'

'Aye,' said Frankie. 'She's no' daft mind. Engineers a war ower some pile ae rocks nae cunt's even heard ae, jist tae take the heat aff aw the pish that she created back here! Ye have tae take yer hat aff tae that kind ae Hitler mind-fuck propaganda, eh?'

They walked further up the hill and into the neighbouring village.

'Remember the days when the train used tae come through here, Frankie?'

'Aye, pal. Ah dae.'

'There wis a wee station here anaw. It wis a lovely wee station. Floo'ers an' seats oan the wee platform. An' a lovely clock, tae. Then the fuckin' thing shut. Ah protested aboot it at the time. No' sure ah could even be arsed noo'.'

'Aye. It's aw away. That must be nearly twenty years ago mate,' said Frankie.

'Bet ye don't remember takin' they two lassies doon tae Irvine oan it. Doon tae the Ship Inn.'

Frankie laughed. 'Fuck sake, of course ah day. Mind ae the fish suppers? Cod the size ae ... *Squalo!*'

'Hey, mind the language. Ah don't speak *tally.*' They both laughed.

'Might come in handy soon, *fratello*,' said Frankie.

'Whit ye talkin' aboot?'

Frankie looked down at his shoes. 'Ah'm thinkin' ae goin' back, pal,' he said.

Washer was stunned. 'Straight up?'

'Been thinkin' aboot it, aye,' said Frankie.

'Oh ... right. When?'

'Dunno. In a wee while, mate,' said Frankie. 'Fuck all *here* for me.'

'*Ah'm* here for ye! Always have been,' said Washer. The evening was turning out worse than he'd anticipated.

'Ah know ye have, an' ah'll always be grateful for the way you an' yer family took ma mam in when ah had tae go away.'

'We're brothers, Frankie ... you an' me. Nothin' gets in the way ae that, ken?'

'Times are gonnae get tougher, Washer, an' muscle has a sell-by date, jist like every *other* kind ae meat.'

'Frankie, it's never been just aboot that wi' us ... you *ken* that!'

'Aye. But ye don't need me as an additional drain oan yer funds. An' wi' this strike rampin' up, the pressure oan aw these punters is gonnae reach breakin' point.' Washer stopped at the bench seat overlooking Knockentiber Amateurs football pitch. They sat watching fifteen or so teenage kids kicking their ball around. Typically, a fat kid was in goal, but untypically, he was making a decent fist of the role. Washer took out his Golden Virginia tin and deftly made roll-ups for each of them.

'Wish we were back that age again, eh?' said Frankie.

'Nae fuckin' worries, eh? Kickin' a ba' an' chasin' the lassies. Life was fuckin' simple, mate. Every bastart wis skint, but we aw seemed much happier. Whit the fuck happened?'

'We jist aw got older, Washer. Older an' less content. Everybody wants shit they cannae have. Thatcher calls it "dreams", but it's jist made everybody fuckin' bone-idle dreamers.' Frankie sighed and blew out a funnel of smoke. 'Ah've just had enough, mate. Ae bloody Thatcher, an' aw her fuckin' dreamers. Ae the bastart weather.'

'Look Frankie, ah ken it's been tough this last year, but hing in there. Somethin's comin'. Cannae tell ye the noo, but ye trust me, don't ye?' said Washer.

'Always, mate ... but ye dinnae need me draggin' ye doon further.'

'Whit ye talkin' aboot?' said Washer.

'Ye're payin' me a retainer ye cannae afford. Ah'm no' even *earnin'* it, mate. Ah'm yer biggest overheid.'

'Fuck that! Ah look after ma ain, Frankie. When this deal comes aff, nane ae us'll need tae piss aboot in the lower leagues again.'

'Ach, ah dunno, mate. Ah need a change ae scenery, ken?' Frankie Fusi sounded like his mind was made up.

Washer sucked the air in through his teeth then pursed his lips. He looked away into the distance. Frankie sensed that something significant was coming.

'Ah've been workin' oan a secret thing,' said Washer. Ah've no' been able tae let oan tae anybody, ken?'

'Don't tell us,' said Frankie. 'Yer the new James Bond?' They both laughed.

'Naw,' said Washer. 'Although ah could be. That cunt Moore's aulder than *me*!'

Another roll-up fashioned. More deep draws. 'It's a thing wi' Don McAllister.'

'Whit ... the *polis*?' said a surprised Frankie.

'Aye.'

'Are ye like ... under cover, then?' asked Frankie. 'Should ah be pattin' ye doon?'

'Don't talk pish! It's no' like that. It's mair ae a ... ah help him, he helps me type arrangement.' It was obvious that Washer was being deliberately evasive.

'Look, Washer, if ye cannae tell me, then *dinnae*. Ah understand. Ah'm gonnae be headin' anyway ... unless this is yer way ae tellin' me ah'm a fuckin' target!' Frankie's demeanour had changed. He never really suspected his close friend would have incriminated him for anything, but in the shifty, uncertain world they both inhabited, you could never be totally sure. Frankie Fusi looked directly into the eyes of his oldest and closest friend, and immediately he was ashamed for even entertaining the thought.

'There's no' much ah care aboot, Frankie. There's Molly, there's the dug … and God fuckin' help me, that eejit ae a boy … an' there's you!' Washer laughed and put his arm around Frankie's shoulder. 'An' no' necessarily in that order, either.' Washer stood up. 'C'mon, lets get somethin' aff that wee van, eh?'

They walked over the road and joined the back of the queue. Steam billowing out of the tiny flue on its roof indicated that on this Tuesday night business was good.

'Ye hear Crosshouse has been twinned wi' Las Vegas?' said Frankie. 'Only two places oan Earth wher' ye can pay for sex wi' chips!' Washer laughed.

'Let's get ours an' get back an' fuckin' spend them then,' he said.

Washer Wishart and Frankie Fusi walked back down Kilmaurs Road into Crosshouse, the tiny village where they had lived, loved and – until very recently – prospered for almost all of their lives. On the way, Washer Wishart told his friend of the deal he, Fat Franny Duncan and Nobby Quinn had made with Don McAllister and Doc Martin a year ago in a Galston barn. He told him of the terms of that deal, of the significant risks, and of the potential rewards of a fully legitimate business in return. He told enough of the story to persuade Frankie Fusi of the benefits of sticking around. For the immediately foreseeable future, at least.

Generally, Norma, things were fuckin' great at this time. Ah wis wakin' up wi' a massive stauner every mornin', an' it wis because everythin' wis sortin' itself oot. Ah paid Hairy Doug for a new mixin' desk, bunged Doc Martin a couple ae thou' for re-decoratin' an' even persuaded Grant tae up the band's weekly wage tae forty quid.

The cunt wis pullin' great songs oot his fuckin' arse, man. Ah'm thinkin' Oor debut LPs gonnae be better than Parallel Lines!

Turns oot he'd kept a book ae fuckin' poetry fae when he wis fifteen. A load ae it wis absolute shite, tae be honest. Ah love you … dae you love me? O how happy we'll always be … kinda pish, ken? Mind you 'Club Tropicana, drinks are free…' well, that's no' exactly Bob fuckin' Dylan either, eh?

Anyway, we've got a great fuckin' set ae tunes, an' for once, every cunt's oan the same page aboot it. Ah pulled in a favour aff some gagdie Washer kent wi' a camera, an he does us some new shots, an that ... an' we've got a contact at the wee studio doon near Glencairn Square, called Shabby Road.

Wan fly in the ointment ... but it wis turnin' intae a fuckin' big fly, ken? Wan the size ae a bastart jumbo jet, as it happens. Aw the money's runnin' oot. The band's bank account wis emptyin' quicker than the Buckfast aisle at Hogmanay ... mainly the cash Grant put in it, 'cos we'd no' actually made anythin' at that point. So, we agreed tae take it aw oot the bank. Ah ken that sounds mental but we jist didnae fuckin' trust the bank, ken? Noo, nae cunt trusts a bank! Mibbe we were jist ahead ae the times.

Ah decided tae tell Washer aboot it, expectin' a kick in the stanes, or at least a three-day bollockin' session ... but naw, the auld tosser says he'd like tae help oot. He says he wants tae invest in the band, an' that he'll become oor 'financial partner'!

Ah'm fuckin' gobsmacked at this, as ye can imagine. Cunt's never expressed an interest before an' noo he's acting aw Richard Branson! Ah wis oan the mushrooms a bit back then, an' the speed ... oan tap ae the medicine for the schizo-gig ... but ah still thought ah wis fuckin' hallucinatin'!

Fair play tae him though. Dosh appears, so ah start Biscuit Tin Records.

34

2nd August 1983

Wullie the Painter wasn't a clever man by conventional standards. He had no school certificates, no educational or training diplomas and, in 1972, he had even failed his cycle proficiency test. However, he was street smart. And he was convinced he had pieced together a cunning undercover plan in which – unfortunately for him – he was a pawn. Wullie had watched a lot of *Columbo*. *That scruffy wee cunt could figure anythin' oot in under an hour,* he'd told Des Brick before revealing his thesis. It had taken him a bit longer, but then the telly detective with the flasher's Mac had a lifetime of experience ... *an' a team ae scriptwriters,* Des had pointed out. Wullie the Painter was a comparative novice.

'Right, here's the script, Des,' said Wullie. Before he launched into it, Wullie outlined the basis of his research. Personal meetings and detailed discussions with Terry Connolly, Benny Dunlop and Ged McClure; the latter of which had ultimately resulted in Wullie getting headbutted. His very explanation of the whole story had been prompted by Des Brick's 'Whit the fuck happened tae *you*?' when he saw the twin black keekers. Wullie kept his covert role as Don McAllister's paid informer to himself though. Some details are best left out, he reckoned.

'Connolly's oan the vans up in Onthank. They're aw goin' like a fuckin' fair. Ye widnae believe it, Des! They ice-cream vans are jist a front for floggin' aw kinds ae illegal shite.'

'Fuck, Wullie ... that's hardly a massive surprise, is it?' said Des.

'Aye, but he's gettin' the gear affa the fuckin' McLartys,' Wullie revealed. 'An' the Fatman's jist lettin' it aw happen! Ah don't fuckin' get *that* bit,' said Wullie. 'Connolly's up front an' open aboot it aw wi' me, tae. Christ, *ah'm* even dain' the odd stint oan them as well.'

'Well, ah dinnae see whit yer problem is then. Yer benefittin', naw? A bit late tae be huvin' a moral dilemma, mate!'

'It's no' that, Des,' said Wullie. He was struggling to avoid blowing his cover and telling Des that his work on the vans was at the behest of – and paid for by – the local cops. 'It's bigger than that though. McClure fae that manky Quinns mob, is getting bags ae skag doon fae Glesga affa this fuckin' Gregor bruiser, Connolly's placing it an' distributin' it, an' – fuckin' get this – that wee Wisharts' prick, Benny Donald ower in Crosshouse is *washin'* aw the money.' Wullie the Painter took a deep breath. 'It's a fuckin' organised racket, Des, wi' the McLartys pullin' the strings. It's a fuckin' takeover, an' the three big knobs are dain' fuck aw aboot it,' said Wullie. He felt his blood pressure rising. Des Brick was impassive. Wullie appreciated that Des had his own personal shite to contend with, but still, his apathy was surprising to say the least.

'Look Wullie, ah dinnae ken whit tae tell ye, mate. If yer concerned for yer ain safety...' Des motioned towards Wullie's eyes, '... then back oot. Ah've done that. It's no' really that difficult. Try an' get a real fuckin' job.' The minute the words were out of his mouth, Des realised how ludicrous they sounded.

'Whit, alang wi' three million other folk! Fuck sake, Des ... it's no' like I've got a folder full ae glowin' references.'

This chat wasn't panning out the way Wullie the Painter had imagined. He'd looked on Des Brick as a mentor; someone to be looked up to. But now he felt little but pity. Des looked a shadow of the man he was a year ago. Effie Brick wouldn't live much longer than the turn of the year, but by all accounts she was upbeat and sanguine despite the care being essentially palliative. Des, on the other hand, looked like he had already given up. The strain had aged him dreadfully. His hair was thinning and grey. The tell-tale scissor marks of his 'short back an' sides' betrayed his current barber as Auld Joe, an eighty-year-old handyman who also washed windows. Around Onthank, an 'Auld Joe number two cut' was a sign of real financial difficulty. Whole families had them, even the women. Des Brick's jacket hung off him like it was two sizes too big for him. He was emaciated and pallid. If anything, Des looked like one dying from cancer.

'Ah'm sorry, Wullie. Ah'm shot ae it aw, noo. It was good while it lasted. Franny's got his ain problems, an' probably his time's came tae. Nothing lasts forever, pal.'

'Aye. Aw'right, Des. Jist one last thing though,' said Wullie.

'Sure, mate.'

'If aw this McLarty business is comin' back, why are the plods no' aw ower it like a rash?' Wullie felt he already knew the answer – *him* – if not the full rationale. But he needed to know if Des did too.

'Fuck knows, Wullie. But they cunts couldnae find their ain arseholes wi' a bullshit detector. How d'ye think we aw avoided the jail aw this time? That's probably yer answer, plain an' simple.'

With that, and Des Brick wishing his former colleague well, Wullie the Painter took his leave. Wullie didn't really do compassion. He felt desperately for Des, and obviously for Effie and the rest of his family, but he couldn't express it properly. Every well-intended comment invariably emerged framed in sarcasm or dripping in cynical humour. He was aware that his concern sounded false, and therefore Wullie the Painter decided that he wouldn't visit Des Brick again.

His next move was a meeting with Charlie Lawson to pass over his observations. He already suspected none of it would come us a surprise to him, and that subsequently, Wullie would still be in the dark about the bigger picture. When the bigger picture got its full Technicolor Cinemascope release, Wullie the Painter had to ensure that he remained out of the blinding searchlights reserved for its stars.

35

30th September 1983

'Ye dae realise how fuckin' difficult it is for me tae get here, aye?' Fat Franny Duncan was wheezing. He'd just climbed up the old stone steps of the keep at Dean Castle. In addition to this – and under instruction from others – he'd had to walk about two miles through the northern undergrowth to get there.

'Fuck sake, man. It's only a few steps. *Jesus!* Dae ye good tae lose a bit ae beef, anyway.'

The others in the room laughed at Charlie Lawson's dig. But Fat Franny Duncan did not.

'Ah wisnae talkin' aboot the *physical* difficulty, ya diddy. Ah wis talkin' aboot the fuckin' *time!*' said Fat Franny, still breathless.

The time and location of this emergency summit had indeed been unusual. Ten pm on a Friday night, at a publicly accessible heritage destination, albeit one that was currently closed to the public, seemed strange to all of them. Nevertheless, the five men – Fat Franny Duncan, Washer Wishart, Nobby Quinn, Charlie Lawson, and his boss, Detective Chief Superintendent Don McAllister – and sole woman, Magdalena Quinn, all sat around a decorator's trellis. A sixth male – Doc Martin – was absent, although why remained unexplained. It was dark in the Great Hall, but they had all brought torches. Franny shone his up to the great vaulted ceiling above them. He'd lived in Kilmarnock all of his life but he'd never been in this six-hundred-and-thirty-year-old building. He had to admit it was mightily impressive. Much more so than the Ponderosie. He briefly contemplated its likely asking price before Don McAllister's voice snapped him back to the meeting's purpose.

'Naebody outside of this room knows the full story, an' unfortunately that's the way it has tae stay for a while longer.'

The three non-coppers sighed in unison. It was like a reunion of Enid Blyton with her Famous Five, after alcoholism, divorce, gout and vanquished dreams had taken their toll.

'Things are developin' up in the East End. But the operation is aimed at takin' out the kingpins, no' just the foot-soldiers. So it has tae be water-tight. Nae loopholes. Nae potential for Donald fuckin' Findlay tae waltz in an' get aw the old guard off. So, ye need tae stick wi' it for a few months longer, right?'

There was no immediate response to Don McAllister. Eventually, Washer Wishart – the most eloquent among them – spoke.

'Look Mr McAllister, we've aw kent each other a long time. Never trusted each other. An' 'cos ae that, naebody went intae this … agreement, wi' their eyes shut. But circumstances are changin'. Personal *and* business.'

'Ah get that…' said Don.

'Wi' respect, ah'm no' sure ye dae!' said Washer. 'Years ago, wi' aw closed ranks an' helped each other drive the McLartys ootae Galston. But we didnae get much assistance fae ye then.'

Don McAllister didn't read books; he read people. It was a vital skill in his line of work. He sought to understand the motivations of those on the opposite side of law from him. To be a good copper, you had to empathise with the criminals. If you could appreciate what drove them to act in the way they did, you could anticipate, inter-cept and then turn that fragile trust to your advantage. Of course, some were way beyond any form of influence, but in Don's experi-ence, these were the exception. Most people drifted into crime as a consequence of circumstance, desperation and opportunity. Only a few chose the life as a specific career path. In Don's opinion, they didn't teach this people-focused analysis in Police Training College enough nowadays. But it had become vital to Don McAllister's strat-egy. He was convinced that some semblance of legitimacy existed in all of those here present. He had to trust his instincts. They had never let him down before, but there was a first time for everything. It was a tense position … for all of them.

'Different times, Washer,' said Don McAllister. 'But have ah no' turned a blind eye tae a lot ae yer collective activities since?'

'Aye. Fair enough,' said Fat Franny, 'but noo *we're* in different times. Ah cannae earn the same way 'cos ae ma mam. Ah'm huvin' tae diversify, an' this tape business ye set up isnae really takin' off.'

'Ah'm also worried aboot losin' ground wi' ma ain distributors,' said Washer Wishart. 'Ah cannae risk this drugs money goin' through these decent wee businesses ah've known aw ma life. We always said "nae fuckin' drug money" an' noo, that's aw there is.'

'And from our side,' said Magdalena Quinn, surprising no one present with her willingness to speak, 'no one can afford the protection anymore. The bettin' holds up a bit but ya need ta understand … most of these poor cuntys are now on strike. We got income fro' Cumnock, Auchinleck and that … no' just Galston.'

'Look, ah know all this. Life's shite for everybody. Ah get it! Ah didnae vote for Thatcher tae get back in either!' said Don. 'But we aw agreed oan a plan. Shook oan it, an' promises were made. Ah'm no' goin' back on these. Everybody here gets protected immunity an' set up wi' legit businesses. Mrs Quinn, Nobby … we're puttin' cash intae a fund for yer regional boxing clubs. It's protected. The licences'll get agreed before the whole McLarty operation round-up. Naebody's even gonnae connect you tae this. McClure is gonnae look like he acted oan his own.'

Nobby Quinn shrugged.

Don McAllister looked at Fat Franny next. 'You've got potentially the best fuckin' deal here! Rental video tapes is gonnae become a massive market, ye'll see … an' no' just for they mucky yins yer sellin' through the vans the noo. We've already sourced ye the players tae rent oot. We told ye we'd fix that after ye complained that Washer's boy's pal … the *singer* … had yer money, an' we did. Naebody welshed oan that deal, did they? Aw we asked is that ye aw kept schtum an' just let that yin go. We'll set ye up wi' a proper shop when aw this is by. Ye can conduct a legit business fae yer house, lookin' after yer ma. 'But we need tae lock Terry Connolly tight in wi' aw the McLartys, no' just that baldy fucker, Gregor Gidney.'

Washer looked up. He knew he was next.

'An' we told you at the beginnin', ye need tae find something totally legitimate and scalable tae "lose" their money in,' said Don. 'That way, when they eventually come lookin' for it aw, an' we make the sting, it'll fall at the door ae Benny Dunlop, an' you an' yer consortium don't get dragged in.'

'Finding somethin' legit … in Crosshoose … these days? More chance ae findin' a virgin at a Young Farmers' do … *after* they've aw been oan the Merrydown leg-openers.'

There was muted laughter. They recognised that the plan originally put forward last year by Don McAllister, via his envoy Doc Martin, hadn't materially changed, even if the timescale had stretched.

'So whit happens next … oan *your* side, ah mean?' asked Washer.

'Ah obviously cannae say too much about the Glasgow side. But it's nigh-oan impossible tae get a similar covert operation going oan up in the likes ae Ruchazie. There's already too much fear. Everybody just boards up their windaes when the gang frighteners come out.' He paused and looked behind him. 'It's called *Operation Double Nougat*. Draw yer own conclusions why. Used to be Single Nougat but noo it's focused on two centres.' Don already felt he had probably said too much, but he acknowledged they were all in a pact, for better or worse. 'We've got an insider just monitering the three individuals doon here. It's no' anybody ye'se know so don't go huntin' an' runnin' the risk ae blowin' their cover.' Don folded his arms. 'End ae the day, this is *aw* about trust. We aw need to completely trust each other.'

Their objective might not have had the far-reaching implications of The Manhatten Project, but if it worked it would change the local landscape forever, and they also had their very own 'Fat Man'. Fat Franny briefly considered suggesting they all get their cocks out, but for the others a stiff handshake seemed to suffice.

36

Max Mojo was unsure what to make of his dad's offer. It had come
out of nowhere. Max even began to think that Washer Wishart
might have been psychic. Like Darlinda from the *Daily Record*.
Washer had raised the subject of a financial investment in Biscuit
Tin Records before Max had even been ready to lay bare the fact that
they were careering uncontrollably towards being skint. His offer
– the equivalent of an advance against any future sales – was fifty
thousand pounds. Max was initially staggered that Washer even had
that to spare, given the number of gloomy faces that currently hung
about the manse waiting for scraps of work.

But Washer had phrased it in accountancy terms that Max didn't
fully comprehend. Bottom line was, The Miraculous Vespas' new
sugar daddy was now Max's actual one. Max would remain manager,
with complete control over all music-related decisions. He simply
had to consult Washer or Gerry Ghee fortnightly on all planned
expenditure. That was good enough for Max, and since he was
facing increasing concerns from Grant about where their adventure was headed, he could now report that it was headed – in the
short term at least – to Glencairn Square, Shabby Road Studios and
a demo-recording date that very morning with owner and erratic
record producer, Clifford X. Raymonde.

Promoted by the bouffant-haired studio boss, a *Battle of the
Bands*-type circuit was emerging in Kilmarnock. In a typical week,
disparate bands, such as Penetration, So What!, Nyah Fearties and
The Graffiti Brothers, played well-attended gigs at The Sandrianne,
The Broomhill Hotel and – as The Miraculous Vespas had only
recently done – The Hunting Lodge. The more established groups

sometimes got to play the Grand Hall, but since a legendary riot at a Sweet gig there in 1973 – immortalised in their song 'Ballroom Blitz' – the council were very wary of making it more widely available. For Max, the Grand Hall was the pinnacle of their immediate aspirations. His current plan was to establish a small but cultish base of operations. Although Postcard's influence remained, it was the only Scottish-based label out there. And since Orange Juice had now moved to London and Polydor Records, the future for the Glaswegian label was uncertain. Max Mojo saw the potential. Maybe the less heavy-metal-orientated of the local bands might eventually become part of the Max Mojo music revolution. Maybe an East Ayrshire *Tamla Motown* philosophy might ultimately shift attention and focus south-west from the current Glasgow scene. For Max, the possibilities seemed endless. But one of the biggest problems was the lack of a supportive, cogent scene. The more accessible venues had their own particular identity and clientele, and although the myriad of local bands that were now filtering through Shabby Road tried to stay close to their home ground, invariably they would have to play difficult gigs in foreign territories. For Max Mojo's band, their potential nemesis was the Sandrianne. In a week-long period in late September, the band had played all of the principal Kilmarnock venues. Only the Sandrianne remained.

The Sandrianne in John Finnie Street was formerly the town's first respectable theatre. When known as *The Opera House*, it had enjoyed a few good years of unusual popularity before punters began to seek their cultural enjoyment further afield. Now, though, the Sandrianne was better known as a biker's pub. It drew the heavier of the local rock bands to its velvety cushioned bosom. A group apparently named after a make of Mod scooter was going to *have* to be pretty fucking miraculous. But the band's growing self-confidence – as well as their ability – meant tough gigs like the Sandrianne weren't the sphincter-tightening ordeal that they might've been only a few weeks before. By the Sandrianne show at the end of September 1983, The Mysterious Vespas had played twenty-two gigs, including one at

Glasgow's Queen Margaret Union, supporting the Glaswegian band Bourgie Bourgie. The gig itself was great, but afterwards Max had lost their fee – and all of the money the band had with them – in an inter-band drinking competition.

Grant Delgado wore leather at the Sandrianne. As did Maggie, although her leather was restricted to a bra. The Motorcycle Boy's full-faced helmet and biker persona made him a hit before a note had even been played. Simon Sylvester made no concession to location and dressed as he did for everyday circumstances. Having given up on the outré clothing styles favoured by the manager, he had his red-and-black Dennis the Menace-style jumper and ripped blue Levis. Max Mojo was the main stand-out. He sported tan DM boots, red trousers and a baggy white shirt with a grey pin-striped waistcoat. The black eye-patch was present and correct, but he had recently started wearing a bowler hat and walking with a new cane. Max justified its flamboyant purchase to Grant with reference to the life-saving qualities of its predecessor. A Crosshouse *Clockwork Orange* was the intended vibe. The music was also tailored to suit. Grant led the band through covers of 'Paranoid', 'Purple Haze' and Led Zeppelin's 'Ramble On', all filtered to fit their own jangly, harmonised sensibilities. But 'The First Picture' was harder edged than it had previously been delivered. The song's underlying melodic grace couldn't be obscured though, and, while not receiving the reception it would have on home turf such as The Hunting Lodge, the night at the Sandrianne was a qualified success. Unfortunately, Max tripped over his cane on the way out to Jimmy Stevenson's van at the end of the night. He fell forward into the first motorbike, and the remainder – parallel-parked down the street – fell like dominoes. The denim-and-leather-clad Sandrianne clientele chased the van as far as the Railway Arches. Max Mojo made a mental note that John Finnie Street was now off limits.

'Well now. What *do* we have here?' Clifford X. Raymonde stood back to get a full view of the four band members.

The studio boss asking the question was an odd mix of styles in his *own* right. He had skin so dark and leathery it could have been coated in creosote. He had a hairstyle that rivalled Barry Gibb in its length and perfectly coiffured structure. A carefully trimmed dark stubble line could have drawn comparisons with Captain Black of the *Mysterons*. He wore John Lennon-style granny glasses, but with two different coloured lens; 'It helps me see the colour of your soul,' he would later tell Maggie. A purple-hued paisley-patterned shirt with the cuffs turned up once, a blue cravat and a pair of beige cords with brown-leather knee patches made up the ensemble. And he was barefoot, Sandie Shaw-style. Clifford had an inch-long fingernail on the smallest finger of his right hand. Despite fierce competition for the accolade, his teeth were perhaps his most striking characteristic. They were terrible. When he smiled – as he did almost constantly – his mouth looked like the result of a prison riot. The studio mirrored its owner's uncoordinated taste. Carpet-tile samples were nailed to almost every surface in the studio spaces. Mould spores grew up the base of the walls in the other areas, and Maggie was convinced a cockroach had crawled for cover under a desk when the studio boss flicked the switch to a bare light bulb in the studio's 'store room'.

'Hmm … nice cheekbones. Hair maybe needs a *wave* or two. Like the make-up, love. *Very* striking,' he said theatrically to Grant Delgado. 'And who do we have under the, em … helmet?' Max Mojo pushed himself to the front. 'Ooh! An *eye*-patch … nice gimmick, son. What do *you* play?'

'Ah'm the fuckin' manager. An' by the by … they dinnae need fashion advice.' He scanned the producer up and down several times. 'They *need* a bastart recording!'

'Well *you're* a bright young thing and no mistake,' said Clifford. 'I'm Clifford X. Raymonde, but everybody calls me X-Ray … or maybe just X, once we've got to know each other better, okay?'

The band nodded. Max Mojo pursed his lips and eventually said 'Aye. Fine.'

Max was way out of his depth in this situation but couldn't admit that to the others, to X-Ray, or even to himself. He had no clue about the technical process of recording. The veteran studio boss homed in on it right away. He had listened to their initial songs with apparent disinterest, but he had heard something startling. His tactical brain kicked into gear.

'Okay, people,' he said. 'Bring your material in and Colum there will get you properly settled.' X-ray picked up the grubbiest, most well-thumbed book Max had ever seen. It was light blue and had a picture of Tony Hatch on the torn and sellotaped front cover. Max had noticed it on the way in because of its title: *So You Want To Be in the Music Business*. 'I'm just away to my office. I'll see you soon,' said X-ray, with a wink towards Max. He headed for a door with 'bogs' scrawled on it.

'Fuck sake, how long ye gonnae *be*?' asked Max.

'Oh, I take me time. Savour the experience, y'know? Sometimes, I even just wait there for the next one.'

'Fuckin' hell, Max ... how much is this aw costin'? Are we payin' this auld hippy by the track, or by the hour?' Grant was unusually rattled.

'Jist as long as it's no' by the shite, eh?' said Simon Sylvester.

'Look, let's jist get fuckin' set up an' started, eh? Dinnae worry aboot the cost ae it. Ah'll deal wi' that. Ah jist want somethin' we can actually fuckin' use ootae this,' said Max, holding the helmeted Motorcycle Boy by the arm to avoid him falling over a large pot plant.

Despite his bizarre appearance, Clifford X. Raymonde had a reputation of note in terms of drawing out hidden depths in the recorded performances of many of the individuals who had passed through the tiny collection of rooms in the refurbished first-floor flat at the back of a Chinese Restaurant that now constituted Shabby Road Studios. The studio had begun in the early 70s as a one-room four-track operation in the converted lounge of the flat in which Clifford was living at the time. He had also played in various blues bands throughout that decade, and while never reaching any recognisable levels of national success, most of them were well-regarded locally. Clifford had developed his interest in sound and recording and had invested his earnings from music first into buying the flat, and then furnishing it with basic recording equipment. His interest in experimentation – with sound *and* with the potential of drug-enhancement – had brought with it equal measures of interest from both musicians and the local drug squad.

Max Mojo wandered around the six small rooms that now made up the expanded Shabby Road Studios. X-Ray might have been a bizarre old tosser, but he clearly commanded entertainment business respect. Signed photos of Jimmy Savile, Mickie Most, Alexis Korner and – bizarrely – STV's children's presenter, Glen Michael, adorned the walls of the fifty-five-year-old producer's studio. Record sleeves were strewn about, and, despite his young Youth Opportunities Scheme-funded assistant Rhona's attempts to tidy up, the studio seemed to be in a state of perpetual chaos. But Max knew decent contemporary bands had recorded here. He had heard a rumour from Hairy Doug that Aztec Camera had been to the studio the year before and had spent so much of their money there that they had to hitch a lift back to East Kilbride.

$$\frac{1}{2}$$

By the end of the first day, X-Ray had noticed that tensions in the band were being exacerbated by Max's unpredictable outbursts and unhelpful suggestions. Despite the manager's interventions, however, the experienced sound man immediately detected something remarkable in the band's spontaneous jams as they warmed up. Max had advocated bringing in a Hammond organ to bolster a part of the chorus. He had even suggested closing off the pavement outside the Chinese restaurant to allow a small crane to transport one in through the front windows of the flat. He even forced X-Ray to look at a crude line drawing he'd made showing how the windows could be removed to allow the organ's passage. This was the last straw; X-Ray expelled him from the studio.

With Max out of the way, X-Ray got to work. He drew out a line of cocaine for each of the band members. The four of them stood in a row in front of his wooden desk like kamikaze pilots about to attain a high level of spiritual training.

'This will relax you all. Get it down ya!' said X-Ray Raymonde. Predictably, Simon Sylvester stepped up first. He took out a ten-pound note he'd pick-pocketed from Max earlier. He flattened it out and, using the base of his right hand, swept the fine white substance onto it. A bemused X-Ray watched him tilt his head back and attempt to funnel the drugs down into his nostril.

'Oooffffor fuck's sake!' He staggered back, choking, his upper lip sporting a powdery moustache.

'Yer meant tae snort it ... ah think,' said Grant, looking at X-Ray for validation. A slight nod, and then Grant and Maggie promptly followed. They all then looked at the Motorcycle Boy. He took the paper currency. He put his head down, opened his visor, snorted loudly and then coughed. He snapped the visor shut again. The others laughed as he visibly shuddered, then held his thumbs aloft like a faceless Paul McCartney.

'Wow, what a strange cat,' said X-Ray.

'Ye dinnae fuckin' ken the half ae it, man,' said Grant. 'He caught aggra-phobia aff a hypnotist an' noo we've had tae paint the inside ae that helmet tae look like his fuckin' bedroom.'

'Boy ... that must be real good ching,' said X-Ray before scooping his rail up with his long, designed-for-the-purpose finger nail. 'Right ... let's make some magic!'

An hour later, and The Miraculous Vespas were bouncing around the studio to New Order's 'Blue Monday' being played at eardrum-bursting volume by Colum Crabbe, the studio's young sound engineer. Simple Minds' 'Love Song' followed, this time with X-Ray joining in with the dancing.

'Are you feeling it?' screamed X-Ray. 'Is it in you?'

'Ah want tae be in *you*?' Grant yelled in Maggie's ear. She pulled him away towards X-Ray's impromptu office. He smiled sagely as he watched them go.

Maggie had smoked dope plenty of times but, like the others, this was her first experience with cocaine. She quickly pulled Grant's cock into her and arched her back over as far as it would go until her arms reached the base of the cistern. Maggie felt that normal amazing sensation of being filled up as Grant went into her as far as he could, and then the equally wonderful rub as he pulled out. It made her want to be stretched and entered forever. Grant actually felt like he would be able to go *on* like this forever. He'd never experienced such an energy rush. It was intense. Grant came before Maggie but continued thrusting into her after he'd recovered his stroke, and she soon reached the same heightened state of euphoria.

'Ah fuckin' love you!' she said to him.

'Ah fuckin' love *everybody*!' he replied.

Grant had no idea how long they had been in the toilet. It could've been hours, or even days. As it was, forty-five minutes had passed. When they came out, the Motorcycle Boy was battering the drums like Keith Moon and Simon Sylvester was lying on his back singing 'What a Wonderful World' into a hand-held microphone.

'Okay, now we've loosened up a bit, everybody ready?' said X-Ray. Grant wondered if he gave this level of personal service to all of his patrons. He began to appreciate why it was called Shabby Road.

Through the remainder of that afternoon, and the majority of the next day, X-Ray Raymonde experimented with the band and the four songs they had to work with. He was really impressed by 'The First Picture', but felt something was missing from their sound. He acknowledged that it would bring him into conflict with the teenage impresario when he returned, as instructed, on the Thursday. Nevertheless, he knew what he was doing. He was now determined to *earn* the £2,000 fee that he'd chanced his arm in asking for. Using the full range of his eight-track machine, he recorded the rhythm tracks separately. X-Ray normally worked this way; building the backing tracks bit by bit. In a move designed to defuse Max's likely aggravation, he added a bit of guide organ to the drums, bass and rhythm guitar parts.

X-Ray got an excitable Maggie to set up her bass drum, snare and hi-hat. Simon Sylvester was told to plug his bass directly into the mixer so they could experiment with a reggae feel for one of the songs.

It all felt unbelievably inspiring to Grant. He stood by X-Ray's side as the producer explained why the drums were being 'bounced' down to one track, freeing up other tracks for 'overdubs'.

Grant recorded his vocals in a number of different ways. He stood, he hunched, he went back into the toilet, and he lay on his back, as Simon – and Marvin Gaye – had once done. The wily producer filtered all of these sounds through his home-made equaliser and compressor units and onto a quarter-inch tape recorder. Once complete, X-Ray mixed each section separately and spliced the parts of quarter-inch tape together manually.

The old producer had gained Grant's trust, and now he pounced. Earlier, when Max and the band had assumed X-Ray was attempting to set a Guiness World Record for the longest time taking a shite, he was actually in the toilet hastily drafting a publishing contract for Grant Delgado to sign. The contract was to a subsidiary company – Mondo Bongo Publishing – and, in return for an advance, Grant would receive 65 percent of applicable future songwriting royalties. The remainder went to Mondo Bongo. This seemed like an extremely good deal to Grant when it was explained to him privately by Clifford X. Raymonde. Max hadn't come back yet, but X-Ray had convinced Grant that since he was, and would most likely remain, the composer of all of the band's songs, the publishing contract only applied to him. What wasn't fully explained was the process of royalty payment – or that Grant, in not fully reading the small print – had agreed to the rights to his songs being owned by Mondo Bongo in perpetuity. Grant *did* persuade X-Ray to subdivide his cut. It was to be 85 percent for Grant and 5 percent each for the others. He felt that was only fair. He had originally intended for Max to receive the same 5 percent but X-Ray persuaded him to drop this. Max would be fine. He'd see to that by helping him with the label. X-Ray conceded the band split, but in highlighting it was highly unusual, said he would only do so if the terms of the contract remained between them at present. The advances were £10,000 for Grant and £1,000 each for the others, but paid only to the others after they had recorded and pressed their first single.

$

At the end of three long, wired days, 'The First Picture' and new song, 'Take It, It's Yours' had been caught on tape. The other two were left for the time being although X-Ray Raymonde had plans for them. 'The First Picture' was The Miraculous Vespas' opening gambit, and the band and their emotional manager were justifiably proud of it. Grant knew it was a good song. Everyone else did too.

'Really enjoyed that, Max,' said X-Ray. 'No hard feelings about earlier, eh?'

'Ah wis' a bit fuckin' pissed off, ah huv tae tell ye. Ah thought aboot comin' back an' fuckin' torchin' the place!' he admitted with a straight face.

X-Ray laughed out loud.

Max Mojo couldn't understand why he was laughing.

'Look Max,' he said after the others had gone. 'I think you might have something pretty special here. Grant's a great, understated singer and his songs are just wonderful.'

Max nodded his agreement adding, 'Aye ... so?'

X-Ray laughed again at what he assumed was simply youthful disdain for experience. X-Ray Raymonde had seen it all before. He had reached an age where he found it charming and endearing. 'Get him on a contract. Tie him in. And then let's make a proper record.' he said.

Max pondered this.

'If you can prove it's commercially viable to release an independent record, the sky's the limit. If anyone can make a record ... anyone can have a record label. Make it yourself, sell it yourself ... cut out all of the middle men. Keep the profits..!'

'Who gives a fuck aboot the money?' said Max. 'We're no' doin' this tae live aff the profits, man!'

'Yeah, you think that now, Max ... but just wait until you see where the money goes if you don't.'

'We dinnae have a fuckin' record deal yet mate,' Max admitted, as if this was a major new revelation.

'You're not hearing me. Put it out *yourself*, son. You told me your dad was subbing the whole show. Biscuit Tin Records, you said. Well ... go for it then! You only live once, Max.'

Unusually, Max Mojo had nothing to say. His brain was doing somersaults.

'It isn't really about whether you can do the recording, or manufacture, or distribution yourself. Anybody with a decent inheritance could do that ... it's about a spirit; an attitude. Have you got that?' pushed X-Ray.

Max responded to the challenge X-Ray Raymonde had just laid down. He nodded his head furiously. No words were necessary. They shook hands. Although he admired Postcard, Max hadn't previously thought about self-financed gigs, recordings and promotions. It would certainly cut out some of the planned trips to London. Soon they would have a proper acetate, and Max had intended coercing Grant back south to follow-up on his Morrison Hardwicke/Boy George connections. If they went to London in the New Year, they could now focus on distribution and trying to get it on Radio 1. He was also visualising another Billy Sloan encounter, although he had already resolved that this next one would be in McDonalds.

Without knowing it, both Clifford X. Raymonde and Max Mojo now had the key to immortality in their hands. They just needed to find the right door.

37

It was the most content Fat Franny Duncan had been for almost two years. He was sat at the kitchen table in the Ponderosie, surrounded by sheafs of complex paperwork and unopened cardboard boxes. *Credit where it was due*, he thought. Don McAllister's predictions about the viability of this new business plan had come to fruition, and at a faster pace than either of them had anticipated. Fat Franny had been permitted to take delivery of a warehouse full of new Philips VCRs. He had then been allowed to distribute these around Onthank and charge a weekly rental for them. Fat Franny could then increase his profits by renting VHS tapes to the same punters. Many of these tapes were being imported from Amsterdam and were pornographic in nature. The ice-cream vans – fronted by Terry Connolly and now also Wullie the Painter – were the distribution mechanisms for the business, with customers ordering titles by number from a monthly updated chart that the local paper boys delivered on their morning rounds. At the end of 1983, around 10 percent of UK households had a VCR. In Onthank – an impoverished, working-class area suffering the worst that Thatcher's Britain could throw at it – the figure was more than four times the national average. And *all* of it down to Fat Franny Duncan's change of business direction.

This had all been achieved by the collaboration with Don McAllister and Fat Franny's part in Operation Double Nougat. The Ayrshire part of the operation sought to lure the fearsome Malachy McLarty and his crime family from Glasgow into a complex trap whereby they would have assumed control of various criminal business interests in order to push hard drugs and other stolen goods in the communities from a network of mobile sources. Increased surveillance and increased fear in Glasgow's East End had seen the operation stall of late but, as the year drew to a close, it seemed that things were heating up again in and around Kilmarnock. The on-off miners' disputes were beginning to cut deep. Initial resolve from many of the peripheral Ayrshire communities had turned to struggle and then desperation around the festive season. Operation Double Nougat's leaders were predicting a ramping up of activity in the first few months of 1984. In Glasgow's East End, hope and despair had long been the catalysts for dependency and addiction, and the violent exploitation with which it goes hand in hand. Don McAllister's squad were as prepared as they thought they could be.

This had all changed Fat Franny Duncan's fortunes, though. He now envisaged – as Don McAllister said he would – a legitimate business rising out of the ashes of the ice-cream van wars. He was grateful. He hadn't been a decent man. He had instructed so many things he wasn't proud of. So many crimes committed and so many people hurt. He had spent many dark nights of the soul during the last six months. He had resolve but was determined to apply it differently. While Fat Franny Duncan couldn't claim it was a wonderful life, he was very thankful for this second chance.

Fat Franny imagined himself controlling a portfolio of shops when the *vermicelli* eventually settled. He was going to name the business *Blockbusters* after his mum's new favourite TV show. Although increasingly frail and house-bound, Rose Duncan's mental condition seemed to have stabilised in the previous few months. Fat Franny knew that she'd never fully recover, but having her able to converse with him periodically and remember things that had happened just days before as opposed to when she was only five, made him blissfully happy. She'd even started saying 'Can I have a "P" please, Bob?' on the occasions when she needed Fat Franny to help her go to the toilet. He couldn't wait to see her face when she saw the Christmas present he'd bought her. It was an electric chair that would be fitted to a rail going up the stairs. It would allow her to recover some independence in getting back up to her bedroom without Fat Franny having to carry her.

He put away his paperwork and smiled. Takings were up on the previous weeks. It was a steady climb in profitability, and he didn't even need to leave the house. He'd handed over full control of his previous business lists, debts and connections to Terry Connolly. That's all it had taken. *Why hadn't he done this years ago?* He smiled at the thought.

'Ma? Are ye ready for yer soup?' It was just about time for a special Christmas edition of *Blockbusters*. 'Can I have a "P & Ham" please Bob?' she had said earlier.

Fat Franny went through to the living room where the theme tune was already playing. Rose Duncan looked like she was asleep, her head simply resting over to one side. But Fat Franny knew. He placed the tray with her soup bowl and plate of bread, buttered and with the crusts removed, down on her small folding table. He lifted her glasses off her face and dabbed the saliva that was dribbling out of the side of her mouth with his sleeve. He leaned over and gently kissed her cheek before wiping away his own tears that had fallen there.

'You jist have a wee sleep, Mam. Ah'll record Bob an' we can watch him later, eh?'

Fat Franny Duncan went back through to the kitchen and telephoned for an ambulance.

05: **EVERYBODY'S ON TOP OF THE POPS...**

Is yer tape recorder still oan, hen? Aye. Right, this next bit goes pretty fuckin' fast, so strap yersel in! Any bits a cannae properly mind ae, ah'll jist make up, aw'right?

Sorry Norma ... but that's the best ah can dae. Ah wis wallopin' that much fuckin' Charlie, ma visage looked like that French mimin' cunt wi' the permanently white face, ken?'

It aw started great. Everybody loved everybody else. It wis like that fuckin' Coca-Cola advert. Perfect fuckin' harmony, ken? The Smiths brought oot 'Charming Man' and we aw freaked oot when it got oan Top ae the Pops. Ah remember sayin' tae them, that'll be us soon. That prick Simon says 'Whit dae ye mean "us"?' aw fuckin' gallus an' that ... but ah let that yin pass. Briefly thought ae swappin' the cunt for him ootae The Fall ... ken the yin that Mark E. Smith had jist punted? Cannae mind ae his name noo.

But the fucker got me a Cabbage Patch wean for Christmas an' ah forgave the cunt. They were as rare as fuck back then. Ah'm certain the bam nicked it oot fae under some poor wee bastart's tree, but still ... it wis the thought that counted, eh?

38

Following a spate of loud and prolonged arguments in the wake of
the Campervan revelation, Grant Delgado decided to move out of
his mother's house. The publishing advance paid to him offline by
Clifford X. Raymonde made up the bulk of the £16,000 purchase
price for a first-floor flat in Barbadoes Road. Its tropical-sounding
name hid the irony of a street regularly flooded by the bursting
of the adjacent Kilmarnock Water banks. While this had left the
ground-floor properties vulnerable, the first-floor ones had always
escaped. Grant took advantage of the low cost of the area and, in the
first week of 1984, said goodbye to the terraced house in Onthank in
which he had grown up. In the months between his decision to leave
home and his actual departure, relationships between him and Senga
had improved. He came across as laid back, but he was a headstrong
and determined young man, and while he had been less than careful
with Fat Franny's money, the threat of serious retribution from the
Fatman had disintegrated along with his reputation and his reach.
Senga could see that the band was more than just a means of *fan-
nying about* and that Grant had a real musical talent. Another early
source of conflict had been his decision to avoid college but she
now understood his reasons for that. It had helped Senga come to
terms with him moving out to know that Maggie wouldn't be automatically moving in. Senga had been a little surprised at that but the
relationship Grant had with his girlfriend was often as strange and
undivinable as her.

Senga too had made some big decisions, pre-Christmas. With
Grant getting on with his life, she had decided to take a burgeoning
but tentative relationship with a widower from Saltcoats to a new
level. They had met at a classical music club in the Dick Institute.

His name was Peter and he was a retired lawyer, some ten years older than her. He'd seemed very keen and initially she'd been a bit overwhelmed by his attention and interest. Peter spoke to Senga in ways for which she had no frame of reference. Her reluctance to let him get closer was solely based on the fear that her background was too incompatible with his and that she would ultimately embarrass herself. But Peter genuinely didn't seem to care about that. He found her great fun. He loved that she spoke her mind and that whatever was inside her just came out unfiltered by any sense of false decorum. It took a while for Senga to be relaxed with this, but now here she was, herself contemplating a move away from Onthank. On Christmas Day, Peter had asked her and her teenage kids to move to Saltcoats. He had a big detached house that he now rattled around in on his own. It had a large tree-lined garden and beyond its fence line, a panoramic view of Arran. Sophie and Andrew had been a bit hesitant at first, fearing losing contact with their friends, but when they saw the size of what would be their new bedrooms, their inhibitions fell away one by one.

Everyone was moving on, and *getting* on. Past lives and past memories were gradually being stored away in locked compartments. With Grant gone, nothing now kept Senga Dale tied to Onthank.

12th January 1984

A play of 'The First Picture' acetate on Radio Clyde's New Music programme was the Holy Grail for The Miraculous Vespas. The programme went out late on Thursdays; so late in fact that it was actually Friday. The programme began at midnight and ran to two am. It was part of a wildly eclectic week, which featured folk, country & western and jazz music on different nights, interspersed with Dr Dick's Midnight Surgery and the charismatic Dr Superbad's Soul Show on the Saturday night. Tom Russell's rock show, featuring metal bands such as Anthrax and AC/DC, made up the vibrant scheduling mix. But Billy Sloan was Max Mojo's only target. The DJ had built a reputation for promoting new, edgier music as far back as his 'Disco Kid' column in the *Sunday Mail*, covering the rise of uniquely Scottish bands such as The Associates and Big Country.

Max knew an endorsement from someone like Billy Sloan would make it much easier to get the eventual record distributed, especially if feedback from his listeners was positive. The programmes were rigidly 'themed', but it was Grant who had noticed that the DJ had been gradually introducing a section in the middle known as 'Ones To Watch'. Max had made another C90 with the two songs recorded by Clifford X. Raymonde. Grant had then used it to make another four. The original first-generation tape got lost because neither of them had labelled it. They scooped up the five and stuck them in a brown envelope.

'So whit's the plan?' asked Grant.

'We head up tae the fuckin' grid th'night. Sloan does this DJ gig thing at Night Moves. We'll see the cunt there, an' he'll take the tape,' said Max.

'Ye seem awfa sure ae that, Max.'

'Me an' Billy Sloan? We're like *that*, man. Ah bought the bastart a fuckin' steak. He owes me!'

They caught the bus up to Glasgow. They went to the Horseshoe Bar for a few pints beforehand and then headed up Renfield Street's slope into the angular driving rain. When they turned the corner into Sauchiehall Street, Grant's hopes dipped. A large queue had formed. It wasn't a night to be outside, though he had at least worn a long coat. Max's bomber jacket was absorbing the water like a sponge, and his hair – a sculpted concoction held in place by a combination of orange juice and sugar – was turning into a sweet paste.

'Max, let's fuckin' go, man! This is pish,' said a miserable Grant. 'It's fuckin' freezin'.'

'Yer a moanin'-faced cunt, *you*! Where's yer fuckin' commitment tae the cause?' Max had spotted interesting activity further up the street. 'C'mon ya walloper,' he said, dragging a sullen Grant Delgado towards the side of a Chinese restaurant.

'Gonnae let us gie ye a hand up the stairs, mate?' Max picked up a guitar case.

'Fuck off,' said a heavy-set roadie.

'Ah'll bum ye a twenty?' said Max Mojo hopefully.

'Gie's peace, ya prick!' said the roadie.

'Look pal, we've got a band…'

'Big wow … Who fuckin' disnae?'

'We jist need a break, man, fuck sake,' Max pleaded. 'Ah've got a tape ah'm try in' tae get tae Billy Sloan … so the cunt'll play it oan his radio show.' Max looked distraught. Grant couldn't be certain he wasn't actually crying.

'Fuck sake, son,' said the roadie. 'If it means that much tae ye … make it forty, an' then grab a drum case each, an' up ye go.'

'Jesus Christ, at least Dick Turpin wore a mask!' Max handed over the cash.

'Anybody stops ye, tell them yer wi' Kenny,' said Kenny, the roadie.

Max and Grant climbed the precarious, wet, metal fire escape stair carefully. Underneath it, and outside in the narrow passageway, chickens were being beheaded by machete-wielding kitchen staff. Once inside the club, they put the drums down near the stage. No one stopped them. No one asked who they were with. They spotted Billy Sloan over at the DJ booth.

'Look,' said Max. 'There's the cunt there!' Billy Sloan was talking to three other people. Max burst through them and addressed the DJ directly.

"Member me, Billy?' said Max, smiling broadly. Billy looked around for a bouncer. His colleagues instinctively took a step backward.

'Aye. Sure, pal. Sure ah dae,' he said, although he looked like he didn't.

'Ah'd just had ma shoes nicked. Ah bought ye yer dinner … aboot six months ago. Yours wis cooked, mine's wis still fuckin' breathin'. Ah spewed ma bastart ring that night, by the way.' Max reached into his pocket. All four strangers took another step back. 'Hey, nae sweat,' said Max. 'It's a fuckin' demo tape, no' a blade, man.'

They all looked relieved. A sodden Grant looked a bit embarrassed. 'Whit ye called, then?' said Billy Sloan.

Max told him.

Billy Sloan was accustomed to any manner of *gallus* corner boys sticking cassettes in his hands or his pockets, but the vast majority were rubbish. Nothing about these two dripping-wet chancers hinted at a different outcome. But like everyone in the music industry, the DJ was driven by the chance discovery of the next big thing. So he took the tape, promising to listen to it, but nothing further.

Max Mojo grunted a profanity, but Grant Delgado politely said thanks.

Max and Grant hung around the nightclub to see a new band called The Big Wheel, led by the Stiff Little Fingers frontman Jake Burns. They rattled through a lacklustre set. Grant knew The Miraculous Vespas had better songs and more attitude already. They should've been playing here on the Glasgow circuit, rather than paying opportunistic roadies well over the odds to jump the queue to get in. They only had enough money for one pint, and they shared it. They had missed the last bus back to Kilmarnock and spent a frozen night shivering in the dark, dead shadows of Anderston Bus Station, amongst the pimps and the prostitutes. With his last pieces of change, Grant finally got hold of Maggie from a telephone box the next morning and she drove up to Glasgow in the Campervan to pick them up. As they drove down Argyle Street, Max looked forlornly out the back window. It was grey, dull and hammering down in stair-rods. He was *still* shivering.

39

18th January 1984

Fat Franny Duncan had filled six bin-bags with his mum's old clothes. He had initially felt that he'd just leave everything as it was. He hadn't entered the room since the day his mum had passed away. It was understandably musty. He opened the curtains, and then the windows behind them. He turned around and saw things that were so familiar they had almost become a part of her. All of these items had a story that Fat Franny could instantly visualise. A frayed blue blanket that Rose had wrapped him up in when he'd come home freezing after falling through ice at the Kay Park lake. He'd have been about eight at the time. Framed photos of Franny progressing through childhood and developing into the man he was now; her pride and joy. An unfinished 1,000 piece jigsaw puzzle of Kilmarnock Cross, which he'd got her to help her remember. Numerous vases containing flowers from Paper Roses, the new florist in town; the flowers having long since died.

Fat Franny Duncan sat in his mum's armchair ruminating on the emptiness he felt. His mum's death had been painless. She had been at peace, with herself if not her turbulent domestic past. It was Fat Franny who had often been awkward and tense near the end. He acknowledged now that feelings of loss about her decline hadn't really been about her at all. They had been about him. For him; the man that he might once have been had he taken a different path.

It had taken three weeks for him to enter this room, because he knew it would force him to contemplate his own mortality and confront all of the choices he had made in his own life. The things he had done that, had she known about them, would've changed the way she felt about him. He was grateful that she didn't know, but equally determined to use his shameful regret as a catalyst for change.

The Ponderosie was massive, having been knocked together years earlier. He had no real need for the extra space, although more and more cardboard boxes filled with dodgy VHS tape stock were appearing by the week. Fat Franny had also felt that gutting the house and removing the traces of his mum's life would have been disrespectful to her memory. When he thought about it further, though, she'd had no real emotional attachment to the place. Rose had grown up in the neighbouring village of Fenwick, just up the A77. She had lived with Abie in Onthank, but not in this particular part of it. When the opportunity to take the house first emerged, Fat Franny had been most attracted to its easily protected position, at the end of a cul-de-sac. Now though, with Rose gone, that just seemed to reinforce his detachment and exarcerbate his dislocated loneliness.

The tipping point had come a week earlier. A letter from the council threatening an enforcement action because he hadn't secured – or had even applied for – planning permission and building warrants to convert the semi-detached house from one into two. Fat Franny had no intention of dealing with this now, and had made the decision to sell the house for cash, probably to Terry Connolly, who was flush with the success of the drug-infused ice-cream business. It was obvious to Fat Franny that Terry was creaming off the top from the McLartys, but Fat Franny was in on the bigger picture and he figured it prudent to strike while Terry was hot. Especially since – either at the hands of Malachy McLarty or Don McAllister – he was certain to get a lot fucking hotter.

Fat Franny Duncan opened his front door. On the other side of it was Theresa Morgan.

'Hello Francis,' she said.

'Hiya yersel,' he replied.

'Ah wisnae sure whether tae chap or no',' she admitted. 'Ah've been standin' here for aboot fifteen minutes, no sure whether tae just go.' She handed Fat Franny a card. 'Ah'm really sorry aboot Rose. Ah ken how much she meant tae ye.'

'Thanks,' he said. 'How've ye been?'

'Aye. Aw'right. Ah went back an' applied for the college efter we ... well, y'ken?' She paused. 'Business, though, no' hairdressin'. Ah'm really enjoyin' it, y'know?'

'That's good,' said Fat Franny. 'Look, ah better be gettin' aff. Need tae get this stuff doon the Cleansin' afore it shuts.'

'Ah missed ye,' said Theresa, touching his wrist.

Fat Franny didn't look up. He was afraid to look directly at her. 'Took me ages tae get ower ye, Theresa,' he said.

'Look, Francis, ah couldnae have coped wi' everythin' Rose wis goin' through. We got engaged an' ah jist never saw the sacrifices ye wanted me tae make, back then.'

'So noo she's deid, yer back an' lookin' tae pick up again, that it?' Fat Franny said this with more bitterness than he'd really meant. In the weeks after their holiday in Margate, he'd confided in Des Brick that he had been far too selfish in assuming that Theresa would simply move in. He appreciated a nineteen-year-old wouldn't want to be tied to an unpaid job as a carer for a demented old woman. But he had been emotionally trapped by the circumstances. He loved Theresa, and, despite everything, felt that she loved him. But he couldn't desert his mum, and he definitely wasn't going to put her in a home, like an old dog going to a kennel ... out of sight and out of mind. He acknowledged he'd handled it badly. Just like so many other situations in his life.

'Maybe ah should go,' said Theresa, turning away. 'Ah just thought that wi' it bein' the anniversary an' that...'

Fat Franny had lost track of the dates. He'd no idea it had been a year since they had got engaged, and also that today was her twentieth birthday.

'Fuck me, where does the time go, eh?' he said. There was a long pause. Neither was quite sure what to do or say next. Eventually Fat Franny said, 'Ah saw ye at the funeral, at the back, an' that. Thanks for comin'.'

'It wis a lovely service,' she said, '...an' a good turnout tae.'

'Aye,' said Fat Franny, although he suspected she'd know many of his former business associates were simply there because they felt they should be, rather than out of any real connection to Rose. She didn't have a lot of friends and her condition had further limited contact with most of them.

'So, whit ye dain'? Are ye goin' oot wi' anybody?' said Fat Franny.

'Naw … whit d'ye think ah am? Ah'm still wearin' *your* engagement ring, Francis.' It was her turn to be hurt. 'Part ae the reason ah'm here noo is tae see if there's any future wi' us. We never totally finished … it jist fizzled oot efter Margate. Ah hated that holiday, but ah still couldnae move oan until ah knew we were ower completely.'

'So whit noo then?' said Fat Franny. He missed her too, but he'd learned to get by without her during the last six months.

'Ah dunno, Francis.'

'Ah'm sellin' the hoose, by the way,' he said, surprising himself by saying it out loud.

'Aye?' She was equally surprised. 'Ah thought ye'd be here forever.'

'Things change, Tre … nothin' stays the same. Ah need a new environment. Ah feel differently aboot Onthank, noo.'

'D'ye fancy a drink sometime? Nae strings, ken … maybe the Coffee Club.'

Fat Franny pondered this for a while. He looked at the black bags containing his old mum's possessions. 'Aye. That'd be nice.'

'Ah'll treat ye tae gammon steak an' chips,' she said, smiling.

He'd missed her smile. 'Naw, ah'm a new man. It's salads aw the way for me noo.' He smiled too.

She turned and walked away. They hadn't made a date. It was too soon for that. And Fat Franny wasn't even sure this new connection between them would even lead to anything more than them speaking to each other when their paths crossed. But nonetheless, he was pleased she'd come around. It reminded him that he wasn't totally alone and for that he was grateful. Anything more could wait.

Nane ae us fuckin' heard it but Billy Sloan played the demo oan his radio show in Glesga an' loadsae folk were askin' where they could get the record, ken? Aw these A&R cunts start phonin' the hoose, an' poor aul' Molly's tellin' them tae beat it, an' tae leave us alane. She thought they were fae a life insurance company. We went back an' auld fuckin' hipster, X-Ray made a record aff the master tapes. We got a thousand ae the fuckin' things pressed at some plant in Cumbernauld. Catalogue no. BT 001. It wis a thing ae fuckin' beauty. Cost aboot two fuckin' grand, mind.

Ah wore oot the bastart shoe leather tryin' tae place it in The Card & Pop Inn doon the street, an' aw other shops like 'Bruce's' in Glesga an' away up in Edinburgh. We sold a few ootae 23rd Precinct in Glesga, an' they asked us tae dae an in-store promotional thing. Aboot six fuckin' folk turned up. Countin' Jimmy and Hairy Doug, there wis fuckin' mair ae us than them! But wan ae them wis the bass player ootae Lloyd Cole & The Commotions ... Lawrence somethin'. Cannae fuckin' recall noo. He wis in buyin' some arsehole dancey import record.

Oor record sold aw'right ah suppose, but meetin' him led tae a tour roon Scotland supporting Lloyd Cole. We got fifty quid a night for it. By this time, ah'd fuckin' gie'd away shares in the band tae just aboot every cunt we met. Jimmy Stevenson got a cut, Cliff the hippy was in, Hairy Doug and Hairy fuckin' Fanny were baith ona wee wedge. Ah wis fuckin' giein' everythin' away back then. An' aw oan top ae the fifty quid a week ah wis payin' every cunt connected. That's when it aw really started ... on every fuckin' front!

40

Gregor Gidney slammed home the black. Its rattling rasp ricocheted around the cavernous basement of the Crown Billiards Rooms.

'Fuckin' shot, big man,' said Ged McClure.

'Aye, ah know!' said Gregor. 'Tenner.' He held out his massive hand.

Ged McClure reached into his back pocket and pulled out the brown. *These two doss cunts better get here soon*, he thought. He was running out of money. Tactical *losing* had cost him forty quid so far, and it was only just past eleven in the morning.

Benny Donald and Terry Connelly zig-zagged their way around the thirty empty tables like a couple of synchronised Pac-Men eating up trails of invisible pellets. Eventually, they reached the furthest table. The one where Gregor Gidney was fleecing Ged McClure. Ever since he'd been banjo-ed by a toilet cistern in London, Ged's anger had built to the point where he was absolutely desperate to hand out some monumental doings. He'd been informed that the two teenage wallopers who were uppermost in his 'to be battered' list were to be left alone for the time being. Gregor Gidney, his handler, had told him just to chalk it up to experience.

'Fuck ae you two pricks been?' said Ged, more tersely than he'd intended. 'Gregor's been here since nine!'

'Sorry pal. Motor widnae start, an' ah didnae want tae roll up Sauchiehall Street in wan ae the Mr Whippy vans, ken?' Terry Connolly laughed at his own intended joke. No one else did though.

Given the nod by Gregor Gidney, Ged McClure racked up the reds again, sighing to himself in acceptance he would soon be down to IOUs.

'Things are gonnae ramp up rapidly boys. Yer Uncle Malachy needs ye tae be ready. Heat's comin' oan up here an' we need tae shift operations doon tae aw you tattie-munchers,' said Gregor. He cracked the cue ball and it scattered the reds like tear gas being fired into an organised picket line. The ball bounced off three cushions before coming to rest behind the green. With his first shot of the frame, Ged McClure was snookered already. Malachy McLarty's was one of the most feared names in Scotland. He communicated with others via hand-written postcards. They were always of Glaswegian landmarks and contained brief, crudely written coded messages. The crudeness of the writing wasn't down to Malachy's illiteracy. In 1964, an attack on his car had left him with a bullet fragment lodged in his hand. With the resultant nerve damage, he had to learn to write with his left hand. That morning, in an empty Glasgow billiard hall owned by his boss, Gregor Gidney had three such postcards written and ready for hand delivered distribution.

Terry Connolly got one with the city's George Square pictured on one side. On the other the words: 'THE WEANS NEED MORE ICE CREAM'. Terry got the message. Increase distribution, increase sales, and – although it wasn't made specific – cut Fat Franny Duncan out of the loop altogether. Benny Donald's card was more direct: 'YOU NEED TO WASH MORE OFTEN, SON'. Gregor Gidney noted that this was an instruction that worked on both levels. The postcard was of the famous Glaswegian coat of arms. 'The bird that never flew, the tree that never grew, the fish that never swam, the bell that never rang ... *an' the gadgie that never washed.*' Benny Donald wasn't coping well with the subterfuge. Since he was also taking an undeclared cut of the funds that Terry Connolly was passing him to pay off mounting gambling debts, he had more reason than most to sweat profusely. The extent of the dark stains under the armpits of his pastel-coloured t-shirt betrayed his anxieties. It wasn't a good look for a person neck-deep in McLarty business dealings. Ged McClure had already failed Malachy McLarty once. He had been instructed to find the missing Tony Viviani from Galston and recover money

stolen from a rigged Quinn family fist-fighting competition. Tony
Viviani was now secure in the comparative safety of Wormwood
Scrubs, and the route to the money had been closed off. 'THERES
ONLY ONE TYPE OF ICE CREAM. NO MORE FUCK-UPS!'
was Ged McClure's written commandment.

Malachy McLarty's longer-term plan was coming together. The
earlier McLarty recce into Ayrshire was aimed at testing the waters,
and also the resolve of the area's operators. Malachy was a very shrewd
judge of every situation in which he found himself. He studied people
closely. He could read their bravado and their fears and, more specifically, weigh up instantly which of these was the stronger force in
influencing someone's likely actions. From Marty's feedback, he'd
assessed Washer Wishart, Fat Franny Duncan and the Quinns, principally Magdalena. He'd gauged the Ayrshire context quickly. Just like
the Joker, the Penguin and Poison Ivy, they all had key strategic weak-
nesses. Get them all on side as part of an apparent pact and gradual
assimilation of their various patches would be pretty straightforward.
Washer Wishart was ultimately too caring. Fat Franny had no self-
awareness and existed in a bubble of gullibility. Nobby Quinn couldn't
make a decision that his wife hadn't ratified. They were all ripe for the
taking, and now, five years on, they were all about to be taken.

Gregor Gidney imparted some additional instructions to all
three. Timing remained uncertain but in the next few months, the
McLartys would take hold of Ayrshire, starting in the East. The
money that Terry Connolly was generating and Washer Wishart was
washing would need to be promptly but secretively recovered from
its various sources. That was Benny's job. In parallel, competing
businesses needed to be put beyond function. Come the order, that
would be Ged McClure's job. For old time's sake, Emporio Viviani
would be first on that particular list. McClure had been assembling
a new team of young local muscle, and he reported positively that
the Quinns had been easier to assimilate than he would've thought.
People just didn't seem to have the stomach for the fight down in
Ayrshire, he'd observed.

The three affiliates climbed out of the subterranean Crown Billiards Rooms into the brightness of Sauchiehall Street. Hopes and fears fought for prominence in each of their thoughts about their immediate futures.

41

March 1984

Having exhausted all potential sources of output, Max Mojo reluctantly decided to head south again. He had assumed that the inevitable national success of 'The First Picture' was a formality. Depite having been lauded by the Scottish musical cognoscenti, the record had only sold 450 copies. X-Ray Raymonde criticised Max's inexperience and blamed the poor sales on his arrogance in not acknowledging the importance of securing a distribution deal with an organisation such as Rough Trade. Rough Trade Records had previously put out seminal records like Stiff Little Fingers' 'Alternative Ulster', and were now readying the first Smiths LP for release. Max Mojo was determined to seek out Rough Trade's main man Geoff Travis, having researched that the record label and its Cartel distribution arm had recently become separate entities. Armed with a bag full of self-financed 'The First Picture' vinyl, a system full of lithium and head full of hopeful dreams, Max Mojo boarded the early super shuttle service from Glasgow Airport to London Heathrow. It was his first time on a plane, but a few G&Ts and a pack of ten Embassy Club would see any on-flight nerves promptly dealt with.

At the same time, Grant Delgado was headed in the other direction. Maggie's sudden disappearances were increasing in spontaneous regularity. She simply packed up the Campervan and vanished without warning or explanation. Any attempts to interrogate these sojourns were met with silence. So Grant did the only thing any reasonable boyfriend would; he hired a car and followed her.

Simon Sylvester was spending his afternoons in prison. Following yet another conviction for petty theft, a lawyer – paid for by Max – secured a reduced sentence of 150 hours community service. The judge heard mitigating pleas and that a custodial sentence would result in a talented young man being removed from his one passion: The Miraculous Vespas. Simon Sylvester was ordered to participate in a music-development programme for the inmates at Carstairs. He couldn't read music or teach it to others but for all concerned parties, it seemed a convenient if opportunistic punishment.

The Motorcycle Boy spent much of time in the early part of 1984 in therapy. The therapist always came to the house in Caprington.

$$\textit{\textbf{\j}}$$

Max chain-smoked his way through the flight. The air at the back of the cabin might've been murky, but the vision in Max Mojo's head was crystal clear. The band needed a far higher public profile. They needed an event. Max landed in London at exactly the same time that Arthur Scargill, President of the National Union of Mineworkers was declaring the previously sporadic walk-out actions in various coal fields was now a national strike. As Max travelled across the UK's capital by tube, the front page of every *Evening Standard* proclaimed 'STRIKE!' It was either a portent of doom, or a call to arms, depending on the reader's perspective. Max took it as a statement of intent. He was headed for Rough Trade in Ladbroke Grove, in an optimistic blur of encountering Geoff Travis. He got off the tube at Notting Hill Gate. He walked up the vibrantly colourful Portobello Road, alive with the possibilities that a tour of towns most affected by the strike might create. The Miraculous Vespas would become a protest band. Their next single would donate a percentage of profits to the families of striking miners. The band would end the tour with a massive, open-air gig in Ayrshire. He walked under the Westway; the same place where Joe Strummer had prospered, and where The Jam's 'This Is the Modern World' cover was photographed. Max Mojo was inspired by standing on the shoulders of such giants. The Striking Miners Benefit Concert would be like The Clash at Victoria Park for Rock against Racism. It would confirm The Miraculous Vespas as a

band with a conscience. It would also see them headline, since Max
Mojo would be the funding organiser. Max's brain was bursting with
ideas. The event could feature all the great current Scottish bands
– Simple Minds, Orange Juice, Aztec Camera, Lloyd Cole and the
Commotions, The Bluebells – and would also be a platform for the
new ones: Friends Again, Fairground Attraction, The Trashcans ...
surely all would do it, and probably for next to nothing, given the
opportunity to stick two fingers up to Thatcher and her new lapdog,
Ian McGregor. He would call it *Louder in Loudoun*. Suddenly, being
in London seemed like a massive distraction.

$$\oint$$

Grant Delgado parked the car at the gates of what looked like an
old Victorian school building. He stared up at a beautiful, stone
clocktower. It was the vertical punctuation mark in a complex col-
legiate campus of buildings near the Old Crookston Castle on Glasgow's southern edges. Grant originally thought that Maggie must
be studying for a degree through the Open University, and that her
covert visits here must be to do with assessments or registrations or
something related to her course. While Max and the others would've
taken the piss, he couldn't understand why she felt she couldn't share
this thirst for knowledge with him. He drove away, satisfied that her
private activities weren't worthy of concern. As he drove out of the
car park, Grant saw a sign that he hadn't noticed on the way in. It
read: NHS LEVERNDALE PSYCHIATRIC HOSPITAL.

$$\oint$$

Despite his lowly expectations, Simon Sylvester was actually enjoying going to prison.

He was now a small part of a new, emergent initiative aimed at
rehabilitating inmates through music. He had been coerced admittedly, but now went willingly. Simon had even vowed to bring

the band back for a free gig, Johnny Cash-style, when the first LP had been recorded. Simon Sylvester had been given a glimpse into a future that, in only slightly different circumstances, could have been his. The Miraculous Vespas had offered an alternative path and since he hadn't taken it seriously enough at the beginning, he now acknowledged the debt he owed it. He knuckled down and quickly learned piano and more advanced guitar. By the time he'd neared the end of his own sentence, he'd taught ten willing kids how to play the whole of The Jam's 'Sound Affects' LP.

⚡

Eddie Sylvester – the Motorcycle Boy to everyone other than his therapist – was faring less well. The sessions were attempting to determine whether he was actually agoraphobic or whether some other veiled condition was the underlying cause. His childlike demeanour anytime his mother's name was mentioned was a clear indication that he hadn't recovered from that trauma a decade earlier. Eddie Sylvester was suffering from a mental disorder that meant he needed constantly to obtain approval from others. He wasn't agoraphobic as such, but the only way he could now function in crowds was to attempt to blank them out and focus on his dead mother as the adjudicator of all of his efforts. Extreme stage fright was the initial catalyst for his current condition, his father was informed. His therapist felt that he shouldn't stop performing with the band. He needed it as an outlet, she'd said. But he also needed to open up more about how he felt about losing his mum. His father had also buried memories of her as a coping mechanism. He had rowed with his wife about cutting the grass in the first place. Now, he was left with the terrible guilt of his last words to her being an insult that prompted her to go out and do something he should have done himself. Talking about it now would be just as difficult for him. So it was left to Simon, with his new empathy for others, to draw the submerged pain out of his brother's broken heart and help him to function as normally as possible in a world full of unsympathetic and judgemental people.

⚡

Grant Delgado's face was stinging from the punch Maggie had delivered to it. He'd tried to find a casual but sensitive way to ask her about the psychiatric hospital visits but it all came out the wrong way. She accused him of spying on her, and of stifling her individuality. She was incandescent and he simply had to acquiesce and take her indignation. Grant was embarrassed and also ashamed that he had followed her. When he tried to explain that it was done purely out of love and concern, he just sounded controlling and desperate. Just before Maggie yelled that she now couldn't trust him and that their relationship was over, she informed him coldly that she went to Leverndale to visit her mother – her *real* mother – whom she'd just found after years of not knowing whether she was alive or dead. Maggie Abernethy had lived with a foster family in Shortlees since she was fifteen. It was the first family that she had felt comfortable being a part of; felt that she belonged to. The previous twelve years had seen her placed with eight different families. Seven different towns; seven different schools. No long-term friendships. No conventional relationships. She told different elaborate – but invented – stories about her parents. How they had met. How unusual her ethnicity was. It was a shield. *Trust and commitment issues.* It took a lot for Maggie to feel relaxed; even more for her to feel loved. Almost from the first time they had set eyes on each other, she had sensed a different potential; a wholly different emotion with Grant. It felt like safety. She would've told him about her psychotic mother eventually, but she was still only coming to terms with it herself. And now he'd gone and fucked it all; the stupid, selfish bastard.

⚡

Max Mojo was on top of the world. The two, foot-long lines of coke hoovered up in the tiny toilet of the British Airways 737 set him on the course, but now he was naturally euphoric. London was the greatest city on Earth. It was Sinatra's New York, Bowie's Berlin and The Blue Nile's Tinseltown all rolled into one. He would head back to Soho and the bar where the boys kissed *other boys*. Only Morrison Hardwicke had been a wasted effort. Predictably, he didn't remember Max having phoned him the year earlier. But since Max couldn't remember Boy George's code words, he perhaps couldn't be too critical. He'd written the phone number in his wee black book, but nothing else. In any case, Max Mojo now had dreams of succeeding on his own merits. He'd do it by the Biscuit Tin Records independent route. The majors could all go and fuck themselves. Do-it-yourself; the punk spirit personified.

Geoff Travis was very accommodating. He liked the record and agreed to place the remaining stock. He also hinted at a wider distribution deal for future records. Max kept four copies of the ones he had brought down. He caught the tube back to Oxford Circus and then walked purposefully up to Broadcasting House. He was way too early to catch John Peel going into BBC HQ, but Geoff Travis had told him about The Smiths' new single and how he had managed to get it past the all-powerful Radio 1 playlist committee. The committee were still in the news weeks after Frankie Goes to Hollywood's 'Relax' had been banned by Mike Read. Max had no prior knowledge that any such committee even existed. But now, thanks to the Frankie furore, he knew that it did, and thanks to Geoff Travis, he knew *where* it did.

Max Mojo paid a window-cleaning team fifty pounds to take him up the side of the old Portland Street building in their cradle. Through each of the four open windows on the targeted fifth floor, Max Mojo deposited a copy of 'The First Picture'. One of them was bound to be *the* room. It had been a great trip, in every sense of the word.

42

April 1984

It was the latest, crucial Biscuit Tin Records shareholders' meeting and Max Mojo had a job on his hands. The frost hadn't thawed between Grant and Maggie, although the fact that she was still turning up for rehearsals was at least something to build on. Max felt that dealing directly with Maggie was like going for a bath with a toaster, never quite knowing if it was plugged in; all risk and no obvious reward. He had tried to treat her differently, but his youthful impatience often intervened. The Motorcycle Boy had regressed further, and was now represented on band matters by his brother, who also seemed to have undergone something of an attitude transformation. Hairy Doug was present, as was Hairy Fanny. They came as a double-act nowadays. She was omnipresent in band matters and since Hairy Doug was a shareholder not only in the band's future royalties, but also in Biscuit Tin Records, she had a Yoko Ono-type effect on the others. As the newest shareholder, Jimmy Stevenson was just delighted that years of ferrying ungrateful bands, DJs and general punters had actually resulted in something approaching ownership. It didn't give him a platform for an opinion that anyone took notice of, but it did constitute the odd arm-raising in support of a motion. It was empowering and Jimmy loved it. Only Clifford X. Raymonde and Max's dad, Washer Wishart were still to show for the meeting.

Max had prepared an agenda, to which he had no real intention of sticking. The main meat of the meeting was to plan activities around the recording and release of the band's next – as yet unidentified – single, and then their debut LP.

'Nae need tae go through intros then, since every cunt kens every *other* cunt...' Max noticed Fanny's hand shoot up. 'Aye. Whit is it?'

'I don't ken *that* cunt!' she said, very politely and with no trace of disdain for the chair.

'Jimmy Stevenson, meet Hairy Fanny. Hairy Fa...'

'Hey you!' Hairy Doug stood up, knocking his chair over. 'Don't you refer to Fanny like that, you little bastart!'

'For fuck sake! Ah dinnae even ken her name. Does it matter? Fuck me!' said Max. It hadn't been a good start. He'd anticipated consternation at the 'accounts' section, not at the introductions.

'Just watch yer mouth. A bit more respect needed, eh?' said Hairy Doug, sitting back down.

'Fuckin' hell. Right ... noted. Can we get oan?'

'It's *Fantasia*, by the way,' said Fanny. 'Fantasia Bott.'

'Fanny *Bott*?' said Simon Sylvester. 'Yer havin' a fuckin' laugh, hen!'

'I'll take ya outside an' kick seven shades of shite out of ya, son!' Hairy Doug stood tall. His chair went spinning again. Max sighed. It was beginning to feel like an Alcoholics Anonymous meeting involving George Best, Oliver Reed and Giant Haystacks.

'Jesus fuckin' Christ! Sit the fuck doon, will ye'se? Item two the new records.'

Grant smiled casually at Maggie. She looked away.

'Right, Delgado, where are we?' said Max, glad to have wrestled the focus away from Fanny the hippy and Biker Doug.

'Aye. It's goin' fine, pal. Got a few ideas, an' that. Once X-Ray shows, ah can go ower some ae them. Jist acoustic drafts at the minute, mind,' said Grant quietly, as he played with the tuners on his guitar.

'Ah telt ye, ah think we need one oot at the start ae May,' Max reminded him.

'It's cool, man. Nae problems,' said Grant. If he had been any more laid back, he would have been horizontal. They were a constant contrast these days. Grant, all 'dopey' carefree laconicism; and Max, a screwed-up ball of wired pulsating energy. Different personalities being exaggerated by different narcotic stimulants.

Washer Wishart stuck his head in to say hello to everyone just as the band's profit-and-loss accounts were being distributed. They didn't make for healthy reading. If Max had been able to convert them into a graph it would've resembled the downward side elevation of Mount Everest. You have to speculate to accumulate in this business, Max implied. He was surprised at Washer's nodding acknowledgment that the spending was part and parcel of the music business. Max simply assumed that his father had bought into the dream just like the rest of them. The Miraculous Vespas' manager had no idea that the dream was being financed by money appropriated from Scotland's most dangerous gangster.

The meeting adjourned less than thirty minutes after its contentious beginning. A few gigs had been set up in Glasgow for the end of April and Max had stated his desire to see the new LP material showcased. Grant saluted. Maggie had stared at her shoes for most of the meeting before leaving sharply without speaking to anyone. The all-new, caring, sharing Simon Sylvester went though to the back of the church hall to report to his brother by telephone. After he'd noted the gig dates, Hairy Doug and the newly identified Fanny Bott left, accepting the offer of a lift from Jimmy Stevenson. Only Clifford X. Raymonde stayed. He wanted to hear Grant's new songs, which Max had told him about weeks earlier. Max hadn't actually heard them himself but he was quickly learning that the music business was 40 percent hype, 40 percent bullshit and 20 percent actual content.

⚡

Washer Wishart was met at the top of his driveway by a tense Benny Donald. Washer had been expecting him.

'Uncle Washer,' said Benny. Washer noticed the beads of sweat on his top lip. He didn't seem out of breath. 'Any chance ae a wee word … in private, like?'

'Jump in, son. Ah'm away tae pick up Frankie. We're goin' a drive doon tae Ayr. Ye can come if ye want,' said Washer, knowing Benny wouldn't.

'Jist a wee five minutes. That's aw it'll take. Drop me at Frankie Fusi's hoose,' said Benny.

When they arrived at Casa Fusi, Benny got out. He was as white as a sheet.

'Fuck sake, son,' said Frankie Fusi, 'get yersel a fuckin' sunbed. Ah've seen healthier lookin' ghosts.'

Benny Donald sloped away without acknowledgement.

'Sup wi' that dozy wee prick?' asked Frankie.

'Well, thereby hings a fuckin' tale,' said Washer Wishart.

On the drive down to the West Coast, Washer told Frankie how Benny Donald had been supplying him with increasing amounts of drug money that had been accumulated through the ice-cream vans on Fat Franny Duncan's Onthank patch. Washer also explained that Benny had taken it for granted that the money was being washed through the Crosshouse consortium.

Frankie Fusi knew that wasn't the case. Too many people asked him desperate questions about how business was for Washer. It was apparent that if business was in fact good, none of that goodness was washing its way downstream. Frankie Fusi was stunned when his oldest friend told him that the McLarty drug money was being invested into his son's band. It seemed a highly risky strategy and although Washer was a wily old fox, Frankie couldn't immediately see the pay-off. And that would put the McLarty spotlight on all of them. Frankie Fusi was hard, but not so hard that he was prepared to face off against the full weight of the McLarty family. He'd had a brief encounter with Malachy McLarty before. The old man had tried to recruit him almost fifteen years earlier. Gregor Gidney eventually filled the role originally scoped out for Frankie. But Malachy McLarty said he admired Frankie's loyalty to Washer, and accepted his respectful refusal. The whole experience shook him. For at least a year afterwards, Frankie Fusi remained vigilant in anticipation of a Glasgow 'send-off' – a severe kicking followed by a shotgun fired up the anus – but Malachy McLarty stayed true to his word.

Washer went on to tell Frankie that Benny had made the situation potentially worse by creaming off a slice of the money, in an attempt to pay back casino debts to organisations controlled by the McLartys. He'd come to Washer to appeal to him to cover for this, but Washer had said he couldn't. When Benny asked what Washer had done with the funds, the old man replied cryptically that he had stored it away safely in a 'biscuit tin'.

It had been the early-morning news headlines on BBC Scotland that had prompted Benny Donald's sudden fears. Several members of a family in the East End of Glasgow had been murdered as part of a gangland turf war being played out over control of lucrative ice-cream van routes. As a consequence of this upswing in national attention, the focus of the McLarty operations was about to take a very immediate turn south down the A77. Benny Donald was suddenly running out of time.

43

The first song he played them was great. But the second song was incredible. They all knew it. X-Ray Raymonde was initially speechless. Max was in tears. The Sylvester brothers both hugged Grant Delgado after he had finished playing them the demo. Even Maggie wasn't immune. Their break-up had sent him into a bit of tailspin. He'd retreated to the flat and, in dopey bursts of reflection his creative juices had burst their banks. Several songs had been written for – and about – her, but their deceptively simple lyrics all aimed at a collection that Grant envisaged to be a universal celebration of the miraculous resonance of love. Grant had gone back to Shabby Road and had taped these demos with the young studio engineer's help. 'The First Picture' was a fantastic record but now, listening to a rough cut of the song entitled 'It's a Miracle', Max immediately understood why it hadn't broken the band nationally. Both of these two new songs sounded contemporary *and* familiar, traditional and unique all at the same time. But it was Grant's voice that demonstrated the biggest surprise. Where only six months ago he had sounded artfully fragile and frail, he now sang with a sighing, richly melodic croon.

He played more. All of the new songs that Grant had written were amazing. They were a leap forward in depth, complexity and lyrical dexterity far greater than any of them could've hoped for. Max was ecstatic. He asked for Grant to play 'It's a Miracle' again.

'Holy fuck, ya cunt! That's like … fuckin' 'Penny Lane', 'Suspicious Minds' *and* 'Hand in Glove' aw mixed th'gither, or somethin'.'

It was astonishing. But it was also incredibly simple. It had long notes and longer intervals, and the chorus went up, as opposed to some indie songs having down-turned minor-chord progressions. Max lifted his eye patch and wiped both eyes.

'It's great, son. It *really* is,' said X-Ray Raymonde. 'That other one, 'Beautiful Mess', was it? That's fantastic as well. Once we've got a bigger multi-tracked backing on *Miracle*, it'll sound unbelievable. Like a Phil Spector record with guitars.'

'Maggie, whit dae you think?' asked Grant.

'Ah really love it, Grant … *both* of them,' she said quietly. '*Really.*'

He had made her happy, at least for the time that the tape was playing. Grant reckoned that would be enough for now. He had missed her more than he could have imagined, but that longing had fuelled the clutch of unpolished songs that would become The Miraculous Vespas' first LP. He too had known 'It's a Miracle' was a brilliant song. It had a deliberately trite and clichéd title, but that belied its sureness of touch and its timeless coolness. It had come to him late at night, as he sat on the hard floor of the flat, sketching out chords and dreaming of what Maggie was doing at that moment. Loneliness and isolation were the context. A muse is a powerful and potent force of creativity. But it can also be most effective when it's just out of reach. In the moment that 'It's a Miracle' was born, Grant knew Maggie was his.

'Sing it for us noo, man,' said the Motorcyle Boy.

'Aw'right. Here goes.' Grant started strumming:

In the streets and houses, lines are being drawn,
There's ghosts in the towers, smearing honey on the lawn,
While the winds are blowing, and the leaves are growing,
From green to gold, it's a miracle.
Here comes love…
The miracle of love.
All my doubts and demons fall at your feet,
Like a bee dreams of flowers, you reach to me,
Now my mouth's betraying what I'm really saying,
If the truth be told, it's a miracle.

Here comes love...
The miracle of love.
It's the miracle ... The miracle of love.

Max had already decided, on advice from X-Ray Raymonde, to delay the release of 'It's a Miracle'. The veteran held the view that even great songs could get as lost in the mush of novelty holiday beach songs of the Costa del Sol as they were in the pre-Christmas rush. Max saw the logic in this. Early August was the target. It gave them time to plan a campaign of sorts. With Geoff Travis's distribution network, Max had already planned for a pressing of 5,000.

The bank account was being replenished at an impressive rate by Washer, without any real constraints on its outgoings. Max simply assumed that Washer trusted his judgement. The band's new accountant – whose task it was to formulate all this financial chicanery into tax statements – was less convinced. But since he too was now a small shareholder, he was firmly holding his tongue.

Another shareholder was Frankie Fusi. Max liked Frankie but the shared interest in the band was something insisted upon by Washer. Washer had given Frankie the role of tour manager, but this essentially meant ensuring nothing happened to Max Mojo when the band was away from Ayrshire. Given where the investment in the band was actually coming from, he also knew that the oblivious investors would ultimately become conscious investors. Frankie Fusi alone wouldn't withstand the might of Malachy McLarty's mob, but until Don McAllister's squad began hoovering up the debris, it would have to suffice.

Violence on their first tour outside of their hometown never seemed far away. The cheek-by-jowl proximity of the band to their audience in these small, sweaty, claustrophobic venues seemed to positively illicit aggression, as if it was the essential component of a great night out. Pay your money, hear some decent music, get bladdered, spit on – and fight *with* – the band; a night to remember and tell your kids about. Grant would come off stage every night,

his face and hair soaked in saliva, beer and – when the beer was finished – the urine of others. The first time this happened, at a hastily
arranged gig in Glasgow's Rock Garden, Grant had walked off stage
after two songs. The band weren't paid. Max had to cajole Grant
into continuing night after night. The manager reasoned that every
band on the rise gets heckled, but only the *really* unlucky ones get
hepatitis.

The biggest gig of The Miraculous Vespas' short career so far
occurred in the middle of the month. It was at Tiffany's in Sauchiehall Street. Max had been contacted – by Billy Sloan no less – to
ask if he'd consider opening for the intriguingly named The Jesus &
Mary Chain, who were part of a Radio Clyde week-long showcase
of new bands. The evening was an open one, but Billy had made it
clear that the hall would be packed with London-based A&R men,
record distributors and various producers.

It was a great opportunity, even though they were way down the
undercard. The band spent the afternoon of their big test at a nearby
Glasgow ten-pin bowling alley. X-Ray Raymonde had provided
some Columbian marching powder, and Simon Sylvester brought
the accompanying vodka. By the time they were due on stage, the
band – with the honourable exception of the Motorcycle Boy – were
hammered. They stumbled onto the famous Tiffany's boards. They
had all watched amazed as Bono from U2 clambered all over the
speaker columns here just months earlier. This realisation seemed
to get them. During the first song, Maggie fell off her drum stool.
During the second number, Simon Sylvester staggered over to his
brother's guitar amps and disconnected his guitar. The normally cool
and calm Grant Delgado spotted someone at the side of the stage
making a 'wanker' motion towards him. Instead of ignoring it, the
chemically aggravated frontman vaulted off the stage and another
mass brawl started. Max Mojo meanwhile had jumped onstage and
continued singing Grant's lyrics. The Miraculous Vespas managed
the four songs they were invited to perform, although the final one
was delivered without a lead guitar part – since the Motorcycle Boy

couldn't find the hole to plug in his instrument – and with a different singer from the one they began with.

In the dressing room afterwards, X-Ray Raymonde said it was the greatest gig he'd ever seen, and they all dissolved into fits of pissed, hiccupping laughter.

The band was travelling around the West of Scotland in Jimmy Stevenson's increasingly rancid van. He'd decided that cleaning it nightly was pointless, and that booking it in for a total valet at the end of the tour – paid for by Max – was the best plan. Jimmy did worry that the lingering smell of Simon Sylvester's farts might never be removed, though.

Three nights later, The Miraculous Vespas finally supported Orange Juice. Prior to the gig, the refined Orange Juice entourage invited their support out for dinner, where they looked on in astonishment as The Miraculous Vespas drank the finger bowls and ate all of the relish, assuming it to be their starter.

Beyond these occupational hazards, the only other notable incident in The Miraculous Vespas' summer mini-tour of Scotland, 1984, was self-inflicted. The band had just played Fat Sam's in Dundee. Bored with being stuck in budget, cell-like hotel rooms night after night, while the band went out drinking post gig, the Motorcycle Boy broke into a vending machine and stole twenty Bic lighters. He was sharing a squalid double room in Dundee city centre with his brother, who had earlier *skelped* him with his bass. Simon Sylvester argued that it was accidental but a fight had broken out between the brothers on the tiny stage at Fat Sam's. Frankie Fusi had been forced to intervene, and Grant had to finish the gig solo.

The band returned to the hotel around two am, and Simon Sylvester's screams woke everyone on the second floor. Unable to sleep, the Motorcycle Boy had spent half an hour heating the metal door handle from the inside by holding the flame of the Bic lighters under it. Simon Sylvester was taken to Ninewells Hospital with severe burns to four fingers and the palm of his hand. The band returned to Ayrshire having cancelled the remaining three dates, and also the planned recording sessions for July.

Max Mojo fined the Motorcycle Boy. Despite previous threats, it was his first ever act of managerial discipline.

With Simon Sylvester unable to play or rehearse, Max Mojo gave the band an official week off. Like a shop steward negotiating terms, the stricken bass player ensured that it would be 'paid' leave for all but his brother before he would accept on behalf of the other, more ambivalent members of the band. Max acceded. The brothers stayed at home in Caprington. Simon was glad of the opportunity to stay in his bed until mid-afternoon, while the Motorcycle Boy spent the majority of the week holed up in the garage teaching himself how to play the piano.

There was a fragile armistice between Grant and Maggie. His new songs had melted her heart. She knew they were about her, and that through the lyrics he was attempting to tell her how sorry he was. But he had crossed a line from which there was normally no return. Maggie found it so hard to open up to people, especially males. She had to remind herself that there were almost five years between them. He was, in many ways, still just a *daft wee boy*. That alone might have been the end of it, but every time she made that decision in her mind, she found something that reminded her that he was capable of genuine sensitivity; of saying exactly the right thing at the right time. Like now, when he suggested they go away for a few days … to get a change of scenery; to allow their relationship to heal and renew itself. *Where did he get these arcane but beautiful terms?* she thought. She agreed, packed up the van and told no one at home where she was going, mainly because she didn't actually know. Grant wanted it to be a surprise.

⚡

They had driven the thirty-five miles to Largs in relative silence. Apart from Maggie making a remark about the Hunterston Power Station on the Firth of Clyde becoming a nuclear target because of the reckless way Ronald Reagan was acting, the only sound was from the Campervan's cassette player. Grant had brought along a homemade C90 with Prince's *Purple Rain* on one side, and Echo and the Bunnymen's *Ocean Rain* on the other. Since it was likely to rain for the majority of their time away, Grant thought the underlying theme was appropriate.

They stopped for ice cream at Nardini's. Maggie marvelled at the Art Deco frontage of the famed parlour. She described it as quaint, a word Grant hadn't heard before. He wrote it down in his notebook for future use. Maggie wanted to look for a souvenir shop where she might be able to buy a picture postcard featuring the building to show her mums, both of them. Grant said she wouldn't need it. He gave her a package. It was a rectangular box wrapped up in an unused promotional flyer Max had made for the 'First Picture' single. Grant had insisted they drop it due to what he felt was a lapse in taste, even for Max Mojo. It read: THE FIRST PICTURE: DON'T DIE OF IGNORANCE.

The poster replicated the stone-cut graphics from the frightening Government Public Health campaign about AIDS. Maggie unwrapped the gift slowly. It was a camera; her first camera. She kissed him tenderly, took it out of the box and with Grant's help, loaded film and batteries into it. She took her first picture, the classic landmark frontage of a North Ayrshire tourist institution. In return, Maggie gave him the tiny gold-coloured ring from her finger. It fitted his right pinky finger. He knew it wasn't valuable, but that it meant a lot to Maggie.

Maggie Abernethy had never been on a ferry before. She was excited about the prospect of staying on an island, even though Grant had informed her that thousands of Glaswegians would be sharing it with them. It didn't matter to Maggie. She was looking at this tiny lump of rock called Bute through a different lens from all the others who had sailed to it 'doon the watter' from the big city. She was also looking at Grant differently now too. He had told her repeatedly how sorry he had been about following her and eventually she'd assured him that it was forgotten.

Prince sang about the 'Beautiful Ones' and it seemed too coincidental for it not to be about a young couple from Kilmarnock on the very edge of their dreams becoming reality. Later that night, they were in the Campervan facing the narrow stretch of water they had earlier crossed. Maggie lay on her front, Grant on his back, blowing smoke rings. He reminisced fondly about the only other time he'd been here; to Rothesay, the tiny principal town on the Isle of Bute.

He'd come with his family around 1972. It was the only holiday they had ever gone on together. He recalled Senga laughing, and his dad being funny – Hobnail dramatically running down the promenade chasing a ping-pong ball blown away from a ludicrous outdoor table-tennis game for the umpteenth time. They were happy in these recollections. They laughed and talked to each other. It was all so different when they were back at home. Grant used to wonder how many actual words had been uttered in the Onthank terraced house they all shared. At times it felt like days could pass without one word being expressed. These passages usually ended with the smashing of crockery. Then there would be too many words, all loudly and aggressively delivered like targetted weapons, aimed to do as much emotional damage as possible.

Grant Delgado loved words but sometimes he'd felt that they didn't love him back. He flipped the cassette. The mood changed. Ian McCulloch now set the tone. It was Maggie's turn at the confessional. She said Annie – her eighth foster mum – was the only person she had ever really trusted. They were very similar. Headstrong and controlling, and likely to explode without any prior warning, but deep down both were very loving. Maggie couldn't imagine her real mum ever being as protective or nurturing. It had been Annie who had encouraged her to try and find out about her past and, particularly, her dad. Annie had been concerned at how Maggie invented past histories for herself, according to her mood, her level of boredom, or her desire to be duplicitous. Maggie had remained with Annie when she was eighteen, even though she had been expected to move out and start adult life independently. Annie had formed a real bond with this beautiful, but belligerent teenager. Experience told her that, like many kids who've moved around, from one destination to the next, Maggie was essentially rootless. Annie feared that she'd simply drift, and most probably into the dark corners of society. But Maggie was funny, and clever, and creative. Beyond the striking looks, she was different in so many other ways to the thirty or so kids Annie had already cared for. Sometimes Annie felt guilty in admitting that Maggie's beauty made her feel more disposed to protect her than the other, less distinctive kids. But Annie knew there was nevertheless some truth in this. So Annie arranged for her to stay on.

That was almost five years ago. Neither had regretted it but Annie had persuaded Maggie to find out more about her real mum, as the only way to address her future.

Maggie told Grant what she now knew; the painful, difficult truths about her real father's violent death, and the psychological effect it had on her real mother. Finally, Maggie wiped her face and smiled at Grant. 'So there ... ye ken it aw noo,' she said. 'Still interested?' Grant didn't answer. He simply pulled her close and held her even more tightly. They lay fully clothed on top of the Campervan's bed, in silence and staring up at the brilliant full shape of the killing moon. Grant pondered how unique it was for all four band members to have lost parents in tragic circumstances. Without them really being aware of it, The Miraculous Vespas had become a substitute family for all of them, maybe as dysfunctional and confrontational as the ones from which they'd joined it.

44

June 1984

'Thanks for comin' boys,' said Des Brick.

'Hey, ah widnae ae missed it,' said Wullie the Painter, then promptly, 'Fuck, Des, that didnae come oot right. Ah didnae mean…'

'It's fine, Wullie,' Des smiled. 'Ah *ken* whit ye meant.' He turned around, aware of someone standing behind him. 'Good tae see ye Franny.'

'Aye, you tae Des. Wish it wis' under better circumstances, ken?' said Fat Franny Duncan.

'Aye. How's Theresa?' asked Des.

'She's good, mate. Past the mornin' sickness stage noo, hopefully. That coastal air, mate. Works wonders fur ye, ken?' said Fat Franny. 'Whit aboot you, Painterman? Keepin' yer nose clean?'

'Aye, Franny. Cannae complain,' he said. 'Well, ah could, but nae cunt would listen,' he added. 'You're lookin' well.'

'Aye, lost a few stone … mostly through cuttin' that ponytail aff, mind you,' said Fat Franny, chuckling.

The transformation in Fat Franny Duncan was remarkable. Not just in the aesthetics, but in the way he now carried himself. Where previously there was the shifty manner of a man anticipating the imminent intervention of the relevant authorities, there was now a calm, assured confidence. Wullie the Painter had heard a rumour that Fat Franny was even paying taxes, but he put that down to scurrilous urban myth. Some things are just too unbelievable to be true.

Des Brick turned again. He took the condolences of someone from Effie's side whose name he couldn't remember.

Fat Franny pulled Wullie the Painter to one side. 'Look Wullie,' he whispered. 'Ah ken whit yer up tae wi' McAllister.'

Wullie's face was a rehearsed mixture of suspicion and bemusement. It changed as Fat Franny Duncan briefly described his own role in the Ayrshire sting.

'Dinnae worry, ah'm ootae it aw noo,' he concluded. 'But you need tae watch yerself, son. Things are gonnae get mental, jist shortly. Don't paint yerself intae corners ye cannae get ootae. McAllister an' Lawson'll drop ye right in it, if it suits them tae.'

Wullie the Painter barely recognised this new caring, sharing Fat Franny Duncan. He looked physically different, and all the healthier for it. But he even sounded different. His voice was softer and more measured, like it had been matured in oak vats over the last two years. He now resembled a fine bottle of red, where before he had been a shook-up bottle of Vimto. It suited him, and, perverse though it seemed, Wullie the Painter was pleased for him. The legitimate business Fat Franny had always craved suited him.

'Des'll be comin' tae work wi' me in a couple ae weeks,' said Fat Franny. 'When aw this shite blows, ah'd like you tae come tae.' Even the phrase 'work wi' me' rather than 'work for me', was strange to hear. 'An' here ...' Fat Franny handed Wullie the Painter an envelope. There were Polaroid photographs in it. 'That's them aw,' he said.

'Thanks, Franny,' said the Painter. 'Ah appreciate that, mate ... and these!' Wullie told his former boss he was fed up taking the scraps from Terry Connolly's table, even though Strathclyde Police were supplementing his income.

'Dinnae worry aboot that prick,' said Fat Franny. 'He's jist a pawn, bein' gied enough rope tae hang himself. When it aw blows, send *his* photies tae the tabloids, if ye want tae!'

Wullie laughed as Fat Franny told him that he'd sold the Ponderosie to Terry Conolly as a 'cash up front, nae questions asked' deal. Connolly had bragged that he'd picked it up for a quarter less than its market value. But Fat Franny hadn't told Terry Connolly about the Planning Enforcement Order that would legally require the Ponderosie's return to two separate semi-detached houses, or retrospective planning applications to secure permission for the way it was now. Neither option was going to be cheap or palatable for the new owner. And legal recourse was obviously out of the question.

Things were good for Fat Franny Duncan. Life was calmer and much less stressful. When he was a bit bored, and worried he might start to miss the old life, he just went for a walk on the beach with his pregnant fiancée and their dog, breathing fresh, clean sea air. Fat Franny Duncan had three new *Blockbusters* video shops. All had opened in the last three months and all were on the rise. Don McAllister *had* been spot on. Sales of VCRs were going through the roof. Fat Franny's shop membership lists were growing faster than Thatcher's unemployment numbers. There was clearly a corollary between the two that Fat Franny hadn't initially appreciated. Still, here he was, fit and happy and living in Troon, out of the way of all the Onthank shite he previously thought he couldn't live without. Life is strange indeed.

'Thanks Franny. For everything, ah mean. Ah couldnae have afforded the service an' aw the caterin' an' stuff. Ah'm really grateful, mate,' said a tearful Des Brick. He had just spent ten minutes with the hospice nurses who'd cared for Effie in the last two weeks of her life.

'It isnae me, ye need tae thank, Des,' said Franny. 'It's yer sister. She sorted everythin' oot. That's the way she wanted it.'

45

Max Mojo and Grant Delgado stood outside the Radio Clyde building. They had nine copies of the 'It's a Miracle' single between them. It now had a bracketed (Thank You) added to its title, just like *(White Man) In Hammersmith Palais*. They had brought ten with them, but Max had given one away to a woman he was convinced was Lulu. Despite her protests to the contrary – and the fact that she was serving tea in the Bluebird café – Max insisted she 'jist gie it a listen. Play it tae Elton an' the rest ae them.'

They had travelled the now well-trodden route north from Kilmarnock because Billy Sloan had been given a new earlier evening radio show in addition to his regular one. It was a two-hour programme reviewing the best of the week's new singles, with Billy and his various celebrity guests from the world of popular music. This week – in what even Grant had to acknowledge was potentially serendipitous – Billy Sloan's guest reviewer on 'The Music Week' was Boy George.

The Miraculous Vespas had only just completed recording the songs for the debut LP. Max hadn't heard the recordings, but, regardless, he had decided the album would be called *The Rise of the Miraculous Vespas*. He'd had this title in mind from as far back as his period spent in Crosshouse Hospital two years ago. He'd regularly reflected back to those fevered days recently; to how much of an insufferable prick he was back then. He could still occasionally be as intolerant, definitely as tactless and foul-mouthed, but he felt far more in control of his emotions. He was being taken seriously now. After hearing 'The First Picture', Alan Horne had phoned *him*. He got into gigs free. He was automatically on the guest list of the main Glasgow bands whenever they played anywhere in Ayrshire. The band had also been featured in an 'up and coming' article in *Melody Maker*. There had even been a couple of messages taken by Molly, from *a Morrison Hardwicke*. He could fucking whistle, though. Max Mojo didn't need the sanctimonius London-centric industry machine. Like Malcolm McLaren before him, he'd win on his own terms.

Max and Grant walked along the elevated pedestrian walkway that connected the Albany Hotel with the building that housed the Radio Clyde studios. It was mid-afternoon. Billy Sloan wouldn't be there, but they were now convinced that he'd listen to the record and, if impressed by it, he'd play it for Boy George to comment on. They entered the small reception. A black pinboard sign near the front door had small, white cut letters plugged into it, spelling out the words:

RADIO CLYDE WELCOMES: CULTURE CLUB AND HAYSI FANTAYZEE.

'Jeezo, the *whole* band's gonnae be oan it!' said an animated Max.

'Aye, but along wi' they "Big Leggy" bampots, anaw though,' said a less enthusiastic Grant.

'Big deal, the more the merrier, eh?' said Max, shrugging his shoulders.

'Didnae, mean that … ah meant that *we* coulda been oan the show alang wi' Boy George. That John Wayne song wis fuckin' pish!'

Max laughed until he realised Grant was being serious.

'You need tae start workin' harder tae get us intae gigs like this, Max.'

'Hey, fuckin' haud oan a minute, pal. Ah'm constantly oan the bastart phone these days. Who dae ye think's gettin' ye'se aw the gigs? Who's payin' the wages *noo*, man? Whit the fuck's the matter wi' ye?'

'Nothin',' said Grant sullenly. 'Let's jist drap these off an' get back doon the road.'

'Yer a miserable cunt, these days, so ye are,' said Max.

'Fuck off!'

'Naw, *you* fuck off!'

'Ah've got an idea,' said the woman behind the desk. 'Why don't ye'se *both* fuck off, before ah phone the polis!'

Max and Grant stopped pushing each other, and looked at Grace, Radio Clyde's front line of defence against opportunistic pricks without an appointment.

'Could ye gie these tae Billy Sloan an' Tiger Tim?' said Max.

'Ah seriously doubt it,' said Grace.

'Ah'll go an' get ye somethin' if ye dae,' said Max.

'Whit like?' asked Grace.

'Dunno. A lamb bhoona or somethin'.'

'Make it a biryani an' ah'll think aboot it,' said Grace.

'Awa' an' get a chicken biryani, Grant. Get me yin tae,' said Max.

'That'll be shinin' bright,' said an angry Grant. 'Fuckin' go yersel'.'

'Excuse me a minute,' Max said to Grace, pulling Grant back through the main door and out into the corridor. 'Whit the fuck's got *your* goat, mate?' said Max. He was annoyed at Grant for this out of character behaviour.

'Fuck all. Jist shut it, right!'

'Is this aw 'cos the Biscuit'll no' move in wi' ye? Fuckin' get ower yersel, an' stop gie'in everybody the jaggy bunnet. It's gettin' borin'.'

Max pushed Grant, but this time Grant didn't react. He simply turned around and walked backwards towards the Anderston Bus Station. Max let him go without any further comments. It took him over an hour to find an Indian takeaway restaurant. When he went back to the radio station, 'Grace' had been replaced by 'Suzie'. Fortunately for Max, she also liked an Indian.

⚡

Later that evening, Grant sat in the front room of the flat. He'd had four cans of pale ale. The radio was on, as it usually was. Billy Sloan had played some great new records, most notably a brilliant one from The Blue Nile. There seemed to be some real tension between the guests and everything Boy George and Jon Moss liked was disliked by Jeremy Healy and Kate Garner, and vice versa. And then, suddenly:

'Here's a new record from a little-known Ayrshire band, The Miraculous Vespas,' said Billy Sloan.

'Oh, I've heard of them,' said Boy George. 'Can't recall from where though,' he added.

'Maybe they stole your look,' said Jeremy Healy.

Billy Sloan played the record. Grant Delgado had tears in his eyes. When it had finished, Billy Sloan lifted the needle and played the song on the other side.

'That's an absolutely brilliant record,' said Billy. For the only time during the show, his guests were in agreement. Boy George said he'd met the singer in London. He'd given him advice, although on the basis of this record, Grant Delgado definitely wouldn't need it.

While Maggie and Grant had been away he'd felt like they had made a massive breakthrough in their relationship, each opening up to the other in ways they couldn't back home. But as soon as they had got back to Kilmarnock, and were in the company of others Maggie had slipped back into cool and distant mode. Grant was frustrated by this. He wanted her to make a commitment to them … to finally feel confident enough to take off the stabilisers. But it seemed like she couldn't.

Grant's front doorbell sounded. When he opened the door, Maggie was on the other side of it. She was carrying a small suitcase. He smiled, and whispered, 'Ma mam says ah'm no' allowed tae play wi' you anymore.'

46

August 1984

'Two fuckin' *rounds!* An irritated Malachy McLarty looked up from his newspaper. He'd lost a bundle on the Hearns v Duran fight the night before. The *Daily Record* was now smugly suggesting insanity for anyone – like Malachy – who, pre-fight, thought that the street-fighting barbarity of Roberto Duran would batter the more refined Thomas Hearns into submission. Malachy had been convinced that brute strength would triumph over crafty finesse. It was a design for life on which he'd built a reputation. You had to watch the crafty fuckers. Give them an inch and they'd take you for everything you had assembled.

The other source of his irritation was the Ayrshire contingent. With the investigative focus now firmly on Ruchazie and Provanmill in the East End of the city, establishment of the McLarty business empire in the less fevered, sleepy towns of the West Coast should've been much more straightforward than it had been.

Malachy partly – but only privately – blamed himself. He was in his sixties. He'd trusted others. If you wanted something done properly you had to fucking do it yourself. Crafty fuckers were everywhere. You just couldn't trust the cunts.

'Right   let's fuckin' hear it, then,' he said.

Gregor Gidney, the Ayrshire campaign fixer, had just come in to the vast living room. It was a little off-putting. Dickie Davies was mouthing silent words from a vast television set in the corner of the room. Although sunny outside, a roaring log fire was increasing the heat in the room to tropical levels. Gregor's boss was in his underpants. Three large sovereign rings glinted in the light from the fire. He wore a loose, silky animal-print kimono but it looked too small to be his. Large-rimmed glasses were bridged on the end of a crooked, mis-shapen nose. He sat back in the brown-leather recliner and lit a cigar the size of a small telescope.

Malachy held a finger to his lips before turning up the volume of the televison via remote control. Dickie Davies's normally soft, comforting voice boomed and reverberated around the tiled floors and bare walls of the room. Gregor watched the large, delicate chandelier above him bounce slightly with the bass levels. Malachy motioned for Gregor to sit closer to him and to whisper.

'Boss, sorry tae say this, but Marty's takin' his eye aff the baw doon there again.' This was an awkward admission for Gregor. Not only was he highlighting a deficit that he was a part of, he was shifting the emphasis of blame onto the boss's lackadaisical son.

'How so?'

'The mechanism's in place. TC an' McClure have taken ower their patches. But the Crosshoose bit's went rogue.' Gregor watched for subtle changes in the bigger man's face. There were none. He continued. 'The money's flowin' fae the regions, mainly Onthank. That Fat Franny gadgie's oot the game, he's no' a factor,' said Gregor, 'but Malky an' his boys should be recoverin' the proceeds noo … in ma opinion.'

'Whit's the problem?' Malachy McLarty was forcing Gregor to spell it out, albeit in hushed tones.

'That wee Wishart walloper, Benny Donald's dippin' the till, an' Malky's lettin' him away wi' it, for some reason,' said Gregor. He was reasonably certain of this. He would've had to have been.

Malachy McLarty blew up a cloud of cigar smoke so large, Gregor briefly lost sight of the old man.

When it he cleared, he spoke. 'Round them aw up. Get them doon the shed,' said Malachy. 'Get a haud ae Marty. Tell him tae get his fuckin' arse back here, pronto.' Malachy pulled a betting-shop pen from the kimono pocket, and a postcard from the recliner's side pocket. It had a picture of a shortbread tin on one side. On the other, Malachy wrote: 'SON, YER TEA'S OOT!'

✦

'Christ, ah huvnae heard that song in years.' The song sounded tinny. It came from a tiny transistor radio over in the corner of the dark agricultural shed.

'Who is it again?' asked Ged McClure.

'Fuck's sake, mate! Marc Bolan an' T. Rex.'

'Aw aye ... ah wis thinkin' Mott the Hoople or somethin',' said Ged quietly.

'Whit d'ye think, son? Ye like this yin? Are ye able tae ... *Get It Oan?*' Gregor Gidney laughed. He was addressing Benny Donald. Benny didn't respond. He couldn't. It would be the last song he would ever hear.

Benny Donald had been fixed to the wooden railway sleeper by two shiny six-inch nails driven through his palms. The excrutiating pain of this had caused him to lose consciouness. A mixture of smelling salts and buckets of water had brought him round again. Initial terror had given way to shock and he was shaking uncontrollably. He had also soiled himself and was lying flat out on his back, literally and metaphorically in shit of his own making. He had already admitted siphoning off some of the Onthank money, but it was to pay back historical debts owed to Marty McLarty. Benny couldn't understand why this alone was worthy of such interrogation. When he was brought, hooded and bound, to this agricultural shed, apparently in the middle of nowhere, he'd appreciated a bigger problem.

'Where the fuck's the money, son?' said Gregor Gidney, impassionately.

'Fuck sake, man ... ah telt ye, Malky's got it aw. Ah jist ... ah jist borrowed a wee bit ae it. Tae pay it back, man ... ah mean, fuck sake ... ma ... AAAAAAAAAAHHH!' The first nail was driven in.

'The money. Where is it?' said Gregor. 'Ah'll no' be askin' again, pal.'

'Aaaah, ah fuckin' ... fuck, telt ... ah dunno, maaaaa!'

Gregor nodded to Ged McClure. 'AAAAAAHHHHH! Bastaaaaa.'

'Christ, the cunt's jist shat himself,' said Ged, disgusted. 'Right, get him up, you two.' Ged watched as his two young cohorts lifted the sleeper with Benny now nailed to it into an upright position. Benny had lost consciouness. Ged, Gregor and their side-kicks left him where he was.

ϟ

'Whit d'ye think, son?' Gregor Gidney said, when they returned an hour later. 'Ye like this yin? Are ye able tae … *Get It Oan*?' Gregor laughed. 'Wan last go, son. Then we'll cut ye doon. Drap ye at A&E. It's jist a lesson yer bein' taught here. Disnae mean yer oot the business. Ye can recover fae this. Look … if ye don't believe me!'

Benny Donald was struggling to move his head. But he opened a swollen eye. He saw the circular scar in the middle of Gregor Gidney's massive hand. Benny sobbed. He whimpered. It sounded like he wanted his mum.

'Where's the money, son?' asked Gregor. He was tenderly holding Benny's head and had put his ear closer to Benny's mouth. Ged McClure was also anxious. He couldn't hear what Benny had just mumbled. Gregor seemed content, though, whatever it was. He rubbed Benny's chin softly and then patted the back of his head, shaking his own, much as Pontius Pilate might've done.

'Finish it. Get rid,' he instructed.

The first bolt from Ged McClure's crossbow hit Benny on the side. It went through his skin. Despite exhaustion he howled in pain. His terrified eyes bulged.

'Fuck sake, finish it, ah said. We're no' the fuckin' Viet Cong, son,' said Gregor.

'Sorry, big man. First time ah've used this yin. Takes time to work oot the sightin', ken?' said Ged. He loaded another bolt, and took aim at the postcard of Glasgow's coat of arms that had just been taped over Benny's heart. He aimed again at the target. 'Feel like ah'm oan the Golden Shot, here.'

Ged's two younger colleagues laughed. This was their first proper mission. Only a year or so earlier, both had been bred to anticipate a life underground; lungs filling with inhaled black coal dust. This was much more exciting. And lucrative.

The second bolt hit its target on the chest area, and Benny Donald's life ended. Minutes later, a third bolt ripped into his groin. Ged's men winced and then laughed. Benny Donald's body didn't flinch.

'For fuck's sake, Ged,' said Gregor. 'Show the poor bastart some respect, eh?'

'Aye, sorry. Cut him doon, boys,' said Ged.

'Get proper rid, okay?' instructed Gregor. 'Nae bits resurfacin' or washin' up oan Irvine Beach for some wean tae find, like it wis a remake ae fuckin' *Jaws*, right?'

'Aye, G … we'll sort it. *The Gadgie Vanishes!*' said Ged.

§

'We should mibbe have taken the cunt affa the wid,' said Ged McClure. 'Ach, fuck it, we're here, noo.'

It had been extremely difficult to get Benny Donald's body loaded into the back of the small van. They had to fold his legs up and over his chest to put him in sideways. Ged was now certain they had actually broken one of the legs in the process. The shinbone hadn't punctured the skin, but it was clearly fractured within its bloodied skin envelope. They had travelled to a remote valley near New Cumnock. It took two hours for them to reach this point. A waterfall flowed over the edge of a perilous, sheer drop into a former quarry that had filled with water after decades of disregard. They had wrapped Benny Donald's lower body in a white towel to avoid getting his *shite* on their hands. It now looked like a nappy. They pushed the cruciform over the edge and watched it gracefully glide down the waterfall. It hit the rocks at the bottom and its previously smooth trajectory ended with it cartwheeling into the murky-brown quarry water. They watched until the weight of the wooden sleeper dragged the body attached to it way down below the surface.

'Fuck's sake, see that? That wis mental, man,' said one of Ged's men.

'Aye. No' half,' said the other. All three clambered back through the trees to where they had left the van. 'Listen, Ah need a bit ae advice fae ye'se. See if some wee hoor fuckin' cheated on ye, it's aw'right tae fuck her maw, intit?'

Benny Donald's lifeless broken shell slowly sank to sixty feet below the surface, coming to rest beside an old truck, several cookers and two other weighted bodies. Simultaneously, Gregor Gidney was heading back to Glasgow. He had the information his boss was seeking. Like many generals before him, Malachy McLarty was now fighting a war on several fronts. The south-west frontiersmen had apparently defied him. Gregor Gidney informed him that Washer Wishart hadn't put the Onthank money through the normal illegitimate routes. He'd used it to start a record label and, furthermore, he'd ploughed vast amounts into some *daft, fuckin' band* managed by his equally *daft, fuckin' son*. Benny Donald had found this out by snooping around his uncle's office. Amounts on the band's bank statements correlated with Benny's drop dates.

Malachy McLarty couldn't decide if this was a genius move on Washer Wishart's part, or whether he was being craftily shafted. Instinct suggested the latter. He needed some insurance. Postcards were written. Gregor Gidney was to be their distributor. All instructed the securing of 'THE BOY' to be held for negotiation and likely ransom.

Ah blame that jug-eared Prince walloper, maself. Well, actually since the wean's always looked fuck-all like him, mibbe it's wisnae his fault after aw.

47

The telephone wouldn't stop ringing. Molly Wishart was becoming demented by it. Newspapers, music journalists, A&R men from countless London-based record labels; all desperate to speak to Max. All thanks to Boy George's endorsement, 'It's a Miracle (Thank You)' had made it into the lower reaches of the national charts. X-Ray Raymonde had pressed it as a double A-side, with 'Beautiful Mess' on the flip-side, so convinced was he of the equal strengths of both. At Max's insistence, every copy of the single had the paradox '*We are nothing, and yet we are everything!*' scrawled onto the run-off grooves. X-Ray had mixed Grant's vocals high up and had used the version on which the singer had sung in a high key. When Max first heard it, he'd wrongly assumed it was Maggie who was singing.

The Rough Trade Cartel of record shops was placing large orders that Biscuit Tin Records was struggling to keep up with. X-Ray Raymonde was given the job of dealing with record-pressing orders, as well as being given an October deadline to have the LP fully mixed and ready to go. For the sleeve design, Max had even approached the celebrated artist Peter Blake, who'd created the legendary *Sergeant Pepper* cover art. Peter Blake was 'considering it', Max had reported at the most recent shareholders' meeting.

Despite the positivity, tensions had recently surfaced between Max and Grant. An inebriated X-Ray Raymonde had let slip to Max the details of the publishing contract he'd signed with Grant. Max hadn't raised it with the songwriter, but had countered by signing a recording deal with his own Biscuit Tin Records on behalf of the band. Although the percentages of royalties were fair and reasonable, Grant had used it as a further example of decisions that affected everyone being taken by the band's manager alone. However, under pressure from the band members, both had been coerced into putting these differences to one side.

As the single received more coverage and critical acclaim, the band – apart from Grant Delgado – appeared to be taking it all in their stride. They had made in-store appearances in a number of national record stores and even the frenetic Motorcycle Boy seemed to be enjoying the attention. Max had even received a bizarre enquiry for the band to license a 'Motorcycle Boy' action figure. He had still to work out if that was a serious proposition.

In the middle week of September though, everything went stratospheric. The record leapt forty-eight places to number four in the UK charts. Max was speechless; no one could comprehend how this had happened. Biscuit Tin Records didn't have squads of A&R men running around London, exploiting the pluggers and bribing them to manipulate the bar codes in HMV. It was truly astonishing. An independent record from a regional band recorded cheaply and at the arse-end of nowhere was selling more than the current David Bowie, George Michael and Shakin' Stevens singles combined.

Two hours after the chart rundown had finished, the telephone in the manse had rung more than fifty times. Mostly they were from wellwishers, some from more record companies; but one was from the BBC looking to book the band for *Top of the Pops* the following Thursday. Grant couldn't believe it. It seemed like some surreal *Jim'll Fix It* episode that he couldn't recall having written in with a request. The Miraculous Vespas met at the church hall just after ten pm. No one spoke initially, but when they eventually sat down, all five – even Grant – simply dissolved into fits of disbelieving laughter.

They sat on the stage, drinking beer to celebrate and playing records on the portable player that had now become a permanent fixture there. Max was smiling contentedly. It felt like a vindication of everything.

Grant was happy but he was also quiet. He wasn't sure it would ever be this good again.

After an hour, X-Ray Raymonde turned up. He joined in, telling them stories of famous bands and their touring exploits. Max sensed most of them were fabrications.

'The Smiths are gonna change everything for independent music. You'll soon be able to buy their records in Boots or bloody RS McColl' said X-Ray.

'Aye ... every cunt sells oot, sooner or later,' said Simon Sylvester. He hurled 'This Charming Man' across the church hall as if it was a frisbee flying across Irvine beach. It hit the far wall and shattered.

'That wis a fuckin' limited edition, you!' shouted Max. 'That's a fine. A week's wages.'

'Break a few more, eh? That bastardin' Queen yin for a starter ... an' ah'll pay it for ye,' said Grant.

Simon apologised, protesting that he didn't think the disc was actually in the sleeve. With the amount of loose, unsleeved vinyl lying around, it was an acceptable – if unlikely – explanation. Max let it pass. He had four copies of The Smiths record, in any case.

⚡

Washer Wishart had also heard the chart rundown. He knew the focus on the band would intensify and that the lumbering prescence of Gregor Gidney would be darkening the Wishart doorsteps again. Washer had suspected that the recent influx of strangers in the local pubs was connected to the Glaswegian hardman. Gidney knew far more about Benny Donald's sudden disappearance than he'd let on, Washer was certain about that. Frankie Fusi had insisted on securing a private chat with Gregor Gidney. Washer was fearful of this, but his old friend wasn't going to be put off. They both knew things were coming to a head with the McLartys, and since Don McAllister was still weeks away from decisive action, he wasn't certain they could all hold out.

Washer Wishart hadn't actually thought through all of the various permutations of robbing the McLartys of their illegally obtained money. With Benny Donald now missing in action, there was actually proof as to the source of the money. Although he felt for the boy, his predicament was one largely of his own making. If the worst came to the worst, Washer could always simply deny Benny made any of the payments. That was Don McAllister's ultimate tactical strategy. But it would require some cast-iron evidence if the combined regional resources of the Cop Squad were to round up the McLarty crime conglomerate. A smoking gun and/or a strong witness willing to give evidence in court remained elusive parts of the prosecution's case.

$

In a call from the *Sun*, Max received an indication that 'It's a Miracle (Thank You)' was likely to be number one, based on early week sales. Max was unaware that a Radio 1 DJ had made it his record of the week. At a time of unruly strikes and IRA mainland bombing campaigns, the DJ had lauded its *upbeat and topically optimistic subject matter*. The song was on everyone's lips at this happy time, Max was told. He was asked repeatedly about his feelings for the Royal Family. Were the band *all* royalists? Or was it only Grant Delgado? Max Mojo was blindsided by these questions, but since he was currently being bombarded by bizarre requests from everyone, they didn't seem too out of place. As the band's principal spokesperson, he'd recently been asked about their – and *his* – sexual orientation, whether Maggie was an illegal immigrant, and if the Motorcycle Boy was an extraterrestrial. Attitudes regarding the birth of a new Royal baby seemed logical by comparison. Max Mojo hadn't yet twigged that 'It's a Miracle (Thank You)' had been wrongly assumed to be about Prince Henry, the newly born Royal baby. Mike Read had changed the key line to have the word 'boy' inserted as he sang over its chorus. The song was surfing a Unionist, blue-rinsed feelgood factor, painting the band as royalists. Max was confused and euphoric. He just hoped Grant didn't cotton on until after they'd done *Top of the Pops*.

The Miraculous Vespas were to be at BBC studios in Shepherd's Bush at lunchtime on the Thursday. There would be a full run-through, and the show would be going out live that evening. In the meantime, Max Mojo was trying to find time to organise the Mine-workers' Support Gig, and more importantly, to get to Shabby Road for a listen to a tape of the full LP.

⚡

'How ye, Frankie? Long time, eh?' said Gregor Gidney.

'Ye could say, son, aye.' The use of the word 'son' was strange. Frankie Fusi was a few years younger than Gregor Gidney.

Both knew this impromptu meeting was going to end in violence. The calmness of the initial exchange was simply a preparatory part of the dance they were both now beginning.

'Drink?'

'Whisky … nae ice,' said Frankie.

'Cheers,' said Gregor as he handed the glass tumbler to Frankie. 'Would've been better tae have avoided this, eh?'

'Ah needed a word in person. There's nae other way,' said Frankie calmly.

'Unfortunately, by the time guys like us get tae talk … like this, face tae face … well, there's nothin' left tae discuss,' said Gregor Gidney.

'Sometimes, yer oan a collision course. Like they wee Scalextric motors. Ye sense that yer goin' too fast but you don't have the controller, y'know?'

'Aye. Ah dae,' said Gregor. He stood up. He moved the glass table in the centre of the room to one side. Frankie Fusi stood and took his jacket off. They faced each other; two solid, rugged blocks of middle-aged humanity. Italian. Scotsman.

Seconds out!

⚡

Forty-five minutes later, one man emerged bruised and battered from the entry to the four-in-a-block in Glasgow's southside. An eye was closed, a tooth had been knocked out and he had a knife wound in his side. But he was still in better condition than his opponent. Frankie had gone to Howwood, and he was still standing. A slightly fortuitous uppercut with a knuckle-dustered right fist had shattered Gregor Gidney's jaw. Just as well, as Gidney seemed intent on ending a fair fistfight with a blade. The knife wound wasn't serious but it would need stitching. Frankie hobbled along the street until a telephone box emerged through his blurred vision. On the balance of probability, it wouldn't work, but he was lucky, with *that* call at least. He dialled. After six rings, a response:

'Speak.'

'Washer, it's me…'

'Ye aw'right?'

'Aye, ah'm fine. Cunt had a chibb, but it's jist a scratch. Can ye sort us oot wi' somebody that can dae a few stitches?'

'Aye. Head back here,' said Washer.

'Listen, ah've picked up a stack ae auld McLarty's postcards. I think they're aw targeting yer boy!'

'Everythin's comin' tae a head, mate. Jist another week, or that. McAllister's guys jist need one more thing tae tie the old man in.' Washer Wishart was scrabbling. It was fortunate that Max and the band would be heading to England the following day. Max had also accepted invites for Grant Delgado to do a photo shoot for *Smash Hits*, and to appear in a bizarre photo-strip adventure for *Look-in*, which would also feature 'friend of the band', Boy George. Those appointments – and other requests for interviews and in-store appearances – would keep Max and the band out of the way, and on the move until the middle of the following week at least. Washer couldn't trust Max with the full knowledge of the threat he was under, so a patched-up Frankie Fusi would have to be the shield.

48

The Miraculous Vespas recorded their *Top of the Pops* debut live on 20th September 1984. Countless VCRs in Kilmarnock recorded it for posterity. It was presented by the Radio 1 DJs Andy Peebles and Steve Wright, whose afternoon show the Motorcycle Boy absolutely loved. Having spent much of his recent life dreaming of this happening, Max Mojo found it all a bit procedural and boring. The dancing audience were herded disrespectfully around the small studio like the extras from a soap opera Grant assumed them to be.

The band spent the three hours between an earlier rehearsal and showtime throwing things out of their green room window to the local kids below. Cliff Richard – in the room adjacent – complained about the noise they were making. Simon Sylvester responded by posting a series of libellous accusatory notes under the Christian singer's door. They all had 'Max Mojo' written at the bottom of them.

Adam Ant spent time with all of The Miraculous Vespas before their slot, and was especially interested in Maggie. Jimi Sommerville appeared more interested in Max, and staying true to his underlying character, Simon Sylvester stole a watch from one of the Sister Sledge sisters.

On arriving Grant had been informed that David Bowie would be on the show. His crushing disappointment at discovering that it would only be in promo video form was clearly detectable during the band's live performance of 'It's a Miracle (Thank You)'. It was a gloriously catchy song but Grant Delgado was the picture of abject misery as millions the length and breadth of the country watched him.

Grant had protested that they weren't ready to play it live. These protests were totally in vain. It was a live recording or nothing, he was told. Max's nonchalance about this important issue only worsened Grant's mood. He suspected Max had been told this days ago, but hadn't seen fit to share it with everyone else. The band played the song as instructed, and against a ludicrous backdrop of a ginger-haired baby's smiling face. Two Hot Gossip dancers were either side of Grant as he sang. Without the proper preparation and the band's own instruments, Grant felt the song sounded totally different to its recorded version. He was worried they would sound amateurish in comparison.

Surreal though the whole experience was, the appearance helped The Miraculous Vespas hit the number-one position in the national UK charts on Sunday 23rd September 1984. They knocked 'I Just Called To Say I Love You' off the top spot – a *rank rotten bucket ae fuckin' sugary puke*, as Max had referred to it in an interview. The double A-sided single from a band of misfits, led by a schizo-additive-suffering twenty-year-old part-owner of the independent Biscuit Tin Records, based in Shabby Road; a converted flat, up a close, behind a Chinese restaurant, in Kilmarnock, in Ayrshire … had sold almost 275,000 records. The world – and everything in it – was theirs for the taking.

24th September 1984

Frankie Fusi appeared. His eye had healed apart from the purple patch around it. He had come down for breakfast from his room on the first floor of the remote Buxton Manor Hotel on the outskirts of Blackpool.

Grant and Maggie were seated at a window table. The other three hadn't yet surfaced. Maggie burst out laughing when Frankie approached. Grant hadn't seen him coming. He turned around and he laughed out loud, too. Frankie Fusi was wearing a t-shirt that read: FRANKIE SAYS RELAX. He had picked it up in London to wear as a joke. It was now the only clean shirt he had. It was the polar opposite of how he actually felt.

Frankie and the band had hired an estate car to get them there from London. They had left the capital two days earlier, but had detoured to Cambridge for the *Smash Hits* shoot, which was to take place with the band on a punt in the middle of the Cam. Predictably, the Motorcycle Boy fell in.

Frankie was keeping contact with Washer Wishart from various telephone boxes. From these calls he understood things were bad and getting worse. As he had anticipated, Ayrshire was being turned over by Malachy McLarty people, led by the equally under-pressure Ged McClure. Max Mojo – or in fact any of the band – were principal targets for abduction. Frankie Fusi had a contract on his head. Washer had moved Molly and Gerry Ghee's growing family out of the area. He was certain they would be next as the McLarty machine worked its way down the available target list.

Frankie Fusi said a polite 'good morning' to his young charges. He ordered a full English breakfast with four slices of toast, and a pot of Tetley's. He then excused himself to make a phone call from the hotel's lobby.

'Frankie, we're fucked,' said Washer Wishart. He had never sounded this nervous to Frankie before. 'The fuckin' McLartys torched the band's studio last night. Totally up in fuckin' smoke. Some poor bastart's been found deid inside.'

'Wis it definitely *them?*' said Frankie, not quite knowing what else to say. He knew that the odds of an accidental fire happening at a location associated with the Wisharts, when Glasgow hardmen stalked the Kilmarnock streets hunting for Max, was a million to one.

'Ah got a postcard through the door. It had DISCO INFERNO written on it. Couldnae be anybody else,' said Washer. 'Auld prick an' his fuckin' cards. He kens ah widnae risk goin' tae the polis wi' just that an' nothin' else. We're ootae time, mate. Even aw the money off their record comin' in isnae gonnae make this yin go away.'

'McAllister?' asked Frankie.

'He cannae act until his bosses up at Pitt Street say so, an' they're

tellin' him he husnae got enough direct shite tae get Malachy con-
victed. Aw their witnesses are retractin' their statements.'

'Whit dae ye want me tae dae, Washer?'

'Ah don't ken, pal. Ah'm *done*. Ah'm fuckin' sittin' here in the
manse, just waitin' on a bloody Molotov gettin' lobbed in through
the windae,' he said.

Frankie was devastated. Washer Wishart, his closest friend,
sounded broken.

'Listen, just keep Max doon there just noo,' said Washer. 'Maybe
if they get tae me, they'll be satisfied. They'll maybe leave Max an'
Molly an' you alone.'

'Washer, listen tae me … these cunts'll never let go. The money
fae the records, they'll make aw that theirs. Malachy's no' gonnae jist
walk away this time, even if it is wi' a few scalps.' There was a long
pause. 'We've got tae bring them doon, mate.'

'Ah don't know how tae, Frankie. Ah'm aw oota masterplans.'

'Washer, leave it tae me. Ah'll sort it oot. Jist stay fuckin' safe,
mate … keep yer heid doon, okay? Ah'll be back the morra.'

They both hung up; neither certain that they would even see each
other again. Frankie Fusi returned to the Buxton Manor's dining
room. The whole band plus its manager was now all present and
correct. Frankie wolfed his lukewarm breakfast, and slurped his tea.
He gazed out of the window at the hotel's beautiful grounds. The
trees were a lovely burnished colour. Their leaves hadn't fully fallen,
but the undressing process had begun. Frankie wished he was back
in the beautiful, rolling hillsides of Tuscany, watching the shimmer-
ing sunsets over the olive groves. He now knew that wasn't an option
for him.

They piled into the car, the helmeted Motorcycle Boy jammed
into the boot along with Grant's guitar case; the *only* instrument
they had brought with them. With Frankie driving, they headed
out of Blackpool, ignoring the Motorcycle Boy's muffled pleas to
stop at the Pleasure Beach en route. The *Look-in* storyline involved
an unlikely meeting between Boy George, lead singer of the UK's

biggest band, Culture Club, and Grant Delgado, frontman with the UK's most talked-about new group. They were to appear at the end of a young fan's birthday sequence, playing 'live' for her, on the stage at the Cavern.

Grant had agreed to do this to appease Max, and also to deflect a bit of focus away from the various phone calls and direct approaches he was getting from the majors, Morrison Hardwicke especially. Max had nailed his colours to the mast by insisting The Miraculous Vespas would never leave Biscuit Tin Records, regardless of the money they were being offered. Initially, Grant admired his single-mindedness. Latterly though, it seemed like *bloody*-mindedness. Max was making unilateral decisions that affected all of them, without consulting anyone. In the beginning, when none of them knew – or really cared – where it was leading, it didn't really matter. Now, though, offers were flooding in; offers that were actually worth thinking about. Substantial advances based on five-album deals. Promo video ideas to be filmed in San Francisco or Tokyo. The opportunity to work with Steve Lillywhite or Stephen Street as producers of the re-recorded debut LP. All of these were things that Grant Delgado now craved. He acknowledged that it was unfair on Max. He'd stayed true to his original ideal. But Grant was having his head turned.

And there was now another factor. Maggie was pregnant. She had only just found out, but already Grant had looked beyond the perceptibly limited lifespan of a band with a variety of personality issues, to a longer-term solo proposition. They weren't The Beatles after all, and their one – admittedly brilliant – hit single now shared a similar associative categorisation as 'Come on Eileen'.

⚡

The photographs for the adventure strip were over quickly. Boy George seemed distant. He said hello politely to Grant, but The Miraculous Vespas singer wondered if he had inadvertently offended the Culture Club star, or – perhaps more likely – that a wired Max had done so.

While the close-ups were being set up, Frankie Fusi pulled Max to one side. Grant could see them talking in animated fashion. Max was waving his arms around; Frankie was generally impassive. And then the bigger, older man leaned in, bear-paw on shoulder. And Max was suddenly calm. It was as if Frankie Fusi had flicked a switch and turned him into an obsequious Stepford Wife; all passive obedience.

'What the fuck wis' aw that aboot?' said Grant. 'Wi' you an' Frankie, ah mean?'

'Eh … nothin'. Jist that we've tae go back doon tae London. Tae get the train. There's a hotel we're goin' tae stay in, for a week or that,' said Max. He looked shiftier than normal, although, regarding Max, Grant found the boundaries of what constituted normality to be increasingly impossible to draw.

'Fuck that, Max. Ah'm goin' hame. Ah'm knackered, man,' said Grant.

'Naw. We're goin' tae London. Orders.'

'Ah'll fuckin' *orders*, ye, ya prick. Ah'm no' takin' orders fae you.'

'They're no' *fae* me, Grant. They're fae Washer,' Max said.

'Max … whit the fuck's goin' oan here?' said Grant.

Max sighed. 'It's the studio … it's been burnt doon.'

Grant laughed at this. Then he realised Max was being serious. 'Whit? Burnt by *who*?'

'Washer disnae really ken yet. He thinks it might be gangsters wi' a grudge against him.'

'Eh? Fat Franny Duncan? Don't talk pish. He's oot the game, noo.'

'Naw … Glesga yins. Bad fuckers. He jist wants us tae lie low a bit the noo,' said Max.

Grant shook his head. 'How we gonnae dae that, Max, wi' a fuckin' record at number one, an' pictures on every bastart tabloid front page?'

Max looked away.

'So whit aboot X-Ray? Is he aw'right? The fuckin' LP tapes?' said Grant.

'They've found a body, but don't think it was him. That wee engineer boy … probably him,' said Max.

'Fuck sake, Max. He's *deid*? Jesus Christ, we need tae go tae the cops!'

'Naw, Grant. Look, fuckin' listen tae me, we've tae go tae London. Keep oot the road.'

'Fuck off, Max,' shouted Grant. 'Ah'm done wi' this shite. Mags an' me are offski. You dae whit ye like.'

Max was hyper again, like he was being jolted by a cattle prod. Propelled by speed and coke, he'd been unable to sleep for almost four days. He'd given countless interviews over the phone to people whose names and publications he now couldn't remember. He felt as if his seams were coming apart.

Grant Delgado felt it too. It was unbelievable how quickly the pressure of the spotlight had affected all of them. Paradoxically, only the Motorcycle Boy now seemed qualified to wear Frankie Fusi's new t-shirt.

They were in a dark corridor at the back of the Cavern. Boy George had scarpered, and his people were still frantically searching for him. Frankie Fusi also seemed to have left. Maggie and the Sylvester brothers – bored at their lack of involvement – had gone to the Pierhead to look for the ferry that crossed the Mersey and, in the Motorcycle Boy's case, to look for Yosser Hughes. Only Grant and Max were left in the lightless bowels of The Beatles' spiritual home.

In the darkness, Grant could see Max staring at him. 'Whit?' he barked, beginning to compete with Max in the shaking stakes.

Max blinked once. Then leaned in and kissed Grant on the lips.

'Ti … fuck!' Grant spluttered.

'Christ … sorry. Grant. Sorry. Ah … didnae…'

'Ya fuckin' prick, ye!' Grant screamed. 'D'ye dae that for? Jesus Christ!'

'Grant.' Max put his hands up to Grant's shoulders.

Grant threw a spontaneous punch at Max. It connected with his throat and knocked him backwards against a wall.

'AAAH! Ma fuckin' wrist, man. YA BASTART!'

Grant looked down at Max. 'We're done. Ah've fuckin' had it! We're finished, you an' me!' He walked out of the corridor.

A fire exit door opened. Blindingly bright light flooded in. Max's eyes couldn't adjust quickly enough. The door slammed closed again. Max Mojo was left slumped in a basement made famous twenty years earlier by four young men on their way to a level of immortality few could ever match. Max Mojo was alone. He was in pain, and in tears. Deep down – and even though it had only just really begun – he knew the dream was over.

Saying silly things that made no sense at all. Trying to sort out the problems, but there were so many of them … You say you love me … through my rise and fall.

Epilogue: The Fall ... & Rise

24th September 2014

Max Mojo, it's an incredible story, but can I ask you why the film starts in mid 82, and then stops quite abruptly in September 1984? You mentioned being dropped from *The Tube* TV show earlier but there's more to say about what happened after that period surely?

Well, Norma, like ah tried tae tell ye, ah cannae fuckin' remember anythin' that happened afore the hospital shite, ken? So even if ah wanted tae, ah couldnae have. As for efter it, well everybody kens aw that. Ah just thought it would be better no' tae bore every cunt senseless wi' stuff they can get aff the internet.

But I think what's missing is your perspective on all of that.

Aye, mibbe so ... but ah made a promise back then that when it came oot, ah'd keep schtum aboot it. Folk could make up there ain minds, y'know? Whether that wis right or wrang, who fuckin' kens, like. But that wis it ... que sera!

I have to ask you, Max. Can you tell me what happened after Grant left? It's an opportunity for you to set any records straight. After the film comes out, it's the question everyone will be asking.

Hmm. No' sure aboot that, mate.

Why take the chance? Where did you go after the incident at the Cavern?

[After a long pause...] Ah went tae London. [Another pause] See that shite wi' Grant? Ah wis' ootae ma fuckin' box then. Ah'd been up for aboot three fuckin' days straight. Hit the brightlights an' that, ken. The night ae the Top ae the Pops thing, ah fuckin' drank champagne oota one ae they Miami Sound Machine's high-heeled boots! Fuckin' mad. An' ah went oot drug-shoppin' wi' Malcolm tae.'

Malcolm McLaren?

Eh ... aye. He kent how much ah thought ae him, like ... an' asked for a meet. Whit a great geezer, he wis.' Ah went tae his send-aff in Golders Green four or five years ago.

Stood at the back, like. No' like aw they false wallopers desperate tae get their picture taken at it. The cunts!

So, you were saying … You went back to London?

Aye. Hung oot doon there for a few weeks. We made up some shite aboot a 'personal bereavement' tae get the band ootae aw the fuckin' PR gigs that were comin' in, ken? Ah hudnae a fuckin' clue whit tae dae next. Ah couldnae get a haud ae Grant. Him an' Maggie fuckin' disappeared tae Mull or some other pile ae muck up the West. Him an' fuckin' islands, eh? Away for three weeks, an' every cunt kens if ye want tae dae a vanishin' act in Scotland, hit one ae they tiny wee bastart islands. Jist ask Paul McCartney, eh?

The Sylvester brothers?

They stupid cunts were jist in the hoose. Waitin' oan a phone call affa me. Nae clue anythin' wis up until the Sun turned up oan their doorstep.

When was that, Max?

[Another pause…] When the whole Boy George thing broke, ken? Mibbe aboot three weeks efter Liverpool.

What's your perspective on the Boy George story now? Were you a party to what Frankie Fusi was planning?

Whit d'ye mean?

How much did you know about what Frankie Fusi did?

[A long pause…] Em … he telt me that he wis gonnae kidnap the Boy George yin, an' he asked me tae cause a wee bit ae a commotion wi' his people that were at the photo shoot. He telt me it wis tae help oot Washer. So ah did. Frankie bundles the dude intae the boot ae the motor … mooth taped up, an' hauns tied an' that ken?

What happened next … in your opinion?

Frankie drives tae the Lake District. Hings aboot tae it's dark, an' then drives up the road back tae Ayrshire. Efter midnight, he sees a car comin' oan the other side ae the road. It loses control an' fuckin' rattles the central barrier. Skelps aff it, an' cowps it ontae its fuckin' roof. Frankie's first oan the scene … nae other cunt aboot. So he gets oot, drags a wumman ootae the motor jist before the fuckin' thing bursts intae flames. He drags her up the hill, runs back doon tae move his ain motor … wi' the kidnapped cunt still in the boot, mind. Then he phones the polis, an' an ambulance. Whit a fuckin' hero, eh?

Do you think Frankie Fusi waited for the police to come to the scene deliberately ... knowing he would get caught?

Aye ... ah dae. Frankie wis totally loyal tae Washer. Washer saved the cunt's life when they were both in the army in fuckin' China or some slanty-eyed shitehole. Anyways, the Boy George yin hears the sirens, an' sterts batterin' away inside the boot. Frankie mustae kent the game was up.

But it wasn't actually the Culture Club singer that he had taken...

Naw. Jist as fuckin' well, probably. Culture Club were absolutely bloody massive in 1984. Biggest fuckin' band in Britain, ken? Their record label used 'Boy George' looky likeys for aw kinds ae shite where the real yin didnae have to sing or speak ... or where the cunt frankly couldnae be arsed. Frankie Fusi had kidnapped a fake yin.

Stroke ae genius, though. He gets arrested. An' tells the cops that he wis instructed tae dae it by his boss ... Malachy McLarty! [A pause...]

He's got aw these fuckin' postcards ... big scribbled, weans writin' oan them. Aw sayin' 'GET THE BOY, G!' an' 'G, BOY FOR RANSOM', ken?

So what happened next?

Instead ae askin' for a lawyer, Frankie asks tae speak tae Don McAllister, a senior polis in Ayrshire. He kent Washer tae, like. So, before ye can say 'dae ye want a flake wi' yer '99?' the polis have rounded up every McLarty-related cunt there is, an' Fusi's the central fuckin' prosecution witness in aw this 'ice-cream war' bollocks. Frankie's claimin' that he wis the guy that fronted the McLarty Ayrshire drug takeover.

Frankie Fusi took that fall for your father, then?

Yeah, ah'm sure he did. Aw they McLarty fuckers, McClure, Terry Connolly, that fuckin' baldy bastart Gidney that followed us doon tae Wembley ... they aw went doon for more than twenty years. Connolly even had pictures ae his knob posted in the Sunday Sport! Bet that worked well for him in the showers at Barlinnie!

The auld man Malachy, he died in the Bar-L. Malky McLarty got ten years, but he wis oot in the early 90s. There wis fuck all crime mob left by then. So he started again ... tried tae get intae politics anaw, the fuckin' diddy.

Frankie got three years for conspiracy tae kidnap the poor 'Boy George' cunt. He got time aff for comin' tae the aid ae the wummin that crashed her motor, an' then the rest ae it suspended on McAllister's recommendation, 'cos ae the vital evidence gie'd against the McLartys. Once he'd done it, other jakeys fae the East End ae Glesga aw came oot the widwork tae. Eventually, Crown Prosecution had more evidence than they kent whit tae dae wi'. Even Donald Findlay couldnae get the cunts aff.

The 'Boy George' walloper writes a book aboot the experience, an' makes a packet. Breakfast telly appearances an' everythin'. Gettin' kidnapped wis the best thing that ever happened tae that prick, man!

Where did Frankie Fusi go?

Ah cannae tell ye that. Let's just say a load ae the cash aff the number one single gie'd Frankie Fusi a new life. Let's leave it there, eh?

So what about The Miraculous Vespas?

Well … the nail in that coffin wis that fuckin' NME article. Efter that, there wis nae goin' back. The record drapped oot the charts like it was a song advocatin' child porn or somethin'.

Do you remember the interview taking place?

Naw.

Nothing at all?

Nothin'. The article got printed near the start ae November. Grant phoned me. Ah wis back at the manse by this time, ken? It wis the first ah'd spoken tae him since, well … Liverpool, y'know? Ah say 'speak', but ah didnae actually say anythin'. Couldnae get a word in. He wis callin' us for everythin'. Sayin' ah'd fuckin' ruined everythin' … any chance ae a solo deal wis whit he meant though.

You hadn't read the article at this point?

Naw, ah hadnae. Once ah got it, ah'm readin' through it an' thinkin' some cunt's havin' a fuckin' laugh here. Ah'm oan the front cover, an' the article's claimin' an exclusive under the headin' 'IS THIS THE MOST HATEFUL MAN IN BRITAIN?'

Ye'll have seen it … every cunt has. But it's got me allegedly claimin' folk that have got AIDS fuckin' deserved it, the miners' strike is just a bunch ae lazy anti-government bastarts, jist wantin' time aff tae fuck aboot in the pub an' the bookies, an' that ah wrote aw the songs … no' Grant Delgado. Didnae matter how fuckin' beezered oan the ching ah'd been, ah'd never ae said they things. Ah wis tryin' to organise a gig tae support the striking miners, for fuck's sake. But then … the fuckin' kicker. The journalist wis a Stevie Dent. He'd used a different name oan the phone. Enough fuckin' said, eh? Remember the cunt at the beginnin' ae the story wi' the tattoo'ed erse? The yin that apparently put me in the fuckin' hospital in the first place? Well did the sponny bastart no' become a fuckin' freelance music journalist. Ye couldnae make the cuntin' luck up, man! [laughs…] Got tae hand it tae the cunt, mind you. As revenge goes, it's much better way than boilin' yer rabbit in a fuckin' pot, eh?

So why didn't you sue if it was all false?

Well, firstly … throw enough shite at a wa', an' it disnae matter how much rain there is, it'll never aw totally wash off. An' anyway, there wis the fuckin' Band Aid disaster an' then ah wis totally fuckin' fucked efter that final fuck-up.

Why did you even go to the recording?

Fuck knows! Honestly. Nae idea, mate.

Was it desperation to see Grant again?

Ah had nae idea Geldof or that other yin … the wan ootae Mary and Mungo, had even asked him.

Are you sure about that, Max? Years ago, you had said the invite came to you originally.

Who kens? Who fuckin' cares? If ye dinnae want tae hear ma side, jist go an' ask him then!

Sorry. Please continue.

Ah went back tae London. Stayed overnight at some decent hotel … the Grosvenor, mibbe. Charged it tae the band's account, naturally. Headed oot early oan the Sunday mornin'. Did a few beefy lines for breakfast … confidence-builders, ken? Studio was ower in Notting Hill. Ah wis wan ae the first there, man. Musicians are a bunch ae lazy cunts, by the way.

Geldof's no' gonnae let us in, but wee Jimi Bronski Beat comes oot an' smooths it. So ah'm in. Grant's no' turned up yet. Ah'm listenin' tae a first playback ae the song … which ah think's total pish, but that's by the by. It's pretty obvious where the key line is, so … thinkin' it'd help … ah tries tae insist that Grant gets it. The Ure gadgie tells me that yin's goin' tae Bono fae U2. Ah tells everybody, Bono especially, that he's no' fit tae lace Grant's DMs. But it aw jist descends intae fuckin' chaos. They claimed ah fuckin' nutted Geldof, but ah didnae. Ah jist fell forward an' ma heid planted one oan his. Amazin' the amount ae cunts since that have telt us they'd wished they'd fuckin' done it! Anyway, ah get thrown oot intae the street, jist as Grant's walkin' up it wi' Paul Weller. The two ae them jist walk past us as ah'm sittin' there in a puddle … in a white fuckin' suit. Grant says nothing tae us. Neither does Weller, although tae be fair, the cunt probably had nae idea who the fuck ah wis.

Did you actually say what the *Sun* reported you as saying?

Probably, aye. But ah wis fuckin' ragin', man. Ah'd jist been kicked oot oan ma erse, an' ah'm dressed like a fuckin' tramp that's jist found John Travolta's clothes dumped in a skip.

This Sun *prick comes up tae an' says: 'Any words for the people of Ethiopia, Max?' an' ah says, 'Aye, sorry we fuckin' missed ye'se oan this tour, but we'll get ye'se oan the next yin!'*

Fuckin' game over efter that, ken?

Jumping forward to 1995, and everything suddenly changes.

Too fuckin' right, man. [A long pause…] *Ah had pitched up in Ibiza. Bobby Cassidy … remember him fae the beginnin' tae? Well, he puts us up in his place ower there. He had a club an' wis makin' a fuckin' mint DJ-ing. Ootae the blue, ah gets a postcard. But a decent yin, this time. It's fae fuckin' X-Ray Raymonde! Ah'm staggered 'cos in the light ae the Shabby Road fire, he totally shot the craw. Everybody originally thought it wis him that set it. Anyway, dopey aul' cunt's aw excited an' desperate tae see us. He flies oot an' Cassidy an' me meets him. Knock me fuckin' bandy, but X-Ray's got the only surviving master tape copy ae The Miraculous Vespas LP! Ah couldnae fuckin' believe it, man. It sounded absolutely magic. Mibbe even more relevant at that time, than in the 80s.*

X-Ray tells me, he had tae lie low, 'cos the stupid aul' prick had let the insurance for the studio lapse, an' he was shitin' it that the kid Colum's family wid sue him. An' also, he tells us that efter aw the shite wi' Grant, an' Band Aid, an' the NME, nae cunt wid ae touched it. He wis probably right, but whit the daft aul' bastart didnae tell us wis the real reason it took so long wis because he'd left the tapes in the back ae a fuckin' hire car, an' it took him aboot three bastart years tae get them back … the dopey aul' tosser.

It must've helped to have Noel Gallagher claiming the band was a big personal influence.

Didnae dae any harm, that's for sure. Efter years ae aw that 'Ah hate maself an' ah want tae die' Nirvana shite, Britpop wis aw upbeat and an' bands like us … ah mean, The Vespas, were back in favour again. But as ye've seen, it's a fuckin' classic LP noo'. Grant's a fuckin' recluse, aye … but that's probably helped his status … in a funny way.

And the smash hit remixed single?

That wis aw Cassidy. Took 'It's a Miracle' an' remixed it. Speeded it up, put aw these effects oan it. Sounded fuckin' amazing, man. Ah'm walloped on the E the night ah first heard it. It wis totally different tae the original but still recognisable, ken? Ah telt they two that it sounded like 'Be My Baby', 'I Feel Love' and 'Blitzkreig Bop' aw rolled intae one. It wis fuckin' massive, man … aw ower the world. It paid for the hoose ah live in noo!

Max, when was the last time you spoke to Grant Delgado?

Other than through lawyers, that day ae the Band Aid fuck-up. As for the last time we saw each other? … The Cavern.

That's pretty sad, don't you think?

It's life, pal … nothin' else. There's poor cunts much worse aff than me, or Grant.

Did you love him?

[A long pause…and then Max Mojo laughs.] *Ah'd have leapt in front of a flying bullet for him.*

Cryptic. Were you *in* love with him?

Dae ye have any other questions or is that us by?

Yes, just one. You have made lots of money, and now a great film. Any regrets?

It was never aboot money, Norma. It wis always aboot chasin' the immortality.

Max Mojo, it's been a pleasure talking to you. *The Rise & Fall of the Miraculous Vespas* is in cinemas around the UK from this Friday. The band's seminal LP is re-released with a bonus special edition seven-inch record of the original hit single, on the same day.

Post Script: Where are they now?

Franny Duncan sold his five Blockbusters video stores to the American Blockbuster Chain in 1986. It made him a millionaire. He bought a bed & breakfast in Troon where he still lives with his partner Theresa, and their son Matthew, who runs the popular guesthouse with his mother. Franny suffers from Alzheimer's.

Wullie Blair (the Painter) still lives in Onthank. Following Strathclyde Police recommendations, he got a job as a social worker specialising in work with addicts in North West Kilmarnock. He was elected as a local Labour councillor for the area in 1992. Detective Superintendent Charles Lawson counter-signed his nomination.

Des Brick committed suicide in January 1989. It was the fifth anniversary of Effie Brick's death. They are buried together in Grassyards Road Cemetery. Weekly, for the last 25 years, fresh flowers from the Kilmarnock florist Paper Roses have been placed on the grave and headstone. The invoices are sent to a post office box in Troon.

Nobby and Magdalena Quinn died in 1996. They were driving back to Ayrshire from Birmingham when their car was in a head-on collision with a lorry transporting livestock. Nobby was driving; Magdalena was in the passenger seat. Both were killed instantly.

Rocco Quinn developed the Quinn Amateur Boxing Club in Galston into one of the most respected in the country. To date, it has provided the impetus for more than 500 local kids to find careers at various levels in boxing or martial arts. The club boasts four Scottish Commonwealth medallists and one Olympic bronze medallist among its previous members.

Don McAllister retired from the police force in 1985. He received numerous citations for his key role in breaking the gangland turf wars that blighted the west of Scotland in the mid 1980s. He was knighted in the Queen's birthday honours list in 1986. He died peacefully at his cottage on the Isle of Arran in 2001.

Charles Lawson was promoted to chief superintendent in charge of the Kilmarnock police station where he had worked under Don McAllister. Now 67, he is an advisor to the Scottish government on violence reduction and prevention strategies in areas of social deprivation.

James 'Washer' Wishart used the remainder of the McLarty drug money to set up an Ayrshire Miners' Benevolent Fund. It continues to provide financial support to the families of redundant miners, and those suffering from pneumoconiosis.

He finally repaired the church hall roof and converted the building into a nightclub and venue for bands in 1988. It was designed at outrageous expense by Joey Miller, a local architecture student. The club – known as the *Biscuit Tin* – closed in 1990 after a local newspaper reported widespread ecstacy use there.

Washer suffered a fatal heart attack in 2007 whilst on holiday in Italy visiting a close family friend. He was 76. His wife **Molly** lives with her son in his villa in the South of France.

Now 84, **Frankie Fusi** remains alive and well and living in ... well, no one is entirely sure where.

Gerry Ghee's youngest child, Annie, won seven million pounds on the UK national lottery in 2010. After years of struggle, Gerry and his wife now live in some considerable style.

The crime organisation run by **Malachy McLarty** was broken by the multiple arrests and subsequent prison sentences following Operation Double Nougat. Malachy's son **Marty** – who received the most lenient sentence of the principal protagonists – attempted to revitalise the family in the early 90s. But, although acquitted of the 1994 murder of prominent Shettleston businessman and politician Robert Souness, on a 'not-proven' verdict, his family name had lost the fear associated with the earlier era. Marty McLarty was stabbed to death in an apparent 'road rage' incident in Glasgow city centre in the early hours of New Years Day, 2000. No one has ever been charged in connection with his death.

Stevie Dent writes a weekly column for the *Daily Mail* featuring celebrity gossip and rumour. He has never used phone hacking as a method for the basis behind his stories. Or so his current legal representation claims.

Farah Nawaz got married six months after the interview with Max Mojo. Now Farah Khushi, she is the founder of The Scottish Circle, a dynamic group of influential women who are passionate about empowering women and fighting poverty in Scotland and across the world. In 1995, on her 30th birthday, she received an anonymous present. It was a 1964 Triumph Tiger Motorbike.

Clifford 'X-Ray' Raymonde moved to Ibiza in 1995. He used profits from The Miraculous Vespas' royalties to build a recording studio on the island. The Ministry of Sound, and other super clubs such as Cream, have recorded acclaimed albums there. X-Ray Raymonde died of natural causes in the summer of 2008. He was facing the sun at the time.

The Sylvester Brothers formed a band of the same name in 1988. The band enjoyed modest success with a well-received debut LP, but Simon's listed convictions prevented the band from touring in

America, and a return of Eddie Sylvester's chronic stagefright saw the band break up after only two years together. Simon is now heavily involved with Jail Guitar Doors, the initiative set up by Billy Bragg to provide musical instruments and instruction to prison inmates.

Both signed away their rights to future royalties from The Miraculous Vespas' songs for £50,000 in 1994, a year before the delayed release of *The Rise of the Miraculous Vespas* LP. The deal was brokered by a lawyer acting for Biscuit Tin Records. After being contacted by Max Mojo, the brothers agreed to appear on the *Top of the Pops* Christmas edition of 1995. They were paid £1,000 each for doing so.

Grant Delgado and **Maggie Abernethy** split up in 1991, following Grant's struggles with depression and alcohol addiction. Both agreed to the live television appearance in 1995, alongside the Sylvester Brothers, on condition that they wouldn't have to meet – or talk to – Max Mojo. After the dissolution of Biscuit Tin Records in 1997, Maggie moved to the USA, eventually settling in Portland, Oregon, with their twelve-year-old son, Wolf. Maggie is now an acclaimed photographer.

The year after The Miraculous Vespas LP was released, Grant Delgado disowned the record in a rare interview with *The Face* magazine. For ten years up until 2007, Grant Delgado disappeared from public life completely. Various contrary rumours surfaced that he was suffering from a muscle-wasting disease, that he was working on an unbelievable new record or that he was dead. None was true. He was living alone in Glasgow's West End writing a novel called *The First Picture*. This only became public knowledge when he was photographed by a tabloid newspaper attending the funeral of his mum, **Senga Dale**. In 2012, his debut novel was shortlisted for the Man Booker Prize. Predictably, Grant Delgado didn't attend the awards ceremony in London. He had moved to Portland three years earlier. Grant Delgado is now universally lauded as the link between New Wave and the Britpop era.

In 2010, *Rolling Stone* magazine placed **The Miraculous Vespas'** only recorded LP at number 86 in their list of the Greatest Albums of All Time.

Boy George remains totally unaware of his part in the rise and fall of The Miraculous Vespas.

None of the following songs were harmed in the telling of this story:

Where Were You?
The Mekons
(Written by Jon Langford)
Available on Fast Product Records, 1978

The Model
Kraftwerk
(Written by Hutter, Bartos, Schult)
Available on EMI Capitol Records, 1981

Should I Stay or Should I Go
The Clash
(Written by Headon, Jones, Simonon, Strummer)
Available on CBS Records, 1982

I Can't Help Myself
Orange Juice
(Written by Edwyn Collins)
Available on Polydor Records, 1982

Let's Stick Together
Brian Ferry
(Written by Wilbert Harrison)
Available on E.G. Records, 1976

Thirteen
Big Star
(Written by Alex Chilton and Chris Bell)
Available on Ardent Records, 1972

The Message
Grandmaster Flash & the Furious Five
(Written by Ed 'Duke Bootee'Fletcher, Grandmaster Melle Mel and
Sylvia Robinson)
Available on Sugarhill Records, 1982

Beat Surrender
The Jam
(Written by Paul Weller)
Available on Polydor Records, 1982

House of Fun
Madness
(Written by Mike Barson and Lee Thompson)
Available on Stiff Records, 1982

September
Earth, Wind & Fire
(Written by Maurice White, Al McKay and Allee Willis)
Available on Columbia Records, 1978

Run, Run, Run
The Velvet Underground
(Written by Lou Reed)
Available on Verve Records, 1967

Roadrunner
Jonathan Richman & The Modern Lovers
(Written by Jonathan Richman)
Available on Beserkley Records, 1972

B-Movie
Gil Scott-Heron
(Written by Gil-Scott Heron)
Available on Arista Records, 1981

I'll Never Fall in Love Again
Bobbie Gentry
(Written by Burt Bacharach and Hal David)
Available on Capitol Records, 1970

Galveston
Glen Campbell
(Written by Jim Webb)
Available on Capitol Records, 1969

What Difference Does It Make?
The Smiths
(Written by Morrissey and Marr)
Available on Rough Trade Records, 1983

Do You Really Want To Hurt Me?
Culture Club
(Written by Culture Club)
Available on Virgin Records, 1982

Stoned out of My Mind
The Chi-Lites
(Written by Eugene Record and Barbara Acklin)
Available on Brunswick Records, 1973

Relax
Frankie Goes to Hollywood
(Written by Gill, Johnson, Nash, O'Toole)
Available on ZTT Records, 1983

Love Song
Simple Minds
(Written by Simple Minds)
Available on Virgin Records, 1981

Blue Monday
New Order
(Written by Gilbert, Hook, Morris, Sumner)
Available on Factory Records, 1983

Perfect Skin
Lloyd Cole & The Commotions
(Written by Lloyd Cole)
Available on Polydor Records, 1984

The Beautiful Ones
Prince and the Revolution
(Written by Prince)
Available on Warner Brothers Records, 1983

Get it On
T.Rex
(Written by Marc Bolan)
Available on Fly Records, 1971

I'm Falling
The Bluebells
(Written by Robert Hodgens & Ken McCluskey)
Available on London Records, 1984

Acknowledgements

I'm extremely grateful to the following people for advice, guidance and support: Kevin Toner, Stuart Cosgrove, Colin McCredie, Theresa Talbot, James Grant, Ian Burgoyne, Clark Sorley, Billy Sloan, Farah Khushi, Billy Kiltie, Lawrence Donegan, Bruce Findlay, Iain Conroy, Hardeep Singh Kohli, Muriel Gray, Christopher Brookmyre, Nick Quantrill and John Niven.

As ever, none of this would be possible without the incredible force of nature that is Karen Sullivan, my friend and publisher who gives me belief that the words I string together are of interest to other people.

I'm thankful once again to my family and friends. Elaine, my ever-supportive missus; Nathan and Nadia, our *dustbins* ... and my mum and sisters, Marlisa and Susan. All of them are patient and accommodating beyond the call of duty.

Finally, I'm hugely indebted to Robert Hodgens ... better known to many of you as Bobby Bluebell. The song 'It's a Miracle (Thank You)' by The Miraculous Vespas, was written, performed and produced by Bobby. Lyrics published by – and reproduced with kind permission of – 23rd Precinct Music/Notting Hill Music.

To listen to 'It's a Miracle (Thank You)' by The Miraculous Vespas, and 'An Interview with Max Mojo' (starring Colin McCredie as Max Mojo and Theresa Talbot as Norma) visit: http://orendabooks.co.uk/book/the-rise-&-fall-of-the-miraculous-vespas/

The final part of the Disco Days Trilogy will be *The Man Who Loved Islands*.